# DAWN
## IN
# DALLAS

## WILLIAM H. VENEMA

*also by William H. Venema*

*Death in Panama*

*Dawn in Dallas* is a work of fiction. Names, characters, places, and incidents are the products of the author's imagination or are used fictiously. Any resemblance to actual events or to any person, living or dead, is entirely coincidental.

ISBN 978-0-9989703-2-5
eBook ISBN 978-0-9989703-3-2

www.williamhvenema.com

# ACKNOWLEDGEMENTS
# AND DISCLAIMER

John D. Rockefeller was once asked to what he attributed his success. He thought for a moment and replied, "To others."

Any success achieved by *Dawn in Dallas* is due, in large part, to the help and encouragement of friends and family members. Several of them read advance copies of my manuscript and offered fresh perspectives and helpful feedback: Greg Bilhartz, Michelle Capezza, Claire Cross, Terry McClenny, Carol McNally, and Lisa Nelms.

I must especially thank my dear friend and former law partner, Sherie Bush. Though we clash over split infinitives and other aspects of the King's English, I owe her a deep debt of gratitude. Ever the perfectionist, she carefully reviewed each sentence of my many drafts and provided an invaluable critique of my work. She even enlisted the help of her husband Walter, a talented and experienced litigator who ensured that I accurately described what happens during litigation.

More than anyone, however, I want to thank my love, my partner, my best friend, my wife, Teresa. She offered her own insights on my many drafts and tolerated my devotion to this project, which at times bordered on obsessive. I could not have finished this book without her.

Readers of my first novel, *Death in Panama*, will quickly see that *Dawn in Dallas* is a continuation of the story of Robert E. Clark, the protagonist from that book. Although there are similarities between the experiences of Robert Clark and those of my own life, both books are entirely works of fiction. Some people who have known me over the years might think certain characters are based on real persons. They are not. Any similarity between the characters in this book and any real people, living or dead, is purely coincidental.

As with *Death in Panama*, this book tells a fictional story, which I hope readers will find entertaining, thought-provoking, and perhaps even meaningful.

# CHAPTER ONE

THE GEORGIA SUN was hot—even for July. The air was heavy and thick with humidity. Major Robert E. Clark and Captain Dan McCormack were sitting on the steps of their office building, a converted, World War II-era, "temporary" wooden barracks with peeling paint. Ronald Reagan's revitalization of the military had somehow failed to reach the Staff Judge Advocate's Office of Forces Command at Fort McPherson. Every window of the building was covered with condensation, as the outdated air-conditioning units perched on the windowsills struggled to keep the inside cool. The two men were bent over, lacing their shoes, preparing for an afternoon run.

"Sir, are you sure we should be running in this heat?" Dan asked.

"If you don't want to, Dan, that's fine. But next week is my last physical fitness test before I leave the Army, and I intend to max it." Clark raised his eyebrows and grinned. "It's cool inside the gym. You can go work out there if you want."

"Uh, no sir, I'd rather run. Anyway, I was hoping to talk to you."

"Okay, but I'll be pushing it. I'm not sure how much I'll be able to talk."

Both men were wearing Army-issue black running shorts and gray T-shirts with "ARMY" on the front in bold black letters. They stood up and began to stretch.

"Sir, I just don't understand why you're getting out." Dan's intensity caused Clark to wonder whether the young captain might be questioning his own decision to remain on active duty, so he chose his words carefully and avoided saying anything negative.

"It's pretty simple, Dan. I'm getting out because the Army is no longer the right place for me."

"What exactly does that mean, sir?"

"Let's just say I have a plethora of personal problems that complicate things. Come on. Let's get going."

As they jogged past the commissary, Clark noticed a family getting out of their minivan to go grocery shopping. The young father held his daughter's hand as they walked across the parking lot. I'll never have that life again, he thought.

Dan persisted. "But you've had such a great career so far. Top of your class at West Point, platoon leader at Fort Hood, and then the Army sent you to law school." Dan jogged a few paces and then said, "And you got to be a prosecutor on your first JAG assignment. What I would have given for that."

"Don't get me wrong, Dan." Clark had picked up the pace, causing him to speak in short puffy spurts. "The Army's been good to me. It's taught me most of what I know. But it's time to leave."

"But, sir, how many Army lawyers do you know have airborne wings and a Ranger Tab and have prosecuted a murder case?"

Clark stopped abruptly and stared at him. "Are you thinking about getting out?"

"I, uh, I've thought about it. My dad wants me to join his firm in Macon. But if I'd been able to do the things you've done, it would be a no-brainer. I'd stay in for sure."

"Well, you need to make your own decision. But let's just say that much of what I did didn't turn out all that well. And right now I need to be running, not talking." Clark took off at a faster pace. "Four times around the parade ground is two miles, right?"

"Right."

The late afternoon sun bore down on them, causing their faces to flush. As their bodies heated up, sweat darkened their T-shirts; their skin glistened. When Dan increased the pace, Clark's expression turned serious and determined, sweat now rolling down his cheeks. But that's what he wanted. He wanted to be ready for the test. It had been several years since he had achieved a perfect score, and he wanted to repeat that performance on his last test.

The two-mile course ended near the gym, so they went inside to cool down. As soon as they sat down on the bleachers, Clark asked, "How was our time?"

"Fourteen minutes and thirty or so seconds."

"Well, that sucks." Clark put his elbows on his thighs and rested his chin in his hands.

"Not as much as this air conditioning."

"Yeah, but it's better than being out there," Clark said, without lifting his head but motioning to the door.

"Can I ask you a question, sir?"

"No, Dan, because I know what it will be." Clark didn't raise his head and almost sounded exasperated. "Look," he said, now sitting up and making eye contact with Dan, "I love the Army. It's made me into the man I am today." He paused as if struggling to decide whether to say more. "This is not an easy decision for me. But I have a multitude of reasons for getting out of the Army, most of which I'd rather not talk about."

"Sorry, sir. I didn't mean to pry. But you know you'll have to talk to Colonel Barnes. He's going to try to persuade you to stay on active duty."

Clark again rested his head in his hands. "I don't know, Dan. I might stay in the Reserve, but I'm not even sure about that right now."

"Okay." Dan paused, seeming to collect his thoughts. "Sir, I understand you don't want to discuss why you're getting out. But would you mind telling me why you're moving to Texas? I mean… You're from Pemberton, Georgia, right? You went to the University of Georgia law school. Those guys dominate the State Bar and all the big law firms in Atlanta. My dad says connections are everything when it comes to building a practice. Why do you want to go all the way to Texas?"

Clark sat up and looked at him with a smirk. "When Davy Crockett left Tennessee, he said, 'Y'all can go to hell. I'm going to Texas.' Or something like that. I kinda feel the same way right now. I'm ready to leave."

"Yeah, but Crockett died at the Alamo."

"Well, *Daniel*, I'm not headed to the Alamo. I've got a lead on a job at a big firm in Dallas." Clark hesitated, trying to decide whether he should continue, and then asked, "Do you know Alan Taylor?"

"Who doesn't? He's that black officer who graduated from Harvard, right? Everybody thought he'd be a general someday. I met him a few years ago at the Employment Law Course at the JAG School in Charlottesville. He looked like a politician—always walking around with a big smile and shaking hands with everybody."

"That's the guy. Actually, he went to Howard and then Harvard Law. We were in the same JAG Officer Basic Course and got to be friends. He's a really good guy." Clark stood up and headed toward the door; Dan followed. "When I told him I was thinking about getting out of the Army and leaving Georgia, he got real excited and said I should come to Dallas. He's out of the Army and is with Underwood & Crockett. Ever heard of them?"

"Isn't that Davy's old firm?"

"Very funny," Clark said.

Dan's face turned serious. "Of course I've heard of them, sir. They're big time. They recruited at Emory during my third year of law school. If I remember correctly, they snagged a few of the law-review types. So, Taylor is with that firm?"

"Yeah. He's in their Dallas office, and as you can imagine, he's already making a name for himself. Says he thinks he can get me an interview. The rest is up to me."

"You're braver than I am. I wouldn't leave the Army without a job offer in hand. But it sounds like your mind is made up."

"Yeah. Listen, I need to get going. I've got to get packed up and ready to move out of my apartment. I'll be headed to Dallas soon." Clark's grin crinkled the corners of his eyes. "See you Monday," he said as he turned and walked toward his car.

"Okay," Dan called after him. "You want me to pace you on the run during your test next week?"

Clark turned and said, "Nah. You've got better things to do. Have a good weekend." He waved and walked away.

❧

Clark knew he had to report to his boss to discuss his decision to resign from the Army, and he wanted to get it over with. As soon as he arrived at his office the following Monday morning, he reported to Colonel William J. Barnes, the Staff Judge Advocate of Forces Command. As he entered the colonel's office, Clark studied the mementos of his boss's long military career, which he'd seen many times before but had never bothered to examine. They covered most of the wall space of his office: pictures of him with general officers and senators and one with President Reagan; plaques from the units he'd served in, including the 82nd Airborne; a cavalry saber; a dress bayonet on a plaque with his Vietnam Service Medal; and a shadow box containing an array of medals, including a Silver Star and a picture of a young officer who must have been Colonel Barnes's father. Considering how broken-down the building was, they made Colonel Barnes's office look rather impressive.

The Staff Judge Advocate was not only a good boss, he was also a leader—something rare in the JAG Corps. Everyone who had worked with him thought he should have become a general officer, possibly even The Judge Advocate General, the highest ranking Army lawyer. It was somewhat of a mystery that he hadn't advanced beyond colonel. Now, here he was, completing his Army career in 1986 in a dilapidated wooden building that was supposed to have been a temporary barracks in WWII.

If this is how the Army treats one of its finest lawyers, Clark thought, why would I want to stay in, especially with everything else I have to deal with?

Barnes pointed to a chair in front of his desk. "You know, Clark, you can skip the PT test if you want to; that is, unless I can persuade you to tear this up." He tossed Clark's resignation across the desk.

Clark shook his head slightly. "No, sir. My mind is made up." He readjusted himself in his seat and looked earnestly at Colonel Barnes. "I do want to say, sir, that I sincerely appreciate all that the Army has done for me. But I have issues to deal with that I can't handle while I'm still in uniform."

"Have you thought about the Reserve?"

"Yes, sir. I haven't made up my mind about that. But continuing on active duty just isn't going to work."

"Okay, Clark." Colonel Barnes sat back in his chair. "I'm sure you have your reasons. And I don't want to pry." He glanced down and to his left, as if pondering something, and then leaned forward and looked intently at Clark. "Let me just say that we hate to lose you. You're a fine officer." He paused to let that comment sink in, waiting for a reaction. When none came, he sat back again and continued. "But I'm sure you'll do well wherever you wind up."

"Thank you, sir."

"Do you have any plans?"

"Nothing specific, sir." Clark did not want to talk about Texas, and he certainly did not want to talk about Alan Taylor. Although Alan had performed well as a JAG trial counsel, prosecuting courts-martial, he departed the Army under a cloud. Clark didn't know the details but had heard that Alan was discharged before his commitment was up, alleging that a highly regarded JAG colonel had discriminated against him. As a result, he had tarnished his reputation among the old guard of the JAG Corps, of which Colonel Barnes was a member.

"Well, good luck to you, Clark. And if you decide you want to come back on active duty, give me a call."

"Thank you, sir. Will do." That was Clark's cue to leave, so he stood up and walked toward the door, pausing to say, "And by the way, sir, I *do* want to take the PT test one last time."

Colonel Barnes smiled and shook his head. "Okay, Clark. Have at it."

Early the next morning Clark took the PT test. He didn't max it. He achieved a perfect score on the push-ups and sit-ups but was forty seconds too slow for a perfect score on the two-mile run. He took the result in stride, though, and didn't mention it to anyone—except Dan, who grinned and reminded Clark that he'd offered to pace him on the run.

For the rest of the day, Clark went to various offices on post to deal with what the Army called "out processing." Although he'd left posts previously in his career, this time was the last time. When he finished, he said goodbye to Dan, Colonel Barnes, and his other colleagues and headed to his car with a box full of his own Army plaques and photographs. He smiled as he looked at the Fort McPherson sticker on the windshield and thought about those that had preceded it: West Point, Fort Knox, Fort

Hood, the JAG School, Panama. I guess I'll have to scrape that off, he thought.

Rather than head directly to the gate, he drove around the parade field, down the tree-lined street known as "general's row," past the immaculately cared-for Victorian homes where the generals of Forces Command lived. The last house on the street was where Colonel Barnes lived. The Commanding General said he always wanted to have his lawyer close by.

As Clark approached the gate, the guard snapped to attention and saluted. Clark returned the salute and, pulling onto the highway, whispered aloud, "And that's the last time I'll be doing that."

It hit Clark that he was thirty-three years old and had just left the institution where he had spent almost half his life. The Army had molded him. Hell, it had practically raised him. Now, everything would be different, and he wasn't sure he was ready.

# CHAPTER TWO

CLARK PULLED INTO the parking lot of River Oaks Club Apartments. Despite the classy sounding name, it was a shabby place. The only river nearby was the Chattahoochee, which was over three miles away, and there were no oaks, just a few pine trees that dropped sap onto the cars in the parking lot. And the only club around was a group of silhouetted figures who routinely gathered by the pool, a glowing joint passing among them. But the place was close to Fort McPherson and it was cheap—all he could afford following his divorce. Having no desire to stumble into a drug deal gone bad, Clark looked around before exiting his car. Seeing nothing, he got out, locked the car, and hurried into his apartment, closing the door and turning the deadbolt in a single motion.

After dropping his briefcase onto the counter, he reached for the phone and dialed a number from memory.

"Hey, Darlene, this is Bobby." He always started calls with his sister that way, even though he knew she never failed to recognize his voice.

"What's up? We haven't seen you in a while. Did you hear about all the thunderstorms down here? Our power was out for two days. We just got it back on today."

Hearing his sister's—or his mother's—voice always made him nostalgic. Both of them had sweet Southern accents that brought back memories of home and a simpler, gentler, better time.

"I processed out of the Army today, Sissy."

"Really? You said you were gonna do it, but it's still hard to believe."

"Well, technically it becomes official when my terminal leave is up, but for all intents and purposes, I'm out."

"Well, well. You've been a soldier since you went off to West Point. When was that?" She paused. "Fourteen years ago?"

"Fifteen. Yeah. I'll have to get used to being a civilian again. Are guys still wearing bell bottoms?"

"Oh Lord no, Bobby. You know that."

"How's Momma doing?"

"She's fine. You know her. She's got her bridge club with Betty Gray and her United Methodist Women. They just had their annual bazaar to raise money for missions. I think they set a record this year. Anyway, she stays busy. So. When are we gonna see you again?"

There was a long pause on Clark's end of the line. "It'll be a while."

"What's keeping you in Atlanta now that you're out of the Army? You don't have a girlfriend, do you?"

"No. That's the last thing I need. I'm interviewing for a job in Dallas."

"Georgia?"

"No. Texas."

"Texas? Why on earth do you want to go all the way out there? It's so far from home."

"It's a really good firm, Sissy, and, well, I just need to get out of Georgia." Clark blurted out the last comment, causing his sister to gasp.

"But this is your home, Bobby."

"Well, it's treated me like shit, so I'm leaving."

"You need to clean up that language, Bobby," Darlene said, momentarily reverting to her "big sister" role. "And surely you're not suggesting *we* mistreated you."

"No. Of course not. I'm referring to the fuc—" He caught the word in his mouth before it fully formed. "I'm referring to the court, Sissy. My divorce was a joke, especially the restrictions on my visitation with Ellie. It was all based on lies. A bunch of damn lies."

Darlene knew her brother was hurting, so she refrained from a second admonishment. "Well, Bobby, everybody was shocked by the judge's order. There's been all kinds of rumors about why he did it."

"That's just the point, Sissy. You said it: 'everybody.' Why did 'everybody' need to know about what was going on in my divorce?" Clark's voice was tense and raised, although Darlene knew he wasn't angry at her. He paused in an effort to compose himself. "When they took my deposition during the divorce, they got into a stupid thing I did in Panama. The only reason I agreed to that visitation order was to avoid having all that come out. Basically, it was blackmail. It was embarrassing enough to have Larry hear all that."

"It's none of my business, Bobby. You don't need to explain to me, but you know Pemberton is a small town. And you know how some people like to gossip. Even so, I don't think anybody thought Ellie needed to be protected from you."

"Well, apparently the judge did."

Hoping her brother would calm down, Darlene didn't respond right away. Then, sounding like their mother comforting him after a bitter disappointment, she said, "I hear you, Bobby. It shouldn't have been anybody's business, other than yours and Janelle's and the lawyers'."

"Well, that judge is an asshole!"

"I know, Bobby. He *is* an asshole."

Darlene's crude language made Clark chuckle. He'd never heard her talk like that. "Why, Darlene, you sound like my platoon sergeant."

"Well, he is a jerk. Nobody knows much about him. Larry said he was from someplace up around Atlanta. He'd been a big-city lawyer and then somehow got appointed to the bench down here when Judge Cochran died."

"I just wish Larry had done a better job in front of him," Robert said. "Do you realize how humiliating it is to have to have you or Momma present when I visit Ellie?"

Darlene could hear the tension in his voice; her response was calm and gentle. "You shouldn't bad mouth Larry, Bobby. He was a big help to us when Daddy died. I'm sure he did his best for you."

"I'm sorry, Sissy. I didn't mean to criticize Larry. I'm sure he did the best he could. I'm just upset."

Darlene paused, knowing her next comment might aggravate her brother again, and then softly said, "And besides, Bobby, you aren't going to make your visitation any easier by moving to Texas."

"Well, Georgia's treated me like crap! I just need to get the hell out of here." The line was silent for almost a minute. "Listen, Sissy, I've got to hang up. I'm getting too angry to talk about this anymore." He didn't wait for his sister's response before placing the receiver into the cradle.

Clark looked around his small apartment. The sun was going down, casting an orange glow through the window blinds, which created long shadows on the living room wall. He stood motionless for almost two minutes, contemplating what to do next. There wasn't much to pack: an old sofa that wasn't worth moving, a floor lamp he'd bought at the Goodwill store, and a portable television sitting on a cheap, pressboard stand he had found next to the dumpster. "A Distinguished Graduate of West Point and a graduate of the University of Georgia School of Law—you sure as hell don't have much to show for all that work," he said out loud. Turning toward his small kitchen, separated from his living room by only a counter, he shook his head and almost laughed outright. There were no pots or pans or dishes, because he didn't cook. There were several unmatched glasses in the cabinet and a few liquor bottles on the counter, but nothing in the refrigerator other than four bottles of Heineken and a moldy package of bologna. His books were scattered around the living room in irregular piles on the floor. There were his clothes, of course, most of which were uniforms or athletic attire, and a couple of sets of sheets and assorted towels. That was about it. He didn't need a moving company: everything would easily fit in a U-Haul trailer.

He poured a glass of Maker's Mark and walked over to his window. Looking out, he could see shadowy figures by the pool, a cloud of smoke hanging about them and their joint glowing in the darkness. "In Panama I would have been prosecuting those guys," he murmured. "Now, here I am living with them."

"Is God punishing me for what I did in Panama?" he asked aloud. "Daddy always said He doesn't work that way. But it sure as hell feels like it." He took a long drink and slumped down onto the sofa. "It makes no sense," he said, continuing his soliloquy. "Many people have done a lot worse and never suffered because of it." He refilled his glass and downed a third of it. The bourbon started to take hold. Slumping back into the sofa cushions, he rested his glass on his stomach. "It's too damn confusing. I need a fresh start."

The next morning Clark awoke, still on the sofa, an empty bottle of Maker's Mark on the floor next to him. His head felt as if his brain were swelling. He could hear his blood forcing its way through vessels that seemed too small. Even his eyes hurt. Heaving himself to his feet, he shuffled to the bathroom, took a shower, and dressed. He drove to a U-Haul pick-up location nearby, where he bought boxes and rented a trailer. After returning to his apartment and loading his few possessions, he asked his neighbor to help him move the sofa next to the dumpster and then returned the television stand to where he had found it months before.

Clark had befriended the elderly lady who managed the leasing office, which was fortunate, because she agreed to wait for him to turn in his apartment keys. It was after 5:30 p.m. by the time he dropped them off. She wished him well and said she would be praying for him.

He drove around the perimeter highway on the west side of Atlanta to Interstate 20 West, which would take him all the way to Dallas. Except for the cities and towns along the way, the scenery scarcely changed. The road stretching west was bordered by tall pines, most of which, at some point, would be harvested for lumber or pulp wood. He could almost hear his father talking about forestry management at the dinner table. "Those trees will soon make some fine family homes," he would say between bites of fried chicken.

The sun was slipping below the horizon as he crossed the Mississippi state line, painting the sky with swirling shades of yellow, orange, purple, and blue. The day is almost over, he thought. Good. I'm glad Georgia is miles behind me. I'm gonna get some coffee and drive straight through.

After dark, the trees seemed to be closer to the road; Clark sensed they were watching him, questioning why he was leaving home and headed west. He knew it made no sense. Why did he want to get farther away from his family, especially Ellie? The divorce. That awful visitation order. It was all so humiliating. Whenever he walked the streets of Pemberton, hand in hand with Ellie, his mother would be close behind them. He would see the furtive glances of people he had known his entire life and watch them whisper to each other, knowing they were speculating about why the judge had ordered supervised visitation. And he knew it was all his own fault. Those looks reminded him of that fact, and they wounded his spirit.

It was midnight when he crossed the Mississippi River at Vicksburg. The tall pines immediately gave way to swamps, creating an eerie landscape in the moonlight. He drove on, wondering whether he had made the right decision but having no desire to turn back. The pine trees returned when he crossed into Texas, and at first it seemed as if he were somehow back in Georgia. But as he approached Dallas, the trees became more sparse and the terrain flatter, eventually giving way to open plains, just like around Fort Hood.

The sun began to show itself in his rearview mirror. It'll be dawn by the time I get to Dallas, he thought. A new day.

# CHAPTER THREE

CLARK ARRIVED IN Dallas as the sun was coming up. The half-gallon of coffee he'd consumed during the trip had necessitated a number of stops, some of them alongside the road—proving he was still a country boy at heart. As he walked into the lobby of the La Quinta Inn and Suites, a young couple was at the desk, checking out. The young woman saw him staring at her with bleary eyes.

"You look tired, mister. Been driving all night?"

"Yeah. From Atlanta."

"Atlanta? Wow. We're from Jackson, Mississippi. We're headed to Los Angeles, California. I'm auditioning for a movie." She practically giggled when she talked and bounced from one foot to the other.

"Well, congratulations. I hope everything goes well for you."

"You, too, mister. Where are you headed?"

"Here. I'm starting over here."

"Dallas is a nice place but not like California."

"Have you been there before?"

"No, but I've read all about it. And I can't wait to get there. I'm Molly Henderson, by the way. This is my husband, Kenny." The young man turned and nodded from beneath a camouflage ball cap. "Look for my name in the movies, mister."

"Oh, I will, Molly. And it's Clark, uh, Robert Clark."

"Well, good luck to you, Robert Clark."

He watched as they walked outside, Molly virtually bouncing as she walked. Seeing her unabashed enthusiasm raised Robert's spirits, almost making him forget how tired he was.

Turning toward the desk clerk, he was met with a scowl that told him it was not going to be easy to obtain an early check-in. But after a few minutes of haggling and, more important, learning that the clerk had also served in the Army at Fort Hood, Robert got a key. Although the room felt used and worn, it smelled clean. He squeezed into the tightly fitted sheets and—despite all the coffee he'd consumed—slept as if he had been drugged. When he woke up, he was disoriented. He looked around the room, trying to get his bearings. The brochure on the nightstand said La Quinta Inn, Dallas, Texas. Right. I'm in Dallas, he thought. He picked up the phone and dialed Alan Taylor's number.

"This is Alan Taylor." He sounded like a radio disk jockey, impressed with the sound of his own voice.

"Hello, Alan, this is Robert."

"Robert?"

"Yeah, Robert Clark."

"Oh, Clark. Yeah, that's right, man, use your first name now. You're out of the Army." Robert could almost hear Alan's politician-style smile, especially when he emphasized the word "out." "How you been, man? When you gonna get to Dallas?"

"I'm here now."

"Now? Why didn't you call me? I don't have your interviews set up yet."

"I was ready to get out of Georgia, Alan. But it's no big deal. I can wait. I'm in no hurry."

"Yeah, well, I'm kinda busy this morning. Hold on just a minute." Robert could hear Alan talking to someone else, though he couldn't make out exactly what he was saying. Returning to their conversation Alan said, "Listen, I can break away for lunch, but it'll have to be fast. Why don't we meet at Dakota's Steakhouse? You can't miss it. It's near the office and across the street from the First Baptist Church. They take good care of the lawyers from Underwood & Crockett. You don't need a tie, but wear a sport coat at least."

"What time?"

"One thirty. That way we'll miss the lunch crowd."

"Okay. See you there. Thanks." Robert hung up the phone, buzzed the desk clerk, and asked for a wake-up call at 11:30 a.m. The instant his head hit the pillow, he was asleep again. When the wake-up call came, he fumbled for the phone, still in a sleepy fog. The hot shower felt good on his face and down his body, washing away his road weariness. He got directions to Dakota's from the front desk clerk and asked about leaving the trailer in the parking lot. After listening to the hotel manager explain how the hotel wouldn't be responsible for it, he headed out.

It took a bit of searching to locate the restaurant at the corner of North Akard and San Jacinto, because neither Alan nor the desk clerk had bothered to mention that it was underground. After finding it Robert took a seat at the bar since he was a few minutes early. The bartender, bald and probably in his fifties, asked if he wanted a drink.

"Just a Diet Coke." The newness of everything—leaving the Army, moving, a new city, the prospect of a new job, all of it—was unsettling. He'd grown up in the Army and understood how things worked in that environment. Now, everything would be different.

The bartender seemed pleasant enough, so Robert decided to strike up a conversation, thinking it might ease his nerves. "Why is it this restaurant underground?"

"That's a good question," the bartender said as he wiped the bar top. "I love telling this story 'cause it points out just how silly lawyers can make things." Robert winced, though the bartender didn't notice. "This spot used to belong to the First Baptist Church across the street. When they sold it to Lincoln Properties, they put a clause in the deed that said no owner could ever sell alcohol on former church property." He stopped wiping and looked at Robert. "Isn't that the silliest thing you ever heard?"

"I guess they really believe in the evils of alcohol." Robert shrugged his shoulders and thought about the folks back in Pemberton, who would probably agree it was a great idea.

"It's a bunch of BS," the bartender said with disgust. "I've seen those church folks in here. And some of 'em are big drinkers. They come in here on Saturday night and then head over there on Sunday morning."

"I don't doubt it," Robert said. "But where's the silly lawyer stuff come in?"

"Oh yeah. Let me get back to that." The bartender's attention turned to a young woman who had just seated herself at the bar. "Let me help this lady first. I'll be right back."

Watching the bartender take the woman's order, Robert pondered his comment about "silly lawyers." *Is that what people think of us—that we just play silly games?*

The bartender returned with a sheepish grin on his face. "That's one of the benefits of this job. I get to talk to gorgeous women. You'd be amazed what they'll tell you when you're the bartender, especially when it gets late and they've had a few."

"I'll bet. What about the silly lawyer stuff?"

"Oh yeah. So, the deed prohibited any future owner from selling alcohol, but as you can see, we're doing that." He looked at Robert with wide eyes, as if expecting a response, so Robert nodded. "Anyway, a lawyer figured out that when the deed said 'on the grounds,' " the bartender indicated quotation marks with his fingers, "it didn't mean *below* the ground. So, Lincoln Properties dug an eighteen foot hole and built this restaurant in it. Ain't that something?"

"Crazy stuff," Robert replied.

"Crazy lawyer shit."

"What's this about 'crazy lawyer shit,' Jake?" Alan Taylor was walking up wearing an impeccably tailored suit and a practiced, politician-style smile.

"Not you, Mr. Taylor. Of course, not you. You help people gettin' sued, don't you?"

Robert thought the bartender seemed a bit too concerned. *What does that mean? Is Alan some sort of VIP?*

"You got that right, Jake," Alan said, slapping his hand on the bar. "But I see crazy shit, too. Listen, I gotta take my friend *Robert* here to my favorite table." Walking toward the table, Alan put his arm on Robert's shoulder. "You're looking good, man. How long's it been? Six years?"

"About that."

"We had some good times, didn't we? The JAG School was a fun place, but we're going to have some good times here, too. Underwood & Crockett is a great place to work."

"I don't have the job yet, Alan."

"A minor detail, buddy. I got your interviews set up this morning. They want you to come in tomorrow at eight thirty, but it's really a formality. I've already greased the skids for you."

"Thanks, Alan, but remember, I don't have that Harvard sheepskin like you do."

"That doesn't matter. I told them all about you. We need associates with maturity and experience. You'll have no problem. But," Alan looked Robert up and down, "you've got to get rid of the Post Exchange wardrobe, man. You look like a soldier on his first leave after basic training. You're going to be big time now. I want you to go to Culwell & Son. It's on Hillcrest. Ask for Mike Culwell. He's the founder's grandson. Tell him I sent you."

Robert looked down at his green plaid sport coat, which in fact had come from the Post Exchange at Fort Hood. "I'm not sure I can afford a store like that, Alan."

"Robert, if you want to make a million bucks, you've got to look like a million bucks."

It was clear Alan had followed his own advice. A model from the pages of *GQ* could not have looked any better. His hair was shorter than when he was in the Army, and he'd shaved his mustache. His suit was a perfectly tailored blue pinstripe with cuffed trousers; his shirt, white and crisply starched. Cufflinks reminiscent of gold swirls of rope peeked out of his sleeves. His tie was a red Hermès, although at that point Robert had no idea what an Hermès tie was. He just knew it looked good. And expensive.

"Stick to blues and grays. Don't get anything too wild with the ties. White and light blue shirts only. And you'll also need a pair of black cap-toe shoes. And remember to always keep them shined." Alan sat up straight and tucked his chin a bit. "What am I saying? I'm talking to a West Pointer about shining his shoes? I've lost it." He chuckled and then motioned for the waiter to come over. "I'll have the usual, Ramón, the grilled salmon salad and ice tea."

"Of course, Mr. Taylor. And the gentleman?"

Robert glanced at the menu and then handed it to the waiter and said, "I'll have the same, please."

The waiter left, and Alan leaned in. "So tell me what's been going on, man? I can't believe you're here in Dallas with me."

"Well, I got divorced. And let's just say it didn't go well."

"I'm sorry to hear that. You've got a kid, right? A little girl?"

"Yeah, but my visitation with her is governed by a court order that requires my mom or my sister to be present. It sucks. So, I decided to come out here and start over. Every visit with her has to be planned anyway." Robert practically spit out the words. "I'll probably see her about as much living out here as I would if I were working in Atlanta."

Although that last comment made no sense, Alan decided it was better to change the subject. "Well, Texas is the land of do-overs, my man. And you're going to love Underwood & Crockett. It's the premier firm in Texas." Alan smoothed his napkin in his lap. "Have you thought about what kind of work you'd like to do?"

"Not really. I did a bunch of trial work in courts-martial, but I'm not sure how that translates."

"Hey, man. Trial work is trial work. That's what I do, and I love it."

The waiter appeared with their salads, and Alan wasted no time before digging in. "Forgive me for rushing, man, but I've gotta get back." He took a bite of salmon. "You tried a murder case, didn't you?"

"Yeah."

"And you got the guy convicted, right?"

"Yeah, but my key witness changed his testimony after the trial, so the commanding general set the conviction aside."

"In other words, your witness went crying to the defense counsel?"

"Not exactly." Robert adjusted himself in his seat. "Could we talk about what I'll be facing tomorrow?"

"Come on, man. You got hazed as a plebe at West Point. This will be nothing. Just don't talk too much. Lawyers like to hear themselves talk. So, let them. Just look at them intently and nod your head. Occasionally say something like 'that's an interesting question.' Stuff like that. You'll be fine. If you get interviewed by Stephan Edgar, don't sweat it. He comes across as a prick to everybody. Just get that suit this afternoon. Tell Mike

I said you need it for interviews with the law firm tomorrow. I've sent a bunch of our lawyers to him. Come in tomorrow lookin' sharp."

"Okay." Robert started to eat but stopped. "Alan, I can't thank you enough. I really appreciate what you're doing."

Alan grinned as he chewed. "All of us need allies, Clark. I mean *Robert*." He wiped his mouth with his napkin and whispered, "When times get tough, we need people we can count on."

"You know, that's what my dad always said about family." A vision of his father flashed through Robert's mind.

"Hell, I probably stole that line from my old man. He nags my ass, but he means well, I guess." Alan sat back in his chair. "Listen, I'd like you to come to dinner tomorrow at my parents' house. It's my night to visit them, and I'm sure they'd like to meet you. I've told them all about you."

"I don't want to impose on your visit, Alan."

"You won't be imposing. You'll be good company. Maybe my dad won't ride my ass so much if you're there."

Robert decided not to ask about that last comment. "Yeah. I'd love to come, as long as you're sure it won't be an imposition." Alan shook his head. As they continued to eat, Robert asked, between bites, "Can you give me some recommendations on where I should look for a place to live? I'm checked in at the La Quinta, but I'd like to find a permanent place soon."

"Well, that ain't exactly the Adolphus." Alan snickered and sipped his tea.

"The Adolphus?"

"Yeah. It an old hotel on Commerce Street. Been around for something like seventy years. But La Quinta is cool, too." Alan looked down at his plate to hide his grin. After a few seconds he looked back at Robert. "You know, you have to live in Highland Park. It's the best neighborhood in Dallas. You can still find some rentals there, and if not, just let me know, and I'll call some people and find one for you. There are some really cool old duplexes."

"Is that where you live?"

"Not exactly. I have an apartment downtown, but—don't say anything around my parents about this—I live with my girlfriend. Her parents gave her a house as a graduation present from college. Can you believe that? A house. It's near SMU. But listen, a duplex rental would be cool for you. And Highland Park is the best." Alan pushed back from the table. "I've got to get back to work, man." He smiled and stood up. "Be at the office before eight thirty, and get that suit squared away today. Make me proud, brother."

As he walked out, Alan said something to the waiter, who came over and started clearing Alan's place. "You not finished, señor? Take your time. Mr. Taylor's always in a hurry. He never finish the lettuce, just the salmon."

"I guess you can bring me the check. Ramón, isn't it?"

"Oh no, señor. Mr. Taylor have an account. He told me to put it on his account. Enjoy your meal."

≼

At 8:15 A.M. the following morning, Robert walked into the offices of Underwood & Crockett, which were located in Lincoln Plaza, adjacent to the Dakota's restaurant. He was wearing a new gray suit, a white shirt with his West Point cufflinks, a maroon tie, and, of course, black cap-toe shoes. The receptionist had him take a seat in the waiting area.

This is so different, he thought, as he took it all in. It looks like a New York art gallery—glass walls looking out onto the cityscape, directional lighting showcasing modern art, sleek Bauhaus furniture, white marble floors, stark white walls. If only Colonel Barnes and Dan could see this place. It's a far cry from Fort McPherson.

In a few minutes a tall, leggy woman approached him. Unlike the receptionist and several other women walking about the office, she did not have big hair, heavy makeup, and big hoop earrings. In fact, Robert thought she could have been a fashion model. Her hair, which was light brown with blonde highlights, was slightly shorter than shoulder length and had only the hint of curls on the ends. She was wearing a white jewel neck blouse, a collarless red blazer with padded shoulders, and a black pencil skirt, which fell just above her knees. The ensemble was topped off by a simple string of pearls and matching earrings. But all that classy attire was totally eclipsed by her stunning natural beauty. She extended her hand and said, "Hi, I'm Megan Miller, the recruiting coordinator. Welcome to Underwood & Crockett." Robert scrambled to his feet. Glancing down at a sheet of paper, she continued, "You have a full schedule of interviews this morning, Mr. Clark, and then lunch with Alan Taylor and Davis Burnet."

"Sounds good." Robert took a deep breath.

"We'll do everything in here," she said as she ushered him into a conference room off the reception area. A table, made from a massive slab of pink granite, dominated the room. Through the floor-to-ceiling glass there was yet another view of the Dallas skyline, brightly sunlit, with a few puffy clouds gliding by. "Help yourself to coffee, juice, or water," Megan said. "Your first interviewer will be here shortly."

Over the next few hours, a stream of lawyers, young and old, came in and talked to Robert, sometimes two at a time. As Alan had predicted, they talked mostly about themselves and the firm and asked only a few easy questions. Fortunately, Stephan Edgar—the partner Alan had warned him about—was not among them. Around noon, Alan walked in with an older lawyer, a distinguished man who bore a striking resemblance to the actor Robert Redford. He had a strong jaw and looked athletically trim, like a runner or a tennis player. His hair was almost blond with a few flecks of gray, mostly at the temples. And, like Alan, he was dressed like a Hollywood actor, playing a lawyer on TV.

"Robert, this is Davis Burnet, the head of our corporate section and the chairman of our hiring committee. He's been anxious to meet you. Like you and me, he was a JAG officer in the Army at one time, although you spent most of your time working for the General Counsel of the Army, right Davis?"

The corners of Davis's mouth began to curl, and he and reached out his hand to Robert. "Why, yes, Alan, I wasn't aware that that tidbit was common knowledge at the firm." Turning back to Robert, he continued, as if he felt the need to explain. "Unlike the two of you, I didn't get to try cases. But I was fortunate to be asked to work in the Pentagon after graduating from law school. I had an ROTC commitment to repay, so I owed the Army four years. Many of my friends had to go straight to Vietnam." He paused, a distant look on his face. "But I'm sure we old Army men don't need to talk about that. Let's go get some lunch. You said you could drive, right Alan?"

The three men took the elevator to the parking garage, and Alan led the way to his late model, black BMW 530.

"Nice car, Alan. We must be paying you too much," Davis said.

"Absolutely not," Alan said with an obsequious grin. "Where are we going?"

"The Petroleum Club."

Alan drove a few blocks down San Jacinto Street to the Chase Tower on Ross Avenue, and the three of them took the elevator to the thirty-eighth floor. When they entered the club, Robert immediately felt out of place, despite his new suit. He'd never been in such elegant surroundings—antique furnishings, oriental rugs, original works of art on the walls, and what seemed like scores of waiters and staff bustling about. And all the guests could have easily been patrons of Culwell & Son.

"We have a private room, so we can talk," Davis said as he led the way through the dining room, pausing to greet some guests and wave to others. After they were seated and ordered lunch, Davis scrutinized Robert for an uncomfortably long time without saying anything. A smile finally emerged, though he seemed to be trying to suppress it, like a British aristocrat talking to a servant. "Tell me about yourself, Robert. Alan says you're almost Superman."

Robert squirmed in his seat while trying to think of something witty to say. "I'm probably more like Clark Kent. I just try to keep my head down and work hard."

"Well, that's just the kind of man we need at Underwood & Crockett," Davis said, smoothing his napkin on his lap. "Our lawyers come from the best law schools in the country, like Alan here, but we're also looking for men of proven accomplishment. I know we don't want to talk too much about the Army, but your record indicates the kind of dogged determination that we're looking for in our lawyers."

"Thank you, sir."

Davis dropped his chin in an attempt to camouflage his grin. "These days we aren't as formal as we used to be, Robert, or perhaps, as you're used to in the Army. So, don't worry about that 'sir' business." He narrowed his eyes to a fixed gaze. "Just work hard and do good work. That's what we want."

The conversation then drifted to a variety of topics, including college football, which Robert learned was even more of a religion in Texas than in Georgia. He also learned that Davis had been the captain of the track team at the University of Texas before attending law school at Yale. It seemed that everyone at Underwood & Crockett was an overachiever. They finished lunch and ordered coffee before Davis returned to the matter at hand. "I've spoken to the lawyers with whom you interviewed this morning, and we are prepared to make you an offer."

Robert sat up straight—almost like a plebe at West Point. He hadn't expected things to move so fast. What he didn't know was that Alan had not only "greased the skids," he had helped the firm conduct a fairly extensive investigation of his background before he ever left Georgia.

"That's fantastic," Robert said, sounding a bit too enthusiastic.

Turning to Alan, Davis said, through another stifled smile, "Have Robert sit down with Megan when we get back." Returning to Robert, he continued. "She'll go over the details and handle the paperwork to bring you onboard."

"I look forward to it."

"We do, too, Robert. Welcome to the firm. Now, let's get back to work, shall we, gentlemen?"

# CHAPTER FOUR

ROBERT FOLLOWED ALAN to the recruiting coordinator's office to complete the paperwork necessary to make him an associate at Underwood & Crockett. Megan's office was small, though large enough to accommodate her desk and a round table with four chairs. The shelves behind her desk bore keepsakes from her days at Southern Methodist University, including a picture of her in a cheerleading uniform. Alan greeted Megan and then said he had to get back to work and left.

"Things certainly moved fast for you, Mr. Clark," Megan said. "I don't think I've ever processed anyone so quickly. Mr. Burnet said he wanted you on board today."

"Please call me Robert."

It had been a long time since Robert had been so close to such a stylish, attractive woman. He consciously tried not to stare and to project a professional image.

"Okay, Robert. Let's get started."

On the table were the various form documents for Robert to sign, concerning medical insurance and other benefits, as well as his offer letter, outlining the terms of his employment. Although he'd been a lawyer for over six years, the firm slotted him as a third-year associate for pay and advancement. He didn't mind: his salary was going to be almost twice what he'd been making as an Army major.

After they finished the paperwork, Megan explained that each associate was expected to bill 2,200 hours every year. "I know that sounds like you'll have no social life, but you'll find that our lawyers still manage to have fun together."

Robert looked up to see her staring at him, doe-eyed, which caused him to squirm in his chair a bit. After some quick mental math, he concluded—erroneously, as he would soon learn—that the 2,200-hour standard meant he'd put in slightly more than forty hours a week with two weeks left for vacation. That shouldn't be too bad, he thought.

The rest of the day was taken up with finding his assigned office, meeting his assistant, ordering business cards, and other administrative matters. His office was on an outside wall, so he had a view overlooking the First Baptist Church. Staring out the window, he thought about the bartender at Dakota's and what he'd said about the people in that church. No wonder so many people think Christians are hypocrites, he thought. Daddy wasn't that way, and Momma certainly isn't. People ought to talk less about their religion and just lead good lives like they did. I hope I can find that path out here.

⟡

That evening, still wearing his new suit, Robert drove to the home of Alan's parents, which was located a few miles south of Dallas in DeSoto, Texas. He parked on the street and approached their modest, but well-maintained, brick ranch. Every light in the house, including the outside floodlights, appeared to be on.

Alan answered the doorbell, wearing his suit trousers and dress shirt but no jacket or tie. "Get in here, man. My dad is giving me a ration of shit." Alan gave Robert the once over and grinned. "You didn't need to come in your new suit, but my dad will be impressed."

"I don't want to get in the middle of a family argument, Alan."

"Don't worry about it. He wouldn't feel like himself if he wasn't giving me shit about not coming to church and not calling my mom. You know the drill. You probably heard the same thing from your dad."

Robert had not, but said nothing. As he entered the foyer, he noticed a desk light on in the room to his left, which probably had been designated the formal living room in the original configuration of the house but had been converted into what appeared to be an office. In the dim light above the lamp, he could make out numerous photographs, plaques, and other souvenirs of a life well spent, including some relating to military service, though he couldn't tell exactly what.

"That's my old man's retreat," Alan said, gesturing to the room. "He goes in there to reminisce about the 'old days' and act like he's doing something important."

Robert stared at Alan in disbelief. Never would he have said something like that about his father. Peering into Mr. Taylor's office, he thought about how much he would give to have even one more day to talk with his dad.

"Come on, man. I want you to meet my family." Alan grabbed Robert by the arm and ushered him into the family room at the back of the house. The aromas emanating from the kitchen reminded Robert of home and how much he missed his mother's cooking. A distinguished older gentleman was seated in a recliner reading the *Wall Street Journal*, which he folded and set aside as he rose to greet Robert. "Dad, this is Robert Clark, the new lawyer I've been telling you about." Alan's father extended his hand.

"Pleased to meet you, Mr. Taylor," Robert said. "Thank you for having me."

"We're pleased to have you, Robert. Alan's told us a great deal about you."

"But I want to hear it from the horse's mouth," said a woman entering the family room from the kitchen wearing an apron and drying her hands with a towel. Her handshake was a virtual embrace. "We are so pleased to have you join us."

"As you probably figured out, Robert, this is my mom," Alan said.

"Pleased to meet you, Mrs. Taylor."

"Oh, please call me Yolanda, Robert. Or is it Bobby?"

"What about us?" two bubbly teenagers asked, almost in unison, as they entered from the hallway on the other side of the room.

"It's 'Robert,' mom," Alan said. "And these are my sisters: Brianna and Jasmine. As you can see, they're twins."

"Pleased to meet all of you. Thank you so much for having me."

"I thought you said he was an old country boy…"

"Shut up, Brianna."

"Alan, don't talk to your sister like that," Mr. Taylor said, drawing down his eyebrows. "Where are your manners?"

"Okay. Okay." Turning to Robert, Alan explained, "I just told them you were from a small town in South Georgia. I never said you were a 'country boy.' " Alan looked back at his sisters. "Didn't that fancy private high school teach you two anything? You need to watch what you say or you're gonna have trouble at Spelman this fall." Alan glanced at his father as if to ask: "Is that better?" Returning to his sisters, he continued. "Robert's a member of the bar—a lawyer like me." And then with his usual smile. "And he looks like it, doesn't he?"

"Enough of this silliness," Yolanda said. "It's time to eat."

As they filed into the dining room, Robert was reminded of how his mother would set the table for special occasions: cloth napkins and the good dishes and silver. There were even fresh flowers and lighted candles on the table.

"You must be special, Robert," Alan said. "We normally eat in the kitchen."

"Now, you be quiet, Alan," Yolanda said. "Girls, help me bring in the dinner."

A feast emerged from the kitchen: fried chicken, black-eyed peas, fried okra, mashed potatoes, and cornbread. As the girls placed the platters onto the table, Robert's mouth began to water, just as it had at Sunday dinner back home. Alan reached for a piece of fried okra.

"Son, wait until your mother is seated and we've said the blessing," Mr. Taylor said. Yolanda walked in, having removed her apron, and Mr. Taylor rose to seat her. After he sat down, he said, in his rich baritone voice, "Bow your heads, please. Our most gracious Heavenly Father, thank you for the many blessings that you have bestowed upon the Taylor family. Please make each of us good stewards of those blessings. Thank you for our new friend Robert Clark. Please watch over him as he embarks on a new chapter of his career here in Dallas. Please guide each of us and direct us in all that we say and do that it may be pleasing unto you. In the name of our Lord and Savior Jesus Christ, Amen."

Everyone repeated, "Amen," and the chatter began. Brianna and Jasmine peppered Robert with questions about where he'd lived, about West

Point, about whether he was married. When they learned he was divorced, it opened a new flood of questions about girlfriends, dating, and nightlife in Dallas.

"The man just got to Dallas," Alan said. "Y'all stop bugging him and let him eat." That quieted the two teenagers, and the gentleman at the head of the table cleared his throat.

"Robert, I would be interested to hear more about your time at West Point," Mr. Taylor began. "In any of your studies, did the name Benjamin O. Davis, Jr., ever come up?"

"You mean, General Davis, the Air Force officer?"

"Yes." Mr. Taylor smiled, clearly pleased with the response.

"Yes, sir. He was the first African-American general officer, I believe."

"Well, not exactly," Mr. Taylor said. "That would have been his father, Benjamin O. Davis, Sr." Mr. Taylor sipped his ice tea and continued. "I had the honor of serving with the younger General Davis in the 99th Pursuit Squadron in North Africa during World War II. He was a young colonel at the time."

"Daddy, Robert doesn't want to talk about Army stuff," Alan interjected. "He's a civilian lawyer now."

Mr. Taylor stared at his son with a look of disapproval and disappointment.

"Oh, no, Alan," Robert said. "I do want to hear about it. My dad was a tanker in World War II."

Mr. Taylor seemed pleased and began recounting a number of stories he'd obviously told many times about how the Tuskegee Airmen, as they were called, flew combat missions in North Africa, Sicily, and Italy. Although Robert knew they had been mistreated in the racially segregated Army of the time, there was no hint of rancor in Mr. Taylor's voice. It was obvious he was proud of what they'd accomplished and proud to have been a part of the legendary unit. His voice was warm and his eyes bright as he told of the bomber crews that specifically requested escort by the Tuskegee Airmen on their bombing runs. Several times Robert glanced at Alan, who continued to eat and occasionally rolled his eyes in reaction to something his father said.

When Mr. Taylor finished and began to eat, Robert asked him if he was still involved in aviation. "Barely," came the response from Alan. "He works at Dallas-Fort Worth Airport, but he doesn't fly."

"I believe that question was directed to me, Alan. You seem to have forgotten your manners this evening." Mr. Taylor looked at his son sternly before turning to Robert. "Alan is correct. I'm a supervisor in the maintenance department at DFW. It's our job to keep the airport's facilities and equipment in good condition. We recently learned that British Airways plans to fly its Concordes—the supersonic passenger aircraft—to DFW as a substitute for its DC-10 service. That's big news, which will require significant adjustments to how we do things." Mr. Taylor took a bite of his dinner and then continued. "In addition to airport maintenance, I also get involved with working on aircraft from time to time. Although I don't fly commercially, I do have a civilian pilot's license and occasionally fly a private plane on weekends."

"You own your own plane?" Robert asked, wide-eyed.

"Heavens, no, son. I have friends who are members of a flying club. They let me fly their plane sometimes. If you're interested, you can come fly with me when I get a chance again."

Robert glanced at Alan, who ever so slightly pursed his lips and shook his head, apparently wanting to avoid another reprimand from his father. The rest of the dinner conversation centered on Robert: where he was from, his family, and his exploits in the Army, including the murder case he'd prosecuted in Panama, a topic Alan brought up. Robert didn't volunteer much about the case, other than expressing his disappointment about how it turned out. When they finished dinner, Alan announced that he had brought cigars, and after fending off his mother's protests and assuring her they would smoke them in the back yard, he and Robert retired to chairs on the patio.

"These bad boys are from Cuba," Alan said as he pulled the cigars from his pocket. "Bet you never had one of these."

"Oh, we had them in Panama all the time. But you're right: they're a cut above anything you can get here in the States. How'd you get them?"

Alan just smiled and raised his eyebrows before producing an expensive-looking cutter and lighter. He clipped the ends off each cigar, lit his, and passed the other cigar and the lighter to Robert. After taking a few puffs, he asked, "So what do you think of my old man?"

"I like him. He reminds me of my dad."

"He's black, Robert. That's a decided difference. He should have been flying those damn planes instead of working on them all these years. They treat him like a yard nigger."

Robert stared at his friend. "I thought we weren't supposed to use that word. My mom always said it was vulgar."

"*You're* not supposed to use it. But that doesn't apply to black folks. It's an epithet only when you're trying to put yourself above somebody else." Alan took a long draw on his cigar, causing the end to glow bright orange. "This is a beautiful evening, isn't it? The perfect way to end the day."

"Yeah. Thanks again for the invitation." Robert savored his cigar, exhaling slowly and forming smoke rings that drifted up into the darkness. "By the way, I signed a lease this afternoon. Like you said, I found a nice duplex in Highland Park. It'll be the shortest commute I've ever had."

"What street are you on?"

"Hawthorne. In fact, I've already moved in, although there's not much in the place yet."

Alan turned toward Robert. "Are you on the part of Hawthorne that's actually in Highland Park, or are you in the city limits of Dallas?"

"I don't know. Does it really matter?"

"Well, you should find out. And, yes, it does matter. You want to actually be in Highland Park. It's important." Alan sat back in his chair.

"Where did you say your place was?" Robert asked.

"It's close to downtown, near The Crescent, which is where I wish our offices were." Alan sat back up and in a hushed voice said, "But remember, I live with my girlfriend, and my folks don't know that. They wouldn't like it, especially my old man."

"Okay. I won't say anything."

"You see, she's a rich white girl. Her daddy—who's a client of the firm—has got more money than God. They bought her a house on Mockingbird Lane. We'll have to have you over sometime."

"That'd be great. What's her name? Your girlfriend."

"Michelle. Michelle my belle." Alan laughed and took another draw.

They were quiet for a few minutes before the conversation turned to the firm and what Robert could expect. Alan tried to describe the personalities of several of the partners, including Davis Burnet. He reminded Robert that Davis is an important partner and that he pronounces his last name as if it were "burn it." He also mentioned a woman named Sharon Alexander who Alan thinks is a lesbian. "Stay away from her," he warned. "She eats young associates alive. There's an associate named Diana Maguire, who's the only one who can work with her. She's probably her secret lover." Robert fumbled with his cigar, causing it to tumble into his lap. He jumped up and brushed off the ashes. Ignoring Robert's reaction, Alan continued. "Don't worry about Alexander, Robert, or any of the rest of that stuff I just told you. Just be careful. Listen, your duplex isn't far from the coolest nightlife in Dallas. You're gonna love it here." And then, though his cigar was only half smoked, he abruptly sat up in his chair. "You know. I need to get going. Talking about Michelle has made me horny." He winked. "I need to get home."

"Okay," Robert said, reluctantly extinguishing his half-smoked Cuban in the ash tray, "let me thank your mom first, and I'll go, too. Should we throw these butts and ashes away?"

"I'll just throw them into the bushes," Alan said, picking up the ashtray and tossing the contents behind a hibiscus bush with magenta blossoms. "Mom will never notice. Organic fertilizer, right?"

On the drive back to his duplex, Robert reflected about his friend. He was grateful that Alan had gone to so much trouble to help him get a job at Underwood & Crockett but puzzled that his relationship with his father—who seemed like an incredible man—was so strained. And why hadn't he told his parents about Michelle? That was weird.

But despite all that, Robert decided simply to be grateful to have Alan as a friend. Alan's relationship with his parents was none of his business. And besides, he thought, I've got plenty of my own problems to worry about. Should I have come to Dallas? Or is it just going to complicate my visitation with Ellie? And what about furniture and housewares? I have no idea of what to get. Alan made such a big deal about being in Highland Park. I guess I'm going to have to step it up a notch from what I had in Atlanta.

Driving through the dark streets of Dallas, Robert couldn't decide whether he was happy or sad. He was starting a new career with a prestigious law firm. But what about his family back home? His mom and sister, his friends, and most of all, Ellie—sweet little Ellie.

# CHAPTER FIVE

"LET'S GO TO lunch at Dakota's." Alan Taylor was standing in the door of Robert's office. It was two days after the dinner at his parents' house.

Robert looked up from his desk, which was covered with stacks of papers and books. "Sure. What time?"

"Let's do one thirty again. That way we'll avoid the lunch crowd. Besides, you look busy, so we need to be quick."

Alan walked away, and Robert returned to the research assignment that had created what appeared to be the aftermath of a tornado in front of him. File folders, papers, and books were strewn across his desk. The morning mail had included an internal office distribution envelope containing a memorandum from a partner he didn't know. It instructed him to prepare and deliver a memorandum by the following morning, summarizing any recent developments in Texas and Delaware law concerning the fiduciary duties of the officers and directors of a corporation. Anxiety churned his stomach, causing him to regret eating the breakfast burrito he bought at a gas station on the way to work. Although he had taken a course on corporations in law school, that was over seven years ago. He didn't remember anything about those fiduciary duties and had no idea how to determine what constituted a "recent development." And, Delaware seemed to have scores of cases dealing with the subject. How could he possibly complete the project on time?

"You look stressed. Is this a bad time?" Robert looked up to see a young woman standing in his doorway, ringlets of blonde hair framing her perfectly symmetrical face, accented by glistening sapphire blue eyes. "I'm Diana Maguire. My office is down the hall." She smiled—a dazzling, captivating smile, complete with dimples. "I mostly work with Sharon Alexander. We do lending and general corporate work. Do you have a minute?"

Robert stumbled to his feet, knocking a book to the floor in the process. "Pleased to meet you. I'm, uh, Robert Clark." He felt his face flush as he extended his hand. "But I guess you know that. The name's on the door, isn't it?" His anxiety had morphed into the awkwardness he always felt in the presence of an attractive woman. He shook her hand, which was soft, though she had a firm grip. "Yes," he said, "I've got time. What do you need?"

Diana sat down in the chair across from him. "I just wanted to meet you. Alan Taylor talked about you incessantly, so I wanted to see if the man matched the legend."

Robert winced and dropped his chin. "I'm afraid Alan might have hyped me a bit too much. I'm new to civilian practice and feeling a little overwhelmed."

They chatted for several minutes, although Diana did not offer much about herself. Instead, she asked Robert about growing up in Georgia, about West Point and the Army, and about where he'd gone to law school. She seemed to be sizing him up and then, out of nowhere, asked, "Are you by chance working on a research memo requested by Stephen Edgar?"

Robert's eyes widened in disbelief. "Yeah," he almost whispered. "How'd you know?"

"He does that to almost every new associate. Gives you a tough research assignment with an impossible deadline and then sees what you come up with. What's yours on?"

"The fiduciary duties of officers and directors."

"Well then, you're in luck, Robert. That one's been done, and I know where it is. Come on. I'll show you."

Following Diana down the hall, Robert could not help but notice her shapely figure as her hips swayed from side to side in a sensuous glide. Not having been with a woman since he left Panama three years earlier, he was unable to keep his thoughts professional. He started to visualize what she'd look like naked, her blonde hair cascading around her breasts. But then he caught himself: What am I thinking? I don't even know this woman.

Diana turned down a windowless corridor and opened what appeared to be the door to a closet. The small room was dark and crammed with file cabinets and boxes. Making her way around a row of cabinets, she opened a drawer, found what she was looking for, and handed it to Robert. "This should help you."

He opened the tattered manila folder and found several memorandums and copies of cases and other materials addressing the fiduciary duties of officers and directors. All the memorandums were addressed to Stephen Edgar. The most recent one was less than a year old.

"This is incredible, Diana. So, it's okay for me to use this stuff? Whose file is it?"

"It's ours. Of course it's okay to use it. That's why I brought you here. It's what we call an 'associate file.' The associates in this firm stick together. You won't find that kind of cooperation at most firms in Dallas, because everyone is worried about the competition to make partner." Robert's puzzled expression prompted her to explain. "Not everyone makes partner, Robert. And if they don't, they're normally asked to leave. Consequently, associates in other firms don't go out of their way to help each other. They view it as helping the competition. We even have a few of those types at Underwood & Crockett. But *they* don't know about this room or these files." She paused to let that sink in and gauge whether Robert understood. "We have all sorts of research we share among those who choose to be collegial."

"So, what do I do with this?" he asked, holding up the file.

"Update the research, which should be easy to do. Just see whether the major cases described in the memorandums were overturned or whether they were cited as precedent in any subsequent cases. If there are new cases, they should be easy to find because they'll probably cite the cases in those memos. And if you find anything new, document it and include it in the file to help the next unlucky soul who gets one of Edgar's memos. You can return the file to me when you're finished."

"This is amazing, Diana. I can't thank you enough."

"You don't need to thank me. Just update the research for the next person." She paused, tilted her head ever so slightly, and smiled. "You want to go to lunch? I can tell you more about the unique features of Underwood & Crockett."

"I would, I would love to, but I have other plans."

"Taylor?"

"Yeah. I sort of owe him. He got me this job. We go back a long way."

Diana's expression went blank. "Okay. A raincheck then."

"Sure."

They walked back to Robert's office, and Diana continued a few doors down the hall to hers. He watched her walk away, exuding sex in a girl-next-door kind of way, but having no clue she was doing it. Alan has got to be mistaken, he thought. Such a gorgeous woman can't possibly be a lesbian. The few gay women Robert had known in the Army kept to themselves and resembled tomboys, not fashion models. He closed his door, sat down at his desk, and stared out the window for a few minutes, trying to get his mind off Diana and back on his research project. But then his thoughts shifted.

He picked up his phone and dialed a familiar number. "Momma, this is Bobby."

"Well, what a pleasant surprise. How's it going out there in Texas?"

Something about his mother's voice always comforted him. In his mind's eye he could see her sitting at her kitchen table, dressed as if she were about to go downtown to shop.

"I got my first big assignment."

"That's wonderful, sweetheart. Are you going to court?"

"No, Momma. This is a research assignment. It deals with corporate law."

"That sounds interesting. Do you like your new job?"

"So far. I can't talk long, because I need to get back to work."

"Okay. Well, it's good to hear your voice, even if it's short."

"Have you seen Ellie lately?"

"Well, I babysit her once in a while. And of course I see her and Janelle downtown from time to time."

"Is she doing all right?" he asked.

"She seems to be. Haven't you talked to her?"

"No, ma'am. Every time I call Janelle's daddy's house, I get the answering machine. I think she's screening my calls."

"Oh, I don't think she'd do that, sweetheart. You must just be missing her. There's a time difference between here and Dallas, you know."

"Yes, Momma, I know. Could you maybe call me at the office or my apartment sometime when you're babysitting her, so I can talk to her?"

"Of course. Are you sure you're okay, sweetheart?"

"Yes, ma'am. I'm fine. I just need to talk to Ellie. Listen, Momma, I need to get back to work. I'll call you when I can, and please call me the next time you're keeping Ellie."

"I sure will, sweetheart. Call me again soon."

"I will."

Robert hung up the phone and opened the associate file, which was bulging with documents. By 1:00 p.m.—and after several trips to the firm library—he had completed an outline for what he thought would be a respectable memorandum.

At 1:20 p.m. Alan appeared, and the two of them headed to Dakota's. As they sat down at a table, Alan said, "You look more relaxed than you did this morning."

"Yeah. Thanks to an associate file."

"A what? Alan's eyebrows pressed together as he stared at Robert.

Think quickly, Robert thought. He doesn't know about the associate files. He must be one of those associates Diana was talking about.

"Isn't that, uh, what you call the folder of materials you put together on a research project?" Robert asked. "I finally got it organized, and now I'm ready to tackle the memo."

"Oh. Yeah. I'm the same way," Alan said. "I just never heard of anyone calling it an 'associate file.' " Smiling, he motioned for Ramón to come to their table. "I'll have the usual, Ramón."

"Me, too, Ramón. The salmon salad was delicious last time."

Alan turned and fixed his gaze on Robert. "So, are you getting settled?" A sly grin appeared. "Got it all figured out already?"

"Hell, no, Alan. I don't have anything figured out. This is completely different from anything I'm used to." Robert took a long drink of ice water, trying to swallow the guilt he felt for failing to be candid with his friend about the associate file and wondering why the other associates thought he was not collegial.

"Okay. Let me explain," Alan said. "There are two basic types of attorneys: litigators, which is what I am, and transactional attorneys, like Davis Burnet. There are also tax attorneys, regulatory attorneys, and other specialists, but litigators and transactional guys are the two basic categories."

"So do you get to try many cases?"

"Well, not really. It's not like courts-martial. We get to court every few months to argue motions, but actual trials are rare. Our clients want to avoid the expense of trying a case. And, they're worried that a fickle jury might screw them. We spend most of our time on discovery—you know, sending questions and requests for documents to the other side. And we use what we find out to negotiate settlements if we can. It's an elaborate, well-developed process, and I love it." Their salads arrived, and Alan continued to talk while they ate. "The firm will have you spend some time doing litigation and some doing transactional work to see what seems to be the best fit. It's important to stay on top of your hours. That is key to making partner."

"Hours?"

"Yeah. Your billable time. You need to bust it while you're an associate or you won't make partner. And being a partner is key. You participate in the profits of the firm. That's big money. And the staff treats you with respect. No more begging a secretary to do her job. Good luck with Carolyn, by the way." Alan took a few bites of salad as he decided what to say next. "Now, back to billable hours. When I started here, the partner I was assigned to told me to keep a yellow legal pad on my desk, to write down the time I arrive and the time I leave, and to ensure that *everything* in between is billable. And that habit has paid off. Last year I billed over 2,400 hours."

"Seriously?" Robert asked. "What about lunch, going to the bathroom, stuff like that?"

A grin spread across Alan's face and grew into a smile. "You're *thinking* about the clients, right? Well, if you're thinking about them, then you're billing them."

Robert felt the need to change the subject. "I'll tell you one thing that's different from the Army."

"What's that?"

"The women. We're surrounded by gorgeous women. And they're all dressed to the nines. You don't see that in the Army, even in a JAG Office."

"Ain't that the truth?" Alan leaned in and whispered, "Have you met Jackie Sullivan?" Robert shook his head. "Talk about hot, man. You should only approach her when there's a fire extinguisher readily available." They began to snicker like two teenagers telling dirty jokes. "And the partners like her, too, if you know what I mean."

Robert half smiled. He wasn't at all certain what Alan meant, and he didn't want to ask. Instead, he said, "Tell me about Diana Maguire."

Alan cocked his head and squinted. "I told you about her. She's a lesbo." He straightened up and winced. "Hey, man, I'll admit she's pretty, but she plays for the other team."

"Are you sure?"

"Yes, I'm sure. What? You got the hots for her?" Robert shook his head. "I told you to stay away from her, man. She works for Sharon Alexander. And I also told you: Alexander is lesbo supreme!"

"I don't know, Alan. Diana seems real nice."

"What? You the expert on lesbians, now? You think they all look like those homely bitches in the Army? This is the civilian world, Robert."

"No. I just thought—"

"Did you see that movie *Desert Hearts*?" Robert shook his head. "Lesbians can be hot-looking. You need to stop thinking and start listening to me. I know what I'm talking about. Besides, Diana went to night law school. She's not like us. The only reason she got a job at Underwood & Crockett was that Sharon Alexander took a liking to her." Realizing he might be coming on too strong, Alan paused. "Look, man, I'm trying to keep you out of trouble. Listen to me. Alexander and Maguire are trouble."

"I hear you." Robert was in auto-response mode. "I appreciate it. But it's just hard to believe she's gay."

"Would you drop that? Can't you see I'm trying to help you? I want you to make partner right after me. And I plan to make it early." Alan finished his salad and pushed away from the table. "Let's get back to billing clients. Did you get a billing number for that memo you're working on?"

"No. Just a memo from the partner requesting the research."

"Who was that?"

"Stephen Edgar."

"Oh, shit, man. How'd you get stuck with that? I got one of his requests when I got here. Damn near killed me. The guy's an asshole. Just finish it as quickly as you can, and then try to avoid him." Standing to leave, Alan whispered, "Listen. I got you hooked up with Davis Burnet on Day One. He's the guy you want to work for. Find a reason to go talk to him. Stay away from Edgar. And Alexander."

As they walked out of the restaurant, Robert noticed a stunningly attractive woman with auburn hair, seated at a table with an older gentleman. She was wearing a stylish business suit, although it was tight and did nothing to hide her décolletage. Alan nudged Robert and then nodded in her direction. The woman smiled and nodded back. When they were safely out of earshot, Alan turned to Robert. "Now you see why a fire extinguisher should be close by? That, my friend, was Jackie Sullivan, having lunch with the partner she's currently screwing."

# CHAPTER SIX

BACK IN HIS office, Robert concentrated on his assignment. The last time he'd done this much legal research was in law school, but he felt good about the final product. In particular, he was pleased to have found three Texas cases that were so new they weren't included in the associate file. After proofreading his work at least five times, and remembering Alan's warning to stay away from Stephen Edgar, he deposited it in an internal office distribution envelope, gave it to his secretary, and went looking for Davis Burnet's office.

He found it on the floor above his office on the side of the building overlooking the Dallas skyline, including an iconic, sixty-story skyscraper, designed by the internationally acclaimed architect I. M. Pei. The building had caught Robert's eye on his first day in Dallas. It resembled a large, multi-faceted prism with slanted sides, causing it to have a different profile from every direction. Despite having an impressive view of such a world-famous example of late-modernist architecture, Burnet's office was anything but modern. In fact, it resembled a room in an old-line London gentlemen's club, like The Athenaeum or the Alpine Club. The floor-to-ceiling windows were framed by heavy brocade drapes, drawn back, with a cornice at the top. An expensive-looking oriental rug covered most of the hardwood floor, even though the other offices in the firm were carpeted. Burnet's massive desk was perpendicular to the windows and had what appeared to be a carved oak relief panel across the front, depicting a cattle drive, complete with cowboys and longhorns. There was a credenza

behind the desk and above it a large oil painting of a cowboy bulldog-
ging a steer. Shelves on either side of the credenza held law books and
bound volumes of closing binders containing documents related to the
business transactions Burnet had closed. And, there were dozens of "tomb-
stones"—announcements of closings, encased in Lucite, commemorating
the transactions. Robert later learned that investment bankers and lawyers
give these tokens to clients as a way of saying: "Remember I worked on
your deal. Don't forget me for your next one." They also display them in
their offices like the notches on a gunslinger's six-shooter.

Burnet was on the phone in what appeared to be a heated discussion.
Assuming that call wasn't going to end soon, Robert decided it would be a
good time to introduce himself to Burnet's secretary, Donna, a tall woman
with a head full of curls so tight they were a virtual cascade of light brown
corkscrews. He noticed that when she mentioned her boss, she referred to
him as "Mr. Burnet," even though most secretaries in the firm were on a
first-name-basis with the attorneys they worked with. When it was time to
leave, Robert asked her to let Mr. Burnet know he had stopped by.

"I'd be happy to." Looking down at a calendar on her desk, she asked,
"Would you like to schedule an appointment? Mr. Burnet is free for fifteen
minutes on Friday, the twenty-ninth, at 9:00 a.m."

"That's over a week from now," Robert said. Donna didn't react to the
puzzled look on his face. She just smiled and stared at him, apparently
finding it perfectly normal that her boss couldn't spare fifteen minutes
for the lawyer he had just hired until over a week from then. "Thanks,"
Robert said, trying to conceal his bewilderment. "Please put me down for
that slot. And if he needs to change it, or something opens up earlier, just
let me know."

On the way back to his office, Robert worried that another random
assignment might be waiting for him. Next Friday can't come fast enough,
he thought. But how am I going to avoid Stephen Edgar until then?
Rounding a corner in the web of office hallways, he almost collided with
Diana Maguire, startling her and causing her to drop an armload of files.
He stooped to pick them up and head-butted her as she knelt down too.

"I am so sorry, Diana. I need to watch where I'm going."

"No problem. Busy lawyers move with deliberate speed."

Their faces only a few inches apart, Robert felt drawn into her eyes—two black pupils, surrounded by rings of sapphire blue, the outer edges of which were jagged silver. He'd never seen anything so beautiful. His thoughts lurched forward: Is she just being nice, or is she possibly flirting with me?

"I've got to finish something for Sharon," she said as she stood up. "We're on a deadline." She turned and hurried away.

Robert was in a fog as he headed back to his office but, recalling Alan's admonition about billable hours, soon began to fret over having no billable work to do. After spending thirty minutes arranging his phone and other items on his desk, he decided a better use of time would be to go to the firm library and learn more about what research materials were available.

Like everything else at Underwood & Crockett, the library was impressive. There were rows and rows of wooden bookcases holding hundreds, if not thousands, of books. He scanned the titles, trying to discern how they were arranged. As he turned to walk between two shelves, he encountered—once again—Diana Maguire. Try to be charming and witty, he thought.

"We've got to stop meeting like this," he said, dropping his chin and grinning at her.

Diana looked up from the book she was holding. "Uh, maybe you should stop stalking me. At least this time you didn't assault me."

Robert felt his face become hot and his confidence vanish. "Diana, I was, I was just kidding around. I'm looking around the library so I know what's here. I don't have any billable work to do," he groaned, "and I don't want to get stuck on another non-billable project from Stephen Edgar."

"I'm just teasing, Robert." She dropped her eyelids and then, reconnecting with his gaze, said, "Let me guess: Alan Taylor told you that you need to bill hours if you want to make partner. Don't let a day pass without filling up a yellow legal pad with a bunch of billable hours."

"Something like that," he muttered.

"Right. Well, come with me. I'll introduce you to Sharon. I'm going there anyway. I'll be surprised if she doesn't have something for you to do." Without waiting for his response, Diana headed for the door, and Robert followed like a school boy. Within minutes they were standing in front of the desk of Diana's mentor. "Sharon, I'd like you to meet Robert Clark, our newest associate."

"Oh, well, please do sit down," Sharon said. Robert tried to examine her without appearing to do so. She was probably in her late forties, had an enigmatic air about her, and looked as if she'd just stepped from the pages of a Neiman Marcus catalog. Everything about her was elegant: her hair (blonde and short), her makeup (tasteful), her jewelry (expensive), and most of all her suit. It was teal blue silk and probably cost as much as an Army captain's monthly salary. Her office looked sophisticated, decorated as it was with modern furniture and artwork, including sculpture and paintings—like something from the pages of *Architectural Digest*, which Robert used to look at in his dentist's office. The common feature of everything about her and her office was that they looked expensive. "Tell me about yourself, Robert." She looked at him as if she genuinely wanted to get to know him; it was not a perfunctory request.

Robert tried *not* to think about what Alan had said about her. "Well, I grew up in a small town in South Georgia, went to college at West Point, and then later the Army sent me to law school at the University of Georgia."

"You must have done well in the Army for them to have sent you to law school." Sharon smiled and cocked her head in a very feminine fashion. "What sort of work do Army lawyers do now?"

Robert raised his eyebrows and said, "Just about everything from environmental law to employment law, criminal law, you name it."

"What did you do?"

"I was a prosecutor. My first assignment as an Army lawyer was in Panama."

"Interesting. So that's how you know young Mr. Taylor."

"Right. Well, we were in the JAG Basic Course in Charlottesville, Virginia, together, although we never served in an assignment together."

Sharon turned to Diana. "You know, Diana, it just occurred to me that we need to get those documents out this afternoon. Do you want to take off and get those drafts finished?"

"Sure," Diana said with a smile and a shrug.

"And please shut the door, will you?"

What does that mean? Robert wondered, fidgeting in his chair as Diana walked by.

"I've been anxious to talk to you, Robert," Sharon said. "I heard almost nothing about you before you came on board. Everything seemed to move so fast." She paused and smiled, as if to reassure him. "Davis Burnet mentioned in our last partner meeting that Alan Taylor had told him about an outstanding prospective hire, and then all of a sudden, you're here. Normally, we do more vetting." Sensing she might be sounding negative, she added, "And let me say, I'm happy you are here. Tell me more about your time as a prosecutor." She made direct eye contact with him, undoubtedly waiting for a response that didn't come fast enough. "What was your most interesting case?"

"Uh, yes. I, uh, tried a murder case involving a thirteen-month old little girl." Robert exhaled heavily. "That was tough. The victim reminded me too much of my little girl."

"My goodness. That must have been difficult. I can't imagine." Sharon paused only long enough to adjust her blouse. "So, you're married?"

"No. Recently divorced." Robert felt strange saying those words and—for some inexplicable reason—embarrassed.

Sharon shook her head and lowered her eyelids. "I know. Divorces are no fun. I went through that wringer almost ten years ago, and the memory still haunts me."

"You were divorced?" Robert asked, perhaps a bit too quickly. Sharon could tell he was surprised.

"Yes. I was married for twelve years. The biggest mistake of my life." Robert didn't respond, and Sharon immediately changed subjects. "I'm sorry, Robert. I didn't mean to get so personal. Let's get back to talking about you. Since you've been a prosecutor, do you want to litigate here at Underwood and Crockett?"

"I'm not sure. I don't really know enough about it."

"Well, the firm will have you do some transactional work, in addition to litigation, to see what the best fit is for you. Are you paired with a partner?"

"Not as far as I know," he said with a half-smile, hoping he didn't sound foolish.

"Well, if you're available, I have a project for you."

"Absolutely." Robert sat up straight. "Do I need to get something to take notes on?"

"Here." Sharon pushed a tablet and pen across her desk. "I think you're going to do well, Robert. Most young associates would listen, write nothing down, and then waste my time with questions I've already answered."

Sharon spent several minutes explaining that her client was loaning millions of dollars to a heavy-equipment rental company. Repayment of the loan was to be secured by liens on the equipment, which was located in twenty different states. Because the laws vary from state to state, she asked Robert to research how to obtain a lien in each state on a list she handed him. She asked if he could prepare a memorandum for her by a week from the following Monday. Despite having absolutely no clue how to tackle such a project, Robert said yes, thanked her, and headed back to his office with his notes carefully tucked under his arm.

For the next several days, including the weekend, he spent most of his time in the library, researching state lien statutes and determining whether any of them had been the subject of litigation. On Thursday, still feeling unsure about whether he was producing what Sharon wanted, he decided to consult with Diana.

"Can you spare a few minutes for a newbie?" Robert was standing in Diana's office doorway holding a bulging file folder.

"Sure. Come in. How's the project coming? Sharon told me she has you doing a memo on lien laws."

"Yeah. But I'm not sure I know what I'm doing."

"Let me see what you have so far," she said, holding out her hand.

Sunlight streaming through her office window made Diana's face and hair, especially the ringlets that framed her face, almost luminous. Robert's mind began to wander. *Damn, she's beautiful.*

"It's good that you have copies of this background research," she said without looking up, "but don't give her that. If she asks about it, you'll have it, but just give her the memo." Diana picked up the document and quickly scanned the pages. "Don't put all these references in the body of the memo. Sharon likes them in footnotes." Diana looked up and saw a hint of concern on his face. "Hey, your legal assistant can fix that. It's no big deal. You're paired with Carolyn, right? I used to be paired with her."

"She barely speaks to me," Robert said. "She always seems to be busy with the partner she works for."

"Well, get used to that. That's just the way it goes. Just be polite but firm with her. Tell her to send it to the word processing pool if she needs to but tell her you need it by noon tomorrow."

"But it's not due until Monday."

"Yeah, but if it still needs revision, you need to have time to fix it—that is, unless you know how to operate a word processor." Robert shook his head. "It needs to be ready to go—and in perfect condition—on Monday. Sharon will get upset if it's late."

"You seem to know her pretty well," Robert said, hoping Diana would elaborate.

"We've worked closely together ever since I started here. I'm lucky. I think she sees a bit of herself in me. She's taught me everything I know about actually practicing law, as opposed to what we learned in law school." Diana handed his file back to him. "I think you've got this."

Robert thanked her, returned to his office, and as she had recommended, told his secretary he needed the document revised and back to him by noon the next day. Carolyn huffed a bit, but when Robert explained that it was for Sharon Alexander, she confirmed that it would be finished on time. Having gotten the revisions underway, Robert sat down at his desk, looked through his mail, and hoped he wouldn't find any more requests from Stephen Edgar.

"Hey, man, you've turned into a library nerd." Robert looked up to see Alan Taylor smiling at him and looking as dapper as ever. "What have you been working on?"

"A memo."

"Another one from Edgar?"

"No. This one's for Sharon Alexander."

"Alexander? I told you to stay away from her, man. She's poison."

"I didn't have anything to do, Alan, and you said I needed to be doing billable work."

"Did you go see Burnet?"

"Yes. I have a fifteen-minute appointment with him at 9:00 a.m. on the twenty-ninth." Robert smirked to underscore his incredulity.

"What?" Alan squinted his eyes as he sat down in a chair across from Robert's desk.

"Yeah. Last week I went to see Burnet as you suggested, and his secretary told me I could have a fifteen-minute appointment with him at 9:00 a.m. on the twenty-ninth."

"Well, Burnet is a bit anal. He schedules everything down to the minute. But he's got the most stroke around here. Even the senior partners don't cross him." Alan could tell that Robert didn't understand him. "He has a great deal of influence, white boy." Alan smiled. "Hey, I'm just messing with you, Robert. I think Davis likes you. That's who you need to link up with. Let me see what I can do." Alan paused to see if Robert was annoyed. "Listen, man, I got to run. I'm meeting a client for lunch." As he was walking out, Alan turned and said, "Make me proud, white boy." He paused. "I'm just kiddin', Robert. Lighten up. You'll get this figured out."

# CHAPTER SEVEN

"DO I HAVE you covered, or what?" Fresh from his lunch meeting, Alan Taylor strode into Robert's office and flopped into the chair in front of him.

Robert glanced up from piles of paper strewn across his desk. His face was haggard. He'd skipped lunch to review—for the umpteenth time—the notes he'd taken while preparing the memorandum for Sharon Alexander. "What are you talking about, Alan?" he asked.

"Hugh and I went to lunch at Dakota's with Randy Donaldson, who has a litigation project for us."

"Hugh?"

"Hugh Williams, dummy, the head of the litigation section. Donaldson is his biggest client. Hey, I found out something interesting about Dakota's. The maître d' told us that the developer's secretary came up with the name. She was a big John Lennon fan. The Dakota was the name of Lennon's apartment building in New York. You remember, that guy shot him right in front of the building. I always thought it had something to do with the Wild West. Funny, huh?"

"Oh, yeah. What was it you said about a litigation project?"

"Aren't you listening, man? I've got you involved in a litigation matter involving Randy Donaldson, Hugh's biggest client. What's all this stuff on your desk?"

"Research for the project I just finished for Sharon."

Alan's jaw clenched. "Well make it your last one," he said, pointing his index finger at Robert. "You don't want to get linked up with her, and you don't want to spend all your time writing memos. Anyway, it's too damn hard to bill hours that way." Alan could tell Robert didn't understand what he'd just said. "Look, when I get a litigation project, there is a whole bunch of routine—and by that I mean easy—stuff to do. I get the file opened. I prepare discovery requests. I know I'm going to have a motion to compel discovery and one to object to the other side's discovery request. So, I just dust off old ones and use them as forms." Robert still looked confused. "Think of a litigation file as the gift that keeps on giving."

"How quickly do you get to court?" Robert asked.

"We're not interested in going to court quickly. Or settling quickly, for that matter. Don't you understand? We don't want to get the matter resolved before we bill some time on the file."

"Seriously?" It was obvious from the look on Robert's face that he hadn't expected such blatant cynicism from Alan.

"Don't go gettin' all boy scout on me," Alan said. "We look after our clients' interests, but we have to be sure we've considered everything. And that takes time." Alan could tell Robert was still perplexed and a bit dismayed. "Listen, man, I'll be the first to admit that the system is inefficient and getting things resolved quickly is not at the top of the list. But that's just the way it's done. Clients need to understand that litigation is just a cost of doing business."

Robert's mind began to race, trying to make sense of what Alan had just said. Is this the way lawyers behave—putting their financial interests ahead of the client's need to resolve a matter? Is that what Alan is really saying, despite trying to disguise it as being thorough?

"Okay," Robert said, trying to regroup his thoughts. "I guess I'm just used to courts-martial. The process is much quicker."

"Well, get un-used to it. This isn't the Army. I'm going to get you on this litigation project for Hugh, so wrap things up with Alexander and then come and see me." Alan stood up and walked to the door, turning to say, "Just relax, Robert. And listen to me. I won't steer you wrong."

After Alan left, Robert stared down at his desk and thought about the strange environment in which he was now working. Maybe the bartender at Dakota's was right. Maybe it's all just silly lawyer stuff. The phone rang, interrupting his thoughts.

"Robert, this is Sharon Alexander. I need to see your memo right now. Would you bring it over please?"

"Uh, sure. But didn't you say you wanted it Monday?"

"You know, I don't remember. But I need it now. Please just bring me what you have."

Robert heard a click as Sharon hung up the phone. What I have? Is she kidding? What I have is a request that Carolyn get it revised and back to me tomorrow. She probably hasn't even started. He rushed to his secretary's desk, but before he could say anything, she handed him the revised version.

"You finished it already?" Robert asked, almost out of breath.

Carolyn smiled. "I know the games Ms. Alexander plays. I figured she'd ask for it early. It's ready to go and in the format I know she prefers. Here, I've made two extra copies, too."

Robert took a deep breath and exhaled. "Thank you, Carolyn. I guess you could tell I was stressed. I really appreciate this."

"You're welcome. We were all newbies once, Robert."

Robert hand-carried the document to Sharon's office. "Here it is," he said, placing the memorandum on her desk.

"Oh, thank you, Robert." Sharon peered over her reading glasses. "Sit down for a moment, would you?"

Robert could feel his skin getting warm. Is the Inquisition about to begin?

"Let me take a quick look at this." She quickly perused the memorandum, pursing her lips from time to time. "This looks good, Robert. You've told me exactly what I need to know. Thank you. And thank you for having it ready early." Robert stood up to leave. "Can you wait a minute?" she asked. Sharon called for her assistant and handed her the document, saying, "Send this to the general counsel with the cover letter I just dictated." After the assistant left, she turned back to Robert. "I have another issue I'd like you to research." Her eyes were wide and welcoming, like a proud teacher who'd just reviewed the term paper of her star student.

As if on cue, however, dark clouds passed in front of the sun, and in seconds Sharon's office went from sunny to gloomy, perfectly matching Robert's changed mood. What should I say? he wondered. Alan said to avoid getting any more projects from her.

"I'm afraid I, uh, have a new litigation project that's going to keep me busy," he stammered.

"Oh? Well." Sharon's face was no longer bright. "Who's it for?"

"Hugh Williams."

"So, Mr. Taylor linked you up with him."

"Yes. I told him yes, because it was an opportunity to get some litigation experience, as you suggested."

"I did indeed. What sort of project is it?" she asked.

"I'm not exactly sure," Robert said slowly, as he tried to come up with a better response.

"So how do you know it's going to make you too busy to assist me?"

"I guess I'm not sure." Robert paused and then said, "Alan just told me to come to see him as soon as I was finished with the memo that you asked me to prepare."

"I see. Did Mr. Taylor say anything else about me?"

Robert twisted his West Point class ring. The muscles in his stomach tightened involuntarily. Does she know what Alan thinks of her? He squirmed in his seat a few seconds before his words tumbled out. "He told me to avoid working for you." Robert studied her face, trying to gauge her reaction, but no longer feeling stressed. It was the prospect of lying to Sharon that had bothered him—especially since she had been so considerate and helpful.

"Well, he's not alone, Robert. You've probably noticed that the only other lawyer you see in my office is Diana. Let me explain." Sharon looked out at the storm clouds, which now reflected her countenance as well. Her sunny openness was gone; her face was now taut and introspective. "You see, I'm gay." She waited for a reaction.

"I... I thought you said you were divorced." Robert's statement was almost a question.

"I did. And I am." Sharon paused briefly and then continued in a weary voice. "Sometimes, Robert, it takes time to understand who you are. That's the way it was for me. I didn't 'come out' until I was thirty-seven." She paused and smiled at him, but the smile was tight, strained. "That's what ended my marriage." Robert said nothing. "Didn't Alan tell you I'm gay?"

"Well, yes, I, uh, guess he said something about that." Robert drew out his words as he struggled to think of what to say next. "But I really didn't pay much attention, Sharon. I figured it was none of my business."

"Well, you would be the first lawyer at this firm to draw that conclusion. My partners seem to think my private life *is* their business." She gazed out the window again and was silent for what seemed like a long time but was less than a minute. Turning back to him, she said, "Don't fall in with them, Robert. Be your own man. Make your own decisions about such matters."

"I always have, Sharon," he said softly.

"Well, go work on your litigation project." She squinted her eyes, and Robert saw the hint of a smile. "No hard feelings. You need to see what that work is like anyway." Robert stood up to leave, but as he reached for the door knob, she added, "You're always welcome to come back, you know."

Walking back to his office, he began to think about the firm. Was Alan right? Was Underwood & Crockett really the right place for him? He'd dealt with personal drama in the Army but nothing like this. He grabbed a yellow legal pad from his desk and headed off to Alan's office.

"Are you finished with the project for the lesbo?" Alan asked.

Robert squirmed in his seat. "Alan, I would think that you would be particularly sensitive about the use of epithets, especially ones that label people in a derogatory fashion."

"Don't get all high and mighty with me, Robert. I'm just trying to help you."

"I know you are, and as I've told you, I really appreciate it. It just makes me uncomfortable to hear you say something like that."

"Did Sharon tell you that she and Diana are lovers?" Alan seemed to enjoy salacious speculation.

"No. And how do you know that's true?"

"Because she's always talking her up at partner meetings."

"Well, Alan, using that logic they might think you and I are gay. After all, you talked *me* up, didn't you?"

"Don't be a smartass." Alan leaned back in his chair and huffed.

"Besides, I didn't know you went to partner meetings," Robert added.

"Of course I don't go to partner meetings. But I hear things. And what I'm telling you is for your own good."

"Okay. Can we just talk about this litigation matter?"

"Right. The fun stuff." Alan pushed a stack of documents across his desk. "These are documents from a case I worked on last year. I'm going to tell you everything I know about our new matter, and I want you to conform all these documents to our facts."

"Are the issues the same?" Robert asked.

"Don't worry about that. I'll figure that out later. In fact, I'm not exactly sure where this case is going. You just revise these documents based on the facts I'm going to tell you. You should have forty or fifty hours of billable work there. Donaldson is always firing somebody or doing something that causes litigation. One time he fired all the outside directors on the board." Alan stopped and leaned forward. "You understand what I'm saying? He's the gift that keeps on giving."

"I guess that's one way to look at it," Robert said.

"You'll learn. Anyway, Donaldson is the chairman of the board and largest shareholder of Donaldson Construction Company. The current matter arose, because he's unhappy with his CEO and wants to fire him. But the CEO caught wind of it and hired a lawyer, so Donaldson contacted Hugh to represent him in the matter."

As Alan continued to explain the situation, it became clear that what Alan wanted Robert to do was grunt work—nothing intellectually challenging, just crank out a bunch of routine documents, regardless of whether they were relevant to firing the CEO.

"Now for the really good news." Alan was almost bubbly. "I've got you a date for Saturday night."

"What? No, Alan. I'm not ready. My divorce is too fresh."

"Bullshit, man! You been talkin' about how fine Diana is, haven't you? But remember, she's gay. I got you a date with Megan Miller."

"The recruiting coordinator?"

"Yeah. She and my lady were sorority sisters at SMU. We're gonna double date, like high school."

"Thanks, Alan, but I'm not sure I'm ready for that. I don't even know Megan."

"You know her well enough. Do you know how many associates would kill to get a date with her? Anyway, she knows all about you. I'm not saying you're going to marry her, Robert. Besides, her family doesn't have any money. But she's Michelle's best friend, so it'll be fun."

"Michelle?"

"My girlfriend?" Alan shook his head as he stared at him. "Do you not remember anything important? You're spending too much time writing memos."

"I don't think you ever told me her name. That's all."

"Don't you remember me saying 'Michelle, my belle'? Well, anyway, it's Michelle Groves. Her old man is a client of the firm. *And*, he's got more money than God." Alan waited for Robert to respond. "So, are we going or not?"

"We're going," Robert replied with a sardonic smile. "Do I need to call her?"

"No. It's all arranged. Like I told you, man. Stick with me. I won't steer you wrong at work or at play." Alan was the image of a kid embarking on a new adventure. Leaning back in his chair, he said, "Now, go back to Culwell & Son this afternoon and get you a nice sports jacket and a pair of slacks. We're gonna go to The Mansion Restaurant on Turtle Creek. It's the best restaurant in Dallas. So, you need to look sharp. Besides, I've told Michelle all about my West Point friend with the sweet Southern charm."

"Right." Robert's tone made it clear he really wasn't agreeing with Alan.

"No, seriously, Robert. Michelle said Megan really wants to go out with you. They're both looking forward to it."

"I hope you're right, Alan. It's been a long time since I was on a date."

"Well then, it's high time. Now, go get to work on this litigation file, so you'll be free on Saturday night."

# Chapter Eight

ON SATURDAY NIGHT everyone gathered at Michelle's house, which was located in a fashionable section of Highland Park. Michelle clearly belonged there—tall and slender, though shapely (perhaps with some surgical help), and, of course, blonde, like almost every other woman who shopped at Chanel, Dior, and the other stores in Highland Park Village. She didn't seem to be a snob, though. She had a confident, engaging smile and went out of her way to put Robert at ease. Watching Alan look at Michelle, Robert was reminded of a poem he'd read—something about "gazing with his heart." My friend has done pretty well for himself, he thought.

Strangely, though, Michelle and Megan seemed to carry on a conversation without saying much of anything, relying instead on fragments of sentences, expressions, winks, and nods that made no sense to Robert. Maybe that's what sorority sisters do, he thought. There weren't any fraternities at West Point, so all the traditions and nuances of Greek life were, well, Greek to him. Despite their obvious close relationship, Megan was nothing like Michelle. She lacked her friend's poise and grace.

"So, Alan said you were from a small town in Georgia," Megan said. "Didn't you get bored?" Robert didn't answer. "Was your father one of those small-town Southern lawyers like Atticus Finch?"

"No. He was the county agent."

"The what?"

"The county agent. He helped farmers decide on planting schedules, fertilizing—things like that. Pemberton is a farming community."

"Oh, God. I bet you were glad to get out of there. Hugh Williams's family owns a big ranch in south Texas. He doesn't do any ranching, though. He just goes down there to shoot birds and deer and whatever other animals they have." Megan and Michelle giggled as if that comment were somehow funny.

"I don't think I'll have much time for that sort of thing," Robert said.

"No you won't," Alan said. "We've got to get you plugged in with Davis Burnet."

"That would be great," Megan said, wiggling in her chair like a little girl. "Davis comes from money. His family owns oil wells out in west Texas. Can you believe it?"

"I can believe this bottle of Mark Swann chardonnay is all gone," Alan said. "It's time to go. I'll drive."

As he walked through the door of The Mansion Restaurant, Robert was reminded of something his friend Barry from Pemberton had said after he ate at an expensive restaurant in Atlanta: "Can you believe it, Bobby? They cook the tomatoes, but they don't cook the green beans!" The Mansion was that kind of place. Small portions, exquisitely presented on fine china. Waiters scurrying about cradling expensive bottles of wine. Soft music and hushed conversations. No loud, boorish behavior.

To no one's surprise, Alan knew the maître d', who proceeded to escort them to their table. But before they reached it, Alan noticed someone at another table and stopped to talk. When he finally arrived at their table, Megan asked, "Who was that, Alan?"

"Randy Donaldson. Robert and I are handling some litigation for him."

"Really? Isn't he that crazy guy who's always in the paper? And his wife is some trashy thing half his age?"

"Be nice, Megan" Alan replied. "He's a firm client."

"Whatever." Turning to Robert, Megan resumed her questioning. "So why did you decide to come to Dallas, Robert, when all of your family and connections are back in Georgia?"

"Well, it's, uh, complicated."

"Don't go scaring him off, Megan," Alan said. "I just got him out here."

"Oh, I didn't mean anything by it, Alan. I'm just curious, that's all."

"I'm divorced," Robert said. There was a long pause. His expression looked as if he'd just bitten into a lemon.

"Aren't we all," Michelle said, breaking the silence and almost laughing.

"I'm sorry. I don't understand." Robert looked back and forth at the others. Had he missed something?

"It appears that all of us—except Mr. Taylor here—have been divorced," Michelle said, raising an eyebrow for effect. "Daddy's investigator found out that my ex was having an affair, and Megan's ex turned out to be, well…" She paused and gave Megan a look. "We're just glad you're here, Robert."

"Oh," Robert said. "Well, I guess I'm just not used to it yet." Robert didn't mention having a daughter; Alan gave him a knowing look but said nothing.

"You'll get there," Michelle said. "What I've learned, Robert, is that love and marriage are like an appetizer and a salad: one gets things off to a great start, and the other is never quite as good as you thought it would be." Michelle and Megan exchanged one of their cryptic expressions, apparently agreeing on the truth of some unstated axiom about divorce—or marriage. Alan was busy scanning the room for other clients and didn't hear what she said.

The rest of the evening was uneventful. Each time Megan began to talk about the firm, Alan would one-up her with a tidbit of gossip she hadn't heard. Robert didn't contribute much to the conversation, nor did Michelle, who seemed bored, often staring across the room as Megan and Alan went back and forth about who was sleeping with whom, who would make partner and who wouldn't, and which partners had the biggest books of business.

After dinner the couples returned to Michelle's house, ostensibly for a nightcap, but it was immediately apparent that Alan and Michelle wanted to be alone, so Robert and Megan said good night and left. As Robert leaned over to open the door of Megan's Honda Accord, she thought he was going to kiss her. When he failed to follow through, she settled into the driver's seat with a smirk.

"You're a funny guy, Robert Clark."

Robert watched as she drove away, wondering whether he even wanted a relationship with a woman like Megan.

At 8:30 a.m. the next morning, his phone rang.

"I hope I didn't wake you, Robert." Though he was groggy, Robert recognized the voice as that of Alan Taylor's father. "You remember I mentioned that from time to time I get the opportunity to fly one of the private planes at Lancaster Regional Airport. Are you interested in flying this afternoon?"

Robert was still trying to wake up and clear his head. "Uh, yes sir. What time did you want to go?"

"Yolanda and I get out of church around twelve thirty. She won't like it, but I'm going to skip lunch, so I can get to the airfield. Do you think you can get there by two?"

"Uh, yes sir. You said Lancaster Regional, right? Is Alan coming, too?"

"Yes. Lancaster Regional is correct. And no, Alan will not be joining us. I haven't been able to reach him. He must be at work. He didn't say anything about coming to church, and he doesn't answer his apartment phone. There's no way to reach him at his office because there's no receptionist there on Sunday."

"Okay, Mr. Taylor. I'll see you at two. Do I need to bring anything?"

"Just yourself and a jacket. It can get a bit chilly up there, even if it's hot down here."

Mr. Taylor sounded excited, which reminded Robert of Alan, discussing their next extraordinary adventure. It was sad in a way. Robert didn't want to be the one to tell Mr. Taylor that his son wasn't answering his phone because he was at his girlfriend's house—a girlfriend his parents didn't even know existed.

Robert arrived at the airfield at 1:45 p.m. and found Mr. Taylor conducting a pre-flight inspection of a Cessna 172 Skyhawk. He had a clipboard and a flashlight and was carefully looking at something on the wing. When he saw Robert walking up, he smiled broadly. "I haven't flown this particular aircraft before, so I thought I'd better give her the once over." Noticing Robert's smile was a bit forced, he added, "Not to worry, though. I've flown many Skyhawks. They are excellent, reliable aircraft. Are you ready? Let's go."

They buckled themselves in and were soon taxiing down the runway. "Don't get me wrong," Mr. Taylor said. "These planes are fun to fly. But let me tell you. The P-47 Thunderbolt. Now, that was an airplane! It was more than twice as fast as this aircraft." Robert said nothing, which Mr. Taylor interpreted as nervousness. "Are you okay?"

"Oh, yes sir. I'm enjoying this," Robert said. What he was not enjoying was the thought of being stuck between Mr. Taylor and his son. He knew what Alan was up to that morning, and it wasn't work-related. He also knew that Mr. Taylor didn't know, and he was worried that this concerned father might start asking questions about his son. That uneasiness, aided by some choppy air, made his empty stomach queasy.

"It's beautiful down there, isn't it?" Mr. Taylor said.

"Yes, sir."

"I never get tired of this. I'm glad you wanted to come. Yolanda doesn't like to fly at all. And she has absolutely no interest in flying when I'm the pilot." Mr. Taylor chuckled a bit. After a long pause he continued. "Alan used to like to come with me, but now that he's at Underwood & Crockett all he seems to do is work. Are you boys that busy?"

Uh oh, here we go, Robert thought. How do I avoid an in-depth discussion of that topic?

"I'm still pretty new, Mr. Taylor, so I'm probably not the best person to ask. But I will say that there doesn't seem to be much time for anything other than billable work. We have to bill 2200 hours in a year."

"Is that difficult?"

"Well, you can't bill for coffee breaks, lunch, going to the bathroom, or office small talk. And, there are a bunch of meetings and administrative tasks that you can't bill for either. It all adds up, which means you have to work longer than you might imagine to get to 2200 billable hours."

"I guess that explains why we don't see much of Alan." Mr. Taylor's face became somber, and Robert suspected something else was on his mind, though he didn't ask.

They were quiet for a few minutes, allowing Robert to take in the view. Their plane was headed south, with the Dallas skyline behind them. Even though it was a Sunday afternoon, the roads below them were crowded with traffic, especially along Interstate 35E.

Where are all those people going on such a pretty day? Robert wondered.

Mr. Taylor cleared his throat. "Alan used to like to fly with me. In fact, I thought he might become a pilot one day. But he had other plans."

"He's done well, Mr. Taylor. I know you're proud of him."

"He has. But I must say I miss having him around. He was quite the athlete in high school—ranked among the best running backs in the state. But during his senior year he injured his knee, so he didn't get any college offers. I think it worked out for the best, though. He really enjoyed his time at Howard. Did you play any sports in high school or at the Academy?"

"No, sir. I'm afraid I'm not very athletic. We all had to participate in intramural sports at West Point. I ran track and played soccer, but I wasn't very good."

"Well, you must have had a distinguished military career to get selected for law school."

"I guess so. I was a good student. I think that's why I was selected. To tell you the truth, Mr. Taylor, I'm really not sure why I went to law school."

"It's certainly a demanding profession. We're lucky to see Alan once a week. And he rarely comes to church anymore. He comes to dinner only because his mother insists on it. And quite often he calls at the last minute to say he can't come."

Robert could feel the sweat under his arms. He knew his face must be a portrait of guilt. What should he say?

Mr. Taylor said nothing for a couple of minutes and then, "Despite his knee surgery, Alan received an appointment to West Point. Did you know that?"

"No sir, he never mentioned it."

"He would have been three classes behind you. I really wanted him to go, but he insisted on going to Howard, which I knew was going to be expensive. So, I encouraged him to apply for an ROTC scholarship, which he did, thank goodness. Then, when he was accepted into Harvard Law School, they offered him a scholarship. He obtained a deferral on his commitment, so by the time he arrived at Fort Hood he still owed the Army four years. For some reason, though, he only served three." Mr. Taylor paused, as if waiting for a response, but Robert just continued to stare through the windshield.

"After the war, I thought about staying in the Army. Sometimes, I wish I had. It was encouraging when President Truman abolished segregation in the military in 1948. That was a colossal step forward for our country. He was a true warrior for social justice."

"I think President Truman was a great president. I know my father always spoke highly of him."

"We've made considerable strides as a country since then," Mr. Taylor said, sounding wistful. "I often think about my fellow Tuskegee airmen. Despite all that we accomplished in the war, it was tough to find good jobs in aviation. Things are much better now, though. My generation fought hard to make it so. Dr. Martin Luther King said he dreamed of a day when his children lived in a nation where they were judged not by the color of their skin, but by the content of their character. I hope we will always continue to strive for that."

Mr. Taylor paused, adjusted the controls, and silently stared at the horizon for a few minutes. Banking the plane to the right, he said, "Let's go west a ways, so we can turn around and approach Dallas from that direction. The sun will be shining on all those skyscrapers like President Reagan's 'shining city on a hill,' but without the hill." Mr. Taylor chuckled at his own joke.

When they were finally turned around and headed back toward Dallas, the view was indeed magnificent. The setting sun made the glass-clad skyscrapers sparkle, as if made of silver and gold. The Dallas skyline seemed to have popped up out of the flat prairie—all man-made and glistening against the low-level sprawl and ruddy brown grass and scrub brush that surrounded it. There were no mountains—or even hills—to obstruct the view for miles. There was only Dallas, in all its man-made splendor.

How different it is from Pemberton, Robert thought. His home town was a farming community that had evolved over hundreds of years, having been established by some of the first settlers brought over from England by James Edward Oglethorpe. It was old. Its roads followed former cow paths and Indian trails. With its tall pines and abundant streams and creeks, it seemed to be a part of nature as opposed to having been implanted upon it by man. Dallas is different, Robert thought. It's a place that rewards men who know how to make things happen. I want to be one of those men.

# CHAPTER NINE

ON MONDAY MORNING Alan and Robert found themselves in rush-hour traffic, headed to the courthouse. Hugh Williams had called them Sunday night and told them to be in the office early on Monday to help him prepare a motion for immediate relief, which was only tangentially related to the litigation project Robert had been working on for him. In fact, Robert really didn't understand why he was involved at all. Hugh had been working from his home office that morning and would be meeting Alan and Robert at the courthouse. Robert was nervous. He hadn't been in court since his days as a prosecutor in Panama several years earlier, and he hadn't had much interaction with Mr. Williams, so he didn't know what to expect.

"Are you ready?" Alan asked.

"What do you mean? Ready for what?"

"Hey, don't be jumpy, man. Hugh will be doing most of the talking."

"So why are we going?"

"To bill hours," Alan said, stifling a grin.

"Seriously?"

"No. I'm just messing with you, man. You're always going on about billable hours and accuracy."

"Well, when you put down time on your timesheet aren't you saying you're providing services to a client?"

"Of course, Robert. And we will be. You brought a copy of that memo you wrote on the fiduciary duties of officers and directors, didn't you?"

Robert nodded. "I gave Hugh a copy last week. If he has any questions about the authority of the board of directors to fire the CEO, he's gonna ask you, and you need to be prepared to answer."

Robert could feel that all-too-familiar anxious tension beginning to take hold in the pit of his stomach. "So why are you going?" he asked.

"I'm driving." Another pause, which ended with a snicker. "Come on, man, lighten up. I might have something to contribute, you know, depending on what comes up. You do know this is an important motion, don't you?"

"Of course."

"Like I told you, Randy Donaldson wants to fire his CEO immediately. I still can't believe what that nut-case did. Incredible." Alan hit the brakes, and the car screeched to a stop. "Can you believe that guy? Get going, you moron!" Alan honked his horn.

"It's pretty congested, Alan. We'll be really late if you rear-end somebody."

"Yeah, I know. I just wish these morons would get going." Alan honked his horn again. "Hell, we could've walked there faster than this. Anyway, as I was saying, the balls of that guy, locking everyone out of the company offices. Changed the locks and everything. I wouldn't be surprised if he took down the Donaldson Construction sign and put up his own."

They arrived at the courthouse with time to spare, but as they walked in, Robert's jitters increased. Hugh Williams was seated on a bench at the end of the hallway, reading some papers. He looked up when he heard them approach.

"Good morning, gentlemen." Gesturing to the document he was reading, he said, "Robert, I'm just looking over your memo on the duties of the officers and directors of a Texas corporation. You did a really fine job."

"Thanks. Are you feeling pretty good about our chances?"

"I was until I saw the judge we'll be in front of. Judge Carter is not known to be the brightest bulb on the tree." Hugh bit his lower lip and glanced at Alan.

"Well, he's certainly no Oliver Wendell Holmes," Alan said.

Hugh looked back and forth at his two young associates. "Let me bounce this off you. I think I just need to argue that under Texas law the business and affairs of a corporation are the responsibility of its board of directors. The officers, including that crazy CEO, serve at the pleasure of the board, of which Randy is chairman. So the board can fire him, unless he has an employment agreement, in which case they'd have to comply with its terms, assuming it addresses termination. That's pretty much it, isn't it?" Hugh studied them with a level gaze. "And the CEO doesn't have an employment agreement, right?"

"I'm not aware of one," Alan said.

"Me either," Robert said.

"Well, I can't believe any judge—including Judge Carter—would disagree with firing a CEO who behaved like this one, regardless of whether he has an employment agreement. It's almost like a mutiny on a ship. Did you ever prosecute one of those, Robert?"

"No mutinies, Hugh. I was in the Army, not the Navy."

"That's right. Well, this guy is a nut. We need to help Randy get rid of him."

After the three of them were seated at their counsel table, they heard a commotion in the back of the courtroom and turned to see an attorney striding into view wearing a blue plaid sports jacket, tan slacks, and a pink tie. He was followed by two attractive young women carrying large briefcases and dressed like they were headed to a bar downtown.

"Oh no," Hugh muttered.

"Hugh Williams, how good to see you!" said the garishly attired attorney with a forced smile.

"Alan, Robert, meet John Dickerson, my law school classmate," Hugh said, standing to shake Dickerson's hand. "Do you have a divorce case in here later, John? We're about to have a hearing with Judge Carter."

"No. I'm your new opposing counsel, Hugh. Got retained only this morning. It seems you spooked my predecessor, so I received a call from Mr. Bevilacqua around six this morning. I represented him in his divorce last year, and he thought I might be of assistance in this matter. So, here I am." Dickerson motioned for his two assistants to put their bags next to the other counsel table. "I see that look on your face, Hugh. I know what you're thinking. But I'm ready to go. In fact, I believe this will be a simple matter. Your client attempted to unceremoniously fire my client after he objected to the board trying to force a new employment agreement on him."

"I'm not aware of any employment agreement, John."

"Well, here's a copy." Dickerson thrust a thick document in Hugh's direction.

After flipping through the pages, Hugh handed it back. "This isn't signed, John."

"Well, let's take that up with Judge Carter," Dickerson said as he and his colleagues arranged documents on their table.

"All rise," said the bailiff. "Court will now be in session, the Honorable James E. Carter presiding."

"Be seated," said Judge Carter. The judge was handsome, probably in his early forties, with the physique of a football running back and a deep, resonant voice. "I have before me a motion for a temporary restraining order, which appears to be seeking to restrain Mr. Jorge Bevilacqua from securing the premises of his company."

Hugh sighed, perhaps too audibly.

"Do you have something to say, Mr. Williams?"

"Yes, Your Honor." Hugh was instantly on his feet. "We would like to set forth the facts that led to the filing of our motion."

"Proceed."

Hugh did a good job of presenting the company's position. Bevilacqua, for unknown reasons, had gotten at odds with the directors, including Randy Donaldson, and then took matters into his own hands and locked them out of the company's offices or—as the judge described it—secured the premises of his company. After describing the timeline of events and discussing the duties of the board of directors and its authority to terminate Bevilacqua's employment, Hugh sat down.

Turning to opposing counsel, Judge Carter said, "Mr. Dickerson, do you have anything to say in response?"

Dickerson stood up holding the unsigned employment agreement. "Your Honor, this document is an employment agreement between my client and the company. Mr. Bevilacqua is prepared to testify that they have been operating under it for over a year. He's been paid as provided in the agreement, and he's received the benefits set forth in the agreement.

But now, the board of directors seeks to terminate his employment without complying with the terms of this agreement. Specifically, the agreement provides that Mr. Bevilacqua's employment can only be terminated for cause, as defined in the agreement, and there is no evidence that such cause exists. Further section 15 of the agreement provides that the company must pay him severance if his employment is terminated for reasons other than cause."

"Do you have anything in response, Mr. Williams?" Judge Carter asked.

"Yes, Your Honor." Hugh rose to his feet. "First of all, the agreement isn't signed. Therefore, it's unenforceable."

"Is the agreement signed, Mr. Dickerson?" asked the judge, turning to opposing counsel.

"It was agreed to and was supposed to be signed, Your Honor. My client has been strung along for over a year by Randy Donaldson and his hand-picked board of directors. Mr. Bevilacqua relied on promises made to him by Mr. Donaldson and at least two other directors that the agreement would be executed. There always seemed to be an excuse for not getting it done." Dickerson wrinkled his face in disgust. "Mr. Bevilacqua feels that he has been wronged by Mr. Donaldson and the board, and he wants them to honor the commitments the company made to him in the agreement."

Dickerson sat down, and the judge turned back to Hugh Williams with an expectant look.

He rose again. "There's a lot to unpack here, Your Honor. First of all, I saw this alleged agreement only a few minutes ago. More important, it's not signed. Therefore, it's not binding. Mr. Dickerson seems to be arguing that this unsigned agreement is enforceable because representatives of the company allegedly made one or more promises to him on which he relied to his detriment—in other words, promissory estoppel."

"Are you saying Mr. Dickerson has failed to establish a case of promissory estoppel?"

"I am, Your Honor. To establish a case of promissory estoppel, Mr. Dickerson would have to show first"—Hugh held up one finger—"that a promise was made to Mr. Bevilacqua and that the person making the promise should have expected that it would lead Mr. Bevilacqua to definite and substantial injury." Raising another finger, Hugh continued. "Second, such injury must have actually occurred. And third"—now three fingers were raised in a fan—"the court must enforce the promise in order to avoid that injury." Hugh paused and looked at the judge to let all of that sink in.

"Is that all, Mr. Williams?"

"Yes, Your Honor, at the present time. In summary, there's been no showing of a promise or of any injury. Mr. Bevilacqua has been paid handsomely for his work. It appears that what we have here is a simple case of the parties being unable to agree on the specific terms of the employment agreement. Therefore, it was never signed, and Mr. Bevilacqua is simply an employee at will"—Hugh's voice was becoming tense—"whose behavior warrants termination of that employment."

The judge turned back toward Dickerson but said nothing.

Dickerson was on his feet immediately. "We'll be happy to have an evidentiary hearing, Judge."

"That sounds like what we need," Judge Carter said, steepling his fingers. "After all, I mean, the CEO is the main man in the corporation, right? So, this is a serious matter. Now, I hear what you say, Mr. Williams, about the board having duties and all, but they also have to honor the promises they make. If promises were made, then Mr. Bevilacqua has a right to continue as CEO. Counsel should be prepared to present their evidence one week from today. Court's adjourned." His gavel came down, and he stood up.

The bailiff immediately called "all rise," but Hugh was already on his feet.

"But, Your Honor—"

"Court's adjourned, Mr. Williams." Judge Carter looked down at Hugh and his two associates with a cold stare. "See you next week." He whirled around and was gone.

Hugh sat down at the table, jaw clenched. Dickerson approached, and Hugh stood up to face him.

"Don't worry, Hugh," Dickerson said. "I'm sure we can work something out." With that, he and his two attractive colleagues walked out of the courtroom wearing the same smug expressions they'd entered with.

"What just happened?" Alan asked.

"Our client just got jerked around by an incompetent judge and the finance chairman of his reelection campaign."

"Dickerson?" Alan asked.

"Yeah. He's raised thousands of dollars for Judge Carter's reelection. In my opinion the judge should have recused himself. But he won't." Hugh rubbed his eyebrows with his fingertips and then stared at the two young lawyers. "And Dickerson runs around town promoting himself on his ability to get Judge Carter to do what he wants."

"That's disgusting," Alan said.

"Disgusting, but real."

"Can't we appeal?" Robert asked.

"He hasn't ruled yet, Robert," Hugh snapped. He rubbed his eyebrows and then looked at the two, wide-eyed associates. "The problem, gentlemen, is delay. At a minimum, it will be a week before we get a ruling. In the meantime, Randy is locked out of his own damn company by this bozo Bevilacqua. It's costing him thousands of dollars a day. And there's no guaranty that Judge Carter will rule right away." Hugh paused as if collecting his thoughts. His jaw clenched again. "What really pisses me off is that the judge didn't even let us get to the question of whether Bevilacqua should be fired for locking the directors out of the company offices. Dickerson would have had to admit that was true. Who gives a damn whether he has an employment agreement?" Hugh paused again, silently shaking his head. "To get this handled quickly, I suspect we'll have to pay that bastard off. What really annoys me is that Dickerson is a low-life divorce lawyer. If he knows anything about the law that's relevant to this case, it's what he learned when we were in law school—where he was near the bottom of the class, I might add. I'm sure he's never litigated anything like this." Hugh gathered his papers and stuffed them in his briefcase. "But so what? He and Carter are two peas in the same intellectual pod. They're both morons. The only thing Dickerson is good at is promoting himself." Hugh started to walk away but turned and said, "I'm meeting a client for lunch. Let's do a *post mortem* this afternoon."

As soon as Robert and Alan were seated in the car, Alan said, "Let's go to Dakota's and do our own *post mortem* over lunch. I'm starving, and we need to be ready to meet with Hugh."

Alan and Robert were silent as they shuffled into Dakota's and sat down at Alan's regular table. "You know this doesn't look good for either of us," Alan said. He stared blankly at Robert before continuing. "I hope it doesn't affect my chances of making partner."

"I don't understand," Robert said. "We drew an incompetent judge and his buddy was our opposing counsel, that's all."

"Yeah. Judge Carter sort of undermines your faith in affirmative action doesn't he?"

"What?" Robert squinted, unsure of what he'd just heard.

"Yeah," Alan said. "The man went to Harvard Law School, like me, and yet he doesn't understand the first thing about how a corporation is run. Or the basics of employment law. He's an idiot. An embarrassment."

"Well, there's nothing we can do about him, is there?" That question hung in the air for a long time before Robert continued. "We just need to figure out what to do now." He paused again, as if trying to decide whether to ask his next question. "Do you really think Carter rules in Dickerson's favor because he's his finance chairman?"

"Of course he does. That's what incompetent judges do. They aren't admired for their judicial acumen, so they raise a bunch of money and scare off any potential contenders to their thrones."

"Well, like I said: What do we do now?"

"The first thing we do," Alan said, "is come up with an answer to what will undoubtedly be Hugh's first question: Why didn't we know about that damn unsigned employment contract? Did you send out the discovery requests like I told you?"

"Yeah, but there wasn't anything in them about employment contracts. The documents you gave me to use as a guide concerned a construction defect case."

"Damn, Robert! You got to think, man! Didn't I ask for all relevant agreements and contracts in those documents?"

Robert could see Alan was upset, so he didn't respond. In fact, the documents Alan had given him to use as guides said nothing about requesting all relevant agreements.

Alan wasn't finished. "You made both of us look unprepared and incompetent in front of Hugh Williams, the man who will probably determine whether I make partner."

"I'm sorry, Alan. I told you I hadn't done anything like that before."

Sensing a lull in the conversation, the waiter approached. "May I take your orders, gentlemen?"

"The usual, Ramón," Alan said. "Thank you."

"I'll take the same, Ramón. Thank you." Robert couldn't decide whether Alan was just blowing off steam or whether he really should feel guilty for not asking about whether Bevilacqua had an employment agreement, signed or unsigned.

But then Alan turned to him. "I'm sorry, Robert," he said in calm voice. "It's not your fault. I should've looked at what you put together. I keep forgetting you're new to all this." Alan stared into space, as if pondering something. "I just can't have this negative shit happen *now* when I'm trying to be considered for partner early."

For the rest of their lunch, they discussed what they would say to Hugh Williams that afternoon. They considered whether to recommend that they ask the judge to recuse himself but decided against it. He wouldn't, and their request would only annoy him. And, it would delay the resolution of the matter, which Hugh certainly wouldn't like. They toyed with their food for several minutes before deciding to return to the office.

Robert went straight to the library and began researching cases dealing with the enforceability of an unsigned employment agreement. A couple of hours later, he briefed Alan on what he'd found, and then the two of them waited for Hugh to summon them. Around 5:30 p.m. Hugh's secretary called, asking them to meet Hugh in his office.

"So, what do you guys think?" Hugh asked, as they sat down at a small conference table.

Alan took the lead. "I think we should file a motion for reconsideration."

"Reconsideration of what, Alan? You know better than that. We don't even have the court's order, yet."

"Well, we all know what it's going to be, so we need to be ready."

"No." Hugh shook his head. "I think we need to file a supplemental brief in support of our original motion and address that ridiculous unsigned agreement. You found some case law on that, right?" He looked at Robert.

"Yes," Alan said. "Robert has put together some good research. I think we can create a supplemental brief that even Judge Carter can understand and, more importantly, can't ignore."

"How thorough was our discovery, guys?" Hugh asked. The room was silent for an agonizingly long time, and then he asked the question the two associates knew was coming. "How did you guys miss that damn unsigned employment agreement?"

"That's my fault," Alan said without hesitation. "I should have looked at what Robert prepared before it went out. But I think we're good. We looked over everything this afternoon, and I don't think there will be any more surprises."

"Okay. I guess we don't have much choice. I want you guys to give me your best effort and have something for me to review by noon tomorrow. That will give me time to review it and file it, so that it'll be on Judge Carter's desk several days before our next hearing. I want to get it before him as soon as we can."

"Got it, Hugh," Alan said.

When Alan and Robert were on their way back to Alan's office, Robert stopped and grabbed Alan's arm. "I'm sorry—"

"Stop right there. No more of that. We both fucked up. You just got here. And I should have known better. Now, we've just got to write a killer supplemental brief."

They worked through the night and into the next morning, creating a mountain of unshelved books on the largest table in the library. To be successful, their supplemental brief would have to convince the judge he would be making a mistake if he refused to grant them their requested relief: control of the company offices and termination of Bevilacqua's employment. It was clear to Robert that, despite Alan's fondness for fancy suits, expensive cars, and high-priced restaurants, he was a serious lawyer with a good legal mind. He crafted persuasive arguments that marshalled all of Robert's research. After reviewing their brief the next day, Hugh said it was "compelling" and filed it that afternoon.

Much to everyone's relief, Judge Carter also found the supplemental brief to be compelling and ordered Bevilacqua to immediately give Don aldson and the other directors access to the company offices. But the issue of whether Bevilacqua had an enforceable employment agreement would have to wait until after the judge considered the evidence that would be presented at the upcoming evidentiary hearing. Randy Donaldson didn't want to deal with another hearing, and he didn't want to wait to get rid of Bevilacqua, so Hugh Williams called a meeting in his office to decide what they should recommend to Donaldson.

"I think we should just pay Bevilacqua the $50,000 severance payment provided for in that unsigned agreement," Hugh said. "The payment would be in exchange for his agreement to terminate his employment with the company and waive any claims he allegedly has."

"I think that's a good result," Alan said.

"What do you think, Robert?" Hugh asked.

"I'm not sure I'm in a position to express an opinion."

"I wouldn't have asked you if I didn't want to know what you think," Hugh said.

"Well, I think we're just caving in. Bevilacqua is the bad guy. Our client shouldn't be paying him. Bevilacqua should be paying the company for the disruption he caused."

Hugh and Alan looked at each other for so long it made Robert feel as if he'd just said something incredibly naive.

Robert continued. "Even if they go by the terms of the unsigned agreement, Bevilacqua should be terminated for cause. He shouldn't get a severance."

Hugh sensed what Robert was feeling. "Sometimes, Robert, things don't work out right. Sometimes, you have to advise your client to do things that are distasteful because the alternative is worse. Alan, draw up a settlement agreement that provides for paying Bevilacqua $50,000 in exchange for him dropping all claims, refraining from disparaging Donaldson, and going away, never to be heard from again."

Such is justice in America.

# Chapter Ten

"HOW DO WE go about asking for time off?" Robert asked. He was standing in Alan Taylor's office door three days after Judge Carter ordered Jorge Bevilacqua to give Donaldson and the board of directors access to the company offices. The settlement with Bevilacqua was still being negotiated. Alan looked up and smiled broadly.

"Oh, I see. Now that you're one of the authors of the brilliant supplemental brief that got Donaldson's company back for him, you think you can kick back."

"No. No. It's not like that. I'm still bummed that Donaldson is offering to pay that jerk anything."

Alan's smile faded. "You look blue, man. You should be happy. You're making a good name for yourself around here. You remember what Hugh said, don't you? Sometimes we have to recommend the lesser of two evils."

Robert looked down and said nothing.

"I'm just teasing about the time off, Robert. You've been working hard. No one will mind if you need time off."

"It's not about kicking back. I need to go home to see if I can get my visitation with Ellie changed." Alan looked puzzled, so Robert continued. "She can't visit me in Dallas, because all my visitations have to be supervised. It's a bunch of bullshit!"

"Shut the door and come in here and sit down," Alan said. "What's going on with you, man?" Robert slouched into the chair in front of Alan's desk.

"It's hard to talk about."

"We're buddies, Robert. If you want me to help you, you've got to tell me what's going on."

"In my divorce…" Robert stopped. He didn't want to go on, but he knew Alan was trying to help him, so he pressed forward. "In my divorce they got into things I did in Panama and made a big fucking deal of it."

Alan leaned toward him with a fixed gaze. "What sort of things?"

"You remember that murder case I tried?"

"Of course. I told everyone here about it. They don't know many young lawyers who've won a murder trial."

"I didn't really win it, Alan."

"Yeah, I know. An asshole witness changed his story, and you did the Dudley Do-Right thing. Whatever. Trying a murder case is still a hell of an accomplishment."

"Yeah. Well, after the trial my company commander—who was a great guy but a bit of a hell-raiser—took me to a whorehouse in Panama."

"Seriously? You, in a whorehouse? Were you wanting to try out a *ménage à trois* or something?"

"It's not funny. Janelle's attorney asked me at my deposition if I'd ever had sex with a woman other than Janelle, and so I told them."

"You're shittin' me! Why'd you do that?"

"Because I was under oath, Alan. You remember? The truth, the whole truth, and nothing but the truth."

"Did Janelle know?"

"Hell no. She'd already left and gone back to the States weeks before that. And, in my defense, I was pretty drunk."

"Damn, man. I don't believe I'd would have confessed to that. But how did that fuck up your visitation?"

"Because my divorce case was in a court in South Georgia in front of an asshole judge. Janelle's attorney threatened to have a jury trial and drag me through the mud. I didn't want my momma hearing all that garbage."

"I see. So where does that leave you now?"

"They insisted on supervised visitation, and I made the mistake of agreeing to it. I can't even see Ellie, unless my mom or my sister is present at all times. They act like I'm some kind of sexual pervert."

"I don't have any kids, but I know that's got to suck."

"Yeah, it sucks. My attorney is trying to get it changed, but he says I have to be present in court if we have any hope of getting the judge to modify the order. And the hearing is the day after tomorrow."

"Well, then, you need to go home." Alan pressed his palms together in front of his face as if he were praying and then continued. "Look, you've worked your ass off here so far. And, you aren't assigned to a partner yet, so I can square things with Hugh. You aren't still doing anything for that lesbo, are you?

"Sharon Alexander?" Robert asked, slightly irritated.

"Yeah, '*Sharon.*' I told you before, Robert, don't get all high and mighty with me. I'm trying to help you."

"I know you are, Alan." Robert paused, slightly shaking his head. "No. I don't have any assignments from her or anybody else right now."

"Okay. Go see Davis Burnet and tell him you have to go home for a court hearing related to your divorce. He won't ask you about it. And I'll square things with Hugh Williams." Alan squinted and looked intently at Robert. "You'll get through this, buddy. You've endured tough times before. And I'm with you, man. I got your back."

# CHAPTER ELEVEN

ALAN WAS WRONG about Davis Burnet not asking him about the need for time off.

"Why is it you need to go to Georgia?" Davis asked, taking off his horn-rimmed reading glasses and carefully placing them onto his desk.

"It's a hearing related to my visitation with my daughter," Robert said.

Burnet stared at him for an uncomfortably long time. "I wasn't aware you had a child." His gray eyes squinted as if he were scrutinizing Robert for the first time. "I thought you had resolved all your personal issues before you moved to Dallas. This firm pays you handsomely and deserves your full attention."

Robert could feel his body getting hot. "I thought I had resolved them, Mr. Burnet. This is something new. My lawyer says I need to come to a hearing."

"Well then, I guess you have to go, don't you?" Robert said nothing. Davis turned and looked out the window for a long time. Without turning back, he said, "But I want you to get back here as soon as you can." Thinking Davis was finished, Robert stood to leave. "Stay for a moment, Robert." Davis turned back to him. "We haven't talked much since you joined us, have we?"

"I've stopped by a few times, Mr. Burnet, but you always seem to be busy," Robert said as he sat back down. "I didn't want to interrupt you."

A self-satisfied smile emerged on Davis's face. "Well, being busy is a lawyer's goal, Robert. Otherwise, we're not making money, are we?" Again,

Davis stared at Robert for an uncomfortably long time before asking, "For whom have you been working?"

"I did a research project for Stephen Edgar—" Davis chuckled, interrupting Robert's flow.

"And you survived the initiation, I see."

"I guess so. And, I did a memo for Sharon Alexander concerning lien law." Davis inhaled deeply and looked out the window again.

"You see that building out there, Robert?"

"The I. M. Pei building? Of course, it's famous."

"Well, actually it's called 'Fountain Place.' It was completed only recently. I was the lead attorney for Underwood & Crockett in representing the Olmstead Group, which built it. That's the kind of clients we have, Robert. And that's the kind of clients I want you working for. Sharon's clients are mostly community banks and S&Ls. Do you understand what kind of work that is?"

"Commercial? Banking?"

"It's working for piddly little clients that we have to harass in order to get paid. They loan money to people to buy houses they can't afford. Most of them are losing money. You read the papers, don't you? We should get out of that business altogether, unless we want to specialize in bankruptcy. The Fed keeps increasing interest rates, trying to wring this damn double-digit inflation out of the economy, which leaves the S&Ls with miserable little portfolios of low-interest mortgage loans. What kind of business is that? And now these financial wizards are getting into commercial real estate, which they know almost nothing about, and junk bonds, about which they know even less. They're going to lose their ass. And that's the bulk of Sharon's business. Do you understand what I'm saying?" Davis paused, apparently to emphasize what he'd just said. "Have you worked for anyone else?"

"I did some research for Hugh Williams related to litigation involving a renegade CEO."

"I heard about that case. That was for Randy Donaldson, wasn't it? And you achieved a good result, didn't you?"

"I guess the client is satisfied. Alan and Hugh are in the process of negotiating the settlement agreement. I helped prepare the motion and attended the hearing." Robert smiled the way people do when they don't know whether they should.

"Right. Hugh's a good man. But I need to get you involved in some good transactional work. Come to see me as soon as you get back from Georgia."

"Yes, sir," Robert said as he stood up.

"And remember, Robert, this isn't the Army. I'm 'Davis' to you, not Mr. Burnet."

"Thanks, Davis," Robert said, although it felt strange. Walking back to his office, he pondered what Davis had just told him.

Is he really interested in mentoring me? Or does he simply want to see for himself what kind of lawyer I am? And all that business about calling him "Davis." Even his secretary calls him "Mr. Burnet." "Davis" indeed. Davis Burnet is about as approachable as a newly promoted four-star general.

When Robert returned to his office, Carolyn could sense that he was stressed. Ever efficient, she quickly made his travel arrangements. After a quick stop at his duplex to pack, he headed to the DFW Airport and by early evening was on a flight to Savannah.

# CHAPTER TWELVE

"CLIMB ON UP in here, pretty boy." Barry Daniel was waiting for Robert at the curb outside the baggage claim area at the Savannah International Airport. His 1972 Ford Ranger pickup was spewing blue smoke and in dire need of a new muffler. "I should warn you that Spot was sitting in that seat about an hour ago. He might've left some fleas behind." Robert stepped back, unsure of whether his high school buddy was teasing him. "I'm kiddin' you, Bobby. There ain't nothing on that seat that's gonna hurt them fancy pants of yours." Robert settled into the front seat and smiled at his old friend, who was sporting a three-day-old beard, a tattered Braves baseball cap, and blue jeans with a hole in the right knee. As they pulled away from the curb, Barry chuckled. "Spot was sitting in that seat, though."

"You haven't changed much," Robert said. "You're still full of shit."

"You sure have, pretty boy. Look at you in your fancy suit and tie. But I guess you gotta do that now that you're a big-city lawyer, right? You ever see J. R. Ewing or Bobby?" Robert grinned, the ends of his mouth stretched down with amusement as if he were resisting a full-on smile. "Yeah, I know," Barry continued, "You probably done forgot where you came from." Barry paused in mock seriousness but couldn't suppress his crooked grin.

"Hell, no, bubba. I'm still just Bobby Clark from Pemberton, Georgia."

They rode along in silence for a few minutes as the cool night air blew past the windows. Barry was smoking a cigarette and had a can of Budweiser between his legs.

No longer teasing, Barry broke the silence. "I'm sorry you're having to go through this, Bobby. I thought my divorce was bad, but this really sucks."

"Yeah. It does. Hey, thanks for picking me up, by the way."

"Glad to, buddy. You've helped me out a bunch, especially hooking me up with Larry Gray. He did a good job for me."

"Thanks, but I didn't do much."

"Now, Bobby, you know the only reason Larry Gray agreed to meet with a redneck like me was that your dad was his best friend. Hell, he treated me like some sort of VIP."

"That's just the way he is, Barry. He's a good man."

"Yeah." An impish grin appeared on Barry's face. "Wanna grab a beer before we go to your momma's?"

"Maybe one. She'll be mad if I don't get home soon. She knows what time my flight was supposed to get in."

Barry pulled his truck into a gravel parking lot in front of a familiar concrete-block building with a neon sign in the window announcing "This Bud's for you." The moment they walked in, Robert realized how out of place he was. Heads turned to stare at the scruffy guy in a baseball cap and jeans standing next to a man in a blue suit, white shirt, red tie, and of course, highly polished, cap-toe shoes. Robert didn't recognize anyone but did notice people grinning and snickering at the city dude who'd just entered Buddy's Bar & Grill. He and Barry made their way to a booth in the back, away from the crowd.

When they sat down, a tired-looking waitress appeared. Her makeup was heavy, and she was wearing skimpy, cutoff blue jeans and a tight, Harley-Davidson T-shirt covering an ample bosom. Though she was probably only thirty-five, she looked more like forty-five, or maybe even fifty. Too many cigarettes and a hard life will do that to a woman, Robert thought.

"What'll it be?" she asked.

"Is Betty here tonight?" Barry asked.

"What? I ain't good enough for you?"

"No. No, darlin'. It's just that we went to high school with her. I wanted to show her what's happened to Mr. Fancy Pants, here."

"You do look out of place, baby," she said, turning to Robert. "But you are kinda cute. I like that suit. You a lawyer or somethin'?"

"Yeah. But I practice in Dallas."

"Georgia?"

"No, Texas."

"Then what in the hell are you doing in this dump?"

"I got some personal business to take care of in Pemberton."

"Hey, sweetheart," Barry said, "we're in kind of a hurry. Could you just bring us a couple of Buds?"

"Well, okay." She seemed annoyed that Barry had interrupted her conversation. "Y'all want something to eat?"

"No. We're good." Barry smiled, exposing his cigarette-stained teeth. But when the waitress left, his face turned serious, bordering on somber, and his eyes fixed on Robert. "So, what's this court hearing all about? I thought your divorce was finished a long time ago."

"It was, but I'm trying to get the judge to modify the visitation arrangement."

"Yeah. I didn't understand why your momma or Darlene had to be there when you was visiting Ellie."

"I sort of got blackmailed."

"Blackmailed?" Barry squinted.

"Here's your beer, boys. Let me know if you need anything else." The waitress plopped two long-neck Budweisers onto the table and walked away with a conscious sway to her hips.

"She's lookin' for a good tip," Barry chuckled. Each man took a long drink, then Barry again levelled his gaze on Robert. "So what do you mean you got blackmailed?"

"They had some shit on me from my time in Panama and threatened to use it in a jury trial if I didn't agree to their demands."

"What'd you do?" Barry asked. "Fuck a hooker?"

"Sort of."

Barry almost choked on his beer. "You? What in the hell were you thinkin'?"

"I was celebrating." Robert's face flushed, and he fidgeted in his seat. "Some guys took me out after I won a big case. We got drunk, and one thing sort of led to another. Janelle had already left me by then." Robert took another long drink.

"Shit," Barry said, stretching out the word. "But you was still married?"

"Yeah. And 'shit' is right. Look where I am now."

"No offense, bubba, but I woulda never pegged you for doin' somethin' like that. I heard the rumors that you did something bad, but I thought that was just people gossiping."

"Well, I'm not proud of it, and now the only way I can see my daughter is with a chaperone." Robert spat out the last word in disgust.

"How'd they find out about the hooker?"

"Janelle's attorney asked me about fooling around when he took my deposition, and so I told them."

"Damn, Robert. I don't believe I'd a said that. Why the hell did you do that?"

"Because I was under oath."

Barry raised his eyebrows and tucked in his chin. "You know, I didn't come clean with everything in my divorce. I didn't even tell Mr. Gray everything." Barry took a long swig and carefully set the bottle back onto the table. "And I still got screwed. So. Don't beat yourself up. You'd a got screwed anyway."

As they sat in silence, Robert began to survey the room. Everywhere he looked there were boots and jeans and ball caps, tank tops and Daisy Dukes—basically, a bunch of country folks having a good time drinking beer and talking loudly over Garth Brooks blaring from the jukebox. There were a few blacks in the back of the bar playing pool, something that would have been unheard of ten years earlier in Pemberton, Georgia.

"Was this place like this when we used to come here?" Robert asked.

"Nah. It's gotten seedier, if that's possible," Barry snickered. After a brief pause, his expression turned serious again. "Is there anything I can do to help you, Bobby?"

Robert took a drink and pondered Barry's offer. He set his bottle down and leaned over the table so he wouldn't be overheard. "Tell me what you know about this guy Junior."

"You talking about the guy Janelle's dating?"

"Yeah. He's not from Pemberton, is he? Do you know where's he's from?"

"Nobody knows anything about him. But you see him and Janelle all over town—at the Walmart and Kroger's and sometimes at the movies or the Swanson Inn. He's a big ole guy. I'll bet he weighs over 250. I think he's older than us. His real name is Rodney White, Jr. Seems like I heard something about him getting into trouble up in Augusta, but I don't know exactly what."

"He's from Augusta?"

"I don't know, Bobby. You want me to find out about him?"

"If it's not too much trouble. I don't want to put you out."

"Hey, man, like I said: you've been there for me. You took care of me with Mr. Gray. It's the least I can do. I'll see what I can find out, if I can ever get away from Old Man Lester."

"The guy with the garage?"

"Yeah. You know that. I've been working for that asshole since high school. I make him a bunch of money, but I sure as hell don't see it in my paycheck. That's the reason my old lady left me." Barry took a swig and smiled. "And that's why I don't have one of them fancy suits."

"Some things never change, asshole."

The conversation drifted to catching up on what had happened to all their high school friends and the current record of their high school football team. All of a sudden they heard a commotion in the back of the bar, where a fight had broken out by the pool table. Three redneck boys apparently didn't like it that blacks were on their turf.

"Let's get out of here, Barry. We don't need to get involved in that mess, and anyway, Momma will be expecting me. She'll be pissed if I don't get home soon."

Robert insisted on paying the check, and they walked out unnoticed. The crowd's attention was directed to the fight, which by then had been broken up by the bouncers but was probably going to continue in the parking lot. They climbed into Barry's truck, which did indeed smell like his dog Spot, and headed for the modest brick ranch house where Robert's mother lived. When they arrived, Robert thanked Barry again and offered to pay him for gas, which he refused. As he drove away, Barry said he'd find out what he could about Junior.

Robert expected to hear his dog Brandy barking as he walked down his mother's gravel driveway, but then he remembered his mother had put her down while he was in Panama. He knocked on the back door, which opened almost immediately. His mother's face beamed in the back-porch light. She was wearing one of the aprons she'd had for years.

"Hey, sweetheart. You're finally home. Get on in here. I've made you some cookies." Robert kissed his mother on the cheek, enabling the detective in her to smell the evidence of where he'd been. "Robert Clark, you've been at Buddy's Bar & Grill! I'm going to take a switch to that Barry Daniel!"

"Now, Momma, Barry wanted to have a beer. How could I say no after he drove all the way to Savannah to pick me up at the airport?"

"I guess you're right. Well, get on in here. I'll put some coffee on."

Walking into his mother's spotless kitchen was like walking back in time. It hadn't changed much since his childhood, although she was quick to point out the dishwasher Darlene and Frank had given her for her birthday—a far cry from the inexpensive necklace Robert had bought her at the Post Exchange. She obviously was proud of it but avoided sounding too enthusiastic, concerned that she might hurt Robert's feelings. "I don't know why they gave me this thing, since it's only me here now. But it does come in handy when I have the bridge club over here."

They sat at the kitchen table for almost an hour, munching on her fresh-baked, chocolate chip cookies and catching up on all that had been happening with their friends in Pemberton. Finally, his mother said, "Bobby, you need to get to bed. You and Larry have to get ready for your big day on Friday. I so hope that judge changes his child-visitation order. I can't understand why he insists on me or your sister being there when you visit with Ellie."

"It's just one of those things, Momma. And you're right: I need to get to bed."

The next day Robert met with his divorce attorney, family friend Larry Gray, in his office, which was two blocks off the town square, across the street from the courthouse. Larry and Robert's father had been best friends since childhood. In addition to being the most successful lawyer in town, Larry was also a member of the Georgia House of Representatives and, like most politicians, carefully guarded his reputation. He'd been shocked by what had come out in Robert's deposition, though he never mentioned it to Robert.

After exchanging pleasantries, they turned to the task of preparing for the hearing. Larry explained that the chances of getting the judge to change the order were slim. He planned to argue that the order should be modified because Robert was now living in Dallas instead of Atlanta—a significantly different situation from what existed when Robert agreed to the order. They finished going over his testimony by noon, so Robert left and strolled around downtown.

The shop windows displayed merchandise that had probably been there for a decade. Like many small towns, Pemberton's downtown was dying. What had once been the commercial center for the county now boasted only a few shops, lawyers' offices, an insurance agency, and the venerable Swanson Inn. The competition from Walmart and an air-conditioned mall with dozens of shops, located only a few miles east on Interstate 16, was too much for the merchants around the square.

As Robert rounded a corner, he was surprised to see Janelle and a large man—most likely Junior—exiting an office down the block. He retreated back around the corner to avoid their notice but watched as they crossed the street to a parking lot, smiling and laughing as they climbed into a car whose primary color was Bondo. I guess she's getting ready today, too, he thought. They sure seem happy. I haven't seen Janelle smile like that in years. Barry was right about Junior being big, but that's mostly fat. And, he's even scruffier than Barry.

On Friday morning, the day of the hearing, Robert woke up early. His mother insisted on making one of her famous breakfasts, including biscuits, gravy, and grits, which he couldn't bring himself to refuse, even though he was worried his stomach might get queasy. He arrived at Larry's office a few minutes late, startling the receptionist, who quickly ushered Robert to Larry's office and announced his arrival. The veteran lawyer was standing behind his desk, organizing files in folders and putting them in his leather briefcase.

"We need to get going, Bobby. Judge Harrington will crucify us if we're late. He already doesn't like me, because he knows I recommended that the governor appoint someone else when Judge Cochran died." As they walked across the street to the courthouse, Larry tried to be reassuring. "You'll be fine, Bobby. Just keep your cool and don't lose your temper if Janelle's lawyer tries to goad you. Walk in there knowing he's going to try, and don't let him be successful."

"Yes, sir. I think I'm ready. I know what losing your temper can do to a case."

Judge Harrington's courtroom was crowded with lawyers. The judge was conducting "calendar call," a proceeding in which the judge asks the attorneys in each case whether they're ready to proceed and how much time they'll need. To Robert it seemed like an archaic way to schedule cases in the late 1980s. His mind began to wander. Wouldn't a computer be more efficient? Are all these lawyers billing their clients, even though—for the most part—they aren't doing anything? Larry later disabused him of both assumptions. He said calendar calls were the best way to coordinate the judge's calendar because things kept changing. As for the lawyers billing time, he explained that most of them were handling DUIs, divorces, and criminal cases, which they billed on a flat-fee basis. When the judge finally finished scheduling the other cases, the courtroom cleared except for Larry and Robert. Judge Harrington looked up over his reading glasses, perched on the end of his nose.

"Mr. Gray, I see you and your client are here, but I have not seen Mrs. Clark's attorney, Mr. Matthews." The judge's clerk whispered something to him. "I can't hear you, Gladys. Come up here and tell me what you're trying to say." Gladys, a heavy set woman with permed hair and long fake fingernails, painted bright red, shuffled up to the judge's bench and stood on her tiptoes, which exposed the tops of her knee-high stockings. "Oh, I see," the judge said. "Well, that sort of ends it, doesn't it?" Gladys returned to her seat, and Judge Harrington turned back to Larry and Robert. "It seems, gentlemen, that Mr. Matthews notified us a little while ago that he's ill with a cold or something and will be unable to be in court today."

Robert whispered in Larry's ear. "I saw Janelle yesterday, Larry. I think she was coming out of her lawyer's office. Do you think he's really sick?"

Larry didn't answer and instead rose to address the judge. "But, Your Honor," he began, "My client has travelled from Dallas, Texas, to be here today. He desperately wants His Honor to reconsider that portion of the court's order pertaining to his visitation with his child, Eloise Clark."

"Well, counselor, he can want it desperately or otherwise, but if opposing counsel is not here, we cannot proceed with this hearing."

Robert whispered to Larry, "Couldn't one of his partners stand in for him?"

"No. He's a solo practitioner." Larry looked down at the table as he tried to decide what to say next. "Your Honor, may I put Mr. Clark on the stand while he is here in Pemberton, so the court will have a record of his testimony?"

"And what good would that do, Mr. Gray?"

"It would preserve his testimony, Your Honor."

"Well, there is this thing called cross-examination, Mr. Gray. I'm sure you've heard of it, and I'm sure Mr. Matthews would insist upon it." Judge Harrington stared at Larry. "Mr. Gray, you know better than to make a request like that."

Larry inhaled deeply and let it out. "Your Honor, Mr. Clark has travelled here at considerable expense from Dallas, Texas. He's currently an associate at Underwood & Crockett, a distinguished Texas firm that I'm sure Your Honor has heard of. It is extremely disruptive to his nascent career with that firm to take time off to come to Pemberton for a court hearing. Mr. Matthews gave us no notice that he was not going to be present today."

"As I said, Mr. Gray, we only received this communication a short time ago. I'm sure Mr. Matthews didn't plan to get sick."

"But that will mean that Mr. Clark has wasted this trip and will have to return from Dallas yet again in order for this matter to be heard."

"The fact that Mr. Clark decided to relocate to Dallas, Texas, is not my concern, Mr. Gray. He'll have to live with the ramifications of that decision. Perhaps you and Mr. Matthews can agree on what changes to the visitation order are appropriate; otherwise, we'll just have to reschedule this hearing. Court's adjourned." The judge brought his gavel down but made no effort to get up. He smiled when the bailiff called "all rise" and then stood up and ambled out the door behind the bench.

"How bad is this, Larry?" Robert asked.

"I'm afraid it means that nothing's going to change for now, Bobby. I'm sorry. Gene Matthews is difficult to deal with. I doubt we'll be able to reach any kind of acceptable agreement with him."

"But Larry, I saw Janelle downtown yesterday. She and that bozo she's dating were coming out of her lawyer's office, and they were laughing. They didn't seem worried about this hearing at all. I think Matthews's so-called illness is nothing more than a ruse."

"It might be, Bobby, but there's nothing we can do about it." Larry stuffed his papers into his briefcase.

That evening Robert took his mother and Ellie to dinner at the Swanson Inn, which they both seemed to enjoy until he broke the news that he was returning to Dallas the next day.

"I don't understand, Bobby. You just got here. You've hardly seen Ellie at all. Can't you at least stay until Sunday?"

Ellie stopped coloring on the placemat in front of her and stared at him, her angelic face now filled with concern. "Why can't you stay, Daddy?"

"I wish I could, sweetheart, but my boss told me to get back as soon as I could."

"Why did you move so far away, Daddy?"

"I needed a good job, sweetheart."

"Your boss expects you to work on Sunday?" his mother asked. Her tone was unusually incredulous.

"Momma, lawyers work all the time."

It pained him to see the look in his mother's eyes. Ellie put the crayons back into the holder and snuggled close to his side.

"I guess we'll have to wait for Thanksgiving then," his mother said.

"I'll try to get home then, Momma."

"Well, I hope you do."

Ruth smiled, but it was tight and strained. Robert knew the announcement of his quick return to Dallas had dampened her spirits, but he kept seeing the look on Davis Burnet's face when he admonished him to return to Dallas as soon as possible. The next morning Barry drove him to the airport.

# CHAPTER THIRTEEN

ROBERT WAS SITTING at his desk, shortly before lunch, wondering why it had been so damned important for him to return to Dallas right away. It was almost 12:00 p.m. on Wednesday, and he had not had a single hour of billable work to do all week. He'd occupied himself by perusing memorandums from the associate files. Some were excellent, written by attorneys still working at Underwood & Crockett. But there were also memorandums that were superficial and trite, written by lawyers whose names Robert didn't recognize. Apparently, Stephen Edgar's weeding-out process was brutal but effective.

"Long time no see." Robert looked up to see Diana Maguire standing in his door with a coffee mug in her hand. "Mind if I sit down?"

"Of course not. Please do."

"Are you working on another memo? I see the associate files."

"Oh. No. I'm just looking for something worthwhile to do. I don't have any billable work," Robert said, staring at her blankly.

"I'm sorry to hear that, Robert. I know what you mean. I'm so thankful Sharon keeps me busy. Without her I don't know how I'd hit 2200 hours this year."

"How do others do it?" Robert asked. "I watch people like Alan Taylor, for instance. He doesn't come in early, he doesn't stay late, he spends a tremendous amount of time socializing with other attorneys and going to lunch, and yet he says he's on-track to meet the firm's billable-hour goal."

"I don't understand it either," Diana said, lowering her voice and leaning toward Robert in an almost intimate fashion. "Jackie Sullivan, for instance. I never see her in the office late or on weekends, and yet, she always makes the 2200-hour goal."

Robert recalled what Alan had told him about Jackie screwing partners, but there was no way he was going to venture into that topic with Diana, so he broached another. "Do you think they pad their timesheets?"

"They must. How else could they do it?"

"Doesn't the firm police that?"

"Are you kidding?" Diana sat back in the chair. "They celebrate it." Her lips curled as in disgust. "As long as the client pays the bill, they don't care how many hours you put down."

"That's bullshit. Oh, sorry, Diana. That just slipped out."

"Don't worry. I've heard worse around here. Stephen Edgar curses like a drunken sailor. Thank *goodness* I spend most of my time with Sharon."

The intensity of Diana's comment gave Robert a twinge. "You really like her, don't you?"

"Absolutely. She's smart, polished, a skilled mentor, and the consummate professional." Diana sighed and shook her head. "I don't know why she keeps working here, though. She's treated terribly."

"What do you mean?" Robert expected Diana to say something about Sharon being gay and perhaps reveal something about herself in the process.

"She's isolated. She has her clients, which she and I service, and she develops new business, but she receives almost no help from anyone around here. She might as well be on her own."

"But Underwood & Crockett is the best firm in Dallas—maybe even the entire state of Texas," Robert said, sounding as if he was trying to convince himself he'd made a good decision in coming to the firm.

"Yeah, well, she gets some benefit from the reputation of the firm, but she never gets any help from her fellow partners."

"Do you think it's because of her lifestyle choice?" Robert asked.

"I don't know what you mean," Diana snapped, her blue eyes suddenly icy. "You know, I need to get back to work." She stood up and walked out without saying anything else.

For several minutes Robert sat at his desk and sulked. Alan must be right, he thought. Diana *is* gay. But I can't believe she's Sharon's lover. Both of them are too professional for that. Sharon probably supports Diana because she respects her ability and her work ethic. He stared at the papers on his desk but was unable to focus. I'm sure I pissed her off with that lifestyle question. What a *dumb* thing to say! She'll probably go back and tell the *one* partner at the firm who's been nice to me and supportive of me that I insulted her. So much for trying to navigate my way around here.

Robert was right: Diana was offended, and she did go to see Sharon Alexander. Her demeanor was uncharacteristically flustered as she rushed into Sharon's office, closed the door, and sat down.

"What's going on?" Sharon asked. Diana's neck and upper chest had red blotches on them, and her face was flushed.

"I thought Robert Clark was a nice guy, but he's just like all the rest of them."

"Why do you say that? What did he do?"

"He started asking about your 'lifestyle'." She punctuated the last word with air quotes.

"What did he say exactly?"

"I told him you were somewhat isolated at the firm, and he asked me whether it was because of your lifestyle choice. I suppose he was referring to your being gay. But what business is that of his? And why would he make that assumption anyway?"

"Because I told him."

"You what?" Diana drew back and her eyes widened. She stared at Sharon for several moments. "Why did you tell him that? I thought you told me you wanted to keep your personal life private."

"You're right. I did say that, and I do want to keep my personal life private. I don't know, Diana." Sharon paused, apparently organizing her thoughts. "Robert came by my office after he finished the memo that I'd assigned to him. And, well, I just felt sorry for him. No other partners are giving him work, and he's stressed about his billable hours because of attorney extraordinaire, Mr. Alan Taylor." She rolled her eyes and shook her head in disgust. "Taylor advised him not to seek out work from me. And we both know where that's coming from."

Sharon slumped back into her chair and stared out the window for several moments before turning back toward Diana. "I hope your affiliation with me hasn't hurt your career."

"What are you talking about, Sharon? You're a wonderful mentor. In fact, I just mentioned to Robert that I didn't know what I'd do if I didn't get assignments and guidance from you."

"That's nice of you to say, Diana, but I'm afraid Robert's comment to me and his question to you were simply echoes of what's commonly said around the firm: avoid working with Sharon Alexander—she's a lesbian, or worse, a lesbo. For some reason I just felt sorry for him. He seems like a nice young man. Obviously, he's naive." Sharon smiled. "I haven't heard 'lifestyle choice' in quite a while." After a short pause her eyes narrowed. "I think Robert is sincerely trying to make his way in this firm. I'm sure he felt conflicted when his friend told him to avoid working with me."

"I see. Well, maybe I overreacted."

"Perhaps. But thank you for letting me know. At least I know you're in my corner." Sharon stopped again and looked at her protégé like a proud parent. "Yes, I know I said we wouldn't talk about our private lives, but what's your sudden interest in Robert?"

The red blotches on Diana's neck and upper chest, which had started to fade, flushed again. "I, uh, I guess I find him attractive."

"I thought that might be the case." Sharon's eyes narrowed slightly. "You should know he's dating Megan Miller."

"The recruiting coordinator? How do you know that?"

"Jackie Sullivan told me."

"Jackie? Why would she be privy to that information?

"Come on, Diana. You know Jackie trades on two things: her looks and gossip. I suspect Megan told her. She said Megan wasn't overly impressed with him, though."

"That's because Megan—and Jackie for that matter—are vapid and empty-headed." Diana looked down and shook her head. "Well, I guess I'd better focus on work and that 2200 hour goal."

"Bide your time, Diana. I think Robert will soon see Megan as you do, if he hasn't already." Sharon smiled. "And don't think things are always rosy for Jackie. She has her troubles, too. She shared something with me just yesterday."

"What? That she's sleeping with Hugh Williams? Everyone knows that. I suspect that's why she's not worried about billable hours. She's sleeping her way to partner."

"No. It's not that," Sharon said. "She actually came to see me in tears. It seems she'd just found out that Hugh is also sleeping with his legal assistant."

"Are you serious?"

"That's what she said. And get this: she was upset that Hugh was 'cheating' on her. It was difficult not to laugh." Sharon stifled a giggle. "I said, 'Jackie, you are aware that Hugh is married, so technically he's cheating with you.' You should have seen her face, Diana. Somehow, I don't think that fact had ever dawned on her."

"It just goes to show that makeup doesn't cover up crazy. And it confirms what I think of her," Diana sniffed. "But it doesn't change the fact that she's still guaranteed to make partner."

"Maybe so. But you'd never go down that road, would you?"

"Absolutely not."

"I didn't think so." Sharon smiled at her. "So, are you going to the firm retreat? Have you heard they're having a costume party in honor of Halloween?"

"I don't know," Diana said. "Can you believe that the retreat starts on Friday, which is Halloween? Did the planners ever think that young parents might want to take their children trick-or-treating?"

"I suspect not. They probably thought a costume party would be 'fun for the young folks.' They're clueless. The only thing they know is that it's the firm—first and always."

"I guess I'll go," Diana said. "You almost have to, don't you?"

"I think you should go, but I'm going to pass. I'd rather get some work done and spend some time with friends. But you need to go. You're going to be considered for partner soon. You should go and smile and make nice with all those old geezers who'll be voting on it."

Diana smiled and stood to leave. "Good advice. As always."

# CHAPTER FOURTEEN

ON FRIDAY AFTERNOON the lawyers of Underwood & Crockett began to gather at the Omni Barton Creek Resort & Spa, located west of Austin overlooking the lush landscape and gently rolling hills of the Texas Hill Country. Robert didn't know many associates at the firm, so he made a point of introducing himself to several of them as they arrived in the hotel lobby. They seemed to fit into two main categories: those who were in awe of the firm and were honored to be among the chosen few, and those who were cocky—including some who were downright arrogant—who acted as if the firm was lucky to have them. Despite his concerns about the firm's apathy toward padded timesheets, Robert was definitely in the former group, and he concluded, reluctantly, that Alan was in the latter.

The lobby area began to clear as folks registered and went to their rooms to get ready for the costume party that evening. Robert had brought his West Point full dress uniform, a pair of high-top leather boots, a maroon sash, and the ceremonial saber he'd received when he became a cavalry officer.

"What in the hell are you wearing that for?" Alan demanded as soon as he saw Robert. Alan was dressed as Robin Hood, complete with a bow and a quiver of arrows.

"I'm supposed to be a Confederate officer, Alan. What's the big deal?"

"Yeah. You look like a Confederate officer. That's what the big deal is."

"That's ridiculous. There's no hidden meaning."

"Well, black folks don't see it the same way. You're being insensitive. But what would you know about our struggle?"

"C'mon, Alan, I didn't mean to offend anyone, especially you. And it's too late for me to change now."

Alan stared at Robert in disbelief, shook his head, and walked away, leaving him standing alone as a parade of costumed lawyers filed past and entered the hotel ballroom. Alan's rebuke only heightened Robert's anxiety. He knew virtually no one at the event, and now his closest friend had abandoned him over a damn costume. He needed a drink.

Entering the ballroom, Robert saw, spread across one entire end of the room, a buffet that could have been in a king's castle. Along with a carving station and a large ice sculpture of a jack-o-lantern, there were all manner of soups, salads, side dishes, breads, desserts, and wines. Deciding he should eat before getting a drink, Robert filled a plate and made his way to a table at which six older attorneys already were seated.

"Now that's a costume!" said a white-haired gentleman wearing a navy blazer, not a costume. "You look like you stepped out of the pages of *Gone with the Wind.*" Robert smiled and asked if he could join them. "You're Robert Clark, aren't you?"

"Yes, sir," Robert replied.

"Well, I'm Robert, too," the man continued. "Rob Underwood." Robert's hands began to sweat as he realized he was seated next to a name partner of the firm. Sensing, from the look on his face, what was going through Robert's mind, Mr. Underwood added, "Don't let the Underwood name bother you, Robert. It was my granddaddy who started this firm with Mr. Crockett. I'm just one of the litigators." Robert knew that Mr. Underwood was being overly modest. He'd been the president of the American Bar Association and had argued cases before the U.S. Supreme Court.

But before Robert could respond, an attractive woman, dressed as a sexy nurse in a very short and very tight white dress, approached their table. "May I sit down, gentlemen?" Noticing that her hands were full with a plate and a glass of wine, Robert stood up and pulled out her chair. She glared at him and said, "If you're going to act like that, I'll sit elsewhere." As she turned to walk away, Robert, speechless, noticed her flaming red hair and realized he had just had his first close encounter with the infamous Jackie Sullivan.

"Aw, sit down, Robert," said Mr. Underwood. "If it'd been me, I'd a decked her." The other attorneys at the table chuckled. "Now, Rob," said one of them. But Mr. Underwood was on a roll. "I can't get used to these women being lawyers. And then they show up looking like a hooker in a nurse's outfit and wonder why guys make passes at them."

Robert sat down. "I guess I don't know how to deal with a feminist."

"Believe me, son," said Mr. Underwood, "she's no feminist. And that red hair of hers? It's just God's warning label." The old men at the table chortled, causing Robert to wonder whether Jackie's reputation was widespread.

With a twinkle in his eye, Mr. Underwood leaned in and asked, "Did y'all hear about Ben Parker's interview of a female law student over at Cook & Simpson?" Underwood's colleagues stopped eating and looked at him, prompting him to continue. "He got in a bunch of trouble over it, but I think it's funny." Mr. Underwood grinned as he paused for dramatic effect. "It seems that when he was interviewing a girl for a summer clerkship he asked her if she could type, and it pissed her off."

"What'd she do?" one of the other lawyers asked.

"Well, she said sure, she could type, and she could screw, too, but she didn't do either one for money. And then she got up and walked out." The other lawyers at the table howled with laughter so hard they attracted the attention of those seated nearby. Robert just grinned. One of the older lawyers asked Mr. Underwood what happened to the girl.

"Hell, we hired her!" he said, causing the laughter to burst forth again.

"Is she still here?" one of them managed to ask while still laughing.

"Who is she?" asked another.

"She sure is. It's Diana Maguire. You know, that good-lookin' girl who works for the lesbian. What's her name?"

"Sharon Alexander," one of them replied.

"Yeah. That's her. How'd we wind up with a lesbian anyway?" Mr. Underwood asked. The laughter stopped, but no one answered. They hung their heads in silence until one of them finally said, "She was married when she joined the firm, Rob."

"Well, she sure as hell isn't married now. It's an embarrassment." Several lawyers at the table shook their heads while looking down at their plates. "We ought to do something," Underwood continued.

"About Alexander?" one of them asked.

"No. About that Maguire girl. Alexander's going to ruin that girl's career. And, hell, anyone who would stand up to old Ben Parker like that has spunk. I want to keep her!"

Again, no one said anything, though several lawyers nodded in agreement. Robert had a sinking feeling he'd heard too much, and it made him sick. Sharon's right, he thought, these men—the leaders of Underwood & Crockett—hide their prejudice beneath a thin veil of superficial courtesy when one of the targets of their bigotry is around.

When the older lawyers left shortly after dinner, things got rowdy. In a separate room off the ballroom, there was an open bar, where already a few lawyers were well beyond tipsy—the kind of inebriation where boring conversations become brilliant, where internal filters erode and jumbled words come out with brutal honesty and overblown sincerity. Boxes of expensive cigars were on a side table, being sampled by aficionados and novices alike. Their exuberant participation in that age-old gentlemen's hobby created a blue haze that hung in the air. Having become a fan of good cigars while stationed in Panama, Robert joined in and began to relax as he conversed with lawyers who were closer to his own age. He didn't seem to notice that few women were present. And no one seemed to be offended by his costume. A few even asked him where Melanie and Scarlett were.

Robert didn't speak with Alan again, although he watched him flit from one group to the next, working the crowd with a cigar in hand and a used-car-salesman smile on his face. Throughout the evening Robert looked for Diana but never saw her. Around midnight he decided he'd seen enough and headed back to his room.

Sleep came quickly, but around 2:00 a.m. he was awakened by raucous laughter coming from somewhere below his window. In the dim light he saw a number of men and women in a large, bubbling hot tub. He couldn't make out whether they were naked or just wearing scanty swimsuits. Some were smoking cigars; all were drinking. Squinting to see, Robert noticed Jackie Sullivan, still in her nurse's costume, crouching next to the tub, holding a martini glass. Suddenly, an arm reached up from the hot tub and pulled her in. She went head-first under the water, which caused the rest of them to laugh even louder. When she popped up, she was soaked but smiling. Her costume, now drenched, became translucent. As she climbed out of the tub, it was obvious she wasn't wearing a bra or panties. Still smiling, she stood up straight, adjusted her dress, which had hiked up her thighs, and announced, "Now I need another drink."

Robert shook his head and went back to bed, happy he wouldn't be nursing their hangovers in the morning.

෬

Following breakfast, there was an "all-associates" meeting with the managing partner and members of the management committee. The ostensible purpose of the meeting was to report on the state of the firm, but the topic on everyone's mind was what the senior associates had begun calling the "duck pond." Historically, the firm had considered attorneys for partner after they had worked at the firm for seven years. But since the last partners' meeting a few weeks earlier, rumors had been swirling that there would now be an interim step to partner called "non-equity" partner—the duck pond. Non-equity partners would not share in the profits of the firm—they would be partners in name only.

Apparently feeling that the rules had been changed in the middle of the game, several senior associates explained, in surprisingly strident tones, why they disagreed with the rumored new arrangement. When they finished, the managing partner turned to his assistant and—in a voice that all could hear—directed her to take careful notes of what had just been said so that he could bring their concerns to the attention of the partners. The members of the management committee who were sitting on the stage with the managing partner nodded their heads in agreement. That comment seemed to placate the group, so the managing partner moved on to another topic.

With considerable celebration and fanfare, he recognized two lawyers who had billed 2,600 hours so far that year. Robert was acquainted with the two attorneys, and although they appeared to work hard, he knew that billing that many hours in ten months was virtually impossible. It appeared Diana was right: the firm didn't police overbilling, it celebrated it. Disgusted, Robert wondered whether he belonged at Underwood & Crockett.

As he was leaving the meeting, Robert saw Davis Burnet, seated immediately outside the conference room. "Robert, could you spare a moment?"

"Of course, Davis. What do you need?"

"Tell me, how's your first firm retreat been?" Davis smiled and patted the seat next to him, indicating Robert should sit down.

"Well, I wasn't sure what to expect. The costume party was a bit of a surprise."

"How's that?"

"Surprisingly raucous," Robert replied with an awkward grin.

"They were just blowing off some steam, Robert. We find that it helps our young lawyers bond together." Davis paused and smiled at Robert the way people do when they're attempting to remind someone he's a subordinate. "Now, sit down. I have something I want to talk to you about."

As he sat down, Robert looked intently at Davis, unsure of where the conversation was headed.

"When we get back to Dallas on Monday, I want you to come to see me. Stephen Edgar told me you did a fine job on a memorandum concerning the fiduciary duties of directors and officers." Robert squirmed, still wondering what was coming next. "And," Davis continued, "I have an important client—Russell Field Services—that's dealing with a matter involving just those issues. I'd like to have you assist me with that. Can you do that?"

"Absolutely," Robert said. "Thank you, Mr. Burnet."

"Remember, Robert, I told you to call me 'Davis.' And you can thank me by working hard and helping me keep my client happy." With that Davis stood up and, looking down at Robert, said, "I'll see you Monday." A practiced smile appeared on Davis's face as if on cue. He walked off in the direction of a group of older partners and, punching out each word with emphasis, greeted Mr. Underwood with, "How have you been, Rob?"

Confusion engulfed Robert. He'd been uneasy ever since Diana told him the firm didn't police overbilling. He knew he couldn't abide what he perceived to be lying to clients, and yet the managing partner had just celebrated what everyone had to have known was overbilling. At dinner the night before, the prejudice of the senior leaders of the firm had been apparent, most likely because a few drinks had eroded their filters. What other prejudices do they harbor? The rowdy behavior after dinner rivaled what he'd seen in Panama; he certainly didn't want to go down that road again. And finally, what would his father think of all this? Would he think Underwood & Crockett is where his son belonged? Is this what's involved with practicing law in a top-tier firm?

But then along comes Davis Burnet—arguably the most important partner in the firm—asking Robert to assist him with his "very important client."

Robert's anxiety began to wane as he imagined what it would be like to work on projects for Russell Field Services. Davis Burnet could be offering him the key to getting a stream of sophisticated legal work. He'd no longer have to worry about finding billable hours, and it certainly wouldn't hurt to be affiliated with someone as prominent in the firm as Davis Burnet. Hadn't Alan advised him to cozy up to Davis? Maybe he did belong at Underwood & Crockett. As long as *he* didn't overbill clients, he wasn't being unethical. Was he? After all, Diana seemed to be highly ethical, and yet she, too, was aware of associates padding their timesheets. She had stayed at Underwood & Crockett and was now on her way to making partner. As for the prejudice and rowdy behavior he'd witnessed, didn't those exist almost everywhere? Surely, if he kept his head about him, he could stay on the straight and narrow path.

He couldn't wait to get back to Dallas.

# CHAPTER FIFTEEN

ALAN TAYLOR IS an enigma, Robert decided after the weekend retreat. The attorneys and staff at Underwood & Crockett see a handsome, ambitious, gregarious young man with a solid education and an incredibly bright future. But it seemed to Robert there might be another man behind that facade. To be sure, Alan had helped him immeasurably, and that fact was never far from his thoughts. Still, Alan had never really opened up to him; he was always guarded. And then there was the rumor about how he had been discharged from the Army before his commitment was up. And why had he been so sensitive about the Confederate costume at the retreat? Robert certainly had not intended to offend him or any other black person. The conflict between Alan and his father was particularly troublesome. Mr. Taylor worried about his son and clearly had his best interests at heart. Yet Alan seemed indifferent to the wisdom that Mr. Taylor might impart, based on his life experience, and dismissive of what his father had accomplished in life. Most of all, though, Robert couldn't understand why Alan hadn't told his parents about Michelle. Was he afraid they would disapprove of her because she's white? But, enigma or not, and regardless of the obvious tension between Alan and his father, Robert would never forget that Alan had done him a tremendous favor by getting him a job at the most prestigious law firm in Texas and then linking him up with the firm's most important partner. Robert couldn't wait to tell him about his conversation with Davis Burnet.

"You coming to apologize?" Alan put his feet on his desk.

"For what?"

"For dressing like a redneck cracker at the firm retreat. You embarrassed me. Remember, I'm the one who talked you up at this firm."

"I'm sorry, Alan. Other people didn't seem to be offended."

"Well, maybe they just didn't say anything. If you look around, you'll see there aren't many black folks at this firm, and there are no black partners. Remember, I intend to change that. And I can't have someone I helped bring to the firm acting like it's the 1950s."

Though he still didn't understand the intensity of Alan's reaction to his costume, Robert decided to change the subject and, he hoped, put the issue behind them. "Davis has asked me to help him on a project for Russell Field Services."

Alan dropped his feet to the floor and leaned forward. "Russell Field Services, eh? Tell me more."

"I don't know much more. Davis just told me to see him today about an assignment. He said Stephen Edgar told him I did a good job on that memo about fiduciary duties."

"Well, well, that bullshit assignment led to some good anyway, didn't it?"

"I guess so," Robert replied.

"Listen. You need to bust your butt on that project for Davis. Russell Field Services is an important client of the firm. We bill them several million dollars a year. Old Man Russell doesn't make a move without talking to Davis. Hell, *I* haven't even worked on any of their files yet." Alan flashed that used-car-salesman smile again. "Maybe you can return the favor and get me in with them."

"I'll try, Alan, but I don't even know what *I'll* be doing."

"I'm just kiddin', Robert. Just do a good job and make me look good for recommending you. Maybe everyone will forget you're an insensitive cracker."

"I told, you, Alan—"

"C'mon, Robert. Can't you take a joke? Now, get going. Make me proud."

Davis Burnet's office door was open, allowing Robert to see him seated at his desk poring over a document. Three neat stacks of papers were lined up in front of him.

"Mr. Burnet is expecting you," Donna said. "Go right on in." Robert was struck again by how much Davis's secretary resembled a robot: always professional, never emotional, pleasant, though not really engaging. Maybe that's what Davis wants, he thought.

Robert knocked to announce his arrival and then approached the front of Davis's desk. Davis continued to examine the document before him and didn't look up. "So, you helped Hugh Williams and Alan Taylor with a litigation matter involving fiduciary duties."

"I helped a bit, I guess."

Davis looked up. "Well, I'll need more than a bit. We have a complicated situation here. Mr. Russell wants to take his company private in a leveraged buyout, so the shares will no longer be publicly traded. As you probably know, these transactions usually result in a shareholder lawsuit. So, you see what the problem is, right?"

Robert's expression revealed his confusion. His weight shifted from one foot to the other. "Not exactly, Davis."

"Well," Davis began, sounding a bit peeved, "because Mr. Russell is the majority shareholder, he essentially controls the board. And the board has to approve the going-private transaction. The minority shareholders might feel that Mr. Russell—and the directors he nominated—are only looking out for him. Surely you remember from your Corporations course that the directors on the board are supposed to look out for *all* the shareholders, including not only Mr. Russell but also all the other public shareholders. So, how do we sort that all out? Is Mr. Russell conflicted?"

"I guess he would be."

"I need more than a guess, Robert. Donna will give you the notes I dictated describing the transaction that Mr. Russell has in mind. I want you to prepare a memorandum for me describing the process the company and the board should go through to approve the transaction and minimize the chance of a viable shareholder lawsuit. And I need it by noon on Friday." Davis looked back down at the document he'd been reading. "That's all."

For a moment Robert stood in front of Davis's desk in silence, not knowing what to do. Although he had questions, he'd obviously been dismissed, so he just walked away. For a guy who insists on being called "Davis," he thought, he certainly has an imperious way about him.

Robert retrieved Davis's notes from Donna and proceeded directly to the file room where the associate files were kept. Unfortunately, he found nothing relevant to going-private transactions. Next, he went to the library and began researching in the digest of court cases for ones that dealt with going-private transactions.

He felt like a law student again. After several hours, he'd amassed a mound of books and a collection of empty Styrofoam coffee cups on the library table where he was working. There was no statute that directly addressed going-private transactions, so he had to look for court cases that were similar to the facts of Mr. Russell's situation, which Davis had outlined in his notes. After reading over a dozen cases, he concluded that a going-private transaction is basically the opposite of an initial public offering. In a going-private transaction, one or more parties buy enough shares to allow the company to terminate its public-company status and the related reporting obligations under the securities laws. The transactions are often challenged in court, usually based on claims that the directors failed to look out for the interests of the public shareholders or the company failed to disclose enough information about the company and the transaction. When a company like Russell Field Services is being acquired by its controlling shareholder, the reviewing court will often apply its strictest standard of review, known as "entire fairness." Under that standard both the price and the process used by the parties to determine the terms of the proposed transaction must be entirely fair to all parties, including the minority shareholders. In other words, Mr. Russell had to establish that the transaction was good for all shareholders, not just him.

By noon on Friday, Robert had finished his research and written the memorandum, which he personally delivered to Donna. Then, exhausted and somewhat anxious, he went to see Alan.

"This is the work you were meant to do, my man," Alan said, smiling at Robert like a proud mentor, "sophisticated corporate work for none other than Davis Burnet."

Robert could sense that Alan was relaxed and shifting into a Friday afternoon mindset. No doubt he'd already planned dinner and an evening with Michelle.

"Why don't you ask Megan to go to dinner tonight?" Alan asked. "We could double. Michelle and I are going to Trader Vic's on Mockingbird."

"I don't know, Alan." Robert sat down in a chair opposite him. "Our last date was kind of awkward. Besides, it's short notice."

"Well, first of all, you are new to the dating scene. Hell, I don't think you ever had a dating scene. And second, this is the eighties man, not the sixties. Girls get asked out at the last minute all the time."

"Yeah. I don't know…"

"What are you doing tonight?"

Robert stared at him but said nothing.

"That's what I thought. You're doing nothing, so you and Megan are going to dinner with me and Michelle. What happens after that is your business. Now, pick up the phone and call her."

Robert looked at Alan and twisted his mouth the way people do when they're resigned to the inevitable, especially when they dread it. He picked up the phone and pressed zero for the receptionist. "Would you connect me to Megan Miller, please?"

"Certainly," said the receptionist. "Is this Mr. Taylor?"

"No, it's Robert Clark."

"Oh, I guess you're calling from Mr. Taylor's office. I'll connect you."

The tone of the receptionist's voice reminded Robert of a high school girl who'd just discovered there was a new "couple" at school. Does this place thrive on gossip? he wondered.

"Hello, this is Megan."

She always sounds so perky and helpful, he thought, but there's something unappealing about her. Is it that she seems fake? He couldn't decide.

"Hey, this is Robert. It seems Alan and Michelle are going to Trader Vic's tonight, and they want us to join them. Sorry for the last—"

"Sure. Sounds like fun. What time?"

Robert held his hand over the receiver and looked at Alan. "Time?"

"Tell her you'll pick her up at seven-thirty."

"Seven-thirty. I'll pick you up at your apartment."

"Sounds great. I'll see you then."

She actually sounds excited, Robert thought as he hung up the receiver. "Okay. We're on for a double date, but I still think we're not right for each other."

"What do you know? You were married during your best years. And remember, I'm not saying you should marry her for crying out loud." Alan leaned forward. His eyes widened, filled with excitement. "Now, tell me exactly what you're doing for Davis."

"Well, I just gave him a memo concerning the risks a majority shareholder has when he decides to take his public company private, including a recommended best course of action for reducing those risks."

"I can see that military mind working." Alan grinned. "Best course of action. Reduce the risks. *Et cetera, et cetera*. I love that shit."

"Are you making fun of me?"

"Hell, no, man. I'm proud of you. I'm sure you gave Davis just what he wanted. And, it won't be the last thing you do for Russell Field Services. I told you: they are *muy importante*. And, you're working for *Davis Burnet*, not Sharon Alexander."

"Come on, Alan. Sharon has been good to me."

"Well, maybe she has, but she'll ruin your career at this firm. I'd venture to say she's already ruined Miss Diana Maguire's chances of making partner."

"Have you heard something?" Robert asked, his eyes wide with concern.

"Don't tell me you've still got a thing for her. You know what I told you. And I'm right about that."

"No. I don't have a 'thing' for her," Robert replied, sounding a bit annoyed. "It's just that I'd hate to think the partners of Underwood & Crockett would hold it against her that she's worked primarily for Sharon."

"Maybe they're just trying to protect the firm's image." Alan pursed his lips and shrugged.

The firm's image? Robert thought. What does that have to do with Diana? Even if the partners don't like having Sharon as partner, why should that affect Diana? Surely they won't deny her partnership simply because she's worked primarily for Sharon. If they do, what does that say about this place? Clouds of confusion began to gather again.

"Hey. Where'd you go, man?" Alan asked. "Are you listening to me?"

"What?" Robert reconnected. "Yeah. I'm listening. You said to work my ass off for Davis Burnet."

Alan chuckled. "Well, you got the important part. Now, let's talk about Trader Vic's. Have you been there before?"

"Yeah, Sharon and I go there all the time."

"Okay, smartass. Now, listen to me. It's a high-end place, so wear a blazer or a sports jacket. Do you have a blazer?"

"No. And don't tell me to go to Culwell & Son. That place is expensive. I'll just wear the sports jacket I wore when we went to The Mansion."

Alan started to say something but stopped. "Okay. But wear a different shirt at least."

The evening went as Robert expected. Alan knew the maître d', scored the best table in the house, and ordered an expensive bottle of wine. No sooner had the waiter filled their glasses than Michelle started talking about an upcoming trip to her parents' lodge in Vail to go skiing during the Christmas holiday. As she and Megan discussed when they were leaving and what to take, it became clear that Michelle was taking Megan with her, not Alan. So, not to be outdone, Alan changed the subject.

"Why don't we all go to Galveston for Thanksgiving?" he asked.

"Galveston?" Michelle and Megan asked, almost in unison.

"Yeah. Galveston," Alan said. "We'll do the family thing on Thursday—Robert you can come to my folks' house; they'd love to have you—and then we could all go to Galveston for a long weekend." Turning to Michelle, he asked, "Your folks would let us use their beach house, wouldn't they?"

"Uh, yeah, I guess they would. But why Galveston?" Michelle asked. "The place will be almost deserted."

"That's the point," Alan said. "We'll have the town all to ourselves. I'll bring some good vino; we can make a cozy fire and just relax."

Michelle and Megan looked at each other, grinned, and then burst out laughing.

"Why not?" Michelle said. "You're right. It'll be fun. Romantic even."

Megan smiled, causing her eyes to narrow as she peeked at Robert to her right.

"I don't know, Alan," Robert said. "I probably should go home. I need to see my mom and—"

"I thought you'd say that. But didn't you say you needed to work on that project for Davis Burnet?" Alan's mien suggested his protégé shouldn't question his proposed weekend getaway.

"You're working on something for Davis Burnet?" Megan asked.

"Yeah," Robert said and then turned back to Alan. "But I really need to see my family, Alan."

"Well, what happens if you get stuck in the Atlanta airport? Davis would not be happy if you're not in the office on Monday. And remember, we can drive to Galveston. We don't need to worry about getting stuck somewhere."

"Come on, Robert," Megan said. "Michelle's right. It'll be fun. And Alan has great taste in wine." She giggled and batted her eyes at him. "And I can show you what an excellent cook I am."

"Uh, okay. I guess so," Robert said, but without the enthusiasm that had now overtaken the other three as they began planning the trip.

Why do I keep letting myself get talked into things? I don't want to go to Galveston. What will my mother say? I told her I would try to get back. And I've seen so little of Ellie. What am I doing? Robert silently stared at the other three, chattering away about what they should take, when they should leave, who should drive.

The evening ended with Alan picking up the check. Although he feigned being discreet, he wasn't, and it made Robert uncomfortable, though he said nothing. The couples said goodnight by the valet stand. Michelle and Alan drove away in Alan's BMW, while Megan and Robert waited for the valet to retrieve Robert's Chevy. Robert fumbled with his wallet to find a tip for the driver, while another valet opened the door for Megan. When they arrived at Megan's apartment, Robert didn't know what to expect, though he knew he didn't want to go in.

When they reached her door, Megan moved close to him and looked up. "Do you want to come in for a night cap?"

"I'd better not. I need to get to the office early tomorrow to do some more research on that project I'm working on for Davis. Alan's made it clear that I need to give it everything I've got."

Megan looked puzzled but shrugged, kissed Robert on the cheek, and said good night.

As he dropped into the driver's seat of his car, Robert couldn't stop thinking about the trip to Galveston. *Staying here for Thanksgiving is a terrible mistake. I should go home. Going to Galveston is even worse. Maybe I can still back out. Is this job that damn important? If Alan is any kind of friend, he'll understand.*

# CHAPTER SIXTEEN

AROUND 9:00 A.M. the following Monday, Donna called. "Mr. Burnet would like to see you in his office." Robert grabbed his notebook and file and headed upstairs.

Davis didn't look up from the document he was reading when Robert knocked. "Come on in and sit down. I'm looking over your memorandum. Generally, it's pretty good, although I noticed a recurrent error."

Robert uncrossed his legs and leaned forward, waiting for Davis to elaborate. His hands began to sweat the way they did when he was taking an exam in school. Not just any exam, mind you, but one of those gut-wrenching exams from a professor who is trying to weed people out by asking obscure questions. What's next? he wondered.

"When discussing the Delaware cases you cite in your memorandum, you repeatedly use the term 'shareholder.' "

Robert's nervousness shifted to confusion. "I'm sorry, Davis. I'm afraid I don't understand."

"Well, you should know by now that the owners of a Delaware corporation are referred to as 'stockholders,' while here in Texas we refer to the owners as 'shareholders.' "

"Aren't they the same thing?" Robert asked.

"Well, no," Davis said, "and I'm concerned that you apparently don't know the difference. Terminology is important, Robert. Professionals, like the lawyers at Underwood & Crockett, always use the correct term. And you also need to pay attention to your punctuation."

"Yes, sir. I see. Was there anything else?"

Davis squinted his eyes and slowly said, "Not that I've discerned so far. But I want you to pay attention to details, Robert. Every firm has its own standard. Underwood & Crockett's is the gold standard. Getting things *precisely* correct is what we expect."

"Yes, sir."

Davis smiled like a condescending lecturer and then asked with contrived sincerity, "What did I tell you about that 'sir' stuff, Robert? We're not that formal here."

No more formal than the coronation of a queen, Robert thought.

"Of course. I remember, Davis. I think I understand what you need. Is there anything else?"

Davis looked astonished again. "Well, for starters your memorandum needs to be rewritten with the changes I've noted. I want to read it again after you correct the shareholder/stockholder terminology. Right now, that just assaults my eyes. I've also noted a few other changes and some punctuation errors." Davis stared at Robert for an uncomfortable few moments. "Do you have a copy of *The Elements of Style* by Strunk and White?"

"Uh, yes. I think I got one in law school."

"Well, you should read it again. In fact, you should almost commit it to memory. I did. Rule Number 2 of Section One says that in a series of three or more terms with a single conjunction, one should use a comma after each term except the last." Davis smiled, apparently awaiting a flattering response from Robert.

"That's pretty amazing, Davis."

"Well, I've found that adherence to the rules promulgated by Messrs. Strunk and White will improve one's writing immeasurably."

"Oh, I'm sure that's true," Robert said.

"Whenever you submit something to me, Robert, ensure that you've given thought to the guidance found in *The Elements of Style*."

"Absolutely, Davis. Will do."

"That's all for now." Davis picked up another document from his desk and began to study it. "Get your memorandum rewritten and returned to me as soon as possible," he said without looking up.

That must be his standard protocol for dismissing a subordinate,

Robert thought. No wonder Donna seems so subservient. He stood up and left without saying anything further.

Robert returned to his office and meticulously changed each mention of a Delaware "shareholder" to a Delaware "stockholder." One day, software would make such a task simple, but in 1986 it was maddeningly tedious. Robert couldn't believe Davis was concerned with something so trivial and decided not to bill the client for the time it took to make those changes. But as he reviewed the memorandum, a deeper, sinking, feeling came over him.

I was so focused on the issue of fiduciary duty—the topic that got me hooked into this project—that I included only a cursory discussion of the disclosure obligations of Mr. Russell and the board of directors. How could I have missed that? Why didn't Davis comment on such a material omission? And how in hell can I insert it now without drawing attention to its absence from my first draft? Screw it. I'll put it in and let the chips fall where they may.

Robert added another section to the memorandum, explaining that Russell Field Services would need to solicit the approval of its shareholders for the going-private transaction by means of a proxy statement that included a disclosure of all material facts. He struggled to define the term "material fact," knowing he had to be "precise," as Davis had advised. His research revealed that the Securities and Exchange Commission has specific rules on such disclosure, but each court decision addressing the issue is based on the specific facts of the case being considered. Unfortunately, because Davis jealously guarded his relationship with Mr. Russell and excluded Robert from the telephone calls and meetings discussing the transaction, he had no way of knowing what the specific facts of Mr. Russell's transaction might turn out to be. Consequently, that section of his memorandum was rather general.

After agonizing over the memorandum for almost three hours, he gave his marked-up draft and notes to Carolyn, who had agreed to stay late. She quickly made the revisions and returned the memorandum to him. He read it at least ten times before he delivered it to Donna, who was also working overtime on another project, and asked her to give it to Davis at the earliest opportunity. Then, he went home and straight to his bottle of Maker's Mark.

# CHAPTER SEVENTEEN

AS SOON AS he walked through the door of his duplex on Hawthorne Street, Robert saw the red light flashing on his answering machine. He pressed PLAY and heard the sweet, though annoyed, voice of his sister.

"Bobby, this is Darlene. You remember me? Have you forgotten you have a sister and a mother in Georgia, not to mention a daughter who misses you? Call us sometime. We're worried about you."

Robert dropped two cubes of ice into a glass, filled it with bourbon, and then dialed Darlene's number. Although it was after nine o'clock in Georgia, he knew she wouldn't mind. She and Frank were probably watching *L.A. Law.*

"Hey, Darlene, this is Bobby."

"Well, hello, stranger. I guess you got my message."

"Yeah. I'm sorry, Darlene. It's just that I've been so darn busy. Is Momma doing all right?"

"She's fine. She gets to keep Ellie from time to time. Momma has helped her with her reading. That little girl loves to read." Darlene paused. "And she sure misses her daddy."

That stung. Robert hadn't seen Ellie or talked to her since his short visit to Pemberton the previous month. Janelle wouldn't answer his calls. His mother had called his office a few times when she was keeping Ellie, but each time he was either on the phone or away from his desk. He glanced at the kitchen table—an unfinished letter to Ellie had been in the same spot for over a week. He took a long drink.

"I miss her, too, Sissy. It's just that that damn visitation order really fouled things up. You should have seen the looks we got when we went downtown. And, Janelle won't let me talk to Ellie on the phone."

"Bobby, I'm so sorry Larry wasn't able to get your visitation changed. I know it must be hard on you." Darlene paused, waiting for Robert to say something, then continued. "Judge Harrington certainly is a far cry from sweet ol' Judge Cochran, isn't he? We all miss Judge Cochran, and nobody likes Harrington. We *never* see him around town. I don't think he even goes to church."

Knowing he would slip into even worse foul language, Robert choked back his opinion of the judge.

"I guess I need to call Larry and see if there's anything else I can do," Robert said. "It's just so hard to get the time to come back to Georgia for a court appearance. Last time Janelle's lawyer didn't even show up. We got nothing accomplished."

"Well, at least you'll get to spend some time with Ellie over Thanksgiving," Darlene said.

The line was silent for almost a minute. "I'm not sure I'll be able to come home for Thanksgiving, Sissy."

"You've got to be kiddin' me. Momma will be upset to hear that. What are you going to do? Are you really that busy? You know how much Momma enjoys having all of us around her table."

"I know. I just don't think I can make it. But let me be the one to tell her. I'm not sure what's happening yet. The partner I'm working for is really demanding. And you know how crazy it gets trying to travel over that weekend. If I'm late getting back, it would not bode well for me."

"Are you sure you should be in Dallas, Bobby?"

"We've had this discussion before, Darlene. I had to get out of Georgia. The firm I'm with in Dallas is the best law firm in Texas. And I'm working for the most important partner in the firm."

"Ellie won't be a little girl forever, Bobby. You're missing so much."

"Don't you think I know that?" he snapped. "If I could get that damn order changed, things would be different."

"I didn't mean to get you riled up, Bobby. I'm just worried about you. And Ellie."

"Why are you worried about Ellie? Has she been sick?" Robert's questions came quickly, his voice tense.

"No. It's just that little girls need their daddy, Bobby."

Robert was silent for a few seconds and then asked, "What do you know about this guy Junior?"

"You mean the fella Janelle's dating?"

"Yeah. Does he seem like a nice guy?"

"I don't know, Bobby, but it seems pretty serious. You see them together all the time. I wouldn't be surprised if they got married."

"Married? She's barely divorced from me!"

"Bobby, I know this has been painful for you, but you need to put your divorce behind you and make the best of the visitation situation."

Robert said nothing for a long time. Darlene knew she'd pushed him enough, so she waited.

"I'll let you know about Thanksgiving when I have a better idea of what's going on here, okay? Tell Momma 'Hi.' I'm going to try to call her tomorrow."

"Okay. You know I love you, little brother."

"Love you, too. Bye."

Tuesday came and went, but Robert didn't call his mother. He tried to convince himself that he was too busy. But the real reason was that he just didn't want to. He didn't want to tell his mother that he wasn't coming home for Thanksgiving and that he wasn't going to see his little girl until Christmas. He didn't want to tell his mother he'd been talked into going to Galveston with a woman he wasn't even interested in.

# CHAPTER EIGHTEEN

ROBERT ARRIVED AT work shortly after 7:00 a.m. on Wednesday. Davis Burnet's silver Jaguar was already in its usual place. As he flipped on his office light, Robert noticed a pink envelope in the middle of his desk, inscribed simply "R.C." It contained a note from Megan on pink stationery. She'd drawn dainty hearts around the border of the page and in the center had written:

*All work and no play will make Robert old and gray. Smile!!!! I can't wait for our weekend! We're going to have SOOOOOOO much fun!*

He groaned out loud. This is not going well, he thought. Why did I agree to this trip?

"I see you got my note." Megan was standing in his door with her cheerleader smile on. "You seemed pretty down at Trader Vic's the other night, and I haven't heard a word from you since then. Is everything all right?"

"Sorry, Megan. Davis has had me busy. You're here early."

"Well, you're not the only one with loads of work to do." Her face lit up, and she gave an excited giggle. "I still can't believe you're Davis Burnet's associate." She put particular emphasis on the esteemed partner's name. "You do know he's the most important partner in the firm. The other corporate associates must be absolutely green with envy. Do you realize how fortunate you are?"

Robert squinted. "I realize it's going to be a slew of work for a guy who's hard to please. Speaking of which, I need to get at it, Megan. Thanks for the note."

"Okay." She spun around, still smiling, and bounced out of his office as if she were headed onto the football field to lead another cheer.

For the rest of the week and the next one, Robert met repeatedly with Davis, who directed him to prepare additional memorandums on every conceivable topic related to Mr. Russell's going-private transaction. Davis said nothing about the section Robert had omitted from his first memorandum concerning the disclosure obligations of Mr. Russell and the board. Instead, he seemed obsessed with whether Mr. Russell's percentage ownership of the outstanding shares would cause him to owe fiduciary duties to the other shareholders. If he owed them those duties, then he could be personally liable to them if they were damaged by the transaction. Davis had Robert prepare at least three memorandums on that topic alone. But throughout this process Davis revealed little about what was going on. He frequently had long telephone conversations, alone in his office with the door closed. Robert wondered how he was supposed to address important issues concerning the transaction if he didn't know the facts.

Megan brought him snacks on several occasions, including homemade brownies that rivaled his mother's. She even brought him homemade lasagna one night when he was working late. She smiled all the time and seemed even more bubbly and bouncy than normal. Robert was gracious and always said "thank you" but was careful not to encourage her attention. For some reason she now made him feel uneasy. Was she beginning to remind him of Janelle? Although Megan was better educated than Janelle, she didn't show it. She never commented on current events or anything else of substance, though she always seemed to be fully apprised of any gossip making its way around the firm. Whenever she started to talk about the latest tidbit, Robert would remind her that he was busy and needed to get back to work. She didn't seem to mind and always left his office as bubbly and bouncy as when she came in.

Robert needed to talk to someone about the work he was doing for Davis. He'd racked up an enormous number of billable hours but wasn't sure he'd accomplished anything of value. He decided he needed to speak with a woman who did have substance. He picked up his phone and dialed.

"Diana, do you have time for a quick chat? I need some guidance."

"Sure. You want me to come over or do you want to come here?"

"I'll come to your office. Thanks."

As Robert shuffled into Diana's office, she looked up, tilted her head ever so slightly, and squinted her eyes. "What's wrong, Robert?" Puffy gray pouches had formed beneath his eyes since the last time she'd seen him. He looked worn and haggard, almost sickly.

"I just need someone to talk to." He stood, waiting for Diana to respond.

"Of course. Sit down."

Robert collapsed into the chair across from her. He said nothing for a few moments—not trying to be dramatic, just not knowing where to begin. "One hundred, sixty-seven."

"Excuse me?"

"That's how many hours I've billed Russell Field Services in the last twelve days."

"Goodness. That *is* a lot."

"And that's not an inflated number. If anything, it's a little light."

"Sometimes, Robert, that's the way it goes. Isn't that what you wanted? Isn't that what Alan told you to do?" Diana arched her right eyebrow.

Robert's eyes widened as he stared hard at Diana. "I know what you're thinking. It's not like that. I really appreciate what Sharon did for me. And, I respect her. I know what people in the firm say about her, and I think it's despicable."

Diana clenched her jaw and looked out the window. Turning back to Robert, she said, "Well, what's this about then?"

"It's about the project I'm working on for Davis."

"The going-private transaction?" she asked.

"Yeah."

"Well, consider yourself fortunate. It's the most high-profile matter at the firm right now. And you know the firm bills Russell Field Services millions of dollars a year."

"So I've heard." Robert's voice carried a hint of disgust. "But I think most of what *I'm* doing is unnecessary. Davis is having me research all sorts of esoteric issues. He's even had me prepare summaries of relevant cases when he could just as easily look in the digest. He said he once found a case misreported, so he no longer trusts their summaries. He has me read the cases and summarize them as if I were the author of the digest. I'd venture to say almost half of what I've billed is useless stuff like that."

"I'd be *very* careful about second-guessing a man like Davis Burnet," Diana said, her voice low and devoid of emotion.

"Well, do you think it's reasonable not to trust the digest of cases? Doesn't that sound a bit crazy?"

"Maybe not on the really important cases. You should read the actual decisions of those."

"Of course, Diana. But that's not all. He's leaving no stone unturned. Another thing he had me do was research whether we could get a lawsuit moved from Texas to a court in Delaware because he likes the 'rich body of case law there.' " Robert made air quotes with his fingers. "That makes no sense. Neither Mr. Russell nor Russell Field Services has any connection with Delaware."

Diana chuckled. "I guess it was a short memo."

"It's not funny, Diana. It's stressing me out. And, that's not all." Robert paused. "The other night I was working late—"

"You mean the night Megan brought you lasagna? I could smell the aroma all the way down here."

"Could we not talk about that now? I'm worried. Like I said, I was working late and went by Davis's office. For once he wasn't there, but there was a stack of bills on Donna's desk. You know, the ones they print on green paper."

"Yeah. They do that to remind us that time is money. Those are the pre-bills the partner reviews before the final bill is sent to the client."

"Well, the Russell Field Services bill was on top, so I took a look at it. Davis has been billing hours upon hours for reviewing the memos I've been writing for him—way beyond what is reasonable. I didn't total it, but I'll bet it was over a hundred hours. And his hourly rate is more than twice what mine is. It's excessive. What if our billing records somehow become public? Or we get fired, and another law firm reviews our bills?"

"Like I said, Robert, I'd be careful second-guessing Davis Burnet."

"What are the ramifications of overbilling?"

"I guess it depends on the situation," she said, "but at a minimum it would make the firm look bad."

"To me, it's like fraud or at least cheating," Robert said.

"I'd be careful throwing that word around. Maybe you should go talk to Sharon."

"Do you think she'll see me? I mean, I kind of deserted her after she was so helpful."

"I don't think she sees it that way. And I'm sure she can help you sort through this better than I can. She's been a partner for a long time, and she always gives me sound advice."

Robert took a deep breath and exhaled. "Thanks, Diana." He stood up and started to leave but stopped. "Can I buy you lunch?"

"You don't need to do that, but I'll be glad to go with you." She sat up straight. "Any place other than Dakota's."

"Okay. You pick the place. I'll come by around eleven forty-five."

Robert walked back to his office, made some notes on a legal pad about what he wanted to discuss with Sharon, and then called her secretary, who said she could see him right away.

"Thanks for seeing me on short notice, Sharon. I know you're busy, so I'll be quick." Robert sat down and prepared to take notes.

As usual, Sharon looked elegant behind her desk, wearing a rose-colored raw silk suit that looked as if it could have come from Princess Diana's closet. A hint of a smile appeared as she dropped her chin the way his Sunday school teacher used to do and said, "I told you that you were welcome anytime, Robert. What seems to be the problem?"

"I'm working on a going-private transaction with Davis Burnet."

"Congratulations. That's what you wanted, right?" She seemed to be genuinely happy for him.

"Well, it is. But it's difficult to describe what I'm worried about." He paused for several moments. "Davis has me researching all sorts of issues and writing memos on things that don't really matter."

"Like what?"

"Like trying to find a way to get a case against Mr. Russell moved to Delaware if he gets sued in connection with the going-private transaction. I don't see how that could happen, and yet Davis has me research every idea he has for trying to make that happen. And as far as I know, there's not even a threat of a lawsuit. He also had me summarize every case I could find in Delaware and Texas where the court held that a shareholder owed fiduciary duties to other shareholders. He even had me make a chart showing the differences between the cases."

Robert studied Sharon's face. Her slight smile was gone. She spoke slowly and softly. "I think I know what you're getting at, Robert. You don't want to be guilty of billing Mr. Russell for what you perceive to be work of limited value."

"Worthless work. And, I saw last month's pre-bill for Russell Field Services. Davis billed an enormous amount of time for simply reviewing the memos I wrote for him."

"I see." Sharon paused. "Although I commend your concern, Robert, I suggest you do your best to ensure you understand the assignments Davis gives you. Sometimes partners have to write off time, especially when it appears an associate didn't grasp what the assignment was about. He might mark down some of the time you saw on the pre-bill. I think you should let Davis worry about the value of the work."

Robert looked down and shifted back and forth in his chair.

"Is something else troubling you?" she asked.

For some reason the floodgates opened up. There was *a lot* that had been bothering him, and until Sharon asked that question with such sincerity, he hadn't felt comfortable talking about it to anyone. "I really don't know where to begin, Sharon."

"Well, let's begin by *me* telling *you* that this conversation is confidential. What you tell me won't go any further."

"I'm just not sure I fit in. In addition to my work for you—"

"Which was commendable, by the way."

"Thanks. I also did a memo for Stephen Edgar, worked on a litigation project with Alan and Hugh Williams, and now this going-private transaction with Davis. I've billed scores of hours, but I'm just not sure I've produced anything worthwhile for our clients. When I was a prosecutor in the Army, I put bad guys in jail. That felt worthwhile. This doesn't."

"Well, much of what civilian lawyers do involves preventing problems, Robert. We research what's gone wrong in the past to try to avoid repeating mistakes. That's probably what Davis is doing. In the long run it saves the client money. Avoiding problems is much better than trying to solve them after they occur." She paused so Robert could digest what she'd just said. "You seem to be quite bothered by how lawyers bill hours."

"Yes, I am." Robert leaned forward, now realizing Sharon understood his frustration. "At the firm meeting Alex, uh…"

"Alex Foreman, the managing partner?"

"Yes. Alex recognized two associates who had already billed 2,600 hours this year. I don't see how that's possible."

Sharon sighed wearily. "It's *not* possible, Robert. Clearly, they've padded their timesheets. And rather than police such behavior, the firm encourages it. I suspect those two will receive handsome bonuses." She paused, considering what to say next; Robert noticed that her normally bright countenance now looked hollow and sad. "Back in the 1940s and 50s," she continued, "when my father was practicing law, attorneys billed using a fee schedule, but as litigation and corporate work became more complicated their compensation fell behind doctors and dentists. By the time I started practicing in the late 1960s, billing by the hour had become the norm. And that system works up to a point. But expecting associates to bill 2200 hours per year is unreasonable. Every lawyer knows that only about two-thirds of your working time is actually billable, so that means they're expecting associates to work 3300 hours per year, which breaks down to over sixty hours a week—every week. It's unrealistic."

"So why does the firm do it?"

"Virtually all firms do it, Robert. The problem is that greed takes hold. That's also why the partners created the infamous 'duck pond'. They don't want to share profits with younger lawyers any sooner than they have to."

"Has that been decided upon yet?" Robert asked. "Alex said he was going to discuss the concerns raised by the associates with the partners."

Sharon pursed her lips and shook her head. "That never happened, Robert. The decision to implement the duck pond was made several months ago. Nothing's changed."

"So, Alex lied to the associates to get them to shut up."

"I'm afraid so, Robert. But it's probably no different at any other big firm."

"What have I gotten myself into?" he asked. His eyes focused on the empty space between them.

"I'll be happy to help you navigate your way through the rules of the firm—both written and unwritten. And, I think you *can* adhere to your ethical principles and still work at Underwood & Crockett. Most lawyers do. But you're not in a position to control the behavior of others, Robert. Just do what you think is right."

"Thanks." Robert stared down at his legal pad. "Do you think it would it be all right if I don't come to the office on Thanksgiving and the following Friday, Saturday, and Sunday?"

"That's fine, Robert. It's not that bad here. I doubt many lawyers will be here then. Are you going home to Georgia to see family?"

"No." He looked down and rubbed his forehead. "I'm going to Thanksgiving dinner at Alan's parents' house and then to Galveston for the weekend."

"That's nice of Alan and his family to include you. Do the Taylors have a family tradition about going to the coast after Thanksgiving?"

"No. Actually, it will be just Alan, his girlfriend, Megan, and me."

As soon as he spoke the words, he regretted it. *Why am I telling her all this? When am I going to learn to think before I speak?*

Sharon looked surprised. "Megan Miller?"

"Uh, yeah. Alan kind of, kind of set it up."

"It sounds as if you're moving on and that your divorce is behind you. That's good."

"Moving on?" he asked. "I'm not even sure what that means. I'm not sure what I'm doing, Sharon."

"Well." She paused to indicate a change of subjects. "Do you feel like you now know what to do with respect to Russell Field Services?"

"Yes, I do. Thank you, Sharon. You've helped me more than you know." Sensing it was time for him to go, he stood to leave.

"Anytime, Robert. Would you please leave the door open on your way out?"

When he returned to his office, another pink envelope greeted him from the middle of his desk. Inside was a note from Megan, complete with hearts drawn around the border.

*You know, Robert, girls won't admit it, but they really like bad boys, not gentlemen. I can't wait for Galveston!*

# CHAPTER NINETEEN

ROBERT STOOD IN the door of Diana's office, watching her work. Sunlight streaming through the window gave the blonde curls framing her face an iridescent glow. Suddenly realizing he'd seem creepy if she caught him gawking at her, he spoke up. "Where are we going to lunch?"

She looked up, her face bright and welcoming. "Campisi's, the Egyptian Restaurant. It's a Dallas institution."

"Why is an Italian name associated with an Egyptian Restaurant?"

"It's a long story. I'll explain on the way. Let's take my car." Always professional, and a bit formal and stiff, Diana was transformed the moment she walked out the door. Her movements became fluid, like a lissome tennis player striding onto the court. She laughed as she talked and gestured with her hands, while steering her Honda Accord through Dallas's lunchtime traffic. The car, like everything else about her, was in perfect order. It wasn't new, but it had that new-car smell. The dash was immaculate, and there were no scuff marks on the doors or bits of trash on the floor.

"Like I said, Campisi's is a Dallas institution." Her voice was animated as she attempted—using a bad Italian accent—to tell the restaurant's story. "You see, after World War II Mr. Campisi introduced Dallas to pizzas. They were such a hit he outgrew his original location and moved to where we're going to have lunch. But after paying for the move and the renovations needed in the kitchen, he didn't have enough money for a new sign. The place had previously been a nightclub called the Egyptian Lounge. So, he took the word 'lounge' off and added 'restaurant.' "

"If he's doing so well now, why doesn't he get a new sign?"

"Like I said, it's an institution. People love the story, and they love the Campisi family."

Diana parked in front of the restaurant, and Robert looked up through the windshield. Sure enough, the word "Egyptian" was there in curving letters with a teal-blue background, while the word "restaurant" appeared in block letters, all caps, with navy-blue backing above red and white stripes.

"Before we go in, let me tell you the rest of the story," Diana said.

"There's more?"

"Yeah. Well, the rumor is that Campisi's is a front for the mob."

"You mean like in *The Godfather*?"

"Sort of, although I don't think there's much organized crime in Dallas. The crime here is more along the lines of crooked bankers or wildcatters or dishonest real-estate developers. Anyway, it seems that when Jack Ruby went to prison... You remember him, don't you?"

"The guy who shot Lee Harvey Oswald?"

"Yeah. Well, supposedly Ruby went to Campisi's and ate with Joe Campisi a few nights before he shot Oswald. And when Ruby went to prison, he asked Joe and his wife to visit him, which they did. So, the rumor is that the mob put a hit on Oswald and used Ruby as the trigger man. Supposedly, Joe Campisi is the one who delivered the order."

Robert was stunned to silence as he stared at Diana but then said, "I would never have suspected that you were interested in this sort of thing."

Opening her car door, she said, "There are loads of things you don't know about me. Let's eat. It's going to get crowded."

The interior of the restaurant echoed a scene from a movie set in New York. The lighting was dim, scores of black-and-white photos adorned the walls, a bar with backless barstools stretched across the back wall. And, it was packed.

"Let's order pizza. It's the best you'll get outside of New York or Chicago."

Robert tried not to stare. In this setting Diana wasn't the professional, helpful colleague. She was an alluring, fascinating woman.

"Do you think all that mob stuff is true?" Robert asked as they settled into their seats.

"Who knows? The Kennedy assassination caused this town to be full of conspiracy theories. It's fun to think about—sort of like living inside a piece of history."

"Have you lived here all your life?"

"No. My dad was in the Army."

"Really? Where was he stationed?"

"I don't know. Fort Benning, I think. Mom and I moved here when they got divorced. I was only five."

The waiter arrived with two large slices of pizza and two drinks. After he left, Robert asked, "Do you still see your dad?"

"Nope. I haven't seen or heard from him since we moved here."

"That must be tough."

"Not really. My mom took good care of me. She worked two, and sometimes three, jobs to support us and get me through school and then law school."

"She must be quite a woman."

"She was. She died last year." The confident lawyer suddenly looked fragile and sad. Her eyes became glassy.

"I'm sorry, Diana," Robert whispered, trying his best to sound comforting. "I lost my dad not long ago, so I have an idea of how you feel."

She looked at him through teary eyes. "Whatever I'm able to accomplish in life I owe to that woman's sacrifice." She blotted her eyes with her napkin, looked down and then back at Robert. "Let's change the subject, shall we? Tell me about you. I know you went to West Point and that you were an Army lawyer in Panama and that you tried a murder case there. I think Alan told everyone in the firm that story before you arrived."

Robert could feel his face flush. "Alan's quite the promoter, isn't he?"

"That's an understatement." She took a bite of pizza.

Robert didn't respond in defense of his friend. Instead, he bit into his pizza and thought about what to say next.

"Well, I grew up in Pemberton, a small town in South Georgia. My dad was the county agent, and my mom was a homemaker. And, I married my high school girlfriend. Huge mistake."

"Why's that?" Diana's eyes were wide with anticipation.

"Well, we had a beautiful little girl together—her name is Ellie—before we both decided that we just weren't right for each other. Now, it's tough for me to see Ellie. My wife left me when we were stationed in Panama. She needs to be in Pemberton, and I couldn't wait to get out. She wants the slow, settled life she has there, and I want to accomplish something."

"And what is that?"

"That's the problem, Diana. I don't know. I thought it was being a partner at a place like Underwood & Crockett. Lawyers at big firms seem to go on to accomplish big things. That's what I thought I wanted, but now I'm not so sure."

"Is that what's been bothering you?"

"Yes and no. I mean… What's bothering me most right now is what I talked to you about. You know, the billing on the Russell Field Services matter."

"Did you talk to Sharon?"

"Yeah. She said to stick to my principles and not worry about other people that I have no control over."

A hint of a smile appeared on Diana's face. "She told me the same thing. I've been trying to do that, too. I don't like some of what I see at the firm—especially how Sharon gets treated. But I know my mother would be proud if I make partner."

"You're up for it soon, aren't you?"

"We'll see." She dabbed her lips with her napkin. "And if either of us is going to have a chance at that, we'd better get back to work."

Robert insisted on paying for lunch, saying, "It's only fair. I invited you, and you drove."

As soon as they arrived at the office, Diana went to see Sharon and found her behind her desk, carefully scrutinizing a document through reading glasses she never used in public. Hearing Diana's knock on the door, she looked up, beaming.

"You look absolutely radiant, Diana."

"I just had lunch at Campisi's with Robert Clark. He asked me."

"Asked you what?"

"To go to lunch." Diana giggled as she moved about Sharon's office. She hadn't yet returned to her professional office demeanor. "And he paid, no less. When's the last time that happened?"

"Oh. That's nice, Diana. Sit down for a moment."

"Is something wrong?" Diana's giddiness ended immediately as she sunk into a chair across from Sharon.

"No. No. Nothing's wrong. It's just that I wouldn't get too serious with him if I were you."

"Don't get too serious with him? Why?" Diana slumped back in her chair for a moment before bolting upright, thinking she understood what her mentor was getting at. "Sharon, I don't think Robert meant anything by that 'lifestyle choice' comment about you. He's just naive. I think it's kind of endearing."

"No. I told you I don't care about that. I thought it was rather quaint. But you should remember that he has an ex-wife and a daughter back in Georgia."

"He told me about that. He said she left him when they were in Panama. Many couples get divorced. You did, didn't you?"

"Yes." Sharon shook her head slightly as she considered the blissful look on her protégé's face. She contemplated telling her that Robert was going away for the weekend with Megan Miller. But she knew she couldn't. She'd promised Robert their conversation would be confidential, and she intended to honor that commitment. "I just don't want to see you get hurt," she said, sounding like the mother of a teenage girl who'd fallen for the local hooligan.

"I'm a big girl, Sharon. Don't worry." Diana stood to leave. "Do you have anything you need me to work on?"

"No. No. Enjoy your weekend." Sharon smiled, but Diana could tell it was strained, leaving her to wonder why she seemed so concerned.

# CHAPTER TWENTY

ROBERT CLARK WAS seated in the backseat of Alan Taylor's BMW, somewhere between Austin and Galveston. Alan and Michelle were in front. Megan was at his side. The two women were reminiscing about their exploits as sorority sisters at SMU—most of it sounding like something from the pages of *Cosmopolitan* magazine.

Feeling separate from the group, Robert stared out the window at the passing scenery. How did I get myself into this spot? I know I owe Alan, but is that more important than my family? Than Ellie? Davis was so insistent that I hurry back to Dallas from my last trip to Georgia, and then I sat in my office with nothing to do until Sharon gave me a project. Are associates supposed to worship at the altar of billable hours? Or is Davis simply a control freak?

Thanksgiving dinner at the Taylors had been enjoyable until it ended badly. Mrs. Taylor had prepared a feast that rivaled his mother's. There had been turkey, of course, but what had impressed Robert most was everything else: the stuffing, the mashed potatoes and gravy, the green-bean casserole, the pumpkin pie. But by far the most incredible dish was her cranberry compote. Just as during his first visit, Brianna and Jasmine peppered Robert with scores of questions, making him feel like a celebrity. After dinner Mr. Taylor had joined Alan and Robert on the patio for cigars, though he didn't partake. Instead, he had entertained Robert with stories of World War II, which again seemed to have bored Alan.

The day ended badly when Mr. Taylor asked if Robert and Alan wanted to go flying the next day or over the weekend. Alan said he and Robert needed to "take care of something" in Galveston and were leaving the next day—a dissembling comment that left Mr. Taylor with the impression they were going to Galveston for work. Mr. Taylor never questioned his son about work after Alan informed him that all his work at the firm was "confidential." That exchange had stunned Robert and caused his Cuban cigar to quickly lose its appeal. What he would have given for one more Thanksgiving weekend with *his* dad.

But then Robert remembered that call to his mother, telling her he couldn't come home for Thanksgiving. That was a lie. He heard the disappointment in her voice, and it reminded him that he'd made a terrible mistake.

When he returned to his duplex from the Taylors, he had called Janelle and spoken briefly with Ellie, who had wished him a happy Thanksgiving but then said she had to get back to her card game with Pawpaw, Janelle's father.

So, here he was, on his way to Galveston with a woman he barely knew in the front seat, another in whom he had scant interest sitting next to him in the back seat, and a man to whom he owed much but in whom he was now sorely disappointed for a variety of reasons, not the least of which was his failure to appreciate what a wonderful father he had.

"How much longer is it, Alan?" Megan asked, sounding like the proverbial kid on her way to the beach.

"About thirty minutes. And then, it's smooth jazz, good wine, and the hot tub on the back porch." Alan smiled at Michelle, and she blew him a kiss.

A half hour later, right on schedule, Alan pulled his BMW into the driveway of an enormous beach house on Galveston Island. Reminiscent of a nineteenth-century Victorian mansion adorned with decorative millwork, it rose four stories and had wide porches that wrapped around each level. Michelle clicked a remote control to open the garage door, and Alan pulled inside. He and Robert unloaded their luggage and the groceries, which included over a dozen bottles of wine, and then the two couples rode the elevator to the main floor.

Alan put on Al Jarreau's album *Breakin' Away* and started singing along with "We're in This Love Together." Although it was only around 2:00 p.m., he started mixing cocktails at a bar that could have come from an Old West saloon. Mirrored shelves covered the wall behind the counter, which had an array of expensive liquor. Robert noticed the distinctive red wax on a bottle of Maker's Mark. The back of the house was an expanse of windows and French doors, which led to a covered porch and then to an uncovered deck. Robert folded his arms as he walked to the rail to take in the view of the Gulf of Mexico and smell the salt air. The beach was not as pretty as those along the Georgia coast, but the house was like nothing he'd ever seen. Being around such a display of wealth somehow made him uneasy.

Alan came out carrying two Bloody Marys, one of which he handed to Robert before taking a sip of his own and settling into a chair. "Ah, this is just what I needed: some honest-to-goodness down time."

Robert sat down next to him, though they didn't converse. He closed his eyes and felt the ocean breeze blow across his face. Memories of trips to the beach when he was a child filled his thoughts. Would he ever have that feeling again? The warmth of family, the joy of being alive. Or, would his future be consumed with billable hours and striving to make partner so he could have dinners at expensive restaurants with people he barely knew in the pursuit of more legal work and more billable hours? All of that, so he could afford a house like this that he would seldom visit. About thirty minutes later Michelle and Megan appeared. They had changed into long, flowing, cotton dresses with spaghetti straps and had traded their Bloody Marys for large, bulbous glasses of the red wine.

"Do we really want to cook tonight, Alan?" Michelle asked. "I know a place that will deliver unbelievable pizza."

Robert's mind flashed back to his lunch at Campisi's on Wednesday, which only deepened his regret about where he now found himself, causing him to become even more withdrawn.

"Fine with me, sweetie," Alan said. "What say you, Robert? Robert?"

"Huh? Oh, yeah. Pizza's fine."

After he finished his Bloody Mary, Alan brought out four more bottles of wine, which flowed freely until the pizza arrived around 6:00 p.m. For the first time in a long time, Robert—along with the other three—got seriously drunk. When the pizzas arrived, Alan stumbled to the elevator to go to the first floor and retrieve them, causing the other three to laugh as if he were performing a vaudeville slapstick routine.

After they finished dinner and three more bottles of wine, Megan wobbled to her feet. Thinking she was about to fall, Robert stood up and caught her under her arms. "Thank you, kind sir. Always the gentleman. See, Michelle. Just like I told you, he's always a gentleman. Now, sit back down, Robert, because, boys and girls, it's time to play Truth or Dare."

"What are you talking about?" Alan slurred.

"You know, Alan," Michelle said. "Truth or Dare. The party game. You get the choice of either answering a question truthfully or performing a dare."

"Oh, yeah. I remember. Are you game, Robert?" Alan asked.

"Uh, sure. Why not?" Robert's head was spinning.

Why do I keep doing this to myself? he thought. I don't want to play this puerile game. Who knows what these three will come up with in their current condition?

"All right, Alan said, "I'm going first. Michelle, truth or dare?"

"Truth."

"Do you love me dearly, sweetheart?" he asked.

Michelle tucked her chin and tilted her head. "Oh, honey, that's a silly question. I change my answer to dare."

"You can't do that," Alan said.

"Yes I can. It's my house."

"Yeah. It's her house," Megan said through giggles that spread to Michelle.

"Okay. Okay," Alan said. "I can't compete with the two of you, so the dare is: show us your underpants."

The giggles of the two women turned to howls of laughter. They slapped their thighs, tapped their bare feet on the floor, and held up their hands in mock protest.

"You don't understand, honey…" Michelle began.

"Oh yes I do," Alan said, the corners of his lips fighting a smile, his eyebrows slightly raised. "You changed to dare, so you have to show us your panties."

"No. No. You don't understand. I can't show you my panties, because I'm not wearing any." Tears rolled down her flushed cheeks, and she and Megan laughed so hard they had to catch their breath.

Still smiling, Alan said, "Oh, to hell with it, Michelle. Forget it. Megan, you take a turn."

Megan smiled in a way that left no doubt she was up to something. "Robert, truth or dare?"

"Truth."

"Have you slept with any women other than your ex-wife?"

Robert could feel a rush of blood to his neck and face. For a moment he thought of his encounter with the young prostitute in Panama, the soft curves of her body, the cushion of her lips against him, the fresh smell of her hair. But then he thought of how that single encounter had affected so much of his life, his divorce, his visitation with Ellie.

"I, uh, I'm going to change mine to dare," Robert stammered.

"That's not how the game is played." Megan feigned a pout, though an air of mischief was still about her.

"Alan let Michelle change hers," Robert said.

"Well, okay. I dare you to take off your shirt and pants."

Whether it was the alcohol or whether, like an adolescent, Robert succumbed to peer pressure, he stood up too quickly, fell back in his chair, and stood up again. With a drunk grin he said, "Okay." Turning around so he wasn't facing the other three, he removed his shirt, twirled it over his head, and tossed it backwards to whoops and catcalls. The ocean breeze felt good on his bare chest. He stopped to enjoy the coolness before attempting to remove his trousers. He struggled to get them off, lost his balance, and wound up on the porch floor wearing nothing but his underwear and his trousers around his ankles. The whoops and catcalls gave way to uncontrolled laughter. After several attempts, he managed to get to his feet and kick off his trousers. But when he turned around, Alan and Michelle were gone, and Megan was standing before him wearing nothing but a smile.

"Drop those shorts, handsome; let's get in the hot tub with our hosts."

Robert stood dumbfounded. He had to admit Megan had a gorgeous body, which easily could have graced the pages of *Playboy*. He could feel himself getting hard.

"Well, well, I guess you do like girls, don't you? Or at least your buddy does." Megan giggled as she ran off in the direction of the hot tub.

Robert staggered after her, still wearing his underwear, and trying not to spill his wine.

"Oh, no, no, no," Michelle said as he approached the hot tub. Alan and Megan were in the tub as well, and Robert could see that all three of them were naked. "Drop those shorts and lose the wine. But don't worry. We've got some weed."

Despite being drunker than he'd been in years, Robert felt a twinge. He'd never smoked marijuana and had caused others to be punished for doing so. But the part of his brain that controlled his behavior was out of commission. He set down his glass, dropped his shorts, and climbed in. Megan slid next to him and handed him a joint. He took a long draw and tried not to cough.

"Damn, man," Alan said. "That's a big hit. Have you smoked weed before?"

"No," Robert said, stifling a cough and starting to snicker, which within moments grew to uncontrolled laughter.

The other three were laughing, too. Robert couldn't tell whether it was with him or at him or neither. But it didn't matter. He didn't care. After several more hits of marijuana, things went black. He awoke the next morning not knowing where he was. It took him a few minutes to orient himself.

Okay, this is the bedroom of the beach house owned by Michelle's parents. I'm lying naked in bed beside Megan, who is also naked. How in the hell did I get out of the hot tub and in bed with her? And what happened after that?

He had to admit it felt good to be lying next to this warm, gorgeous, naked woman. But where was this headed? Did he really want a relationship with a woman who was so comfortable smoking pot and jumping in a hot tub with naked people? But then, so had he. He tried to think clearly.

Although she sometimes seems superficial, I know she's educated, completely unlike Janelle. And in fairness, I've never really talked to her about anything of substance: I only listened to her and Michelle go on about their days as sorority sisters. Maybe all women talk that way with their old college friends. She seems competent as the recruiting coordinator, and she certainly is clued in on everything that's going on at the firm. Maybe I'm not being fair. And, unless she was faking it, she seems genuinely interested in me.

Megan rolled over and looked at him with drowsy eyes. "Good morning, handsome. A hell of a night, wouldn't you say? I wouldn't mind a repeat performance, Soldier Boy. Your other soldier manages to stay at attention for a long, long time."

Megan pulled her body close to his and put her arm across his chest. He rolled over and kissed her. The taste of wine and marijuana was still on her lips, but it was pleasant. She thrust her tongue into his mouth and squeezed her arm around him. Pulling back she whispered, "Fuck me like you did last night."

No woman had ever talked to him like that. But he liked it. He could feel himself getting erect, and so could Megan.

"Well, well," she said, "he's at attention again. He needs to get going."

Robert slid down to her breasts, kissing and sucking them. He'd never done anything like that with Janelle, whose breasts were small, almost adolescent. Megan's were full and round and soft. Her nipples were high on her breasts, giving them a perky appearance despite their size. He was captivated.

"Enough foreplay," she said. "Roll me over and fuck me doggie style."

He paused. What did she say? Doggie style?

Megan grinned and squinted her eyes. "Don't tell me you don't know what that means."

"Uh, yeah. I do. It's just that—"

"Where'd you learn about sex, Robert? Church camp?"

She rolled over and got up on her knees. Placing her head down on the pillow, she spread her legs and arched her back. Robert stared at the white flesh of her butt and the tan line created by what must have been a tiny bikini.

"I'm waiting, big boy."

He'd never had sex in this position, but he obliged her. His stomach, now wet with sweat, slipped against her backside. She was so different from Janelle, so tight. Was it because she'd never had children? The feeling reminded him of the woman at Club Iguana in Panama-the only woman, other than Janelle, he'd ever been with. Although several years had passed, his memory of that night was still intense, still wonderful. Megan made him feel like that again. She moved her hips the way the ravishing Panamanian had done, creating a sensation unlike anything he'd ever experienced with Janelle. Within seconds, he released into her, causing her to moan softly into the pillow. After a few more thrusts, he backed out of her, and she rolled over, her eyes still dreamy.

"That's more like it," she said. "You're huge. Michelle's got nothing on me." Robert felt his neck and face flush. "Aw, did I embarrass you, big boy?"

He flopped down on his back, savoring the bliss.

They finally went downstairs to breakfast—or rather brunch—around 11:30 a.m. Megan and Michelle went out onto the deck while Alan cooked.

"Need any help?" Robert asked.

"No, but this will make you feel better." Alan handed him a Bloody Mary. "Quite a night, wasn't it? Didn't I tell you to stick with me? Megan's awesome, isn't she?"

"Yeah, she's special all right. Nothing like any woman I've ever been with."

"We hit it pretty hard last night," Alan said. "Today, I plan to slow down and chill."

"I couldn't agree more." Robert took a sip of his Bloody Mary.

For the rest of the day, the couples lounged on the back porch, drinking cocktails before switching to wine around dinnertime. There was no Truth or Dare, no hot tub, no marijuana. They listened to the waves, shared the latest firm gossip, and snuggled in the cool salty air. Megan was extremely attentive to Robert, though she didn't tell much about herself, despite his questions. She deflected each question about her family with a joke or a question back to him. She clearly didn't want to be forthcoming, and Robert didn't press. They all retired early, and Robert and Megan had sex again. He couldn't believe how passionate Megan was—moaning, thrusting herself against him, wrapping her arms around him, pulling him close. Janelle had always been so passive. Sweet, but passive.

Sunday morning the two men loaded the luggage into Alan's BMW, while Michelle and Megan made brunch. Megan cozied up next to Robert at the table but didn't say much to him. Instead, she and Michelle carried on an incessant conversation that covered a variety of what he thought were trite topics: the latest fashions at Northpark Mall, the men their friends were dating, the ones who were having affairs, the best places to take hot yoga classes. Their prattling continued on the drive back to Dallas, while Alan seemed content to hum along with the songs on the radio.

With no one to talk to, Robert stared out the window at the passing landscape, fascinated by its diversity. Galveston resembled many of the beach communities near Savannah. But the scenery quickly changed to rolling hills as they skirted the edge of the Piney Woods and then, as they approached Dallas, to flat prairie.

Robert's mind wandered, and he became deaf to the chatter and humming of the other three occupants of the car. An hour into the drive, he began to reflect on the events of the last couple of days. *Am I getting in too deep? Should I have even had sex with her? God, I hope she's on birth control. She certainly acted like it. I must admit that sex with her* was *incredible. But is that enough?*

They passed a field with several longhorn cattle, which distracted him temporarily. "What do people do with those longhorns, Alan? Do they eat them?"

"Oh, hell no. University of Texas fans keep them as pets."

"Really?" Robert asked, his voice incredulous.

"Different strokes for different folks, my man." Alan resumed humming to "My Girl" by the Temptations.

It wasn't long before Robert's thoughts turned philosophical again. *Where does libido come from anyway? It's done nothing but get me into trouble—a bad marriage and a bad divorce.* He took a deep breath to clear his head. *But then, there* is *Ellie. Despite all that's gone wrong, there is still sweet, precious Ellie.*

Robert looked over at Megan. The sun shone on her high cheek bones as she smiled and jabbered like a schoolgirl. Her eyes sparkled. *She* is *captivating,* he thought. *But what the hell am I doing? And what about Diana? But then, I really don't know her either. But if I'm dating Megan, I certainly can't date Diana.*

Abruptly, his thoughts turned cynical. Why was Megan so vague in answering questions about her childhood and her family? Could she be using sex to draw me into something? I'm sure as hell not ready to get married again—to her or anybody else. Besides, a long-term relationship with her would be no better than marrying Janelle: we simply don't go together. Surely, she wouldn't be trying to get pregnant. No. She'd be risking a firm scandal. Maybe she's just a fatuous party girl. If she was really interested in me, she'd want to talk now, instead of continuing her banal dialogue with Michelle. Yeah. That's it. She's probably just a party girl.

I wonder what she thinks about the sex we had. She seemed to enjoy it and want more. Is that so wrong? Hell, the guys in Panama screwed anything and everything in a skirt.

He looked over at Megan again, chattering away. Damn, she's sexy.

# Chapter Twenty-One

AFTER THE WEEKEND trip to Galveston, one thing led to another, and a week and a half later Megan moved into Robert's duplex. He wasn't sure how it happened so fast or whether it was the right thing to do, but she kept showing up, staying late, and then saying she was too tired or too "tipsy" to go back to her apartment. When she finally asked him for a key, he simply handed it to her, no questions asked. She didn't seem to want a serious relationship with him, just his company.

At first he enjoyed the intimacy she brought to his life, which had been absent for so long. Sex with Megan was easy. She had an insatiable appetite and was always ready. But it wasn't long before things began to feel different. The coarse talk that at first seemed so sexy began to sound just coarse. Worse, Robert began to feel he was with a detached stranger.

Movies and the media have spread the lie that great sex is virtually all a man and woman ever need. But Robert knew that wasn't enough. And he knew that, once again, he found himself in a bad situation because he'd failed to think clearly about consequences. His relationship with Megan was a relationship by default. Nothing—other than sex—bound them together. Never once did she open up to him about her childhood, her family, her hobbies, her religious beliefs, her future plans, anything. She was always up on the latest law-firm gossip and whatever news there was about Mel Gibson or Madonna, but nothing about her seemed to have any depth.

One evening, while reading an article about AIDS in the *Dallas Morn-*

*ing News*, he asked her, "Do you think the Reagan administration is doing enough to combat the AIDS epidemic?"

Megan fidgeted in her seat on the couch. "Why'd you ask me that?"

"I was just reading this article written by a doctor. It says that the Reagan administration has no real policy, and when medical experts called for explicit AIDS education, administration officials gave a ridiculous answer. The article says they preferred to let Americans remain uninformed rather than address such a taboo subject. That's unbelievable, don't you think?"

"Well, isn't AIDS something only gay guys need to worry about? I mean… I feel sorry for them, but shouldn't they just use a condom?"

"It's not that simple, Megan. Some people get AIDS from transfusions. Drug addicts can get it from dirty needles. It's an epidemic, plain and simple. It just disproportionately affects gays."

"Well, they should be more careful."

"Megan, we weren't careful in Galveston."

She gasped and whirled around to face him, her fingers touching her parted lips. "Oh my God, you don't have it, do you?"

"No. Of course not. I don't have anything."

"Thank God. You scared me. Michelle said Alan told her you were the straightest of straight arrows, so I wasn't worried."

"I don't need to worry about you getting pregnant, do I?"

"What do you take me for, Robert?"

"I'm sorry, Megan. I didn't mean to offend you." He walked over and kissed her forehead. "But like Alan said—and as I'm sure you observed—I'm new to all this."

A relaxed, thank-goodness smile appeared. "You're just fine, Robert. You just scared me with all that talk about AIDS. Would you pour me another glass of wine? *Married with Children* is about to come on. I don't want to miss it. *Cheers* comes on after that. Wanna sit with me and watch them?"

"No. I think I'm going to take a shower and go to bed early."

"I'll join you if you want me to." She faced him with a look that Marilyn Monroe could not have matched.

"I need to get up early tomorrow, Megan. Just enjoy your shows." She looked at him with a mock pout.

As he walked through the kitchen, he saw her dinner dishes in the sink. His were already in the dishwasher. Entering the bathroom, he almost tripped over her clothes on the floor. Her makeup was strewn across the counter, leaving no room for him. He finished his shower and went to their bedroom where it seemed more of her clothes were on the floor than hanging in the closet, even though she always looked professional when she left for work. He began to wonder whether he even liked her. Again and again he asked himself: Why am I living with her?

Although they attempted to keep their relationship confidential from people at work other than Alan—fearing that firm management wouldn't like it—most of the associates and staff knew something was going on. Megan was frequently in Robert's office, and judging from the looks between them, they weren't talking about firm business. Robert knew Diana was no fool and, like many others in the firm, had probably concluded he and Megan were in a serious relationship. That worried him the most. Despite Alan's warnings, Robert began to believe that Diana was the woman he wanted to get to know better, and he feared that would never happen now.

Work prevented him from engaging in too much introspection, however. Davis Burnet left on a ski vacation two weeks before Christmas, so Donna, his assistant, frequently brought Robert faxes and other correspondence to see if they needed immediate attention. One fax in particular caught his eye. Davis had been copied on a letter to Mr. Russell from Scott & Cranston, a small investment bank in Dallas. The letter stated that Scott & Cranston had completed their valuation of Russell Field Services and determined that Mr. Russell could make a tender offer of $13.00 per share for the minority interest, which was publicly traded. Nothing in the fax indicated it was time-sensitive, so Robert told Donna it would keep until Davis returned and made a mental note to discuss it with him.

♾

"It looks like I'll be able to go home for Christmas after all," Robert announced as soon as he set down his briefcase in its usual spot, just inside the door of his duplex. It was Thursday evening, December 18. Megan was lounging on the sofa with a glass of wine, watching a *Happy Days* rerun.

"We're not going to spend it together?"

"I haven't been home since early October, Megan."

"O-Kay, I guess." She did her fake pout routine, which Robert had learned wasn't serious. "Do you want me to watch this place while you're gone?"

"Aren't you going to spend the holiday with your mom?"

"No. She and her husband are going to the Caymans for the holidays. That's what they do every year. And remember," she let out an excited giggle, "right after Christmas I'm going to Vail with Michelle. I can't wait."

"Oh, yeah. Well, have fun."

"Do you want to have some fun tonight?" Her eyes were bright above a devilish grin.

"I can't, Megan. I need to get caught up on work tonight, so I *can* go home for Christmas tomorrow. And, I'll be getting up early."

"Oh, okay," she said, again with her mock pout. Turning back to *Happy Days*, she continued, "Let me know if you need anything. One of these days you need to get a life."

No kidding, he thought as he picked up his briefcase and headed to the extra bedroom, which doubled as his office. He stopped in the kitchen to pour a generous amount of Maker's Mark in a glass of ice and grab a bag of pretzels. Megan didn't bother him, content as she was to enjoy her wine and the antics of Richie and The Fonz.

He worked late into the evening, woke up early, and left for work while Megan was still asleep. He wanted to finish his latest research memorandum before leaving for the airport. Despite being absent, Davis's presence could still be felt. Donna was anxious that no one would be in the office to ask about incoming faxes and phone calls, and Robert could almost hear Davis's voice telling him to return to Dallas on December 26. He wrapped things up by noon, stopped by Megan's office to tell her goodbye, and then headed to DFW Airport.

His flights to Atlanta and then Savannah were uneventful. He slept most of the trip, having gotten little rest in the days before his departure. Barry showed up at the Savannah airport with his sly grin and jokes about Robert's suit. And again, they went to Buddy's Bar & Grill, where again they attracted attention—one guy in scruffy jeans and a leather jacket and another who looked like he worked for President Reagan. But it was good to be home.

Robert smiled as they drove up to his mother's house. The holiday decorations were the same as they'd been for years: Santa in his sleigh in the yard, lights strung around the edge of the roof, and a wreath on the front door, illuminated by a spotlight in the yard. When Robert was growing up, his father always put up the decorations in just the same way, because he knew his sweetheart wanted them that way. Personally, he couldn't have cared less, although he never complained.

"You got some time to get together over the next few days?" Robert asked as he climbed out of Barry's truck.

"Day after tomorrow, I got nothin' but time, brother. Just give me a ring."

Barry pulled away quickly as if he had someplace to go, but Robert knew that wasn't the case. He had no steady girlfriend, his parents were dead, and his daughter had almost nothing to do with him; that is, unless she wanted some new clothes or money for spring break. But since it was almost Christmas, she might be in one of her good moods, in anticipation of a gift from her dad. Maybe that's where he's headed, Robert thought. I need to remember that I'm not the only one whose personal life is a mess.

Robert's mother heard them drive up and met him at the back door with outstretched arms. She was beaming.

"Don't you look handsome in your suit? I won't say anything about you stoppin' at Buddy's, even though I know y'all did."

"I never could fool you, Momma." Robert hugged her like a lost child who'd just been found.

"It's good to have you home, baby. I've missed you so much. But it seems," she said in a mock scolding way, "that I need to give you instructions on how to call long distance." She smiled, and for a moment Robert saw a hint of the old twinkle in her eye.

"Aw, Momma. I've told you how busy I am. The partner I work for is tough. He doesn't miss a thing. If I make a mistake, he always catches it. And then he wants something else."

"Well, you don't need to worry about that tonight. I'm gonna pop some corn, and we can watch *It's a Wonderful Life*. I rented the video down at Blockbuster."

"Whoa! Look at you, Momma. Gettin' all high tech. Rentin' videos and playing 'em on a VCR."

"Darlene and Frank bought me the thing for Mother's Day. I told them it was too much, but they insisted. And I must say I do love it. I watch all the old movies your daddy and I went to see when we were datin'. I don't like all these horror movies and Rambo stuff that are at the picture show now. Give me John Wayne and Gregory Peck."

Robert felt a twinge of guilt. He'd just sent flowers on Mother's Day. No card. Just flowers.

The familiar aromas of his mother's house brought back memories of growing up—home-cooked meals, canning garden vegetables, cleaning the kitchen to her exacting standards, Saturday nights watching old movies on TV and "popping corn." He carried his suitcase down the hall to his old bedroom and changed into blue jeans. The room was almost the same as it had been when he left for West Point so many years ago. The blue chenille bedspreads were still on his twin beds, and his high school diploma was still hanging in the same spot. The only thing missing was the framed copy of Kipling's poem, *If*, which his father had given him when he entered high school. He'd taken it with him when he returned to Panama after his father's funeral. It now hung in the bedroom he used as an office in Dallas—a reminder of the man who raised him, the man he looked up to, the man he aspired to be.

Robert and his mother settled in and watched the Jimmy Stewart classic, munching popcorn and drinking grape Kool-Aid. His mother wasn't a fan of Coca-Cola: she believed the old wives' tale that it could eat a hole in your stomach. They didn't discuss the elephant in the room—his visitation with Ellie—because his mother knew it was a sore subject. Tomorrow will be soon enough, she thought. Tonight my boy needs to relax.

The next morning Robert awoke to whiffs of his mother's cooking: coffee brewing and bacon frying. He dressed quickly, washed his face, and headed for the kitchen, entering just as his mother was taking biscuits out of the oven. He wolfed down his food and finished eating first—owing to a habit he'd developed in the Army of eating fast—and then sat back, sipping his coffee, as his mother slowly finished her meal. Ever the lady, her manners were impeccable, even here in her own kitchen with only her son present to observe. She was still pretty, despite the silver in her hair, but the old sparkle that had always brightened her face seldom appeared anymore. Losing the love of her life had taken its toll on her over the last few years. And then there was the topic she dreaded discussing with him but knew she must.

"What are your plans concerning Ellie? Have you talked to Janelle?" His mother looked down at her plate, not wanting to see his expression.

"I tried to, Momma, but I can't ever seem to get ahold of her."

"Would it be all right if I called her? You know either Darlene or I have to be present when—"

"Yes, Momma. I do *not* have to be reminded of that." His harsh response erased his mother's smile. "I'm sorry, Momma. I didn't mean to snap at you. It's just that this order is terrible. Nobody seems to understand that it is harming my relationship with my daughter, and when we tried to change it, Janelle's lawyer didn't even show up."

"I know, sweetheart." She looked down and silently stirred her coffee. "I don't know quite how to tell you this." She smoothed her apron and then stood up and walked to the coffee pot, her back to Robert. "Ellie acted a little strange the last time she was here."

"Strange? What do you mean, Momma?" The anxiety in his voice was palpable.

"Well, she wasn't her normal, happy self." His mother turned to face him. "She didn't smile much, and she was real quiet. And…"

"And what, Momma? Don't leave me hanging."

"Well, she wet the bed." His mother paused but, sensing her son's anxiety, continued. "Now, Bobby, you know I don't mind, but it's just not like her to wet the bed. She hasn't done that in a long, long time."

"Well, maybe she's upset about our divorce."

"I don't think that's it, sweetheart. That was a while ago."

"What is it, then?"

"Well, when Junior came to pick her up, it was like she was scared to go with him."

"Scared? How?"

"Well, I don't know. I mean… She just seemed sorta scared. And I don't like to say things like this, but he looks evil, like a bad guy in one of those gangster movies. His hair is all greasy, and he's got a sneaky lookin' smile. I think Ellie's scared of him, and it makes her nervous."

"Have you said anything about this to Janelle or the social worker?"

"I don't know what I'd say, sweetheart. I mean I told Janelle about her wettin' the bed, and she said she'd done it a few times at home, too. But I didn't say anything about Junior, because it's just a feelin', you know." His mother turned, picked up the telephone receiver, and began dialing a number.

Robert poured another cup of coffee while his mother talked to Janelle and arranged for Ellie's visit.

"She's gonna bring her over today after lunch," his mother said as she hung up the phone. "And, she said she can spend the night."

"That's great. What shall we do? Watch a movie? I wonder why Janelle is being nice for a change."

"Well, that's the good news, sweetheart. The bad news is that she and Junior are going to visit his family up in Clayton day after tomorrow and won't be back until after New Year's Day."

"And they're taking Ellie," he said. His mother nodded. "So, she's not gonna let me see my daughter on Christmas?" His voice shook as if he were about to cry.

"Now listen, Bobby. We just have to make the best of it. My Christmas tree is already up, so we'll just have Christmas tomorrow. We can pretend tonight is Christmas Eve. We'll just tell Ellie that Santa has to come early because she's going on a trip."

"Oh, crap! Santa. Momma, I need to run to town and get Ellie some presents."

"Well, the Walmart down on U.S. 25 has the best selection now. Do you want me to go with you?"

"No. If you wouldn't mind, just get ready for Ellie's visit. Maybe get a kid's movie at Blockbuster or something."

"You'll have the car, sweetheart."

"Oh, yeah, that's right. I'll get a movie. What should I get her?"

"If you go to Walmart, go find Marie Majors. She's a friend of mine, and she knows all about what little girls want."

"Thanks, Momma. I need to get going so I can get back. And Momma, we gotta talk more about this strange behavior business."

Robert slowly backed his mother's Chevrolet out of the driveway, but as soon as he was out of her sight, he hit the gas. He wanted to finish his errands quickly, so he could go by Lester's Auto Repair where Barry Daniel worked. With the help of Marie Majors at Walmart and a teenager at Blockbuster, he bought Ellie's Christmas presents and rented a movie— *A Charlie Brown Christmas*—in a slightly over an hour. As he pulled into Lester's Auto Repair, he could see Barry beneath a car that was up on a lift. He was covered with grease and crushing out a cigarette.

Barry saw him and grabbed a rag to wipe his hands. "Fancy meeting you here, Mr. Lawyer. I thought you was gonna call me."

"I was, but something's come up."

Barry could see Robert was distraught. "Let's go to the break room. I don't think anyone's in there." They sat down at a folding table, and Barry lit another cigarette. "What's going on, man?"

"Did you find out anything about this Junior guy?"

"Not really. I tried, but nobody knows anything about him, and I didn't want to seem nosy."

"Yeah. I know. Thanks, man. I really appreciate you trying." Robert took a deep breath and let it out. "Momma says Ellie acts like she's afraid of him. And she also said he looks evil. Now, you know my momma. It's like she's got some sorta sixth sense about these things. If she's uneasy about Junior, then I'm real uneasy. Didn't you say you heard he got into trouble up in Augusta?"

"Yeah, but I didn't know how to look into that. I don't remember exactly who I heard it from."

"Well, I got a law-school classmate in Augusta named Billy Pardue. His family's been there forever. I suspect he'll know or could find out. Would you mind calling him, tell him I asked you to, and see what he knows or can find out?"

"I'm happy to, Bobby. But why don't you just call him yourself?"

"I'm afraid if something blows up, they'll ask me about whether I was checking on Junior." Robert rubbed his hand across his mouth. "I know this sounds stupid, Barry, but I've been screwed so much in this deal that I've got to be extra careful."

"Yeah. I get it. Give me his phone number, and I'll call him."

Robert pulled out his pocket address book and wrote Pardue's name and phone number on a napkin.

"Sorry to rush, man, but I gotta get back to Momma's. Ellie's coming over after lunch."

"Okay. Listen to me: enjoy her while she's young. When they get to be teenagers, they turn into little shits." Barry smiled and took a long draw on his cigarette before crushing it out in an ashtray overflowing with butts. "I gotta get back to work anyway. Old Man Lester hasn't given me my Christmas bonus yet. I don't want him to think I'm goofing off."

"Okay. Well, I'll call you before Christmas. Maybe you can come over for Christmas dinner. Janelle's taking Ellie up to Clayton—which, by the way, is apparently where Junior is from; you can tell Billy that—so anyway, Ellie won't be there. It'll just be me and Momma and Darlene and Frank." Barry could hear the disgust in Robert's voice.

"Well, enjoy her while you got her."

"Thanks, man."

Quickly making his way back to his mother's house, Robert was pleased to learn Ellie had not yet arrived. As he unloaded his packages, he thought about Mrs. Majors, the sweet Walmart clerk who'd helped him. His mother was right: she seemed to know exactly what little girls want. Robert knew Ellie already had a Cabbage Patch Doll but decided to get her another one anyway. Mrs. Majors told him a little girl couldn't have too many dolls and recommended he also buy a Strawberry Shortcake Doll. Robert had no clue how popular they were. Knowing how Ellie liked to pretend she was a princess, he had bought her a Crystal Castle Playset and, to balance the scales on the serious side, a Fisher-Price Medical Kit and some books, crayons, and coloring books. After hiding the gifts in the top of the hall closet—the same spot where his mother used to hide his and Darlene's Christmas presents—he went into the living room and plopped down onto the couch, exhausted from his hectic morning and anxious over the troubling news his mother had dropped on him at breakfast. He had just settled in when the doorbell rang.

# CHAPTER TWENTY-TWO

WHEN ROBERT OPENED the door, he was overwhelmed by a flood of memories. He hadn't seen Janelle up close since their divorce. Although she was still attractive, any hint of sophistication was gone. Wearing faded jeans, an Atlanta Falcons sweatshirt, and no makeup, she had all the hallmarks of just another country girl shopping at Walmart.

He felt two diminutive arms wrap around his waist and looked down onto the face of his precious Ellie, smiling up at him.

"Merry Christmas, Daddy."

"Merry Christmas to you, too, baby."

"We need to get goin', Bobby," Janelle said. "We gotta get the car worked on today. We're headed to Clayton for Christmas."

It was only at then that Robert noticed Junior, standing behind Janelle on the sidewalk. Momma is right, he thought. He is evil-looking. Junior's hands were in the pockets of his jeans, which looked as if they should've been thrown away years ago. Long, greasy hair oozed out from underneath a dirty John Deere ball cap, above an uneven, scruffy beard. And he squinted so much behind a cloud of cigarette smoke that Robert could barely see his eyes.

"Well, as you can see, she misses you," Janelle continued.

"I miss her, too." Robert bit his tongue to avoid telling her how angry he was that she was taking his daughter away for Christmas. He tried not to look annoyed. "Thanks for bringing her over, Janelle."

"She likes comin' here. Your momma's been real good about keepin' her when I need a babysitter. You know Daddy couldn't handle that." A hint of a smile began to appear on her face but faded before it took hold. "Well, like I said, we need to get goin'."

"Don't you want to say 'hi' to Momma?"

"Sure, but we gotta go pretty quick."

Robert looked down at Junior, who was eyeing the ground while crushing out his cigarette. Turning in the direction of the kitchen, he called out, "Momma, Ellie and Janelle are here."

Robert's mother appeared, drying her hands on her apron. She bent down, hugged Ellie, and kissed her on the cheek. "There's my little darlin'. Are you ready for Santa Claus to come?" Wide-eyed, Ellie just grinned and bobbed her head so eagerly one would have thought St. Nick had just landed onto the roof.

"We just wanted to say 'hi' and Merry Christmas, Ruth," Janelle said, without really making eye contact.

Hearing Janelle call his mother by her first name hit Robert hard—another reminder that a chapter of his life was over. Janelle had always called her "Mom," probably because her own mother had died when she was young. Now, it's "Ruth."

Janelle continued, "We gotta get the car worked on today. Junior doesn't have the tools he needs, and his back's been acting up, so we're taking it to Lester's. It won't make it to Clayton if we don't get it fixed."

"Well, Merry Christmas to both of you," Ruth said, her smile so sincere and warm it melted the tension. "We're gonna have some Christmas fun here, too." Looking down at Ellie, she whispered, "I heard that Santa Claus is gonna come here *tonight* because you won't be at your house for Christmas." Ruth and Janelle exchanged smiles, but Ellie gave her mother a puzzled look.

"You said he was gonna come to Junior's momma's house," Ellie said, wrinkling her nose.

"He is, sweetheart. But since you live in Pemberton, he's gonna stop here at Nana's house, too."

Ellie let out an excited squeal and ran into the living room.

"We'll pick her up tomorrow afternoon, if that's okay."

"Sure," Ruth said. "Around five o'clock?"

Janelle didn't say anything. She just pursed her lips, nodded, and turned to walk to Junior's car, which growled as he pumped the accelerator, causing blue smoke to billow out the tailpipe.

Robert watched them drive away and then returned to the living room, where he found Ellie in front of the TV watching *She-Ra: Princess of Power*.

"What would you like to do, sweetheart?"

Ellie shrugged her shoulders and pursed her lips just as Janelle had done—a reminder that he would be forever linked to the woman who just left.

"You wanna play *Candy Land*, baby?"

"She's too old for that, Bobby," his mother said. "Ellie, why don't you show your daddy how we play Crazy Eights?"

Ellie jumped up and ran down the hall toward the back of the house, returning with a tattered box of Bicycle Playing Cards and an innocent smile that lit up her face. For the next hour or so the three of them sat around the kitchen table playing a card game that Robert had learned—probably with the same deck—more than twenty-five years before. Every few minutes, Ruth would jump up to tend to something on the stove or in the oven and, when it was time to eat, set out a meal that was almost as elaborate as the Christmas dinners she'd prepared when Robert was growing up. When they finished, they went into the living room—shockingly leaving dirty dishes behind—and watched *A Charlie Brown Christmas*. For a few short minutes Robert was overcome with a feeling that something magical and sacred was temporarily restored from a distant memory. And it was good.

After much persuading, including threats that Santa might not come, Robert tucked Ellie into bed in his mother's room and read her *The Night Before Christmas*. As he kissed her goodnight, she gazed up at him with her bright blue eyes full of love and broke his heart: "When are you comin' home, Daddy?"

He struggled to keep his composure. "I live in Texas now, sweetheart."

"Why can't you live here?"

"That's where my job is, but I'm gonna try to get back to visit more. Now, you get to sleep. Santa won't leave presents if you're still awake."

Ruth was waiting for him in the kitchen. "You wanna have a little Christmas cheer?" She held up a glass of eggnog, which he knew was only mildly spiked with bourbon.

"Sure, Momma."

"What's wrong, baby?"

Robert stared at his mother for a long time, unable to speak. He could feel tears welling up. "Ellie asked me when I was comin' home."

"I know this has been hard on you, Bobby." She paused for almost a minute, and then, as if she were a child asking for permission, she continued, her voice soft and tender in a way only mothers can express. "Is there any chance you could get a job in Savannah or something?"

"We've been through this before, Momma. I'm never going to have a normal relationship with Ellie because of that damn court order. I'm sorry Momma. I didn't mean to say that. It just makes me so angry. People whispering about us when we go downtown. Everything having to be so arranged. I might as well live in Dallas. And you remember what I told you? I'm with the best firm in Texas, and I'm working for the most important partner in the firm. I couldn't replace that in Savannah or even Atlanta."

"Well, I know I don't understand all that lawyer stuff, sweetheart. You just gotta do what you think's right. Hey, I bet Ellie's asleep by now. Let's put her presents under the tree."

His mother's enthusiasm was contagious and always capable of changing the mood. They tiptoed down the hall, Robert stopping to ensure Ellie was asleep, and then gathered up her presents and arranged them under and around the Christmas tree, just as Ruth had done for so many years. It was another reminder of his connection with this woman and this place. His mother added a few presents of her own, having better prepared for Ellie's Christmas than he had. After they'd settled onto the couch and sipped their eggnog for a few minutes, Robert knew he needed to address the sensitive topic his mother had raised at breakfast.

"Momma, thank you for doing all this—the dinner and all."

"It was my pleasure, sweetheart. That little girl of yours is so precious. I'd do anything for her."

"Would you talk to the social worker?"

All the holiday sparkle left his mother's face. "I told you, Bobby, I don't know what I'd say other than Junior makes me uneasy in a way I can't explain. If I were Ellie, I wouldn't want to go with him either."

"But what if he's hurting her, Momma? Like you said, he makes you uneasy, like he's evil or something."

"Oh, I don't think because of that we can assume he's hurtin' her, Bobby. If we did, they'd be investigatin' half the daddies in town. Most of 'em come to town lookin' like bums—old, worn-out clothes, dirty ball caps, and even dirtier hair. Even when we were poor as church mice, your daddy always dressed nice." She sipped her eggnog.

"I know what you mean, Momma. Junior would fit right in with them. But like you said, there's somethin' else about him that's just not right."

"Don't borrow trouble, sweetheart. I'll keep an eye on things and look for any sign that there's a problem."

"I know you will. I just think we need to have a professional talk to Ellie."

His mother's face fell. "I may just be an ordinary housewife, Bobby, but I'm also a mother who raised two children."

"I'm sorry, Momma. I didn't mean to offend you. There's nothing ordinary about you. Everyone knows you have that sixth sense. If you're bothered by Junior, then I'm concerned. That's all."

"Well, I'm afraid if we go contactin' the social workers it would just make things worse. I've got a pretty good relationship with Janelle, and I get to keep Ellie several times a week."

"Really? Well, it looks to me like you're just a free babysitter for her."

"Are you kiddin'? I love keepin' that little girl of yours. She's so smart and sweet. You need to have her read to you. We have the best time." Ruth paused and looked at her son. She knew he was still worried. "Sweetheart, I'll keep watchin' for anything suspicious. Now, you said I had a sixth sense. Let me use it." She smiled and patted his leg. "We need some more eggnog." She stood up and headed to the kitchen. Robert was right behind her, hoping to spike his glass a bit more than his mother would. But before he could, he watched as she tilted the Old Crow bourbon bottle until both glasses were over half full. She topped them off with eggnog and handed Robert his. His grin made her eyes sparkle.

"Here's to you, Momma." She took a tiny sip and winced, which made him snicker. "Say, Momma, do you care if Barry Daniel comes over for Christmas dinner? He doesn't have any family anymore, and his daughter really doesn't have much to do with him."

"Of course. We'd love to have him. It's just gonna be you and me and Darlene and Frank."

"I know. But I think he needs a little Christmas cheer, too. Thanks, Momma."

≼

The next morning Robert awoke to his daughter sitting on his chest.

"Get up, Daddy. Nana said I can't go see what Santa brought me until you get up. So, get up."

"Okay, sweetie. Give me a minute to wake up. Go wait with Nana."

Robert dressed and went down the hall to get Ellie and his mother. For the first time he noticed that his mother had repainted the master bedroom and rearranged the furniture, probably an effort to erase the mental images of when his father died in that room. At first he thought he might have opened the wrong door, until he saw the two of them wiggling and giggling beneath a blanket—the woman who'd shaped the man he'd become and was always his biggest cheerleader and the precious child who'd captured his heart the moment he first saw her.

"Let's go see if Santa came, shall we?"

Ellie bolted out of the bed and dashed down the hall. Robert and his mother were right behind, laughing as Ellie squealed with delight when she saw the presents beneath the tree. She hugged her Cabbage Patch doll and said, "Now, Molly will have someone to talk to."

"Who's Molly, sweetheart?" Robert asked.

"My other Cabbage Patch baby," she said, a bit frustrated that he didn't know who Molly was.

For the rest of the day, Robert and his mother played with Ellie and her new toys, stopping only briefly for lunch. She especially liked her Fisher-Price Medical Kit and insisted on operating on Robert and his mother, as well as her new Cabbage Patch doll.

When the doorbell rang at five o'clock, Robert could feel that all-too-familiar sinking feeling overtaking him, knowing that the precious few hours he'd spent with Ellie were over. Janelle came to the door, while Junior stayed in the car smoking a cigarette. Robert almost said something to Janelle about exposing Ellie to secondhand smoke but decided not to. His mother was right about not stirring things up. He forced a smile and held back tears as he hugged Ellie and told her goodbye. But he couldn't stop the sadness welling up in him as he watched her walk with Janelle to Junior's junk heap of a car. Not wanting his mother to see him in such a state, he rushed to the bathroom and washed his face.

❧

Robert slept late on Christmas day, eventually awakening to the comforting sounds of his mother in her kitchen. As he approached, he could hear her singing "Joy to the World."

"You have such a pretty voice, Momma."

Startled, she turned around and smiled. Her cheeks flushed.

"I didn't mean to wake you up, Bobby."

"You didn't. I needed to get up. And I'm hungry."

"Well, it will be Cheerios today, mister. I've got to get this dinner underway. There's fresh coffee in the percolator, though."

Robert sat down at the table and flipped through the local paper, which didn't offer much: an unenlightening report on the last meeting of the county commission and several obituaries of people he didn't know. In a way it was refreshing—evidence of how things in Pemberton proceeded at a slower pace. He sipped his coffee and worked the crossword puzzle, while his mother buzzed around the kitchen humming Christmas carols. Shortly before noon, Darlene and Frank arrived, smiling and full of Christmas spirit. Darlene donned an apron to help their mother in the kitchen, while Robert and Frank went into the living room and channel surfed for something to watch. Barry showed up around 12:30 p.m. with a bottle of Blue Nun, which Ruth went out of her way to thank him for. She always made a big fuss over such things—her way of trying to make people feel welcome in her home.

When they sat down to dinner, it was almost like old times. As usual, his mother's cooking made his mouth water the instant the aromas reached his nose. The only thing missing was the man who used to sit at the head of the table. The five of them drank the bottle of wine Barry had brought, as well as another. After a dessert of pecan pie, the ladies shooed the men into the living room and said they would clean the kitchen. Even though Frank hadn't met Barry before, he made him feel at home, asking about car repairs and when he should rotate his tires. Barry patiently offered his advice. When the ladies joined them later, Barry stayed only a few minutes before thanking Ruth and saying he needed to get going. Robert walked him to his truck.

"Thanks for coming, man."

"No. Thank you. Your momma's still the best cook in the county. I'd forgotten how good her dinners were. But I need to get goin'. I might be able to see Misty today." Barry climbed into his truck and rolled down the window.

"She's not with her momma?" Robert asked.

"Yeah, she is. But I got her a little present and told her I'd bring it by. She actually sounded like she was happy to be seein' me."

Robert didn't say what was on his mind. He just smiled and said, "That's great, man."

"Hey. I called your friend, Billy Pardue. He didn't know anything about Junior but said he'd ask around. I'm supposed to call him back on Friday."

"Thanks."

"He sure likes you." Barry started his truck and pumped the accelerator. "He said he wouldn't have made it through law school if he hadn't studied with you. I always knew you was smart, Egghead. All right. Well, let me get goin'."

"Thanks, man. And thanks again for comin'."

# CHAPTER TWENTY-THREE

HIS MOTHER WAS upset that he had scheduled to fly back to Dallas on Monday, but Robert knew Davis would be back. He'd spent only a few days in Pemberton, and yet it felt as if he'd been there a long time. His visit with Ellie had been painfully short, of course, but the rest of it—visiting with Barry, his mother, and Darlene and Frank—just seemed like a continuation of what had always been.

All the lights were off in his duplex when he drove up, which was strange. Normally, Robert could see the glow of the television through the front windows, but then he remembered that Megan was in Vail with Michelle. So, he was surprised when he flipped on the lights, to see one of Megan's pink envelopes on the table in the kitchen.

*Hi Robert,*

*As you will see when you look in the closet, I've moved out. I've accepted a job offer from an awesome firm in New York. I was going to tell you about it, but I didn't think I was going to get it. Anyway, I have always wanted to live in New York, and I'm soooo psyched! I hope you're not mad at me. I want to still be friends, but this job is awesome! I just had to take it. Michelle & I had a terrible time in Vail, so we came back early. It totally sucked. The guys were sooo lame! Not like you! I'll call you when I'm coming back to Dallas.*

*Love,*
*Megan*

There were no dainty hearts around the border this time. Clearly, Megan had moved on, despite the way she signed the note, and Robert was unsure of how he felt. He'd had serious doubts about their relationship but had no idea what to do about it. And now she was gone. She'd made it easy—just like sex with her. He knew he should be pleased, but somehow he felt rejected.

Since New Year's Eve was on Wednesday, most of the associates and many of the partners were still on vacation. But not Davis Burnet. Robert walked by his office to see if he was in and saw him poring over pre-bills, the telltale being the green paper. Stacks of green paper covered his desk. Those pre-bills needed to be turned into invoices before the year was out. Davis's bonus depended on it. Not wanting to get pulled into that vortex, Robert decided to keep walking and wait to be called.

As he set his briefcase onto his desk, he saw the voicemail message light flashing on his phone. "Hey, Bobby. I tried you at home but got no answer. I hope you're on the way to your office. I heard back from Billy Pardue. Call me right away. It ain't good." Robert frantically looked for the phone number of Lester's Auto. In his haste he used the wrong billing codes for a long distance call and had to start over twice. Finally, the phone rang.

"Lester's Auto."

"Could I speak to Barry Daniel, please? It's urgent."

"He's working on a car right now. I'm not supposed to bother him."

"Would you tell him Bobby Clark is on the phone?"

"Oh, hey, Bobby. This is Shirley. I work the front desk now. I didn't recognize your voice. I was so sorry to hear about you and Janelle."

"Yeah. Thanks. I'm sorry, Shirley, but this is real important. Would you please get Barry on the phone?"

"Oh. Yeah. Well, sure."

"Hey, man, I got some bad news." Barry's voice sounded uncharacteristically tense.

"What? What'd you find out?"

"Your buddy called me back. Hang on a sec, Bobby. Shirley, could you give me some privacy. It's important, sweetie. Yeah. I'll tell him you said hello. Sorry, Bobby. So, it seems that Junior was investigated for child abuse."

"Goddammit!"

"Yeah, I know."

"Did he get convicted?"

"No. That's the thing. He didn't even get arrested. Billy said Junior's daddy knew some folks in the sheriff's office and got the whole thing dropped. One of the social workers up there went to high school with Billy. She made him promise not to use her name but said she knew Junior was guilty. Apparently, he diddled his girlfriend's little girl."

"Fucking motherfucker! I need to call Larry."

"What's he gonna do, Bobby? I mean, I know he's a good lawyer and all, and he's a friend of your family, but we got nothing. That social worker ain't gonna tell us anything. Billy wouldn't even give me her name."

"Fuck! Well, I need to call Larry anyway. Is there anything else?"

"No. I think they're still in Clayton. I haven't seen them around town. I worked on that piece of shit car of Junior's and told him to bring it back, because I had to order some parts. I mean, it runs and it's safe, but it'll never pass the state inspection."

"Yeah. I don't give a shit about that."

"All I'm saying, Bobby, is that I think they're still in Clayton, because Junior hasn't come back with his car."

"Oh, yeah. Sorry, Barry. I'm not thinking straight. Thanks, man. I can't thank you enough. I'm gonna call Larry. I'll let you know if he has any ideas."

❦

"Gray, Reed and Donaldson. How may I help you?"

"I need to speak to Larry, please. This is Bobby Clark."

"Mr. Gray is not in the office, Bobby. Can someone else help you?"

"No. I'm afraid not. Would you please have him call me in Dallas as soon as he can? It's urgent."

As the day dragged on, Robert stared at his phone, waiting for it to ring. Finally, around 1:30 p.m. it did. He snapped up the receiver. "Larry?"

"Larry? No. This is Davis. Would you come to my office please?"

"Uh. Yes, sir. Right away."

Robert left instructions with his secretary, Carolyn, to track him down if a lawyer named Larry Gray called and then headed to Davis's office with a slug of dread in the bottom of his stomach.

"Thank you for watching over things while I was away, Robert. Donna tells me you were a tremendous help."

"Thanks."

"How was your visit to Georgia?"

"It was, uh, it was good. I was able to visit my mom and my daughter."

Robert paused, wondering whether he should tell Davis about the sickening news he'd just received. Based on past experience, he didn't think Davis gave a damn about the personal problems of Robert or anyone else, so he changed the subject.

"Do you think the Russell transaction is going to heat up?" he asked.

"Not for a while. I haven't even finished reviewing the correspondence that came in while I was away. Everyone is still in a holiday mood, so I suspect nothing will happen until after the New Year's celebrations are over. Are any of your teams in a bowl game?"

"Uh, yes. Georgia was in the Hall of Fame Bowl. They lost to Boston College, though. And, of course, Army's not in any of them."

"Baylor is playing Colorado in the Bluebonnet Bowl," Davis said. "And Texas A&M is in a bowl, but Texas didn't make it to post season. I can't believe it. Texas was five and six this year. They lost to A&M *and* to Baylor. The Texas Exes are going to have Coach Akers's head if he doesn't get that program turned around." Davis stopped. "You seem agitated, Robert. What's going on?"

"Oh, nothing, Davis. I was just expecting a phone call from home. Something my mom wants me to take care of."

"Well, don't let me interfere with that. In fact, I was going to tell you that if you want to take the rest of the week off, go ahead. I assume you have your billable hours for the year."

"I believe so," Robert replied.

"I *would* like to meet with you on Friday, however."

Robert struggled to focus. If I have to be in the office Friday, how am I going to deal with this situation with Junior? Should I just come clean with Davis? No. He already thinks I have too many personal problems.

"You know what?" Davis was talking again. "I forgot. My wife's cousin is being sworn in as a County Judge on Friday." Davis chuckled. "That's what we Texans call the head of our county commissions."

"That's what I've heard," Robert said, his stomach tightening into knots as he agonized over what to do or say next.

But Davis continued, "So, let's just plan to meet on Monday the fifth. I'll spend some time with the correspondence and the other documents in the file, and I recommend you go over any materials you have, so we can have a productive planning session on Monday."

Thank God!

Robert consciously tried to keep his composure. "Will do, Davis," he said calmly, as he stood to leave. But once outside, he rushed back to his office. He wasn't going to trust Carolyn with these flight arrangements. In fact, he wasn't even going to tell her or anyone else that he was making a quick trip back to Georgia.

As soon as he walked into his office, he called Larry. "I hate to bother you again, but is Larry there?"

"He just walked in, Bobby. Let me tell him you're on the line."

"What's going on, Bobby?" Larry had a smooth Southern drawl that spoke with authority without sounding pompous or condescending.

"I just found out that Junior—the guy Janelle's been living with—"

"She's living with him?"

"Well, dating, I guess. I don't know, Larry, I think they're living together. Anyway, I found out he was investigated for child abuse in Augusta."

"Really? Where'd you find that out?"

"A law school friend did some checking for me. But his source is confidential, and Junior didn't get convicted or even charged."

"Well, I'm not sure what we can do with that information. If we go to court, we'll need more than that, especially since he wasn't even charged."

"Larry, we've got to do something. Couldn't we get the court to order a social worker to investigate? Maybe have one of those interviews with Ellie where they use the doll and all."

"I don't know, Bobby. Judge Harrington hasn't exactly been our friend. And I don't think the Division of Family and Children Services can do that kind of interview unless Janelle consents or the court orders it."

"Can we at least try to get an order? Maybe put Junior on the stand as a hostile witness and confront him with what we know."

"I don't think that's a good idea, Bobby. There are far too many ways that could backfire on us." Larry paused, sensing Robert's distress. "Let me give it some thought and see if I can come up with something."

"Well, I'm coming home regardless. But I have to be back in Dallas on January fifth. Do you think we could get into court on an emergency basis on Friday?"

"I doubt it, Bobby. We don't have anything that would justify asking for it." Another pause. "Let me talk to the clerk. I'm on pretty good terms with him. I'll call you back."

Robert made flight arrangements to fly to Savannah that evening and then headed home to pack. He was almost finished when the phone in his duplex rang.

"Are you mad at me?"

"No, Megan, I'm not mad. I'm just dealing with something right now."

"You sound mad. I can tell."

"No, Megan, I'm not mad. I wish you all the best. I want to hear all about your new job, but I can't talk right now. I gotta go. Sorry."

No sooner had he hung up the phone than it rang again.

"I don't mean to be short, Megan, but—"

"This is Larry Gray, Bobby."

"Oh. I'm sorry, Larry. I thought someone was calling me from work."

"I see. Well, we got lucky. The clerk can get us in on Friday morning, assuming you can be back here by then."

"I've already made my flight arrangements. I'll be in Pemberton late tonight."

"Can you tell me any more about this business in Augusta?" Larry asked.

"I told you everything I know, Larry. Can we just say we don't know what the living arrangements are, so we want DFACS to look into it?" As did everyone in Georgia who'd had an encounter with DFACS, Robert pronounced the acronym as if it were spelled dee-fax.

"DFACS?" Larry asked.

"Isn't that what folks call the Division of Family and Children Services?" Robert asked.

"Oh, yeah. I guess that's right. What did you say about DFACS?"

"Say that we want DFACS to investigate the living arrangements."

"Actually, Bobby, that's not a bad idea. If we can get a social worker in the home, we might be able to find out what we need. One of the ladies in my Sunday school class is the head of the office here in Pemberton."

"Well, that's some good news. I'm flying out this evening. I can see you tomorrow morning, if that's okay."

"I'll clear my calendar. See you at eight o'clock."

# CHAPTER TWENTY-FOUR

"I'LL SAY ONE thing for you: you don't mess around."

Robert climbed into Barry's truck, which was double-parked outside of baggage claim at the Savannah Airport. Despite the late hour, there he was. No questions asked.

"You wanna go to your momma's right away?"

"No. I didn't tell her I was coming. I didn't want to get into all of this with her yet. Can I stay at your place?"

"Sure. But it ain't as nice as your momma's. And I don't cook." Barry smiled, but could see his friend was in no mood for lighthearted banter. He paused until Robert looked at him. "I'll do anything I can to help you, Bobby."

"I know you will."

"But your momma's gonna be pissed off if you don't tell her you're home. Don't you go gettin' me in trouble with her."

"I'll surprise her tomorrow afternoon. I'm meeting with Larry in the morning. We have a hearing on Friday."

"Wow! That's fast. My divorce took over a year."

"Yeah. But I don't know if it will do us any good. The judge is an asshole."

"Yeah, I heard that about him. Some stuffed shirt from Atlanta. Nobody likes him. He don't go to church or the country club. Far as I know, he goes home every night and drinks."

"How do you know that?"

"One of my customers is a clerk at Crossroad Package Store. She says Harrington is in there almost every week. And he drinks high-dollar scotch."

"Well, it doesn't help his disposition."

"Speaking of liquor, Old Man Lester gave me some of your fancy bourbon for Christmas. Let's open that bad boy when we get home."

"Sounds like a plan," Robert said. "Did you get your bonus?"

"Not yet. Lester says he's got to do some taxes or something first."

Barry was right about his trailer. It smelled like an ashtray; dirty dishes were piled in the sink; and Robert gagged when he went to the bathroom—mildew ringed the toilet bowl and the bathtub, and a foul odor emanated from the sink drain. It was as bad as some of the poorest places he'd seen in Panama. When Robert walked back into the living room, Barry was pouring two tall glasses of Maker's Mark. He threw the bottle cap across the room and set the open bottle onto the coffee table.

"Let me tell you about my visit with Misty," he began.

Barry was not just a good friend; he was the brother Robert never had. Although his attempt to get Robert's mind off Junior was pretty transparent, the process was aided by several drinks, consumed in quick succession. But drinking on an empty stomach is never a good idea. It is worse when a person is stressed, and he drinks too much because the bourbon seems to calm his nerves and create a warm glow of contentment. Unfortunately, it also removes filters on what he says and erodes his reason, which can cause his baser instincts to come forth. On that evening—in Barry's trailer—it did both.

After they'd started their fifth tall drink, Barry shifted the conversation back to the purpose of Robert's return to Pemberton.

"So, tell me about this hearing." He took a long draw on the cigarette he'd just lit.

"I really don't know, Barry. Larry has some ideas. Says he knows the lady who's the head of DFACS in Pemberton."

"I heard she's a bitch. A couple of the guys at work said DFACS is always on their ass about child support and not drinking when their kids are around. Shit like that."

"Well that might work to our advantage. Maybe she'll get on Junior's ass."

"You know, Bobby, there's nothing worse than a son of a bitch that would hurt a little girl."

"I hear you."

"When my daddy was a boy"—Barry's speech was slurred; the Maker's was having an effect—"folks knew what to do. The men would either kick a man's ass or run him out of town." Barry took another draw, causing the end of his cigarette to glow bright orange. "You know the Klan wasn't all bad."

"Now you're talking crazy, Barry. The Klan was a bunch of cowards in bedsheets, terrorizing poor black folks to make themselves feel important. I'm talkin' about a goddamn child molester."

"You're right. You're right." Barry paused as a new thought occurred to him. "You know what the Godfather would do, don't you?"

"The Godfather?"

"Yeah, you know, the movie. Remember when that undertaker told the Godfather he wanted justice for those punks that beat up his daughter, and the Godfather had their asses kicked. That's what fucking Junior needs. Some Godfather justice."

Barry wasn't the only one getting drunk. The bourbon was clouding Robert's judgment as well. "And how," he asked, "could we arrange for Junior to get some Godfather justice?"

"I'll show you." Barry opened the drawer of the end table next to him and pulled out a .45 caliber 1911 Springfield pistol."

"Where'd you get that?" Robert asked, unfazed by the presence of a weapon he had seen and used many times.

"The Army's gettin' rid of 'em. I bought this one off of a guy over by Fort Stewart. The women in the Army can't handle a weapon like this, so they're changin' to a pussy nine millimeter Beretta."

"No shit." Robert took the pistol from him and cleared it. "So, is it registered to you?"

"Nah. I don't even know the guy I bought it off of. Just paid him cash." Barry took a drink and then another draw on his cigarette. "You know, it's like that gun that Michael Corleone shoots the cop and the Turk with. It's droppable. You could drop it, just like Fat Clemenza said in the movie."

"Man, we are fucked up. We can't be talking about shooting somebody, even if he is an asshole."

"Aw, I wouldn't kill him. I'd just blow out his knees so every time he took a step he'd think about not being a fucking child molester."

"Barry, we need to stop. Being drunk and talking like this is stupid."

"You're right. Let me put on some Cash. That's one tough motherfucker."

Barry stumbled to his portable stereo and scratched the album with the tone arm as he attempted to place it into position. The song began with Johnny Cash's trademark pulsing beat, reminiscent of a train.

"My daddy always liked Johnny Cash," Robert said. "But I ain't interested in shooting a man in Reno—or anywhere else—just to watch him die."

"You remember that song? 'Folsom Prison Blues'?"

Barry slumped back into his chair. Fading fast, he attempted to sing along but mostly mumbled. His chin drooped onto his chest, and he started to snore. Robert reached over and crushed out Barry's cigarette and then picked up their glasses and added them to the pile in the sink. On his way to the bedroom in the back of the trailer, he picked up the pistol and its loaded magazine and slipped them into the pocket of his overcoat.

# CHAPTER TWENTY-FIVE

BARRY WAS SITTING at his kitchen table smoking a cigarette and drinking a cup of coffee when Robert emerged from the back of the trailer the next morning. "How'd you sleep?" he asked.

"Fine," Robert replied. "Did you make it to bed or did you sleep on the couch?"

"The couch. It seems like I wind up sleeping there more than in the bed. Listen, I can drop you off at Mr. Gray's but I need to get going. Are you ready?"

"Yeah. Just let me grab my jacket and coat."

They didn't talk much on the way to Larry Gray's law office, owing to the residual effects of the prior evening's activities, which had also left Barry's Christmas present empty on the coffee table.

"Do you want to stop at McDonald's for a sausage biscuit?" Barry asked.

Robert smiled. His friend always pronounced the name of the restaurant the same way he sang the name of the farmer in the children's song. E-I-E-I-O.

"I don't think my stomach could handle it, Barry. I'm sure they'll have coffee at Larry's."

"If y'all are finished when I take my lunch break," Barry said, "I can take you to your momma's, but don't you get me in trouble with her by telling her about last night."

"I won't. And I'll buy us some lunch at Swanson's Inn."

"Now that's high class, buddy. But I'll be all dirty from work. Let's just go to McDonald's and get us a couple of Big Macs." Barry paused a moment and then smiled while looking straight ahead. "You can still buy, though."

~

Larry got down to business as soon Robert sat down.

"After you and I talked, Bobby, I spoke with Frances Hopkins about this matter. She's the woman I told you about—the one in my Sunday school class who is the head of the Division of Family and Children Services here in Pemberton. She checked with her colleagues in Augusta and found out, as you did, that Junior—whose full name Rodney K. White, Jr.—was *investigated* by their Augusta office, although he was neither charged nor arrested."

"Did they say why?"

"No. And there's not much in the case file, other than a statement from Mr. White's former girlfriend, which sets forth the sordid details of her allegations against him, and a statement from him, denying the allegations. Nevertheless, Frances thinks it would be appropriate to interview your daughter and Janelle and Mr. White."

"He'll just deny doing anything wrong, Larry. I thought we were on the court's calendar for Friday?"

"We are, Bobby, but—"

"Well, can't we get the court to order Janelle to permit Ellie to undergo one of those forensic interviews, you know, with an anatomically correct doll?"

"DFACS usually only seeks a court order when they're wanting to retain custody. I'm not sure we need an order for a forensic interview."

"Janelle will never agree to it voluntarily, Larry." Robert was almost pleading.

"Let me talk with Frances again and see what she thinks. We haven't sent a notice to Janelle or Junior, so neither of them would be present. We'd be asking the court to give us a ruling without notice to Janelle or Junior, which I know Judge Harrington doesn't like to do. As far as I know, he's never granted *ex parte* relief."

Larry paused as he studied his young client's face. He recalled going to the hospital when Robert was born. He'd watched him grow up and saw how proud his parents were when he graduated from West Point and then law school. He knew how painful it had been for Robert when his father died a few years ago. And, of course, there was his divorce and the hurtful visitation order concerning Ellie.

"Listen to me, Bobby, I understand your feelings, and I'll do everything I can to help you." Robert said nothing, and Larry continued, "I'm aware that your mother keeps Ellie from time to time. Has she noticed anything?"

Robert's eyes were watery and his nose runny. "Nothing definite, Larry, although she did say that Ellie sometimes seems to be afraid to go with Junior, and she's wet the bed a few times lately, which she hasn't done in years." Robert grabbed a tissue from a box on the table next to him and blew his nose. "I don't think Momma would be willing to testify. She told me she wouldn't even talk to a social worker because she didn't have anything specific to say. And she's worried about ruining the relationship she has with Janelle."

"Well, that *is* a risk, Bobby. It could make matters worse."

"Would you worry about that if you were in my shoes, Larry?"

Larry paused and rubbed his forehead. "I guess not, Bobby. Let me give some thought to how we should proceed. If I need anything, can I reach you at your momma's?"

"Yes, but give me a couple of hours. Things moved so fast I didn't tell her I was coming. Barry Daniel is going to take me home on his lunch break."

"Well, you can make yourself at home in the conference room until then, if you'd like. How's Barry doing after his divorce?"

"Okay, I guess. I think his daughter yanks him around a bit."

"Well, tell him I asked about him."

"Will do."

Robert spent the remainder of the morning in Larry's law library, researching the Georgia law on child abuse. Nothing in either the statutes or the court rules described when and how a court should review a petition for *ex parte* relief. He was encouraged to learn that judges have discretion to decide on granting *ex parte* relief based solely on the written allegations of the petition asking for relief. Or, they can decide after reviewing the petition and considering what the person asking for relief has to say. Robert made copies of what he found and highlighted the important passages. After explaining to Larry's assistant that he was trying to be helpful—not second-guess Larry—he left the copies with her and went outside to wait for Barry.

Shortly after noon, he drove up.

"I'm as hungry as a horse," Barry said as Robert climbed into his truck. "You're gonna regret agreeing to pay for all I can eat."

They'd only travelled a short distance when Robert asked him to pull off the road.

"I need to give this back to you," Robert said, pulling Barry's pistol out of the pocket of his overcoat.

"Why in the hell do you have that?"

"Because I'm an idiot, Barry. The bourbon got to me last night. I'm disgusted with the situation I've gotten myself into, and what you said about the Godfather started making sense."

"Damn, Bobby. That was drunk talk. You don't need to be getting messed up with anything like that. It would ruin your life."

"What about my little girl's life, Barry? Living with a damn pervert."

"Well, you don't know that for sure. And you do know that Janelle wouldn't put up with any bullshit."

"She might not know what he's doin'."

"C'mon, Bobby, put that shit out of your head and listen to Larry. That's why you hired him, ain't it?"

"Yeah. I guess you're right."

"They're home, by the way."

"Who?"

"Janelle and Junior and Ellie. He brought his car in this morning for me to finish working on it."

Robert didn't respond right away; he just stared out the window. "Well, we'd better go get you some lunch," he said.

During their twenty-minute stop at McDonalds, Barry ate two Big Mac meals with fries. Robert had a Diet Coke. After that, Barry dropped

Robert off at his mother's house, where, as expected, she was surprised and delighted to see him.

"Oh my goodness, sweetheart! I sure didn't expect to see you at my door."

Robert hugged his mother tightly. "It's not good news, Momma."

"Come on in, sweetheart. What's the matter? What's wrong?"

"I found out that Junior was investigated for sexually abusing a little girl in Augusta."

"Oh, my." Ruth sat down hard in her chair.

"I should have called you, Momma, but everything's happened so fast. I got in late last night—"

"Last night?"

"Yes, Momma, Barry picked me up in Savannah. It was real late, so I stayed at his place. I met with Larry this morning and told him what I know. He's deciding what we should do next. We might have a court hearing on Friday."

"Oh my goodness." Her chin dropped, and she shook her head. "This is terrible news." When she looked back at her son, there was an intensity in her blue eyes that he hadn't seen in a long time. "Bobby, I am sure Janelle doesn't know anything about this."

"I don't think she does, Momma. When she decided she didn't want me and my life, she hooked up with the first man that showed her any attention. And, we don't know for sure what happened in Augusta. Junior's girlfriend accused him; he denied it; and he wasn't charged or even arrested. So, we don't know whether he was guilty or not."

"What did Larry say you should do?"

"He's not sure. I'd like to get the court to order an experienced social worker to interview Ellie to see what she could find out. You know how they use those anatomically correct dolls to get children to open up about what might have been done to them."

His mother sighed deeply. "This is awful."

Tears began to stream down her face; the muscles in her chin trembled like a little girl. Robert could tell what she was thinking. "Momma, there is no way you could have known, even with your sixth sense."

"No, no. I feel so bad. That precious little girl. What if he's abusing her? What did Larry say, again?"

"He knows the head of DFACS in Pemberton—"

"Frances Hopkins."

"Yes, Momma. She's in Larry's Sunday school class."

"I've known Frances for years."

"So I guess we're in good hands. I don't know what's going to happen, Momma. I'm kinda grasping at straws. I just feel like I have to do something."

"I understand, Bobby."

"Hey, let's think about something else," he said. "Why don't I take you to lunch at the Swanson Inn?"

Ruth smiled, though it was lopsided—reflecting her conflicting emotions. She was happy her son had returned for a visit and they were headed to her favorite restaurant, though the ominous news he brought with him prevented her smile from reaching her eyes. "Let me freshen up a bit first."

Although they had a pleasant lunch, Robert could tell that his mother was stressed. She wasn't herself when friends stopped by their table to say hello. Gradually, the shock of the news subsided, and she began to compose herself. They avoided talking about Ellie, and instead discussed her plans for New Year's Eve and New Year's Day. She even smiled and said she felt blessed that this year she'd be celebrating with both her children.

On New Year's Eve, Frank and Darlene joined Robert and his mother as they watched Dick Clark's televised celebration from Times Square in New York. The show also chronicled what a tough year 1986 had been, beginning with the Challenger shuttle disaster and ending in a morass involving Iran, hostages, and Nicaraguan Contras. Robert's life, over the last twelve months, reflected the same dismal tone. His divorce, along with its terrible child visitation arrangement, had become final; he'd struggled with a new job in an environment that was vastly different from the military; his personal life was a mess; and worst of all, his daughter might be living with a sexual predator. When the clock struck twelve, he hugged his mother tightly so she couldn't see the tears in his eyes and went straight to bed.

Ruth's New Year's Day dinner was normally a joyous occasion with talk of football games and the good luck that comes from the Southern tradition of eating black-eyed peas. Not so this year. It didn't take long for Darlene to discern something was wrong. When Robert told her and Frank what he'd learned about Junior, they had the same stunned response as his mother and immediately suggested that he contact Larry Gray, which of course he already had. So, there was nothing else to do but pretend to watch football games and wait until Friday.

# CHAPTER TWENTY-SIX

THE HEARING DIDN'T start well.

"So, Mr. Gray, you are back again on behalf of your client, Mr. Clark, and you'd like me to order a forensic evaluation of the child, Eloise J. Clark."

"Yes, Your Honor."

"The last time you were here, Ms. Clark's attorney was sick, as I recall. So, this time you've decided to dispense with notifying him and simply seek *ex parte* relief?"

"No, Your Honor." Larry paused and stared at the judge, more out of disbelief than protest. "As reflected in our petition, we have recently received disconcerting information concerning Mr. Rodney K. White, Jr., the boyfriend of the former Mrs. Clark, the mother of my client's daughter, Eloise Clark. Given the nature of this information, Your Honor, we believe time is of the essence."

"Well, your petition merely recounts allegations that were made against Mr. White in Augusta, and I note that he was neither charged nor arrested in Augusta. He wasn't, was he?"

"No, Your Honor."

"So why am I to conclude these are exigent circumstances?"

"Your Honor, Mrs. Frances Hopkins is here and can testify. She is the head of the Division of Family and Children Services office in Pemberton."

"Yes, Mr. Gray, I'm well aware of who Mrs. Hopkins is. I'm also aware that you two are in the same Sunday school class, are you not?"

"Why yes, Your Honor, that is correct." Larry must have appeared surprised at the judge's comment.

"As you well know, Mr. Gray, there are no secrets in small towns. But let me be clear: I don't need to hear from Mrs. Hopkins, unless she can explain why I should ignore this report from Augusta, which to me exonerates Mr. White."

"If it please the court, Your Honor—"

"It does not. Just listen, Mr. Gray. The statute requires you to allege specific facts indicating an occurrence of abuse. The court must find that probable cause exists that such abuse has occurred in the past and may occur in the future. All you've offered me are the disgusting allegations of Mr. White's *former* girlfriend, which he denied, and pursuant to which he was neither arrested nor charged. I don't think you've made your case for probable cause."

"Your Honor, Mrs. Hopkins spoke with her colleague in Augusta—"

"I don't care, Mr. Gray. I don't need Mrs. Hopkins to tell me how to do my job. Your petition is denied. And Mr. Gray, this marks the second time you've asked this court to do something unreasonable. Don't do that again. You may have been able to get away with that when your old friend Judge Cochran occupied this bench. But I'm not Judge Cochran, and I expect you to know the law and follow the law. Court's adjourned."

Robert couldn't move. He couldn't think. It was a struggle to breath. He kept seeing images of the sneer on Judge Harrington's face as he berated Larry. He looked over at Mrs. Hopkins, who looked as if she'd just been kicked in the stomach. Larry turned to them and said, "Let's reconvene in my office."

⁓

"He is an awful man. What does he know about protecting children?" Mrs. Hopkins had just seated herself on the couch in Larry's office, holding a cup of coffee and a saucer. "I'm going to do everything I can to get him off that bench. I so miss Judge Cochran."

"He is challenging. That's for sure," Larry said.

Larry was doing his best to be professional, but Robert could tell he'd felt the sting of Judge Harrington's remarks.

"Larry, I'm sorry if I—"

"You don't need to apologize to me, Bobby. You're my client. I made the decision to go forward with the petition. It's my responsibility, not yours."

"I never dreamed he'd be so negative, Larry. It's as if he hates me."

Neither Larry nor Mrs. Hopkins said anything. Larry had been careful not to reveal to anyone that Robert had agreed to the child visitation arrangement solely to avoid having Janelle's lawyer make a public record of his dalliance with the prostitute in Panama. It was supposed to be confidential, although almost everyone in town, including Mrs. Hopkins and probably Judge Harrington, had heard all about it because Eugene Matthews—Janelle's attorney—ran his mouth after he'd had a few drinks in the country club lounge.

"What am I going to do, Larry?"

"I don't know, Bobby. I'm just—"

"Well I know what I'm going to do." Mrs. Hopkins became animated and raised her voice. "Judge Harrington isn't going to tell me how to do my job either. I'm going to have one of my staff pay a visit to Janelle and Mr. Rodney K. White, Jr., so we can see for ourselves what's going on. And if things don't look proper, we'll begin a full-scale investigation. If Judge Harrington had bothered to let me testify, I would have told him that the staff of the Augusta office were uniformly dismayed that nothing was done as a result of their investigation. Apparently, Junior's father is a good friend of the Richmond County Sheriff. The rumor is their fathers used to run moonshine together during Prohibition."

"Good grief," Robert muttered.

"Now, Frances, be careful," Larry said. "Judge Harrington will be watching what we do and what you do."

"Larry, I've been doing this for a long time. I've known Ruth Clark for over forty years, and I've known Bobby since he was a baby. Janelle's father is a no-count. And from what I can tell, this Junior fellow is worse. We have our ways of getting at the truth."

"How long will that take, Mrs. Hopkins?" Robert asked. "What if Junior's abusing her?"

"Bobby." She paused. Her dark eyes radiated an intensity that left no doubt about her resolve. "We don't know that for sure. But I'm going to send Eunice Wilson to talk to him. She could put the fear of God in General George Patton. Mr. Rodney White will be no match for her. Don't you worry, Bobby." She patted Robert's knee. "We'll be watching him like a hawk. And I'll talk to your momma, too. Now, gentlemen, if you'll excuse me, I've got to get to the office."

Robert thanked Larry again and followed Mrs. Hopkins out the door. Driving back to his mother's house, he tried to make sense of what had happened.

We'll never get anywhere with that judge. He wasn't just rude to Larry, he was rude to Mrs. Hopkins. Maybe he hates everybody in Pemberton, not just me. He sure as hell doesn't care what Junior might be doing. He wouldn't even listen to what Mrs. Hopkins was going to suggest. Maybe Barry's right. Maybe I just need to deal with this myself. I wouldn't mind meeting that lying jerk Gene Matthews in a dark alley, either. He probably put Janelle up to asking for that damn visitation arrangement. I'd like to kick the shit out of his skinny ass and then kick him in the nuts, if he has any.

Robert drove for a few minutes trying to calm down and clear his head. What am I thinking? This is insane. I'm not the Godfather. I'm Robert E. Clark from Pemberton, Georgia. My parents didn't raise me to think like that. One thing is for sure, though: Judge Harrington is an ass. Larry was kind to say the petition was his decision, but he wouldn't have done it for anyone but his best friend's son. I know that. I just hope it didn't damage his reputation. I guess I'm going to have to trust Mrs. Hopkins. She sounded like she isn't going to rest until she gets to the bottom of it.

Unfortunately, no amount of positive self-talk could take away Robert's worry. In a few minutes, his doubts returned.

But what if Ellie is being abused? Didn't Mrs. Hopkins say the social workers in Augusta were upset that nothing had happened to Junior? And what about Momma's sixth sense? She's never wrong. Junior looks like a guy who would hang out at the playground to lust after little girls. But even if Mrs. Hopkins gets right on it, she won't be able to get to the bottom of things very fast. What else can I do?

Janelle's gonna go ballistic when she finds out what I tried to do with the court order. I just hope she directs her anger at me and not Momma. If she doesn't let Momma keep Ellie anymore, we'll have no idea what's going on.

Robert pulled his mother's Chevrolet into the driveway and put it into park, but he didn't get out right away. He knew he needed to calm down before he went in, so he slowly said the Lord's Prayer, ending it with, "Jesus, I hope you heard me."

# CHAPTER TWENTY-SEVEN

WEEKENDS AT THE Clark house were normally filled with household chores, maybe a trip to the movies on Saturday night, and church on Sunday, followed by one of Ruth's famous Sunday dinners. But on this weekend, none of that happened. Instead, Robert and his mother ambled about the house in a disconnected daze, going through the motions of living. It was reminiscent of the days following his father's funeral. Neither of them wanted to talk about the subject that was foremost in their thoughts, as if somehow that would prevent reality from taking hold.

On Sunday afternoon, Barry drove Robert to the Savannah Airport for his flight back to Dallas. They were mostly quiet during the trip. Barry refused to let Robert pay for gas and, as Robert was getting out of the truck, reiterated his offer to do whatever he could to help him. Barry was always thinking of others—even when his own life was a mess. Despite his troubles, Robert at least had his mother and sister who loved him and worried about him and Ellie who seemed to still want him around. Barry had no one but Robert.

It was only when he was driving to work on Monday morning that Robert remembered he was supposed to meet with Davis Burnet for a planning session on the Russell going-private transaction. No sooner had he settled into his office than he received a call from Donna, Davis's secretary, summoning him. I guess I'll just have to wing it, he thought, as he grabbed the file and a legal pad and raced upstairs.

"Have a seat, Robert," Davis said, gesturing to his conference table. "I understand you just returned from a quick trip to Georgia. Is everything all right?"

How the hell does he know that? Robert wondered. Am I being watched?

As Robert struggled to find words to respond, Davis sensed his confusion. "Stephan Edgar said he saw you at the airport last night. Said you were in the baggage claim area for a flight from Atlanta, so I assumed you took a quick trip back to Georgia. I hope everything's all right. Last week you mentioned needing to take care of something for your mother."

"Oh yes, uh, it's nothing, Davis." Robert hoped his expression didn't betray his true thoughts. "Just some personal matters I needed to attend to."

"Well, I hope you have them resolved, because I need all your focus and attention." Robert noticed Davis's jaw tighten. "Mr. Russell has been sued, and I fear his attempt to buy out the public shareholders is now in jeopardy." Davis took a legal pad from his desk and slammed the drawer shut as he stood to walk to the conference table. "These minority shareholders are so selfish, so greedy. After all Mr. Russell has done for them. They're parasites!" Davis's lips curled as he spat out the words. "They take avarice to a whole new level."

For several uncomfortable moments Robert sat in silence and then asked, "What exactly is the nature of the suit?"

"They think Mr. Russell's tender offer of $10.00 per share is too low."

Having no idea of what to say, Robert sat up in his chair, pen in hand, awaiting directions. Davis sat down and pressed his fingertips on his temples. It was so quiet Robert could hear the antique clock on the bookshelf behind Davis's desk. Tick-tock. Tick-tock. Finally, Davis raised his head and looked to his right, not making eye contact with Robert.

"Get this down," he snapped. "I want you to prepare a resolution to be adopted by the board of directors of Russell Field Services, appointing Lewis Johnson as a special committee to evaluate Mr. Russell's tender offer and to prepare and present a recommendation to the full board and the minority shareholders concerning the company's position on Mr. Russell's offer. Also, the board should authorize Lewis to hire Scott & Cranston to advise him."

That name sounded familiar to Robert, but he was too busy taking notes to give it much thought. He wanted to be certain he had everything he needed to prepare the documents Davis was requesting. "Will Mr. Johnson be the only one on the special committee?"

"Yes. The other directors are Mr. Russell's children and his accountant. Lewis is the only independent director."

"Should the resolution authorize Mr. Johnson to hire his own legal counsel, since we represent Mr. Russell?"

"Why on earth would we do that? We're not in the habit of giving work away, Robert. Besides, I've known Lewis for over twenty years. He's an experienced businessman. I doubt he'll need much legal counsel, and if he does, I certainly can assist him. We can get waivers of the conflict."

The next three weeks were hectic. Davis directed Robert to prepare not only the resolution for the board, but also a formal notice of the meeting, which he sent to each of the directors, and a script that included everything each director needed to say and discuss prior to the board's vote on the resolution. Every document went through numerous drafts, as Robert seemed to be unable to please Davis, no matter how hard he tried. Davis also had him research and prepare legal memorandums on a host of issues he thought might be relevant to the litigation, including the duties of officers and directors, what constitutes a conflict of interest, and the effect of conflicts of interest on the process of approving a resolution recommending a buyout of the public shareholders of a corporation.

Under normal circumstances Robert would have found this work interesting. After all, it was what he thought he wanted for his career: high-stakes corporate work at a top-tier law firm. But these were not normal circumstances. His thoughts were clouded by the shadows cast by that infernal investigation in Augusta. And, he kept seeing Judge Harrington's sneer as he lectured Larry Gray prior to denying his petition to have DFACS conduct a forensic evaluation of Ellie. At times, Robert felt as if something was constricting his lungs, making it difficult to breathe. Worst of all, visions of Ellie being abused by a filthy degenerate kept creeping into his thoughts. He called Mrs. Hopkins several times but only managed to speak with a staff person who each time said, simply, that the matter was still under investigation—whatever that meant. It gnawed at him that for the first time in his life, he couldn't "make it happen."

The stress and worry weighed heavily on him. He ate irregularly, drank way too much coffee, and popped aspirin tablets like candy, trying in vain to relieve an incessant headache. Late evenings at the office were rarely followed by dinner. Exhausted, he would go home late to pretzels for dinner—and his bottle of Maker's Mark. He was polishing off a large bottle each week. The gray smudges that always appeared beneath his eyes at times like these turned into dark, fleshy pouches, adding ten years to his appearance. He stopped caring about how he looked. His shirts or suits or both were often wrinkled, his shoes scuffed, and his hair longer than it had been at any time since high school. If others noticed, none of them said anything—that is, except for one.

"What's going on, Robert? You don't look well." He looked up from his desk to see Diana framed in his doorway, as if she were gracing the cover of *Vogue*. For a fleeting moment he thought about what might have been.

Stop, he told himself. There's no time for that now.

"I'm getting pulled in so many different directions, Diana. I don't know what to do."

"Can I help?" Her voice sounded like a mom, comforting her child with a scraped knee.

"No, thanks. It's just Davis has me busy with the Russell litigation—"

"Yeah. I heard about that." She smiled in a way that made him think of his mother.

"And..." He stopped. Should I tell her about Ellie?

He paused too long. "And *what*, Robert?" Her blue eyes narrowed.

"Things aren't going well at home."

"I thought Megan moved to New York."

"Not her, Diana. That was never serious. It was... I was an idiot. It's about my daughter back in Pemberton."

"What's wrong, Robert?" Diana shut the door and sat down.

He could feel the emotions that had welled up in him begin to spill out. "It's about Ellie. She's living with her mother. Janelle. That's my ex's name. Anyway, Janelle's got this boyfriend—"

"You didn't expect her to stay single, did you?"

"No. No, I don't care about that. It's just that a few years ago this boyfriend was investigated for child sex abuse."

"Oh my goodness."

"I went back to Georgia to try to get the court to order a forensic evaluation of Ellie, but I got nowhere."

"Robert, I'm so sorry."

"Yeah. And now, I've got to focus on this damn Russell litigation."

"Have you told Davis?"

"Does he strike you as someone who cares about anybody's personal problems?"

"No, I guess not. I think he finds it helpful to be insensitive." She closed her eyes for a moment, recalling something. "When I was in situations like this, my mom used to always say: 'When you come to the end of your rope, tie a knot and hang on.' "

Robert tried to smile. "I'm trying, Diana. I just don't know what to do. I can't stop thinking about what that degenerate could be doing to my daughter."

"What does your lawyer say?"

"Like I said, he tried to persuade the court to order an evaluation, but the judge just insulted him. He's a jerk." Robert paused and exhaled to compose himself. "Junior—that's the guy's name—was investigated based on his former girlfriend's complaint but was never even arrested. Somehow, his dad got him off. But the social workers who were involved in the investigation think he was guilty."

"Is Social Services looking into your ex-wife's situation?"

"Yeah, well, the head of the local DFACS office—that's what they call it in Georgia; it stands for Department of Family and Children Services— she said she was going to look into whether any abuse might be taking place, but I haven't heard anything, and it's been almost four weeks."

"Those things take time, Robert. You should feel good that someone in a position of authority has taken notice. Believe me, my mom had her run-ins with social workers after my dad left, but I think most of them want to help people. And you have the head of the office looking into things."

"I know. I guess I'm lucky in that respect. I'm just scared."

"I'm sure things will work out." Her brow wrinkled as she studied his face. "Are you taking care of yourself?"

"Yeah. I guess so."

"Any trouble sleeping?" Her expression was sincere and concerned.

Robert struggled to decide whether he should answer and then said, "Actually, no. I'm not doing okay. I get to sleep all right, but then I wake up in the middle of the night and can't go back to sleep. I lie awake and keep replaying, over and over, all the foolish things I've done in my life: marrying Janelle, things I did in Panama that I shouldn't have, not spending enough time with my family, and..." He paused, and his face relaxed. "And, Megan—one of the stupidest situations I ever got myself into." Diana's expression gave no hint of what she was thinking. "In other words," he continued, "all the bad decisions that have made a mess of my life."

"You have a good life, Robert. You're an outstanding attorney who has a successful career going at the leading firm in Texas."

"Yeah. How's that working out for *you?*"

"Okay, you've got me," she said. "We both know Underwood & Crockett has its challenges. But we do get to work with some of the best attorneys in the country, and the work is interesting—cutting edge. And, of course, we're well paid, aren't we?"

"There must be more to it than that, Diana." He dropped his head and stared at the floor for a moment before looking up. "But, you know, right now I don't have the time or the mental energy to think about it. I feel like I'm failing as a father—the most important job a man can have."

"You're not failing, Robert. You're doing everything you can. Listen, I know you need to get back to work, but how would you like to go to dinner tonight so we can talk?"

Damn it, he thought. Damn it. Damn it.

"I can't, Diana. Alan wants me to go to dinner with him tonight."

Her expression left no doubt what she was thinking.

"I know you don't like him, Diana, but—"

"I don't dislike him, Robert. I think he's out for 'number one.' I know you think you owe him, but you don't. Alan Taylor doesn't do anything unless it's going to help him be the first black partner at Underwood & Crockett."

"He's not that shallow, Diana."

"Well, I'll leave you to him." She stood to leave.

"Can I get a raincheck?"

She didn't quite smile, but her eyes betrayed a hint of sparkle. "Maybe."

Around eight o'clock that night, Robert and Alan went to Dakota's. Alan headed straight for the bar.

"Jake, give me a Macallan eighteen-year old on the rocks. Make it a double."

"Sure thing, Mr. Taylor. Can I get you something," Jake asked, turning to Robert.

"I'll have a Makers on the rocks, please. A single is fine."

Alan paid the tab, and the two of them went to an empty table and sat down. As the waiter approached, Alan held up his hand. "We're gonna need a minute before we order. Thanks." Alan took a long drink.

"What's going on with you, Alan?" Robert asked. "You seem restless."

"Michelle left me."

"What? What do you mean she left you?"

"I mean she said we're through." Alan took another long drink and stared into space for almost a minute. "I don't know what those girls did out in Vail. First, Megan leaves you, and then Michelle tells me we're through. I should have known it wasn't going to last."

"Why do you say that?"

"Michelle wasn't serious about our relationship, Robert. I think she just liked showing off her black boyfriend to her friends. She thought I made her look cool—burnished her credentials as an enlightened liberal." He finished his drink.

"Alan, I don't think—"

"No, man, I was just her token Negro. Her folks would never have allowed her to get too serious with me." He motioned for the waiter and then turned back to Robert. "But hey, I don't mean to be having a pity party. I mainly wanted to talk to you. Are you doing all right?"

"Yeah. I'm all right."

The waiter approached, and Alan began straight away. "Tonight I'm gonna try something different, Ramón. I'll have some of your steak tartare, medium rare."

Ramón said nothing but rocked from left to right. Robert could see the look of concern on his face and knew he didn't know what to say.

"Alan, I think steak tartare is, by definition, raw," Robert said. "Are you sure you want that?"

"Oh, yeah. Yeah. Of course. What was I thinking?" Alan fiddled with his shirt cuffs and then put his hands flat on the table. "I guess I'm just tired, Ramón. Um. You know what? I'll have a nice sirloin, medium rare, baked potato with extra butter, no sour cream, and a side salad with blue cheese. Oh, and we'll have a bottle of… Let's see…" Alan perused the wine list. "We'll have the Beringer's 1985 Private Reserve Cabernet Sauvignon."

Glancing at the wine list, Robert noticed that Alan had just ordered a bottle that cost almost $100. Is he compensating for not knowing what steak tartare is? he wondered.

"Very good, Mr. Taylor," Ramón said. "And for you, Mr. Clark?" he asked with a look that said: "thank you."

"I guess I'll have the same, Ramón, but I'd like my steak medium, please. Thanks."

When the waiter left, Alan continued. "You gotta start moving towards rare, Robert. You're in Texas now."

Robert's cheeks raised, as if he were about to smile, but he pressed his lips together to fight the urge.

Alan leaned toward him. "Are you sure you're okay? Folks are starting to talk."

"What do you mean 'talk'?" Robert asked.

"Well, some of them say you're starting to look like someone who's drinking too much or doing drugs."

"Bullshit, Alan. You know I'd never do drugs." Robert could feel his face flush. His voice was sharp. "That joint I had with you down at the beach was the first time I ever even tried marijuana. And I haven't touched it since." He paused a moment for Alan to respond and then added, "You're the one who's just gulped down a double of expensive scotch."

"Hey, man. I didn't say I believed any of it. I just said people are starting to talk. You need to watch yourself. You've got a good thing going. Don't screw it up." He studied Robert for a moment. "Are you upset over Megan leaving?"

"Is that what people think? Really? Hell, no. I'm glad she's gone." Robert took a drink. "We weren't right for each other, anyway."

"I don't know, man. She had a fine lookin' body. Was she good in bed?"

"There's more to a relationship than that, Alan."

"I suppose. Well, what's wrong with you then?"

Should I tell him about Ellie? Would he even understand? Probably not. All he thinks about is making partner at Underwood & Crockett. He'd probably tell Davis all about my problems back in Georgia, if he thought it would help his chances. No. That's not fair. Alan would never do that.

"Hey. Did you hear me?" Alan asked.

"Yes. I'm sorry, Alan. I can't seem to think straight these days; Davis has been incredibly demanding."

"I never told you he was going to be easy. I just said he can do more for your career at the firm than anyone else, especially that lesbo you're so fond of."

"Can we just not talk about Sharon?" Robert finished his drink. "It's this damn Russell litigation, Alan. It's unlike anything I've ever been involved in."

"Welcome to the big leagues, my man. Make me look good for recommending you. You do remember the partnership vote is in March, don't you? Davis can make or break that vote for me."

"I remember, Alan. You want to be selected for partner early."

"You know it," Alan said.

"Well, you know I'll do my best. But Davis keeps asking me to research things and do things that make no sense."

"There you go again. You shouldn't be second-guessing someone like Davis."

"Well, think about this: he's obsessed over whether Lewis Johnson, the only independent director at Russell, hires Scott & Cranston to advise him in connection with his evaluation of Mr. Russell's bid for the company. He had me include it in the board resolution, and now he asks me about it at least twice a day."

"That's because Davis is tight with Scott & Cranston. He uses them all the time."

"Really?" Something about that didn't sound right, but Robert decided not to pursue the topic with Alan.

"Anything else?" Alan asked.

"Yeah. Davis also told me that he would serve as counsel for Mr. Johnson. Doesn't that sound like a serious conflict of interest to you? How can we represent both Mr. Russell and the person who is evaluating Mr. Russell's bid?"

"Davis knows what he's doing, Robert. Besides, you never have a conflict if you put yourself first."

Robert recoiled. "What?"

"I'm kidding, man. Lighten up. Davis isn't going to do anything that would get the firm in trouble. Stop doubting him. Just do what he says. Stop worrying and just focus on doing a good job."

"Okay. I guess."

# CHAPTER TWENTY-EIGHT

OVER THE NEXT two weeks, Robert tried to follow Alan's advice. He kept his head down, didn't ask questions, and concentrated on what Davis asked him to do. And Davis asked him to do a lot. In addition to requesting several more research memorandums on various topics related to the Russell litigation, he also had Robert assist with discovery.

That process brought back bad memories of his divorce case. He recalled how, before trial, he and Janelle had had to produce evidence to each other. Larry had said the goal was to enable each party to assess the relative strength and weakness of each side's case, so they would decide to settle the case without a trial. It led to settlement all right—one based on blackmail. When Gene Matthews, Janelle's attorney, asked Robert a routine question about whether he had had sex with anyone other than Janelle, it all went downhill. Matthews knew Robert would never let that information come out in public. He used it to get Janelle all of their meager savings and alimony and child support. But the worst of it was the visitation order. Robert couldn't decide whether Janelle had really wanted that arrangement or whether it was Matthews—something he wanted to crow about. Janelle had never been vindictive before. But what does it matter now? he thought. The result is the same.

Robert tried to refocus and employ those same discovery tools in the Russell litigation. He'd gotten a taste of the process when he helped Alan with the Donaldson Construction matter. But there was so much more at stake now. And he didn't want to repeat the mistake of being wedded to form documents, which had caused him to fail to ask about whether the renegade CEO had an employment agreement. This time he needed to think carefully about the case. He drafted interrogatories, which went through multiple revisions from Davis and Hugh Williams, and he prepared requests for documents and requests that the minority shareholders admit or deny certain facts.

Davis seemed to be more concerned about what Robert proposed to produce to the other side, in response to their discovery requests, than he was with what Robert was proposing to request of the other side. He gave Robert a folder of documents and directed him to determine which ones were responsive to the requests made by the attorneys representing the minority shareholders and whether any of them contained privileged material, such as attorney-client communications, which did not have to be produced. While he was reviewing the documents, Robert remembered where he'd seen the name Scott & Cranston. It was on the letter that had been faxed to Davis in December while he was away on his skiing vacation. Not finding that letter among the documents Davis had asked him to review, Robert concluded Davis must have decided it didn't have to be produced.

On Friday the thirteenth Robert returned home late, completely drained. Just as he finished pouring himself a drink, the welcome silence of his duplex was interrupted by the jangling of his phone. He almost dropped the bottle.

"Hello, this is Robert Clark."

"Hey, Bobby, this is Darlene."

"Well, this is a pleasant surprise. What brings you to call so late?"

"I'm afraid it's not good news."

Robert's blood turned to ice water. "What? What? Is Ellie okay?"

"Oh, sorry, Bobby. Yes, Ellie's okay and Momma's okay. It's Junior."

"Junior?"

"Yes. Junior. He's dead."

"What? Oh, my God! What happened?"

"Well, it's all very mysterious. He died in a car accident last night. Fortunately, no one was with him, and no other cars were involved. He just ran off the road and hit a tree. From the looks of things he had just left Buddy's. You know, that bar."

"Was he drunk?"

"Nobody knows for sure, but there weren't any skid marks. It was like his brakes just failed."

Robert's hands began to sweat. Surely, Barry wouldn't have, he thought. No. That would've backfired if Janelle or Ellie had been in the car. He would've never taken that chance.

Darlene was still talking. "They've been looking for Barry Daniel because he'd recently worked on Junior's car."

Robert said nothing, though he could hear Barry's drunken voice from that night in his trailer: *What Junior needs is some Godfather justice.*

"You don't know where he is, do you, Bobby?"

"What do you mean?"

"Well, no one has seen him for a couple of days. The police went to his trailer, but nobody was there, and his truck was gone. They even talked to his ex-wife."

Robert's hands were now wet with sweat, his voice strained. "Uh, no. I haven't talked to him. I've been too busy with work to talk to anybody back home."

"Well, if you do talk to him, I hope you'll tell him to call Chief Staples. The longer he stays away, the more suspicious it seems."

"They don't think Barry had anything to do with it, do they?"

"I don't think so. Everybody's known Barry his whole life. He's always been such a sweet guy. And nobody liked Junior, anyway. I mean… Not that anyone wanted him to die, mind you. It's just that he was always so sour lookin'. Janelle even stopped going to church because of him."

"How's she doing?"

"She seems okay. I've only seen her once recently. She was gettin' a prescription filled at the drug store, so I didn't talk to her."

"So if they don't think Barry had anything to do with it, why does he need to call Chief Staples?"

"Apparently, Junior's daddy is a bigwig up in Clayton, and he's raising all kinds of Cain down at the police station. He wouldn't let them perform an autopsy on Junior, so nobody knows whether he was drunk or not. His daddy just keeps saying that his son would never drink and drive and that there weren't any skid marks. He's the one pointing the finger at Barry. He says Barry worked on Junior's car just a few days before the accident. Mr. Lester is nervous, too. People are saying Mr. White is likely to sue him, claiming he was responsible for the brake job on Junior's car, even if Barry did the work."

"Yeah. I know all about Junior's daddy and how he covers for him."

The line was quiet for so long Robert thought it had gone dead. Then, Darlene said, "Yeah. Momma told me."

"What?" Robert's voice was stern, though he sounded more hurt than irritated.

"Now, don't be mad at her, Bobby. She needed to talk to somebody. She said Mrs. Hopkins was investigatin' Junior because of that business up in Augusta."

Again, the line was silent for a few moments. "Well, I guess it doesn't matter now, does it?" Robert said, his voice now quiet and resigned.

"No. I guess not." After a short, respectful pause, Darlene attempted to change subjects. "Janelle and Ellie are stayin' with her daddy."

Robert's mind was still focused on Junior. "Do you know anything about the funeral arrangements?"

"The memorial service is gonna be on Sunday. They're having it at the Thompson Funeral Home."

"They're not going to have it at Janelle's church?" Robert asked. "She's been going there her whole life."

"Well, you know how people talk. After she moved in with Junior, she'd get all kinds of funny looks when she went to church. You know that bothered her daddy: Mr. Pierce has been a deacon in that church for as long as I can remember. But Junior didn't want her to go anyway."

"I'm gonna come."

"No, Bobby. I don't think that's a good idea. And, it would be sorta odd, don't you think? I mean, you and Janelle were married, and then she left you and took up with Junior. I just called you because I thought you should know. Momma was too upset to call."

"Well, Monday is Presidents' Day, so maybe I'll fly home just to make sure Janelle doesn't do something crazy."

"Are you sure you want to do that?"

"You remember how she left me in Panama with no warning, don't you?"

"Of course, but what are you worried about now? Where would she go? She's only got her daddy, and he's not going anywhere."

"I don't know, Darlene. I don't know. But I don't have time to think about it if I'm going to get on an early flight. I need to make the reservations right away."

"All right. Well, do what you think you have to do. Want me to pick you up at the airport?"

"Yes, please, since Barry normally does."

"Okay. Just let me know when."

After he hung up, Robert called several airlines to find the earliest flight he could get to Savannah. He loaded his gym bag with his shaving kit and three pairs of underwear and socks, put his dark suit and a shirt and tie in a hang-up bag, and went to bed. The next morning he phoned Darlene shortly before boarding his 7:00 a.m. flight to Atlanta to tell her when he'd be arriving in Savannah. She and Frank were waiting for him in baggage claim with somber looks.

"Are you sure it's a good idea for you to go to the memorial service, Bobby?" Frank asked, as they walked to Frank's car.

"I don't know, Frank. I can't seem to think straight these days. Something just tells me I should be there, you know, to remind Janelle that, hey, I'm still Ellie's father, and I'm still here. I'm sure Ellie is totally confused by all this."

"Okay. Well, we were going to meet your momma for dinner at Swanson's. Is that okay with you?"

"Sure."

Ruth had a troubled look on her face when she first saw Robert. Obviously, she was happy to see her son, but her smile was strained. Robert's spirits brightened when he saw Ellie sitting next to his mother. When Ellie saw him, she bolted from her seat and ran to him, throwing her arms around his waist.

She looked up at him. "I've missed you so much, Daddy."

"I've missed you, too, sweetheart. I think you've grown a bunch since I last saw you. Did you get your hair cut? It looks nice." He hugged her back and thought about all that he was missing.

"Do you really like it? Momma took me to get it cut yesterday." Her normally bright and engaging face was somber. "Daddy, I need to tell you something. Junior's gone to be with Jesus."

"That's what I heard, sweetheart. I'm so sorry."

"Momma said we're gonna live with Granddaddy again."

"Is that good?"

"I guess so. Granddaddy takes me fishin', and we go to the Dairy Queen."

"Well, that's good. Let's go see what Nana's doing."

Holding his hand, Ellie led Robert back to their table. He bent over, and Ruth hugged him tightly.

"I don't know what all this means, Bobby," she whispered. "I can't believe he's dead."

"Me either, Momma."

"I won't lie," she continued in a hushed voice. "I never did like Rodney White. But this is awful. And I see now why he went by Junior, instead of using his daddy's name. Mr. White is even worse. He's makin' all sorts of accusations about Barry and Mr. Lester." She looked down and shook her head. "That boy would've never done anything like that."

"I know, Momma. Barry wouldn't hurt a fly."

"Well, why hadn't anybody seen him since the accident?" she asked with a sidelong glance. She scanned the room to see if anyone was listening.

"I don't know, Momma. I haven't talked to him."

The five of them sat down and ordered dinner, which was served family-style. And although the atmosphere felt like old times, they were guarded in what they said, in part because Ellie was there, but also because they didn't know who might overhear them.

After dinner Darlene and Frank headed home, and Robert drove to his mother's house. Ruth called Janelle, so Ellie could say goodnight, and then put her to bed. By the time she joined Robert in the kitchen, he'd made a pot of coffee and was sitting at the table, his father's favorite mug nestled in his hands in front of him.

"Janelle asked me to keep Ellie until next Tuesday. She doesn't want her around Mr. White and his family. They're going to have a memorial service at Thompson's Funeral Home after church tomorrow, but Mr. White wants Junior to be buried in the family plot up in Clayton. Janelle feels like she needs to be there."

After a couple of minutes of awkward silence, Robert finally said what was on both their minds. "Well, I guess Mrs. Hopkins can stop her investigation."

"Oh, Bobby. Don't say such a thing. A man is dead. And besides, we don't know that he ever did anything."

"Just the same, Momma, I'm relieved." Robert could tell his mother still wasn't pleased. "I know, Momma. I'm not happy Junior's dead. I'm just relieved that I don't have to worry about my little girl."

"Well, son, there's still plenty to worry about."

"What do you mean?"

"Well, I'm not sure what Janelle's gonna do. She hasn't worked since y'all got married. I don't think she wants to move back in with her daddy, and he don't have much anyway."

"I don't think she'll want to get too far away from Mr. Pierce, Momma. She'll find something to do." Robert took a sip of coffee. "She could always get an apartment in Savannah and work in a department store or something."

"Maybe. But then there's this business about Barry."

"Momma, that's all Mr. White's blow. Barry Daniel would never do anything like that."

"I know, Bobby. But why's he been gone since right after the accident?"

"I don't know. I'll try to call his ex-wife and see if she knows anything."

"You know the police already talked to her."

"That's what Darlene said." Robert took another sip of coffee and, as if to signal a change of subject, carefully, and somewhat formally, placed his mug back onto the table. "Momma, I need to ask you a question." She looked at him and waited. "Do you think I should go to the memorial service tomorrow?"

"Oh, I don't know, sweetheart. Mr. White is even stranger than Junior was. And you know Mr. Pierce. He's been strange ever since his wife died."

"I just want Janelle to see me. I want to remind her that I'm still here, and I'm still Ellie's father, regardless of what she thinks of me."

"Are you sure about that?" she asked.

"I don't know, Momma. I've been confused about so many things lately. Something just tells me I should go."

"Son, if you're worried she's gonna run off with the first man who shows her attention, don't be. I'd be surprised if she ever marries again."

"Why do you say that?"

"I don't know. It's just a feelin'." A genuine Ruth Clark smile finally appeared. "You're the one who said I have a sixth sense."

"I hope you're right, Momma. Ellie doesn't need any more turmoil in her life."

"Well, if you're set on goin' to the memorial service, do you want me to go with you?"

"No. You need to take care of Ellie, don't you? I'll go, and if things get testy, I'll just leave."

On Sunday morning Ruth fixed breakfast, and then she and Ellie left for church. Robert was anxious about the memorial service, so he busied himself by cleaning the kitchen, ironing his shirt, and polishing his shoes. Those everyday tasks turned his thoughts to his childhood. He poured another cup of coffee and walked from room to room, sipping his coffee and examining the house as if he were a stranger.

Reminders of the love they had for each other were everywhere. His sister's room was just as it had been for years. Pictures of her in her high school cheerleader's uniform and cap and gown were on the bureau, and the magazine rack he'd made in shop class for her eighteenth birthday still held old copies of *Seventeen* magazine. The walls of his room were covered with the awards and certificates he'd received growing up: delegate to Boys State, 4-H awards and ribbons, his Boy Scout merit badges in a shadow box his mother had put together when he made Eagle Scout. Only his parents' bedroom was different. The changes his mother had made reminded him of how, in her own quiet way, she had coped with losing the love of her life.

I don't know how Momma does it, he thought. Despite all their hardships, she and Daddy gave us a wonderful life, and just when they thought they might be able to take a breath, relax, slow down, and retire, he was taken from her. How does she go on after that—after losing the love of her life? If only I'd had a marriage like that, none of this would have happened. There would have been no divorce, no Junior, no Janelle and Ellie involved with God-knows-what kind of family. I've made a mess of so many things.

# CHAPTER TWENTY-NINE

THE THOMPSON FUNERAL Home was in a converted residence that could have been a movie set from *Gone with the Wind*. The only time Robert had been inside was when he came to the viewing for his father several years earlier. The place smelled the same as he remembered—stale and musty. It was too cold outside to open any windows. The floors creaked beneath rugs that had probably been laid out before he was born.

He made his way to the room where Junior's casket was on display but didn't enter. Through the door, he surveyed the room to see who was there, recognizing only a few. Janelle was seated near the casket. She looked pretty, though her expression was weary and strained. She had on a stylish blue dress and was wearing the pearls he'd given her as a Christmas present when they lived in Panama. Deciding it was a bad idea to be there, Robert turned to leave.

"What do you think you're doing here?" It was Junior's father, so close Robert could smell tobacco and bourbon on his breath. He must have just returned from a smoke—and maybe a drink—outside. "I know who you are."

Before Robert could say anything, Janelle's father joined them. "You need to leave, Bobby. You got no call to be here. You're not welcome."

"Mr. Pierce, I—"

"You heard him, Clark," Junior's father spluttered. "You need to get on out of here. And don't be surprised if the police want to talk to you. They're still lookin' for your friend Barry Daniel. I heard you two was hangin' out before Daniel worked on Junior's car."

"Now, Rodney. This ain't the place to get into all that," Mr. Pierce said, putting his arm around Rodney to move him away. He turned back toward Robert. "Like I said, you need to get outta here."

Robert said nothing and hurried to the front door. It had begun to rain, so he ran to his mother's car, fell into the driver's seat, and started the engine but then paused to catch his breath. The rain pounded the roof of the car; wind gusts gave the sound a rhythmic quality. Water collected in large drops on the windows like thousands of glass beads, refracting the light and obscuring his view. A hand slammed against the driver's side window. Robert jolted straight up. He strained to see the face of the dark form outside the car. As he rolled down the window, the phantom spoke: "You was told to get out of here. That was a pass. Take advantage of it and go. There won't be another." Before Robert could say anything, the shadowy figure turned and left. Shifting the car into gear, he backed up and then drove away.

As soon as Robert walked through the back door, his mother, seated at the kitchen table with a cup of coffee, could tell something was wrong. "Are you okay, Bobby?"

"Yes, Momma. It was just as you expected." He shook the rain off his coat and hung it on a hook by the door. "I didn't even go in the viewing room. Junior's father saw me, said I wasn't welcome, and told me to leave. Mr. Pierce was there, too. He backed him up."

"Well now, son, you're the one who first told me that Janelle's father was strange. And I warned you about Rodney White. He's even worse."

"You did. And, as usual, I should have listened to you. It was a bad idea to go up there." Robert poured a cup of coffee and sat down. "You know, Momma, up close Mr. White is even stranger than Junior was. His clothes looked like he'd been sleeping in 'em. His hair was long and greasy; he hadn't shaved; and yet there he was at his son's memorial service. I think he and Mr. Pierce had been outside drinking on that back porch. They were coming back in, just as I was leaving. Mr. White had a real evil look in his eyes." Robert paused when he noticed the concerned expression on his mother's face.

"Don't say anymore, Bobby. I don't want to think about those men."

"I'm sorry, Momma. I didn't mean to upset you." He leaned over and kissed her forehead. "I'm kinda tired. I think I'm gonna go to bed." He didn't want his mother to start using that sixth sense of hers and somehow learn of his encounter in the parking lot. She had enough to worry about.

# CHAPTER THIRTY

A STACK OF pink message slips in the center of his desk caught Robert's eye as he walked into his office on Tuesday morning. Three were from Donna, Davis Burnet's secretary, asking Robert to call Davis as soon as possible. They were dated Saturday, February 14. Eight more were dated Monday, February 16. Those were from his secretary, Carolyn, referencing calls from Donna, telling Robert to see Davis as soon as possible. I guess the firm doesn't observe Presidents' Day, he thought.

"Where have you been?" Carolyn barked, sounding every bit like a female drill sergeant.

"I had to go to a funeral in Pemberton."

"Well, you should've told me. Mr. Burnet's been looking for you since Saturday. Donna says he's really upset."

Robert shuffled through the message slips. "Saturday was Valentine's Day." Carolyn just looked at him with an I'm-glad-I'm-not-you smile. "And the office was open yesterday?"

"Of course," she replied. "Why wouldn't it be?"

"I thought it'd be closed for Presidents' Day."

"Didn't you look at the firm personnel manual? It lists the firm holidays."

"I guess not carefully enough, Carolyn," he replied, pushing back a bit.

"Well, you need to see Mr. Burnet right away." She spun on her heel and walked out, leaving Robert with the feeling that she was somehow on a different team—the firm team, perhaps—and he wasn't. He located his Russell litigation files and a legal pad and headed to Davis's office.

"Where have you been, Robert?" Davis asked, his gray eyes squinting in disbelief.

If Carolyn had sounded like a drill sergeant, Davis sounded like a pissed off brigade commander.

"I went home for a funeral."

"To Georgia again?"

"Yes, sir."

"Well, I'm sorry for your family's loss, Robert, but you should've told someone. I needed you on Saturday, and no one knew where you were yesterday."

"I'm sorry, Davis. I thought yesterday was a holiday."

"We're not the government, Robert. We're in the business of making money. Now, have you thoroughly examined the documents I provided you? Are there any of them that we don't have to produce to opposing counsel pursuant to their discovery request?"

"Yes. I think so."

"Well, I don't need an equivocal answer. I need to know for certain. When I couldn't find you on Saturday, I had Diana Maguire help me. She was the only associate I could find in the office. Get with her and Donna and ensure everything is ready to submit to opposing counsel and that we're certain of what we don't have to produce." Davis looked down at the papers on his desk and waved his hand, dismissing Robert without looking up.

After checking with Donna, who assured him that Diana had all the documents, he headed downstairs to her office.

"Knock, knock." Robert stood in the doorway of Diana's office, feeling like a kid summoned to see the principal.

She looked up, and, for a moment, her incredible, made-for-TV smile made him forget how much trouble he was in.

"Come in and shut the door." Shaking her head, she continued, "Why did you take off and not tell anyone where you were going? I was worried. I even called Alan."

"I thought Monday was a holiday. I guess I should've checked the personnel manual." He exhaled heavily. "Anyway, I needed to go to a funeral in Pemberton."

"Oh my gosh," she said, touching her throat. "What happened? Who died?"

"My ex-wife's boyfriend."

"The guy who was—"

"Yeah. That guy. Apparently, he drove off the road and hit a tree. Thank God he was by himself and no other cars were involved."

Diana squinted as she asked, "Why on earth did you want to go to *his* funeral?"

"I don't know, Diana. I guess I was worried about my daughter and how my ex might react. A dumb decision, I know."

"How's your ex taking it?"

"I didn't even get to talk to her. Things got tense at the funeral home, so I left. She and Ellie are going to move back in with her father."

"Well, you have a lot on your plate here, so let me bring you up to speed about this weekend." She reached for a stack of files on the side of her desk. "I looked at the documents in the file and your memo concerning the ones we should not produce to opposing counsel pursuant to their request for documents. I didn't see anything I disagreed with, but I did find something missing."

"What's that?"

"Well," she began, her expression suddenly serious, "there was a letter in one of Davis's files that wasn't in the file of documents he gave you to review. It was from Scott & Cranston, a small investment bank in Dallas, dated sometime in December. I don't remember when exactly."

"I remember that letter. It came in while Davis was on vacation. He was just cc'ed on it, right?" Robert looked out the window, his brows furrowed. "But Davis said he gave me all the correspondence related to the Russell matter." Turning back to Diana, he continued, "Come to think of it, Scott & Cranston is who Davis told me to arrange for Lewis Johnson to hire."

"Johnson? You mean the independent director the board appointed to evaluate Mr. Russell's tender offer?"

The tone of Diana's voice ratcheted up Robert's anxiety, and then clarity struck him like a thunderbolt.

"That's a problem, isn't it?" he said.

"It could be a big problem. The letter was to Mr. Russell, and you're right: Davis was cc'ed. Scott & Cranston was informing Mr. Russell that he could offer as much as $13.00 per share for the publicly traded shares of Russell Field Services."

"But he's only offering ten," Robert said, rubbing his forehead. "He doesn't have to offer more, does he?"

"No. But why is Scott & Cranston advising both Mr. Russell and the director who's supposed to be making an independent evaluation of Mr. Russell's bid? And why would that letter be privileged anyway? It's not an attorney-client communication."

"Yeah, I see what you mean." Robert looked out the window again. "They're advising both damn sides—essentially evaluating their own work. Do you know if Mr. Johnson has reported to the board yet?"

"I doubt it," she said. "Davis would probably have had you draft a resolution for the board or something like that." She put her elbows onto the desk and cradled her chin on her fingers. In almost a whisper, she said, "I'd be careful, Robert. There might be some funny business going on."

He exhaled sharply. "What do I do now?"

"I don't know. I guess you need to ask Davis about it. Maybe he has a reason he thinks the letter's privileged. Maybe he forgot about it when he gave you the documents to review or when he told you to get Johnson to hire Scott & Cranston."

"He doesn't miss much, Diana."

"Well, that's the only open issue I found. The rest of it looks fine. You did a good job."

"Thanks." Robert shook his head. "Damn it," he groaned. "I guess I've got to go talk to Davis again."

On his way to Davis's office, he was confronted by Carolyn, who stopped him in the hallway. "Did you know that a Mr. Thomas Jackson is waiting for you in the Crockett Conference Room?"

"No. Who's Thomas Jackson?"

"I don't know, Robert." She sounded exasperated. "He told the receptionist that he was supposed to meet with you, so she told him to wait in the conference room."

"Okay. Would you check on him and tell him I'll be right there? I need to go see Davis first."

Davis's door was closed, and Donna explained that he was on a conference call, so Robert decided to leave him a note:

*I've checked with Donna and Diana and have confirmed that all the documents we intend to produce are responsive and not privileged. Diana agrees with me on the ones that should not be produced because they're attorney-client privileged communications.*

*There might be another document we should produce, however. It's a letter to Mr. Russell from Scott & Cranston, dated back in December. You were copied on it. In it they advise Mr. Russell on the price he should offer for the publicly traded shares.*

*Please let me know if you want to speak further. I've been told that a client named Thomas Jackson is waiting for me in the Crockett Room.*

Robert put the note in an envelope and asked Donna to give it to Davis as soon as possible.

Mr. Jackson was looking out the window when Robert entered the room. He was wearing what was obviously a custom-tailored suit, although it was not a staid blue or gray, which were commonplace around the office. Instead, it was a brown glen plaid with double vents in the back, like one might see in London. The collar of his shirt was French blue. As he turned around, Robert was dumbstruck. The hair was longer and sprinkled with gray, but the smile was unmistakable. Somehow, for some reason, Captain Elmer T. Jackson had shown up at Underwood & Crockett in Dallas, Texas.

"Oh my God. What in the hell are you doing here, Elmer?"

"Good morrnning, Counselor," Elmer grinned, stretching out the word "morning" as was his trademark greeting in Panama.

"How the heck did you find me?" Robert asked, still trying to process seeing his buddy from Panama after so many years.

"I have my ways, Counselor. I wouldn't mind a cup of coffee. Been smelling it while I was waiting."

Robert poured two cups—black, of course—and sat down. "So, how've you been, Elmer? What's it been? Four years?"

"Almost five. And it's been unbelievable, partner. But now I use my middle name: 'Thomas.' But buddies like you call me 'Tom.' Thomas is too formal, and Elmer's long gone. I seem to remember you didn't like the name Elmer, even though that's your middle name, right?"

"Now, Elmer, I mean Tom, I didn't mean any—"

"Oh, bullshit, Clark. You can't fool me. You thought it sounded redneck, didn't you?"

"Well, maybe, I—"

"Yeah. Well, I found out real quick you were right about that, when I got out of the Army and started selling life insurance. I decided 'E. Thomas Jackson' sounds more professional than 'Elmer T. Jackson'. "

Robert stared at his old friend in disbelief. "I can't believe you're here, Elm—, I mean Tom. You look great. It's amazing to see you after all these years." Robert was reluctant to pursue a sensitive topic but decided to forge ahead. "How'd your marriage situation work out?"

"It worked out." Tom's blue eyes sparkled. "Tracy's the best thing that ever happened to me. I went back to Fort Benning after Panama and threw myself at her mercy. She was skeptical, you know, but she gave me a chance."

"No shit," Robert said. "You and Jaime were a pretty rowdy twosome."

"Rowdy? Hell, we were crazy. Well, I've turned the page on all that. So did Jaime, by the way. He and his wife are back together, too."

"Yeah. I saw them together before I left Panama."

Tom's expression turned solemn, as if to respect his next topic. "I understand things didn't work out for you and, uh, Janelle, right?"

"No, they didn't. But it's probably for the best. I don't think we were really right for each other."

"Ol' Watkins had that pegged. She said you and your wife were a complete mismatch. Said she couldn't understand why you married her."

"Watkins talked about me like that?"

"I think she had the hots for you." Tom's devilish grin was back.

"Bullshit."

"Now, Clark—"

Robert held up his hand. "You're not the only one who's changed his name. I go by 'Robert' now. Thank you very much."

"Well, Robert." Tom said each word with staccato precision. "Let me just say that my life is nothing like it was in Panama. No. It's more than that. You see, I figured out that I'm an alcoholic, just like my old man, although unlike him, I'm sober and have been since I came back to the States. I don't care if other people drink, mind you. It's just not right for me."

"My hat's off to you, Tom," Robert said.

"And Tracy took me back." Tom's eyes brightened, and Robert thought he detected the glistening that comes before tears. "She'd gotten active in her church by the time I got back to Columbus, so I started going, too. They had an AA group that I started going to. And, I guess this time it sorta stuck."

"What do you mean?"

"You remember I told you I went to Oral Roberts University, don't you? Back then, all that stuff was just a bunch of nice-sounding words. But when Tracy forgave me for all the hell I put her through, I knew there must be something powerful in it. So, believe it or not, I've been walking the straight and narrow and trying to be a good dad to Sally, Jessica, and Amanda. In fact, let me show you some pictures."

Just then, the door to the conference room swung open and in strode Davis Burnet. Robert stood up and cringed in anticipation of a reprimand from his boss in front of his old friend.

"Thomas Jackson. It is indeed an honor, sir," Davis said, extending his hand.

"And who might you be?" Tom asked.

"I'm sorry, Tom," Robert said. "I should have introduced you. This is my boss, Davis Burnet."

"Well, pleased to meet you, Davis. I guess you know you have a helluva lawyer here," Tom said, gesturing toward Robert.

"We think so, Thomas. How do you two know each other?"

Tom grinned. "He used to keep me out of trouble in Panama."

"Oh, so you're Army buddies."

"You could say that, although I'd say it goes much deeper, wouldn't you, Robert?" There was a sarcastic lilt to Tom's voice that Robert hoped Davis didn't notice. "No, seriously, Davis. We're very close. Robert and I conducted all sorts of operations together. There was a lot going on in Central America back then."

"Mind if I join you for a moment?" Davis asked, as he and the other two sat down. "Robert, you should have told me you knew the founder of one of the largest term life insurance companies in the U.S."

"I've got to correct you there," Tom said. "We're *the* largest term life insurance company in the U.S."

"Quite an accomplishment. Did I read in the *The Wall Street Journal* that you only formed the company four years ago?"

"You're quite astute, Davis. But actually, I bought the company and built it up."

Damn! Robert thought. Is Tom tweaking Davis, or is he serious?

"What I found out, Davis, is that most companies have no leadership. There's no mission, no strategy, no courses of action to achieve objectives. I simply took what the Army taught me and applied it to business."

"Amazing," Davis said. "Well, what brings you to Underwood & Crockett? Just reminiscing with Robert?"

"Oh no. I want to hire him to help me sell my company."

Robert and Davis were stunned to silence as Tom cocked his head from one side and then the next, his trademark grin on full display.

"Well normally, Thomas, I would supervise a project of that magnitude—"

"Let me stop you there, Davis," Tom said, holding up his hand like a traffic cop. "I'm only here because I trust this man implicitly. Otherwise, I would be at one of the Atlanta firms that have gotten more of my money than I care to think about." Tom pointed to Robert and paused to let the importance and authority of his comment register with both of them. "I've seen him in action, and I want him to run this deal. He can involve any of your other lawyers he wants to, but he needs to run this deal. And, it's going to be around a hundred-fifty-million-dollar deal if everything goes well."

Robert almost choked on a sip of coffee. Davis set his cup down and sat up straight in the chair, a dazed look on his face.

"Uh, of, of course, Thomas. It's important to know you're in good hands. And, we certainly have confidence in Robert. But a deal of this magnitude will require a team of lawyers to—"

"That's fine, Davis, but Robert runs it."

"Of course. But we'll need to have a partner on the engagement."

"That's fine." Tom smiled and shook his head. "You know, Davis, we have a lot of catching up to do. Would you mind if I get back to you later on the details of the engagement?"

"Oh, uh, no, not at all, Thomas." Davis stood up and turned to Robert. "I saw your note, Robert, and that looks fine. I'll talk to you about that later. Nice meeting you, Thomas."

As soon as the door closed, Robert leaned in. "What the hell, Elm—, I mean Tom? You're a famous business tycoon, now?"

"I'm sorely disappointed you haven't kept up with my exploits, Robert."

Tom sounded just as Robert remembered Elmer sounding—simultaneously mocking and grandiloquent—just as he had when he kept a bevy of lieutenants enthralled with tales of Ranger school and other Army exploits.

"Well now, in fairness, Tom, I never connected E. Thomas Jackson with Captain Elmer T. Jackson. And besides, between work and dealing with my absurd divorce, I didn't have time to read the *Wall Street Journal*."

"I'm just messin' with you, Robert. We weren't in the news much. I'm surprised Davis had read about us. But I am serious about you running this deal."

"I don't know, Elmer." Robert was so flustered he forgot his friend was now "Tom." He shook his head. "This is a big deal, even for Underwood & Crockett, and I haven't been in civilian practice that long."

"Yeah, but I trust you. And you know bullshit when you see it. You can do this. Just like you tried that murder case in Panama. You remember you were worried about that, and I told you you could do it. Right?"

"You're right. And I'm honored that you have that much confidence in me. You know I'll give it my best." Robert took a sip of coffee and relaxed in his chair. "Now you've *got* to tell me how you built a hundred-fifty-million-dollar company in four years."

There was a knock at the door and Carolyn appeared. "Mr. Burnet asked me to see if you want to have lunch brought in."

"I can't stay for lunch, Robert. I need to get back to Tracy."

"No thank you, Carolyn," Robert said. "Thanks for checking."

"As I was saying, Robert, it was easier than you think. When I got out of the Army, I started selling life insurance. It didn't take long to figure out that they didn't know what the hell they were doing. I developed the concept of telling people they should buy term insurance and invest the rest. Most people pay a bunch of money for whole life insurance that isn't worth a damn. They'd be much better off buying term insurance and investing what they would have otherwise spent on premiums."

"But surely other folks knew that, too."

"They did, and they do. But they believe the insurance company bullshit. I didn't. And, I knew how to lead and motivate people. We kicked ass. Most of my guys were new to the industry. They didn't have anything to unlearn. No bad habits. They just did what I told them to do. And, we focused on military folks—senior NCOs and officers. We talked their language. We sold so much insurance I was able to buy a small life insurance company and move all my sales force to it. Sales took off. As long as you treat people fairly, get rid of those who don't want to work, and put God first, you can't fail."

"That's an incredible story. I'm really proud of you, Tom. And I'm really happy your marriage worked out."

"Well, I'm proud of you, too. Underwood & Crockett is a hell of a firm. I'm sure you're gonna do big things here. As for my deal: just make me a bunch of money, and we'll go celebrate. Now, however, I need to get going. Tracy's at that fancy mall you have here in Dallas. Northpark, right? I need to get back to her before she spends whatever I might make on this deal."

Robert walked Tom to the door and then went back to his office. No sooner had he sat down at his desk than he heard a familiar voice.

"How in the hell do you know Thomas Jackson?" It was Alan Taylor with a look of disbelief on his face.

"We were in Panama together."

"You do realize he founded one of the most successful life insurance companies in the country?"

"So I've heard. How'd you know he was here?"

"Are you kidding? The whole firm's talking about it. Davis has been crowing about how the Atlanta firms will be annoyed that we're handling the sale of a company based in Georgia."

"Is it that big a deal?"

"Are you kidding? Of course it is. And listen, man, whatever problems you might be having with Davis won't matter now. This could be your ticket, Robert."

"I'm not looking for a 'ticket,' Alan. I just want to do a good job for an old friend."

"Well, if you need a litigator's help, call me. This is good news."

# CHAPTER THIRTY-ONE

TWO DAYS AFTER Tom Jackson's visit, Robert was sitting in his office, staring out the window at a cityscape that resembled an old black-and-white photograph. It was as if the overcast winter sky had sucked out all the color. The gloom was so profound he could feel it draining his energy. Fear had eroded the excitement of seeing his old friend. Six months in private practice hardly qualified him to manage the sale of Tom's company. He knew he wasn't up to that task. And, of course, he was worried about Davis Burnet. Was he falling short of Davis's expectations? More important, was Davis up to something unethical? If not, why had he been so keen on having Scott & Cranston advise Mr. Johnson? And why had he withheld the letter Diana found in his files concerning the financial advice Scott & Cranston had given Mr. Russell?

Sensing there were eyes on him, he turned to see Diana Maguire, her expression so positive, so dazzling, it pushed back the gloom.

"Well, well, Mr. Clark. You are quite the celebrity. Who would've thought you were buddies with someone like Thomas Jackson."

"That was a long time ago, Diana." With that reminder of his most recent source of stress, the gloom returned. He motioned to a chair before shuffling behind his desk and collapsing into his own.

"Well, the firm is buzzing," she continued. "The word is you're going to assist him in selling his company."

Robert just stared at her, wondering whether she realized how inadequate and overwhelmed he felt.

"What's wrong, Robert? You should be happy. You *are* a celebrity—of sorts, anyway."

Robert reached into his drawer and pulled out a tattered piece of paper. "Let me read something to you." Holding the paper in front of him, he read aloud:

*Fame is an illusive thing –*
*here today, gone tomorrow. The fickle, shallow mob raises its heroes to*
*the pinnacle of approval today and hurls them into oblivion tomorrow*
*at the slightest whim; cheers today, hisses tomorrow; utter forgetful-*
*ness in a few months.*

"That's depressing. Who wrote it?"

"Henry Miller."

"The guy who wrote those sexually explicit novels?" Her nose wrinkled in disgust.

"Yeah. But they're tame by today's standards. Anyway, I think he nails it. It's something I had to learn the hard way."

"You keep that in your desk?" She squinted her eyes and cocked her head.

"It's a habit I picked up from a boss I had in the Army. Keep reminders around of important lessons in life." Robert carefully slipped the paper back into the drawer. "Fame. Celebrity. Recognition. Distinction. None of them are worth a damn thing."

"You don't seem like the type who chases fame," she said.

"Not now. But I had to learn that lesson the hard way."

"So what are you worried about, then?"

"I have a dear friend who doesn't understand that I'm totally unqualified to help him sell his company, and Davis is clearly interested in having that friend as a client. And then there's that damn letter you found, which Davis should have produced in discovery. We could be subject to all sorts of court sanctions for that, couldn't we? Not to mention that it's unethical."

"Slow down, Robert. First of all, if you haven't discussed the letter with Davis, you don't know whether he has a good reason for not producing it. And, with respect to your deal, we always do these projects with a team of lawyers. You'll have all the help you need."

"Yeah, but Elm—I mean Tom wants *me* to run the deal. He thinks I'll protect his interests, but I don't have a clue of how to do that."

"Davis can help you, can't he?"

"I'm not sure I want him to, Diana. Besides, he's consumed with the Russell shareholder litigation."

"You could talk to Sharon." Diana studied his face for a reaction.

"I thought about that," he said, eyebrows raised. He knew what she was thinking. "Do you think she'd help me?"

"Come on, Robert. What does she have to do to convince you?" Diana's look was stern but not annoyed. "But your friend Alan won't approve."

"My job is to do a good job for Tom. That's all I care about."

"Well, start by talking with Sharon. You should also check the associate files. I think there are several memos and task lists that would be useful in organizing the work. And, you'll need insurance regulatory help, too."

"Oh, yeah, I—"

"Right. I'm not sure what the rules are in Georgia, but Sharon will know what to do." Diana stood to leave. "And I hope you know that I'll help you in any way I can."

"Thanks, Diana. I'll see if Sharon will see me this afternoon."

"Congratulations, Robert." Sharon, elegant as always, was sitting at her desk, a vase of fresh flowers behind her on her credenza. "This is exciting news. What can I do for you?"

"Well, Tom Jackson and I served together in Panama, and now he wants me to handle the sale of his company simply because he trusts me. But I'm afraid he doesn't understand how little I know."

"Don't be too quick to discount the importance of trust, Robert. It will enable you to manage the sale process much better, because Mr. Jackson will trust what you tell him."

"But that's just it, Sharon. I don't know what to tell him."

"No lawyer knows how to deal with every issue that arises in a transaction. That's why we use teams. If you're a good manager, you can manage that team. However, you *will* need team members who will accept you as the leader."

"I don't even know who that would be."

Sharon's eyes narrowed as she smiled. "Let me give it some thought. I helped a client sell an insurance company a few years ago. If you want me to, I'd be glad to help you."

"That would be fabulous, Sharon." Robert paused a moment to reflect. "But I should warn you: the Tom I knew in Panama was a bit rough around the edges. Don't get me wrong: he's a good guy, but he's not exactly what I'd call open-minded. He does seem to have turned over a new leaf, but I don't know for sure. He's now kind of religious, too."

"Don't worry, Robert." Sharon knew what he was getting at. "I can handle myself. And anyway, you'll be the one talking to him most of the time, not me." She looked at him in almost the same manner he'd seen her look at Diana. "Now, let me give you a few suggestions. Take this down."

For the next half hour Sharon gave him a detailed roadmap for planning and organizing the legal work that needed to be done to sell Tom Jackson's company. She suggested attorneys at Underwood & Crockett who she thought should be on the team, and she even knew a lawyer in Atlanta who could help with the insurance regulators in Georgia. Although Robert left her office feeling as if a weight had been lifted off him, his good mood was short-lived.

"You need to let me know where you're going to be, Robert." Carolyn sounded annoyed. "Mr. Burnet wants to see you."

Gloom enveloped him again as he trudged up the stairs to Davis's office.

"Carolyn didn't know where you were, Robert. Let's not make that a habit," Davis said, though he didn't seem irritated—perhaps because he was thinking about getting Thomas Jackson as a new client. "We'll need to ensure we don't have a conflict in representing your friend and his company. Did he say who he thinks the likely buyer will be? We represent a number of large insurance companies, so that might create a conflict that would prevent us from representing him. But if it turns out there is no conflict which I hope will be the case—then I need to be the billing attorney on the file because the firm rules require that role to be filled by a partner. But rest assured, you'll receive due credit."

Robert cleared his throat. "If it's okay, Davis, I'd like to have Sharon Alexander be the billing attorney." He sat down in front of Davis's desk.

"Sharon?"

"Yes. I thought you were pretty busy with Mr. Russell's litigation, so I consulted her on how to get organized. She was extremely helpful."

"Oh. Well. Okay." Davis's jaw jutted out a bit. He nodded, as if accepting something he didn't like. "Of course. Sharon is a good choice. She's a fine lawyer. And if I remember correctly, she sold an insurance company for one of our clients a couple of years ago." Davis paused for a moment and then looked intently at Robert. "I didn't realize you were still doing work for her."

"Well, I'm, uh, I'm not actually. You've been keeping me pretty busy after all." Robert half-smiled and studied Davis's face, looking for a reaction. As usual, he was inscrutable.

His focus still on Robert, Davis continued, "I wanted to let you know that we're going to be in court on Monday on the Russell matter. We'll be in front of Judge Carter, so I've asked Alan to assist me. Hugh Williams said he did a good job in front of Judge Carter on a matter that I believe you said you assisted with as well—the one involving Randy Donaldson and that crazy CEO he had."

What is Davis talking about? Robert thought. Alan didn't do anything in court other than sit at the counsel table. And all Hugh Williams ultimately did was buy the crazy CEO off with a $50,000 settlement on what should have been a clear winner for our client.

Davis was still talking. "So, I need for you to brief Alan and get him up to speed on our case. He needs to be prepared to respond to a motion to compel filed by counsel for one of the shareholders."

"What's the substance of the motion?"

Davis's gaze shifted up and to his right. For a moment Robert wondered if someone had entered the door behind him. Was Davis trying to remember something or come up with a response?

"It's a… It's a motion to compel disclosure."

"Anything in particular?"

"Correspondence, I believe." Davis was now looking down at the documents on his desk—the mannerism he used whenever he wanted to conclude a meeting and send Robert on his way. This time, Robert persisted.

"Does it involve that letter from Scott & Cranston?"

"You'll have to be more specific, Robert."

"The letter to Mr. Russell." Davis gave him a look that said tread lightly. "The letter to Mr. Russell concerning how much he should offer for the publicly traded shares. I believe it was $13.00 per share."

"I'm not sure what you're talking about, Robert."

"You know the letter. It's the one I mentioned in the note I left you when I went to meet with Thomas Jackson. Scott & Cranston copied you on the letter to Mr. Russell. It came in while you were on your ski trip."

"Yes. Well, I don't recall that. I had another associate remove anything he thought was privileged before I gave you the files. Just tell Alan to look through the files. And tell him that Donna can help him with that. Everything he needs should be in there. Now, if you'll excuse me, I need to get back to reviewing this document."

Robert left, wondering whether he should have pressed harder. He went straight to Alan's office where he found him hunched over his desk, surrounded by stacks of files.

"You look busy," Robert said, standing in the doorway. "Davis told me to stop by and see if you needed anything in connection with your hearing on Monday."

Alan looked up and motioned for him to sit down. "Well, I think I have a handle on things." He was all smiles. "See, you thought that silly little Donaldson case with the crazy CEO was good for nothing. But that's what got me this assignment. And this is what's going to get me selected for partner early. Davis takes care of people who take care of him."

Robert shrugged. "What's the substance of the motion?"

"Oh, plaintiff's counsel says we haven't produced all the documents we're supposed to in discovery. But I've looked through the files and can't find anything for them to complain about."

"So, Donna's already given you all the files?"

"Yeah. She brought them to me this morning. There's not much in here."

"Did you see a letter from Scott & Cranston to Mr. Russell advising him on how much he could pay for the publicly traded shares?"

"A letter concerning what?"

"How much he could offer for the publicly traded shares."

Alan's eyebrows pressed together. "No. I haven't seen anything like that."

"Are you sure? I remember it came in while Davis was on his ski vacation. It should be in the correspondence file. Diana saw it, too."

"Diana? Diana Maguire? What's she involved with this for?"

"She was helping Davis while I was in Georgia. She came across the same letter."

"Well, she's not a litigator. Besides, I doubt if she looked through the files as carefully as I have. Donna assured me this morning that she'd brought me everything. And I haven't found anything like that."

Robert had a sinking feeling the letter from Scott & Cranston had not so mysteriously disappeared. But what now? He hadn't made a copy, and neither had Diana. And Alan certainly didn't want to talk with Diana.

"I'm sure I saw that letter, Alan," Robert said, shaking his head. "But I don't know what to tell you. It should be in the correspondence file. I don't know why it wouldn't be."

"Could you be confusing it with another case? I mean... That was months ago."

"I don't think so. The letter had a detailed analysis of Scott & Cranston's valuation of Mr. Russell's company, and it said he could offer as much as $13.00 per share."

"Well, I can only work with what I have, and I don't have any such letter. And I don't need you and Diana confusing things."

This conversation is going nowhere, Robert thought. I'm not sure Alan even wants to know about that letter. See no evil... I can't believe Davis would have destroyed it, especially after the minority shareholders filed their lawsuit.

Robert stood to leave. "Okay. Well, good luck on Monday. Let me know if you need anything from me."

"Listen. Let's go to Javier's tomorrow night," Alan suggested. "Just you and me."

"Javier's?"

"Don't tell me you don't know about Javier's. It's the best Mexican restaurant in Dallas."

"Dallas has no shortage of Mexican restaurants."

"No. This is no dump. It's high-end Mexican. And it has the coolest bar, including a cigar humidor. But the best thing is there's a tremendous amount of talent that comes strolling through there."

"So, I take it you're over Michelle."

"Of course. I knew that whole thing was bullshit." Alan's eyes widened. "But we did have some fun at her daddy's beach house, didn't we?"

Robert just smiled and shook his head. "Okay. Javier's it is. I'll just follow you there after work."

❦

Alan wasn't kidding about Javier's. A Ferrari was conspicuously parked out front next to a sign that said "Proprietor." Inside, it seemed as though they had been transported to Mexico City. Javier himself was there, impeccably attired in a gray suit and burgundy tie—probably from Culwell & Son. With his wavy black hair slicked back in dramatic fashion, he strolled through the bar, chatted with customers, and generally played the role of the gracious, elegant host. Hemingway would have felt right at home. Exotic animal trophies hung on the walls, evidence of the days when collecting them had been Javier's hobby. And there were other trophies—of sorts. Gorgeous, young, fashionably attired women were seated at the bar and in large leather chairs in the cozy corners of the room, apparently unfazed by the cigar smoke that hung in the air.

"What was I telling you? Is this place cool, or what?" Alan was in his element.

"It's impressive, all right. Are these women looking to get picked up?"

"Probably. But be careful, my friend. They're used to high-rollers who drop C-notes like they're Hamiltons."

"I'm content just to take in the eye candy," Robert said.

They settled into a corner where they had a good view of the scene. A waiter with a white shirt, black vest, and black bow tie took their order for drinks—and cigars. In a few minutes he returned with their drinks and, with elaborate fanfare, lit their Montecristo No. 2s.

After Alan's second single malt scotch took effect, he turned toward Robert and, somewhat glassy-eyed, said, "I've been worried about you, my friend."

"I'm okay, Alan."

"No. No, you're not." His words were beginning to slur. "Davis says your performance is slipping. He says you're spending too much time running back to Georgia. I thought you put that shit behind you, man. Isn't that why you came to Texas? I stuck my neck out for you."

"What does he mean slipping? I've been busting my ass for him." Robert paused. "No. I know what this is about."

"It's not about your fucking letter, if that's what you're thinking," Alan said. "It's about you and Davis Burnet, the most important partner at the firm who says your performance is slipping. And Dude," Alan took another long drink, "you've got no race card to play."

"What do you mean by that?"

"C'mon, man. We both know they're not gonna mess with me. Can you see the headlines?" Alan held up his hands as if he were reading a marquee. "Renowned Texas firm discriminates against black Harvard Law grad. They don't want that shit. But you, white boy, don't have that card."

"Alan, I think the scotch is getting to you."

"Maybe, but it's the truth."

"Well, Davis wasn't complaining when Tom Jackson showed up," Robert said.

"Yeah. That Jackson thing is good for you." Alan took a long draw on his cigar, blew smoke rings, and then looked around the room to see if anyone noticed, especially those with cleavage on display. "Yeah. The Jackson thing is good for you. It could be your ticket. But you need to get other important people at the firm involved. Like Davis." Alan stared at an attractive woman walking by who was obviously checking him out and then turned back to Robert. "Look. Davis told me you want Sharon Alexander to be the billing partner. What I want to know is: Why the hell do you want that? What'd I tell you about her? She's nothing but trouble. And so is her lesbian lover Diana."

"Alan, you don't even know Diana. I don't think they have a relationship like that. And Sharon's private life is her business, isn't it? Why do you care?"

"She's an embarrassment to the firm, Robert."

Robert could see Alan was getting drunk. "Did you eat anything today?"

"Who needs to eat?" Alan's smile was borderline goofy.

"I just want to do a good job for an old friend, Alan. Sharon sold an insurance company a few years ago, so she has relevant experience."

"And she can't do a damn thing for your career. She's probably ruined any chance Diana had of making partner." He looked at Robert and took another long draw. "You think I don't know anything, but I do. I know Diana's a good lawyer, but the firm will never make her partner. One lesbian is enough."

"Can we just talk about something else? Look at all the lovely ladies in front of you. Doesn't that inspire you to think of something else?"

"You are right, *mi amigo.*" Alan smiled and tapped his cigar on the ash tray. "They *are* good-looking women, and it inspires me to get laid."

# CHAPTER THIRTY-TWO

"ALL RISE." THE bailiff sounded as if he were announcing the arrival of a king. "The Court of Dallas County is now in session, the Honorable James Carter presiding."

Alan Taylor arranged the documents on the table in front of him. This was the first time he'd gone solo in a court proceeding. He alone would be representing Mr. Daniel Russell, the longtime client of Davis Burnet, the most powerful partner at Underwood & Crockett. And Alan was convinced that this hearing was his ticket to becoming the first black partner at the firm. He felt ready to handle anything opposing counsel or the judge might throw at him.

Judge Carter grinned down from the bench like the Cheshire Cat. "Are counsel ready to proceed?"

"May it please the court, my name is Randolph Navarro. I am counsel for William Ramsey, the shareholder of Russell Field Services who is bringing this suit on behalf of the corporation against Daniel Russell and the other directors of Russell Field Services."

"So, this is a derivative action, Mr. Navarro?"

"Yes, Your Honor.

"Has your client filed a demand with the board of directors?"

"Yes, Your Honor, and the board has failed to act upon that demand."

"So, are you ready to proceed, Mr. Navarro?"

"May it please the court, I would like to ask the court's indulgence." Judge Carter nodded. "On Saturday, as my colleagues and I were preparing for this hearing, our client asked us to associate a lawyer with whom he has had a prior relationship."

"And who might that be?" Judge Carter asked.

"Mr. John Dickerson, Your Honor, who I believe has been before Your Honor previously."

"Indeed he has. Welcome, Mr. Dickerson. You may join your fellow counsel at his table."

Alan hadn't noticed Dickerson in the court room. Now, he watched him amble from the gallery through the railing, finally joining Navarro at his counsel table. Same swagger. Same flashy attire. Alan recalled how Dickerson's last-minute appearance before Judge Carter in the Donaldson matter had upended what should have been a routine proceeding. He ran his finger around the inside of his shirt collar as if it were too snug. His mouth was suddenly parched. Reaching for the water pitcher, he bumped it and spilled water onto his documents. Blotting them with a napkin, he looked up to see Judge Carter grinning at him.

"Are you ready to proceed, Mr. Taylor?"

"Yes, Your Honor."

"And you, Mr. Dickerson, will you be presenting on behalf of the plaintiff?"

"Yes, Your Honor."

"You may proceed."

"Your Honor, plaintiff has filed this motion to compel, because neither Mr. Russell nor any director of Russell Field Services has produced certain documents that plaintiff requested as part of pretrial discovery. Moreover, Your Honor, defendants have not claimed any privilege with respect to these documents—that is to say, they were not listed on the privilege log provided to plaintiff's counsel."

"What do you have to say, Mr. Taylor?"

"Your Honor, the attorneys at Underwood & Crockett painstakingly reviewed numerous documents in connection with plaintiff's discovery request and have produced 419 that are responsive and are not privileged. The privilege log to which Mr. Dickerson refers is a complete list of all documents that we believe are privileged, most of which are faxes and other correspondence between the firm and our clients, which are protected from discovery as attorney-client communications."

"Well, plaintiff is not alleging that you produced nothing, Mr. Taylor." Judge Carter peered over his reading glasses. "He's saying you left some things out. What do you have to say to that?"

"I am certain, Your Honor, given how carefully we reviewed plaintiff's request and our clients' documents, that we did not omit anything that should have been produced."

"You're sure of that?"

"Yes, Your Honor."

"Well, Mr. Dickerson, I realize you are new to this case, but Mr. Taylor says they provided you everything they were supposed to. Do you have any reason to doubt him?"

"We do, Your Honor."

"Well, let's hear it."

"Your Honor, we offer Plaintiff's Exhibit A, which is a photocopy of a letter from Scott & Cranston, addressed to Mr. Daniel Russell with a copy to Mr. Davis Burnet, who is a partner at Underwood & Crockett. The letter summarizes their valuation analysis of Russell Field Services and concludes that Mr. Russell could offer as much as $13 per share." Dickerson handed copies of the document to the judge and to Alan.

Alan reached for his water glass and took a sip. As he read the document he'd just been handed, he realized it was a copy of the letter Robert had been talking about.

Judge Carter took a couple of minutes to read the letter. Without looking up, he asked, "Do I remember correctly, Mr. Dickerson, that counsel's brief states that Mr. Russell has offered only $10 per share?"

With a smirk, Dickerson answered: "That's correct, Your Honor."

"Well, he didn't have to offer precisely what Scott & Cranston recommended, did he?" The judge appeared to be amused.

"No, Your Honor, he did not," Dickerson replied. "The reason this document is important is that the board of directors appointed a special committee to evaluate Mr. Russell's tender offer of $10 per share. That special committee was comprised of the only independent director on the board: Mr. Lewis Johnson. The other directors are Mr. Russell, his children, and his accountant. At the recommendation of the lawyers at Underwood & Crockett, Mr. Johnson also hired Scott & Cranston to advise him in connection with his evaluation of Mr. Russell's $10 offer. In other words, Your Honor, Scott & Cranston was on both sides: they advised both Mr. Russell and Mr. Johnson."

"Was their prior relationship with Mr. Russell disclosed to Mr. Johnson?"

"Based on the answers to our interrogatories, Your Honor, we do not believe it was."

"Well, that doesn't sound like an objective analysis to me." Judge Carter looked first at Dickerson and then Alan.

Every muscle in Alan's body began to tighten.

Dickerson continued, "What counsel did produce in discovery, Your Honor, is the report that Scott & Cranston provided Mr. Johnson, which concluded that an offer of $11 per share would be reasonable."

"Oh, I see." The judge turned his gaze back to Alan.

"Your Honor, this… this is, uh, the first time I've seen this letter." Alan stared at the document, hoping it would trigger a response. Nothing. "To respond to Mr. Dickerson's claim, Your Honor, I'll need to consult with other attorneys at Underwood & Crockett."

"I expect you to be prepared when you come to my court, Mr. Taylor. Unless Mr. Burnet did not, in fact, receive a copy of this letter, and was unaware of its existence, it should have been produced pursuant to plaintiff's discovery request. Moreover, your answers to plaintiff's interrogatories indicate that the prior relationship between your client and Scott & Cranston was not disclosed. I'm going to adjourn this hearing at this point. We will reconvene on Friday, February 27, at 9:00 a.m. At that time, Mr. Taylor, I expect you to have answers. Court's adjourned."

The gavel's impact, as it struck the bench, exploded in Alan's ears. *What in the hell have I gotten myself into? Where did they come up with that damn letter? And if Davis received it, why didn't he tell me? Robert saw it. He said Diana saw it, too.*

"See you Friday, Alan," Dickerson sneered as he strolled by. "Just like old times, right?"

Dickerson's slight, close-lipped smile made Alan want to rearrange his face with a quick left jab. He wanted to tell Dickerson just what he thought of him: that he is a lousy lawyer whose only value is his influence with Judge Carter. But then, Dickerson did have that damn letter. Where did he get it?

❧

Alan barged into Robert's office. "Do you have a copy of that god-damn letter?"

"What are you talking about?"

"I'm talking about that damn letter you said that Scott & Cranston sent to Davis. You said Diana saw it, too."

"No. I don't have a copy."

"Well, why the fuck not?" Alan glared at him in a way Robert had never seen before.

"What's going on, Alan?"

"I just got my ass handed to me by Judge Carter. That slimeball Dickerson was there, too. They have a copy of that letter you were talking about. How'd they get it? Do you think Diana sent it to them? She's never appreciated what being in this firm means."

"Hold on, Alan. She's one of the most ethical people I know."

"Really? How the fuck do you know that? I told you to stay away from her. Now, she's sabotaged my fucking career."

"You don't know that she gave them the letter."

"Okay, then how'd they get it? Did you give it to them?"

"Of course not. Maybe Mr. Russell did. It was addressed to him."

"Don't be ridiculous, Robert. We represent Mr. Russell. He would have asked us about it." Alan began to pace back and forth. "My first solo appearance in court, and it's a fucking disaster."

"You need to talk to Davis," Robert offered.

"Right, Robert. I'm supposed to go to the most powerful partner in the firm and tell him I fucked up the hearing he entrusted me with. Not a chance. Not until I find out how the hell they got that letter."

"Isn't the real question why Davis failed to provide it?"

"I don't know." Alan sat down and twisted his head from one side and then the next. "Did you prepare the answers to the interrogatories?"

"No. Davis did that himself."

"Yeah, well, they're fucked up, too. I didn't know that Scott & Cranston had advised Mr. Russell."

"I tried to tell you, Alan: that's what the letter was about."

"I never saw the fucking letter, Robert!" Alan stood up and began to pace again.

"What's next?" Robert asked.

"I have to be back in court on Friday morning with an explanation for that moron Judge Carter."

"You're going to have to talk to Davis. I'll go with you if you want."

"I don't need a fucking wing man. I can handle this myself." Alan stared out the window. His voice softened. "But I can also see my career going down in flames."

"It's not your fault, Alan."

He turned back to Robert, his eyes now glassy. "Who gives a shit, Robert? You think Davis gives a shit? He probably destroyed the goddamn letter so he wouldn't have to produce it."

"Destroying evidence could get the firm sanctioned by the court, couldn't it?"

"Well, no shit. But I know this: Davis Burnet will do anything to win. That's why he's the big dog around here. And now I've got to figure out what I'm going to do." He stormed out, leaving Robert reeling.

For almost an hour Robert sat at his desk, gazing out the window at the bleak Dallas skyline, twisting his West Point ring. If Davis somehow thought the letter was privileged, why didn't he list it on the privilege log? Was that just an oversight? Why was he so evasive when I asked him about it? Is it possible he destroyed it? The Texas Rules of Professional Conduct can't possibly permit that. It might even be a crime. And what about the intended recipient of the letter: Mr. Russell? Where's his copy? Davis wouldn't tell him to destroy it, would he? Are all those firm presentations on professionalism just more bullshit from firm management?

~

"Can I talk to you for a minute, Davis?" Robert stood in the hall outside the office of the "big dog," as Alan had called him.

"I'm really busy, Robert. Is it about Mr. Russell or Thomas Jackson?"

"It's about Mr. Russell."

"Come in and have a seat. I guess you've heard that Alan made a mess of the hearing in Judge Carter's court."

"That's what I wanted to talk to you about, Davis. He's pretty upset."

"Well, so am I. Mr. Russell is my oldest client. I've represented him ever since I joined the firm. And now, because of Alan's mishandling of this matter, we've let him down. Fortunately, Judge Carter directed Alan to be back in court on Friday, thereby giving us a second chance. I can no longer trust Alan to handle it, however, so I've decided to have Hugh Williams take the lead."

"I don't think this is Alan's fault, Davis."

"And what would you know about it, Robert? Are the rules of discovery something you pondered on one of your many trips to Georgia?"

Robert shifted in his chair and took a deep breath. The hazing at West Point had prepared him for moments like this: focus on doing what's right and press ahead.

"Alan didn't know about the letter, Davis."

"What letter?"

"The one that caused all the trouble. I mentioned it to you the day Tom Jackson showed up."

"There was so much going on that day, Robert. I don't remember any such conversation."

"I mentioned it in the note I left for you with Donna."

"I never received a note from you. Donna just told me you were meeting with Thomas Jackson." Davis shuffled the papers on his desk. "Are you and Sharon getting that transaction organized?"

"We're working on it." Robert paused, wondering whether to press ahead. "I came here to talk to you about the letter you were copied on."

"I told you, Robert. I don't recall any such letter. Do you have anything else for me?"

Robert began twisting his ring again. Should I tell him Diana saw the letter, too? No. Don't involve her in this. "Uh, no, Davis. I don't have anything else."

"Then I suggest you and Sharon get going on the Jackson transaction and let me handle this matter. That'll be all."

# CHAPTER THIRTY-THREE

ROBERT WENT TO bed that night but couldn't sleep. *What is Davis up to? Will Diana get dragged into this mess because she looked at the document, too? And poor Alan. I've never seen him like this. He was like a kid on Christmas Eve when he got the assignment to go to court. Now he's acting like a crazy man.* Robert glanced at the alarm clock on the nightstand. *Shit. I've got to get to sleep.*

The night dragged on, and though the room was cool, the sheets felt hot against his skin. The alarm clock startled him at 6:30 a.m., so he must have dozed off at some point. With a groan he rolled out of bed, dressed, and headed to work, more tired than he had been in weeks.

He attempted to get organized on how to staff and handle Tom Jackson's transaction but accomplished almost nothing, other than going back and forth to the break room for one cup of coffee after another.

At 10:00 a.m. his phone rang. "Would you like to go to lunch?" The sweet voice of Diana Maguire made him smile.

"Uh, yeah, sure, Diana. Do you want to go to Campisi's again?"

"No. And I don't want to go to Dakota's either. Let's go to El Fenix."

"I heard it was a mediocre chain restaurant."

"Oh no. They've been around forever. They have a cool old building right down the street."

"Okay, I—"

"I'll drive again. It's easier. I'll stop by around eleven forty-five." She hung up.

I wonder what that's all about. She didn't sound upset. Maybe Davis pulled her back into the Russell litigation. Maybe he's playing games because she's Sharon's primary associate, and Sharon is helping me with Tom's transaction.

⁂

Although it was located just down the street from Dallas's modern sky-scrapers, El Fenix had the look and feel of a place that had been around awhile. Plastic menus with pictures of all sorts of Mexican—or, as Robert soon learned, "Tex-Mex"—dishes were on each table.

"They have a bunch of these restaurants around town," Diana said as they sat down, "but this is the original. I think it's the best." If she were about to give him bad news, her face certainly didn't show it. "It's too bad we can't order margaritas. They're fantastic." She smoothed her napkin in her lap. "So, how are you doing?"

"Aw, I don't know, Diana. I think Davis is annoyed that I asked Sharon to help me with the sale of Tom's company instead of him or somebody he recommended. But frankly, I just don't trust him."

Immediately Robert wondered whether he'd said too much, been too forthcoming, too candid about his thoughts concerning the most powerful partner in the firm. Diana quickly dissuaded him of any such concerns.

"Well, between you and me, I don't like him either. He's one of those people who talks nice to your face—like a politician—and then talks *about* you behind your back. I know for a fact he's undermined Sharon. "

"Yeah. Well, the last thing he said to me was to get to work on Tom's transaction, so that's what I'm trying to do."

"Sharon won't lead you astray." Just then the waiter arrived with their lunches. "Watch out for the salsa, Robert. It always seems to find its way onto the front of whatever you're wearing."

There was that smile again. Even her eyes smiled. Robert wished he'd never had anything to do with Megan Miller. If he hadn't, this might be more than a friendly lunch.

"Anyway," she continued, "I wanted to let you in on some news that Sharon told me. It's not common knowledge yet, but I didn't want you to get caught by surprise."

"Am I getting fired?"

"Of course not. Don't worry about Davis. Partners get grouchy all the time. No. I wanted to let you know that Alan did *not* get picked up for partner early."

"Oh shit. He's not going to like that."

"Well, I didn't either. The only one who did was Jackie Sullivan."

"You've got to be kidding me. She's nothing but—"

Diana held up her hand to stop him. "I know. I know. We all know. But that's not the reason I wanted to talk to you. Despite what he thinks, Alan doesn't have many friends at the firm. I think he's going to need one when he finds out. But you have to wait until *he* tells you. Sharon and I would both be in trouble for saying something before it's officially announced."

"Oh, yeah, you're right about that. He's going to be devastated. But what should I say?"

"Yeah, well, I've given it considerable thought, because I'm in the same boat." Diana grinned and raised her eyebrows as if to say: Have you forgotten that?

"Oh, right, of course. I'm sorry, Diana. But you seem to take things in stride better than Alan does. He went nuts after his hearing yesterday. He stormed into my office, all hot under the collar, asking about that letter from Scott & Cranston."

"I suspect we'll both get asked about that." She took a sip of her drink. "I hear that Hugh Williams's strategy is to say that no one at the firm received a copy of the letter, and the client didn't understand that it was something we should have reviewed in response to plaintiff's discovery request."

"Well, both of us know that's not true," Robert said. "What are you going to do?"

"If they ask, I'll tell the truth. I just hope they don't ask. I think it was terrible of Davis to send Alan into court so misinformed. I suspect he thought Alan's race would keep him from getting into trouble with Judge Carter."

Robert snorted. "I can tell you that's not true. Judge Carter gave us a terrible ruling in the Donaldson matter involving that crazy CEO. And Alan was sitting at the table right in front of him."

"Maybe Davis thought it would be different if Alan was in court by himself—not just window dressing." Diana poked at her enchilada. "Oh, I don't know what I'm talking about, Robert. I'm speculating. I just thought you should know about Alan, so it doesn't catch you by surprise."

"Thanks." Robert smiled as he watched her bite into her taco, which promptly fell apart. She was the epitome of a kid, thoroughly enjoying her messy lunch. "Aren't you annoyed that Jackie was selected and you weren't?" he asked.

"Not really. I value my freedom too much."

"Your freedom?"

"My mom used to say that freedom is not so much about being free to do what you want to do, as it is about not being *controlled* by something or someone else, such as material possessions or a job. If you're too worried about having a big house and a fancy car, it's not long before they control you." She took another bite.

Why couldn't I have met this woman years ago? Robert thought.

"So, I'm not sure what you want me to tell Alan," Robert said. "That he's better off not making partner because he would be less free? That'd be a surprise to him."

"No. Not that," she said, shaking her head. "It's just… I think he worries too much about having a fancy car, fancy suits, making partner early, being 'Mr. Big' at the law firm. And not just any law firm: Underwood & Crockett, 'the most prominent firm in Texas.' I've heard him say that a million times."

"You really think he's that shallow?"

"Not shallow. Just too focused on things that don't have enduring value. Momma used to say, 'What's important is to do the right thing. If you do that, you don't have to worry about anything else.' "

"Your momma sounds like a wise woman," he said. Diana's lips pressed together, but she smiled anyway—ever so slightly. "You know, my dad used to say something similar." Diana perked up, her blue eyes bright with anticipation. "He quoted the Bible. Something Paul said about Christ wanting us to experience freedom, so he set us free from sin. But dad was quick to add that true freedom comes from having a desire to please Jesus—kinda like your mother saying you should do the right thing and everything else will take care of itself."

"I guess. Do you know what verse that is?"

"No." Robert shook his head. "My dad would, but I don't."

"Well, we need to get back to the office. I hope you can help Alan get through this. Try to get him to focus on all that he's accomplished, all that he has to be thankful for."

"I thought you didn't like him."

"I don't dislike him, Robert. I just don't care for some of his behavior, or the way he tries to manipulate you. But he's still a human being—not a bad person. I hate to see anyone hurt."

What does she mean "manipulate"? Robert pondered that for a second but decided not to ask.

On the way back to the office, he remembered that he hadn't spoken with Barry. If nothing else, he should warn him that Junior's dad thinks he sabotaged Junior's brakes.

❧

"You've reached Tracie and Misty." It was the voice of Barry's ex-wife on an answering machine. "She ain't here, and I ain't either." Then, a raspy, smoker's laugh. "Leave your number, and we might just call you back. Bye."

"Tracie, this is Robert, uh, Bobby Clark, Barry's friend. I'm trying to get in touch with him. Would you mind calling me at…" Robert slowly stated his phone number twice. He didn't want to give her an excuse for not calling him back. Then, he decided to go see Alan.

Alan's office door was closed, and his secretary was furiously typing away on her word processor. She looked up as Robert approached. "He's left for the afternoon, Mr. Clark. Is there something I can help you with?"

"Uh, no. I just needed to chat with him for a minute."

"Well, he said he was going to work from home. Do you have that number?"

"Yes. Thanks."

Back in his office, Robert phoned Alan. "What's up, man? Your secretary said you're working from home."

"I, uh, I just have some things to tend to. Listen, why don't you stop by for dinner? I'll make us a salad, baked potatoes, and a couple of steaks. I just bought a 1985 Burgess Zinfandel, which they say is destined to be a classic."

"Okay, but—"

"Be here at seven thirty." Click.

ॐ

Robert had never been to Alan's apartment and didn't know what to expect. As soon as he walked in, he could see that it was a reflection of its occupant. Alan greeted him at the door wearing a Williams-Sonoma apron and told him to make himself at home in the living room. A large, white leather and chrome sofa—like something one might see in a Manhattan high-rise—dominated the room. The lights of the city glistened beyond the floor-to-ceiling glass that comprised the outside wall in front of him. Skyscrapers and small buildings stretched out to a congested freeway where a string of white headlights glowed in one direction, red taillights in the other. Prominent among the skyscrapers in the distance was Lincoln Plaza, the building that housed the offices of Underwood & Crockett. The wall to the left, painted whitewash white, showcased original modern art paintings—not Robert's favorite but tasteful nonetheless. Alan was busy in the kitchen, which overlooked the living room. Jazz music was on the stereo. Robert smiled as he thought about the women Alan must have impressed with his pad.

"How do you like your steak, my man?"

He seems upbeat, Robert thought. Maybe he doesn't know.

"I'm not particular."

"That's your problem, Robert. When you have a choice, take it. Now, how does medium rare sound?"

"Sounds good.

After a few minutes, Alan called from the kitchen, "Come get you a glass of this zin. It's spectacular."

"I think I need a glass of water first." Robert's throat was dry, and his chest began to feel tight. He didn't like knowing something so critical to Alan and yet being unable to tell him.

"Let's eat," Alan said, handing Robert a plate.

"Thanks. I didn't know you were such a cook."

"I'm not really. Steaks are pretty easy, as is making a salad. The most important thing is to pick the right wine. Then you can't go wrong."

They ate silently while jazz continued to play in the background. Alan spoke first. "So, what have you heard about this hearing on Friday?"

"Not much. Just that Hugh Williams is going to handle it."

"Yeah. I had to get out of the office. I can't believe Davis set me up like that and then handed it off to the great Hugh Williams. He'll pull something out of his ass on Friday."

Robert took a sip of wine and carefully placed his glass back onto the table. "I heard that Hugh is simply going to say that no one at the firm ever received that letter, and the client didn't understand that he should have produced it."

"That makes sense." Alan cut off a piece of steak and popped it into his mouth.

"But that's not true, Alan. I saw the letter, Diana saw it, and so did Donna."

"Davis's secretary?"

"Yeah."

"Well, she'll say whatever Davis tells her to say. I suspect Hugh is going to want to talk to you and Diana tomorrow. You'll have to decide what you're going to do."

"Do they know Diana saw it?"

"How the hell should I know? I never saw the fucking letter."

"Well, I don't intend to lie."

"Then say you can't remember." Alan took a sip of wine and closed his eyes. "I can't believe how good this is."

"Is that how's it's done? People just lie?"

"How the fuck would I know? I'm not partner material apparently."

"What do you mean?"

"I didn't make it. Probably because of that damn hearing. The only one who did make it was that fucking whore Jackie Sullivan. They had to make her partner, or she'd blackmail a third of the male partners. And like I told you, your precious golden girl didn't make it either."

"So that's why you came home?"

"I guess so. I'm pissed. It's pretty damn clear Davis had me go in front of Judge Carter because I'm black. That is apparently my main value to the firm. And then he fucks me over." Alan took another sip of wine. "Yeah. They promote whores but not a qualified black man."

"You really think race entered into it? We know why Jackie got promoted. Nobody else did."

"Well, I've seen this shit before. I'm considering filing a lawsuit."

"Really? Maybe you should talk to your dad first."

"My dad? What the fuck would he know about this shit? He's just an Uncle Tom, Robert. Can't you see that? My dad's just a nigger."

"Oh, God, Alan. Don't say that."

"Why not? He is. He talks all that shit about the Tuskegee Airmen, but what did he do after the war? He worked in shitty maintenance jobs that had nothing to do with being a pilot. He just talks about that shit all the time because it's the only thing he ever did that was worth a damn."

"No, Alan. Countless men worked at jobs beneath their ability after the war. My dad worked as a farm hand while he went to school."

"Yeah. But then he graduated and wound up as the county agent, respected in your community. My dad never finished college and never did anything except be The Man's nigger."

"Shut up, Alan. Stop saying that."

"Who do you think you're talking to, Robert?"

"I'm talking to a guy who doesn't appreciate his father, who worked his ass off to support him and the rest of his family. How many times do you think he had to swallow his pride so that you and your sisters could have a better life than he did? Did you ever think about that? You should be happy you still have him." Robert's voice cracked as those last words caught in his throat. He took a deep breath. "And you damn sure shouldn't refer to him with a filthy epithet."

Alan looked away and said nothing, but Robert wasn't finished.

"And don't give me that bullshit about it being okay for you to use that word but not a white person. That's absolute bullshit. A filthy epithet is a filthy epithet. And even if it weren't, you damn sure shouldn't be referring to your dad with that word." Robert could feel his skin getting warm, certain his pale skin had flushed.

Almost a minute passed before Alan finally said, "You're right. I know you're right. I shouldn't have said that. But it doesn't change the fact that he didn't fight for social justice. He didn't fight to get a better job."

"Maybe he thought his first priority was taking care of his family. That's what my dad always said. He'd done his duty for the country during the war. When he returned home, it was time to look after his family."

"Yeah, well, my dad did his duty, too. And he came home to segregation, discrimination, and Jim Crow. And he didn't do a damn thing about it."

"Not everyone is Martin Luther King, Alan—who, by the way, never served in the military, during war or peace. Your dad provided a good life for you and your sisters. You're a lawyer for crying out loud. Do you think that would have happened if your father hadn't busted his butt for you and got you a good education?"

"He didn't pay for my college. He wanted me to go to West Point because it was free. He made me enroll in ROTC at Howard because I could get a scholarship. And I hated it."

Sensing the need to lighten the mood, Robert grinned and said, "Don't be knockin' my school, Alan. And remember, if you hadn't been in the Army you would've never met me."

"Okay. You're right." Alan grinned. "I'm just glad I avoided West Point. You would've probably been one of those upperclassman hazing my ass."

They enjoyed their steaks and wine until Alan's thoughts returned to the topic that had started this conversation.

"I just can't believe Jackie Sullivan made partner early, and I didn't. Your golden girl Diana should've fucked her way in the way Jackie did. She's pretty enough." Alan virtually spit out the words. "There's no way I could've done that."

"Do you realize how foolish you sound right now?" Robert said. "You'll make partner on schedule, for all its worth."

"What do you mean?"

"I mean you'll be in the duck pond for a year, and that's nothing more than a glorified senior associate—a partner in name only. You won't be sharing in the profits of the firm. You'll still just be getting a salary."

"I thought Alex said at the associates' meeting that he was going to bring our concerns to the attention of the partners."

"That never happened, Alan." Robert shook his head slightly and tried to avoid sounding condescending. He knew Alan considered himself to be the man with his finger on the pulse of the firm.

"How do you know it never happened?" Alan asked.

"Because Sharon told me."

"The lesbo again. When are you going to stop consorting with her? Diana's career is going nowhere because she's associated with her. And didn't I tell you to stop worrying about Diana?"

"I can only answer one question at a time, Alan. First, you should stop calling Sharon a lesbo. That's as bad as calling someone a nigger. And second, I'm not consorting with her. I just happened to be talking to her about the project I was working on for Davis."

"Why didn't you talk to me?"

Alan was angry again, and Robert didn't want to tell his friend that he knew what his advice would have been. He knew Alan would have simply told him to do what Davis said, even if it made no sense and seemed to be causing the client unnecessary expense. But he couldn't tell his friend that, especially not now. So, he punted. "I don't know Alan. I guess you weren't around, or it came up in conversation. It was a while back. I don't remember."

Alan looked at him as if he was processing what Robert had just said. "Well, I'll tell you what I do remember: I have an office to go to tomorrow, so you need to get your happy ass out of here so I can go to sleep."

"You want me to help you clean up?" Robert asked.

"Nah. The maid will get it tomorrow."

# CHAPTER THIRTY-FOUR

ON WEDNESDAY MORNING Robert found a pink message slip taped to his office door. The date and time on the slip indicated that it had been left at 10:30 p.m. the prior evening. It was signed by Donna, Davis's secretary, and said, simply: "See Mr. Burnet as soon as you arrive."

Robert bit his lower lip. "I know what this is about." As he set his briefcase onto the desk, he noticed a thick fax in his in-box. The cover sheet showed it was from Martin & Howard, a large Atlanta law firm. The comment section indicated they were representing Darden Industries, a multi-billion-dollar conglomerate located in Atlanta. He flipped to the next page and discovered it was an eighty-three page stock purchase agreement. Darden Industries was proposing to buy all of the outstanding shares of Tom Jackson's company for $163 million. Robert's chest felt tight. *Damn. I guess it's game on. Maybe Davis will at least be happy to hear this news.*

Even though Davis's door was open, Robert knocked twice. "Donna left a note last night saying you needed to see me."

"I do. Come in and sit down. Hugh Williams and I were working late on this hearing that's taking place on Friday. I need to speak with you about that but first let me ask how the transaction with Thomas Jackson is going."

"Funny you should ask, Davis. A law firm named Martin & Howard—"

"I'm familiar with them. It's an old-line Atlanta firm."

"Right. They faxed me a stock purchase agreement, indicating that

Darden Industries wants to purchase all the outstanding stock of Tom's company for $163 million." Robert paused, hoping Davis would say something like "Congratulations!" or "How can I help?"

"Darden Industries, huh? I've read about Mr. Darden. He's a self-made multi-millionaire—a true rags to riches story. If I remember correctly, he was a friend of Lyndon Johnson." Davis cocked his head and jutted his chin. "Do you have your team identified?"

"Yes. Sharon helped with that. As you mentioned, she previously handled the sale of an insurance company."

"Right. Well, I wish you the best of luck." Davis began sorting through the documents on his desk, apparently looking for something. "So, the plaintiffs in the Russell litigation are claiming that we received a letter from Scott & Cranston that we should have produced in discovery. Do you know anything about that?"

Where is Davis going with this? Robert wondered. *Of course he knows I'm aware of the letter.*

"Yes, that's the letter I mentioned to you previously—the one where Scott & Cranston was advising Mr. Russell on how much he could offer for the outstanding public shares."

"So, *Mr. Russell* received the letter," Davis said.

"Yes, but you were copied on it. Don't you remember? It came in while you were on your ski vacation. I left a note with Donna concerning the letter on the day we met with Tom Jackson."

"I'm sorry, Robert. No one remembers receiving any such letter. I had Donna check with support services to ensure there was no record of receiving any such letter. And she doesn't remember it either. Are you sure you're not mistaken? Did you file it properly?"

"I didn't file it at all, Davis. Donna asked me about it, and I said it would keep until you returned."

"So, why did you say you brought it up when Thomas Jackson was here last week?"

"Because..." Robert almost mentioned Diana but stopped, knowing that would drag her into the mess.

"Because what, Robert?"

"I was, uh, I was just following up."

"Well, it seems you are the only person at the firm who has any recollection of receiving any such letter. Hugh plans to tell the court that no one at the firm received that letter or knows anything about it. Are you okay with that?"

Robert's heart started racing; he could feel his body getting hot—some sort of primal response to stress. "Uh, actually, no, Davis. I'm not okay with that. I distinctly remember seeing that letter."

"You realize you're putting the firm in an awkward situation."

Awkward situation? Robert thought. What is he talking about? I'm causing a problem because I won't lie for him the way Donna does?

"I fail to see how I'm doing that, Davis."

"Let me cut to the chase, Robert. I need you to sign this affidavit, which Hugh has prepared, indicating that you don't know anything about that infernal letter."

"I can't do that, Davis."

"What do you mean, you can't do that?" His gray eyes narrowed into an intense stare. "You mean you *won't* do that."

Robert hesitated, suddenly flooded by a tsunami of emotions. Words and thoughts flowed through his mind: "silly lawyer stuff"; padded timesheets; dumb judges, concerned with politics, not justice; pompous judges who show scant regard for the human tragedy unfolding in front of them; prevarication from the managing partner instead of candor; repeated instances of lawyers being disingenuous with colleagues or outright lying to them. He decided he had had enough.

"No, Davis. I mean I won't lie for you."

"I beg your pardon?"

"I said I won't lie for you. You know damn good and well that that 'infernal letter,' as you call it, was in your files. Donna saw it. Have you told her to lie for you, too?"

"You forget yourself, Robert. No one at this firm talks to me like that." He tossed his Montblanc pen onto the desk. "You're fired, effective immediately." Davis's gray eyes no longer looked merely stern; they looked possessed. "And if you attempt to cause any trouble in this matter, I'll see to it that you never practice law in Texas again." Davis looked down at his desk and continued without looking up. "I'll arrange for two weeks' severance. Now, get out of my office." When Robert stood to leave, Davis looked up, the same possessed look in his eyes. "Oh, and by the way, Robert, good luck with handling Jackson's transaction. Those boys in Atlanta will eat you alive."

Robert said nothing. He just walked out.

What have I done? he thought as he headed back to his office. Better let Alan know.

"What?" Alan squinted so hard his mouth pulled up under his nose. "You got fired? What in the hell did you do?"

"Davis tried to get me to lie about that letter, and I told him I wouldn't do it."

"Didn't we talk about this, Robert? Didn't I tell you to just say you don't remember?"

"But I do remember, Alan, and I'm not going to lie about it."

"Okay, Mr. Boy Scout. How did that work for you in that deposition where you admitted to going to a whorehouse? A whole lot of trouble, right?"

"Yeah. But I'm sick of the bullshit, Alan. I'm sick of parsing the truth. I'm sick of the managing partner of the firm lying to us about when associates would be considered for partnership and looking the other way when associates bill hours they didn't do. I'm sick of the whole goddamn thing."

"Slow down, man. You're on an emotional roller coaster. Go back and tell Davis that you were wrong. You're not sure about the letter. What does he want you to do? Sign an affidavit or something? Who gives a shit? That's just to cover Hugh Williams's ass. They're not going to enter it into the court record."

"Fuck it, Alan. I'm done. This whole place is built on bullshit. Lawyers lie. Secretaries lie. They parse their comments instead of being forthright. They talk about people behind their backs." Robert could feel his body getting hot again. He took a deep breath. "There are only three people in this firm I give a shit about: you, Sharon, and Diana."

"Well, don't put me in the company of those two. I've got my own troubles."

"Listen to yourself, Alan. You're the one who's always talking about prejudice. Don't you think Sharon has been the victim of prejudice because of something that's nobody's business? And, contrary to what you might think, Diana is not gay."

"Well, do what you gotta do, man. But I hate to see you go. I think you're making a terrible mistake."

"You know what? I'm gonna be fine." Robert stared out the window. "I just need to figure out how to make my child-support payments and what to do about Tom Jackson's transaction." He rubbed his chin as he turned back to Alan. "Ironically, I just received the stock purchase agreement. I even told Davis about it before he fired me. Darden Industries is offering $163 million."

"Damn." Alan's eyebrows went up, and his mouth fell open. "That's a big deal. And Davis fired you after you told him that?"

"Yup."

"Shit. He must be really pissed. I wonder how pissed he is at me over that hearing?"

"You're even asking that question, Alan? He set you up. He thought you might be able to smooth talk Judge Carter. Davis is a sanctimonious prick. I'm glad I'm leaving."

Alan stared at Robert for several moments but said nothing. "Well, good luck, man. I hope you can figure it all out." As Robert stood to leave, Alan continued. "Listen, if you can get out of your lease, you can stay with me for as long as you want."

"Thanks, man, but I don't think that'll be necessary. But I might take you up on another steak dinner." Robert grinned and walked out.

Heading back to his office, Robert could tell that already the word had spread. Donna probably had called every secretary in the firm. He didn't care. The people staring at him and whispering were just minions—minions of Davis Burnet and partners like him. They'd sold their souls to Underwood & Crockett.

Robert turned a corner and almost collided with Robert Underwood. "Well, if it isn't Stonewall Jackson. How have you been, Robert?"

"Not so good, Mr. Underwood. I just got fired."

"Fired? Step in here a moment." Mr. Underwood guided him into a conference room, where they sat down at the conference table. "What's this all about?"

Maybe I'm being hasty, Robert thought. Maybe Mr. Underwood can set things right. Slow down, like Alan said. Be careful what you say.

"Davis Burnet wants me to sign an affidavit saying I don't remember seeing a letter that should have been produced in discovery."

"Well, what's the problem?"

"I do remember seeing it."

"Are you sure? We see lots of documents during the course of our work. If you aren't absolutely certain that you remember it, shouldn't you just say you don't recall?"

So this is the way the game is played, Robert thought. Mr. Underwood is no different from the rest of them. They'll swear to anything, so help me dollar sign.

"I'm certain, Mr. Underwood. I definitely saw the letter."

"Son, if Davis thinks you should sign the affidavit, I'd think long and hard about it. He carries a lot of weight around here."

"I'm afraid my mind is made up. I can't sign it."

"Well, we hate to lose you, but I'm afraid I'm in no position to challenge Davis Burnet, the man who determines my compensation, especially since I don't bill as many hours as I used to. Well, good luck to you, Robert." With that, Mr. Underwood stood up and walked out.

So much for the great litigator, Mr. Robert Underwood, pillar of the legal community. Robert decided he needed to seek the counsel of the one partner he trusted.

"Sharon, do you have a minute?"

"Of course, Robert. Come in."

Sharon was always gracious and genuine—a female Atticus Finch in the midst a bunch of disingenuous schemers.

"Davis just fired me."

"Wait. What? What happened?"

"He wanted me to say I didn't remember seeing a letter he should have produced in discovery in the Russell litigation. But I did see it, and I think he destroyed it. Anyway, I told him I wouldn't lie for him, and he fired me."

"Oh, Robert, I'm so sorry."

"I'm okay with it, Sharon. As I've told you before, I'm not sure Underwood & Crockett is the right place for me anyway. But I am worried about

Tom's transaction. I just received a fax of a proposed stock purchase agreement. It's eighty-three pages long, and I have no idea of where to begin."

"Well, the firm has no basis for abandoning a client. Thanks to you, I'm the billing partner. So, I think you should just establish your own practice, in a manner of speaking, and we'll work on it together."

"I don't know, Sharon. I have no idea of how to do all that."

"I told you before that Mr. Jackson wants you involved because he trusts you. You can still fill that role, provided you trust me to guide you."

"You're the only partner at this firm I do trust."

"Thank you for saying that, Robert. Well then, we can work on this together if you at least have a place to receive faxes, a telephone, and a computer. You won't be accepting any other clients, will you? Robert shook his head. "Then, you can work out of your home." Robert stared at her vacantly. "Listen, Robert. After the transaction is finished, you can decide what to do next. But right now, we can't let Mr. Jackson down, can we? You should call him, explain what happened, and ensure he's still comfortable with us handling the transaction."

In an instant, Robert felt as if a huge load had been lifted off him. His fear and anxiety washed away as he looked at the warm and welcoming expression on the face of a much maligned partner. "I can't thank you enough, Sharon. I had no idea what I was going to do."

"Well, let's first ensure Mr. Jackson is comfortable with the arrangement. In the meantime, let me see that fax." Robert handed it to her. "Martin & Howard, huh? I know that firm. I'll look this over and prepare comments, which I'll go over with you before we send them out."

Robert stared at her, his eyes glistening with gratitude. "You are an angel, Sharon. I mean… I mean with the utmost respect, you are an answer to prayer."

"Don't get maudlin on me, Robert. Let's just get this deal done. Now, go tend to your departure from the firm and get set up at your place. And don't forget to call Mr. Jackson."

Robert was met in his office by a young man from the Human Resources Department. "Mr. Burnet says we are, uh, we are to escort you out, Robert." The young man stood at the door of Robert's office, shifting his weight from one foot to the other and avoiding eye contact.

"Don't worry about it," Robert said. "Sometimes, things just don't work out." He could see the young man relax immediately. "Just give me a minute to pack up my personal stuff."

Carolyn appeared at his door. "You're probably going to need these." She'd assembled four boxes for him. "I don't know what happened, Robert, but I wish you all the best. You're a good guy. And," she smiled, "I'll always remember that your shoes were always shined." With that, she turned and walked back to her desk.

It took less than fifteen minutes to collect his personal things: his diplomas from West Point and the University of Georgia; several framed photographs of Ellie, his sister, and his mother and father; and a few books and files. The young man from Human Resources helped Robert load the boxes into his car. But rather than head to his duplex, he walked down to Dakota's.

"You're in here early, Mr. Clark." It was Jake, the bartender, engaged in his typical activity of continuously wiping the bar top. "You want me to get Ramón for you?"

"No, Jake, I want you to get me a double Maker's Mark on the rocks. I just got fired."

"Damn. What hap—. Never mind. None of my business. This one's on me." Jake put ice in a glass, filled it to the rim, and placed it in front of Robert.

"Can you have one with me, Jake?"

"Oh, hell no. I'd get fired."

"Yeah." Robert took a long sip. "No. It's okay, Jake. The first day I was here you told me about 'silly lawyer stuff.' Well, you were right."

"Oh, you mean about this restaurant being underground. Well, I—"

"No, Jake, you were more right than you know. There's too much silly lawyer shit that goes on at Underwood & Crockett. And it's more than that. It's lying and deceit and backstabbing and using people. The place makes me sick. I'm glad to be done with it. I have no idea where I'm going, but it won't be to another firm like that."

Jake said nothing but continued to wipe the bar, as if trying to remove an invisible spill. "We're going to miss you, Mr. Clark. You're a good guy."

"Thanks, Jake. But it's Robert to you." Robert downed the rest of his drink. "And before you tell me to be careful, let me say that I'm fine. I just need to go home."

Jake smiled and extended his hand. Robert shook it and said, "I should have listened to your warning, Jake. You're a good guy, too. Take care of yourself."

When Robert got back to his car, he didn't leave right away. He sat and thought about all that had happened that morning and decided he was satisfied with the way things had turned out.

*It's funny how I told Dan McCormack that the Army wasn't the right place for me. Well, apparently, Underwood & Crockett isn't the right place either. But what do I do now? No. I can't think about that. I've got to get Tom's deal done first. Then I can think about it. Right now, I need to go buy a fax machine and a computer.*

# CHAPTER THIRTY-FIVE

THE BLINKING RED light on the answering machine greeted Robert as he walked through the front door of his duplex. The recorded voice told him he had two messages. The first was from Barry Daniel, who left a number and told Robert to call him back. No other details. The second was from Mr. Taylor, inviting him to go flying on Thursday. Alan must have told him what had happened at the firm. Robert called Barry first.

"Suncoast Automotive. Glenda speaking."

"Uh, hi. This is Robert Clark. I'm trying to reach Barry Daniel. He left this number on my machine."

"Oh, yeah. Sure. Let me see if he can take a call. What'd you say your name was?"

"Robert Clark."

Soon, Barry's familiar voice was on the line. "Well, well. Mr. Fancy Lawyer tracked me down."

"Where are you, man? I've been worried about you."

"You talkin' about that Junior business? I done talked to Chief Staples. He knows I didn't have nothing to do with it."

"Well, why in the hell did you leave Pemberton, then?"

"You're asking me? You did the same thing."

"You know why I left Georgia, Barry."

"Yeah, well, I needed to get the hell out of there, too. Old Man Lester didn't give me no bonus—not a damn penny, after all these years. All I got was that whiskey you and I drunk."

"That *is* pretty shitty," Robert said.

"You're damn straight. After all the years I busted my ass for the man. He said he had payroll tax problems or something and couldn't afford to pay nothing. I think it's bullshit myself. He's just cheap. Anyway, I decided to go to Panama City. Brought Spot with me. He likes it down here, too. Hang on a second." Barry put his hand over the receiver, though Robert could still hear him. "I'm on the damn phone. I'll be back in a minute." His hand now off the receiver, he continued, "Where was I?"

"Talking about how much you like Panama City."

"Oh. Yeah. Well, you know, I always did like the beach, and I got myself a good job down here. Makin' good money—more than I was makin' at Lester's."

"That's wonderful, Barry. But what about your trailer and your stuff in Pemberton?"

"What stuff? I ain't got nothing but Spot and my truck and my trailer. I let my ex have the trailer on account of she got evicted from her place. Didn't pay her rent for four months. And I've been sending her child support all this time." Barry raised his voice on that last comment, triggering a coughing fit. "Gotta quit these damn cigarettes. Anyway, Misty's still livin' with her, and they needed a place to stay, so I said she could have it. It ain't worth much, no way."

Robert sensed Barry's bitterness ran deeper than not getting a year-end bonus. But now was not the time to talk about it. Instead, he said, "Well, now I have a reason to come to Panama City."

"You sure as hell do. Come anytime. And let me tell you, Bobby: there's a lot of good lookin' women down here."

"I might just take you up on that. But I've got to get a project finished first."

"You'll never change. Always workin'. When you gonna relax, man?"

"Soon, probably. I just got fired."

"Fired? You? What happened?"

"It's a long story. Let's just say I'm not gonna lie for those assholes."

"Then come on down here."

"Like I said, I can't, Barry. I have this project I've got to finish for an old friend. You remember that crazy captain I told you about from Panama?"

Barry chuckled. "You mean the one who fucked everything in a skirt?"

"Yeah, him. Well. He turned over a new leaf. You ever heard of Jackson Life Insurance Company?"

"Just them late-night ads on TV."

"Well, that's the guy. He left the Army and built that company."

"No shit?"

"Yeah. And he asked me to help him sell it."

"Damn. You *are* big time, ain't you? How you gonna do that now you been fired?"

"Well first of all, I'm not big time. A partner at the firm is going to do the deal. I'm just involved because Elm—I mean, uh, Tom Jackson trusts me."

"That's high praise, buddy, but I'm not surprised. You never let a friend down."

"You don't either, Barry."

"I ain't done nothing."

"You've been there for me. I owe you big time. And I'm gonna come down to Panama City soon and see how much beer we can drink. I just need to get this project done first."

"Okay. I'm gonna hold you to that. And, hey. Thanks for checking up on me. There ain't nobody else who gives a shit."

"Yeah? Well, I give a shit. And you damn well better show me a good time if I come all the way down there."

"Count on it."

"Take care, buddy. I'm happy for you."

Robert hung up the phone, relieved to learn his good friend was not the target of a criminal investigation. Then he started to think about returning the call from Mr. Taylor, which he really didn't want to do. What would he say? That he's happy to be gone from a firm that encourages its lawyers to lie under oath? The firm his son is so proud of it practically defines him. After all, Mr. Taylor seemed pretty proud of it, too, when he talked about Alan.

Robert decided to call Tom Jackson instead. As Sharon had suggested, they needed to be sure Tom was still comfortable with being represented by Underwood & Crockett, since Robert was no longer with the firm.

"So, why'd you get fired," Tom asked when Robert finally reached him.

"It's a long story, but basically my boss asked me to sign an affidavit that wasn't true. When I refused, he fired me."

"That's why I sought you out, Robert. I'll never doubt your integrity."

"Well, you know I'm no choir boy."

"Neither am I. But I also know you'll never let me down and you'll do your best to look out for me. That's why I came to the firm, and as long as you're going to manage the transaction, I'm fine."

"I won't let you down, buddy," Robert said.

"I know. See you soon."

Robert hung up the phone and slumped into his chair. Tom was the same good friend he had been in Panama. Against impossible odds he had gotten Robert out of Panama on the next available flight when he learned that Robert's father was dying. And now, without knowing it, Tom had given him a sense of peace and direction that he sorely needed. For several minutes Robert sat quietly in the chair, smiling and wondering what he had done to deserve such a good friend.

But there was still work to do, so he got up and busied himself with unpacking the fax machine and computer he had just purchased and setting them up. Around 5:30 p.m. he called Mr. Taylor.

"Taylor residence. This is Yolanda."

"Hello, Mrs. Taylor. This is Robert Clark, Alan's friend."

"Why hello, Robert. What a pleasant surprise."

"Mr. Taylor left a message on my answering machine."

"Well, he just got home from work. Let me get him for you."

Robert could hear her calling Mr. Taylor to the phone.

"This is Bill Taylor."

"Hello, Mr. Taylor. This is Robert Clark."

"Are you ready to go flying?" Mr. Taylor's enthusiasm was apparent.

"Thank you *so* much for the offer, Mr. Taylor. I really would like to go, but I have so much I need to take care of. Among other things, I need to start looking for a new job."

"I understand, Robert," he said, the enthusiasm now gone from his voice. "Alan called and told me what happened. I thought you might want a diversion. And it just so happens that the flying club's plane is available on Thursday. The weather is supposed to be good, so I'm going to take off work and fly out to Abilene and back. Are you sure you can't join me? I could really use a navigator on such a long flight."

"You know what, Mr. Taylor? You're right. Getting away for a few hours would be a good idea, although I'm not sure I know enough to be your navigator."

"Sure you do, Robert." His enthusiasm was back. "We'll fly out of the Lancaster Regional Airport again. When we reach altitude, it will be a bit colder than last time, so wear a sweater in addition to bringing a jacket. Be there around ten. And bring a sack lunch. We'll be gone a while."

"Yes, sir. Thank you. I'll see you then."

Robert's alarm went off at 7:30 A.M. He knew he should get up and eat a hearty breakfast, but his bed felt too good. Somehow, he'd slept soundly for the first time in a long time—no tossing for hours, no sweat-dampened sheets. He turned off the alarm and rolled over. When he awoke again, it was 8:30 A.M., barely enough time to get ready and make it to the airport by 10:00 A.M. and certainly not enough time to make a sack lunch. He scrambled out of bed, brushed his teeth, threw on a West Point sweatshirt, and raced out the door. At 9:57 A.M. he pulled into a parking place at the airport and ran to where he knew Mr. Taylor would be inspecting the Cessna 172 Skyhawk, owned by the flying club. Sure enough, Robert found him closely examining the rudder of the plane they would be trusting for the next five hours.

It was a beautiful day. The sky was bright—a pure, uninterrupted azure blue that stretched as far as he could see. A crisp, cool breeze carried the hint of burning leaves. Robert paused to watch Mr. Taylor, as he paced around the plane, carefully conducting a pre-flight inspection he had performed hundreds of times before, but nonetheless reviewing his checklist at each step.

Careful and thoughtful in everything he does. No shortcuts. Follow the rules. Experience life and soar among the clouds, but be smart. Be safe. Mr. Taylor embodies all of that. Why can't Alan see what a remarkable man his father is?

Mr. Taylor noticed Robert as he approached the plane. "So, I'm going to have a West Point navigator, am I?" He was beaming like a kid.

"Sir?"

"Your sweatshirt, Robert."

Robert looked down at the West Point crest on his chest and chuckled. "Oh, yeah, I forgot. And, I'm, uh, afraid I didn't get a lunch packed."

"Don't worry about that. Yolanda prepared enough food for an entire squadron. She's just happy I have someone to fly with. She won't even consider it, and of course Alan is working and the girls are away at school."

"Well, I am more than happy to keep you company, Mr. Taylor, as I am currently unemployed."

"You'll get through this, Robert. I can tell you're made of tough material. Alan told me you were a Ranger."

"Well, I graduated from Ranger School, but I never served in a Ranger unit. I'm what they call a 'tab holder.'"

"Still, you've soldiered through adversity before. That's what counts." Mr. Taylor paused. "Listen. I'm counting on all that map-reading skill you learned in the Army. It's a long way to Abilene."

"I hope I'm not too rusty," Robert said.

"I'm sure you'll be fine. Let's get going, shall we? It's going to be a great day."

They climbed into the cockpit, and Mr. Taylor briefed Robert on the flight plan, which was marked on the map with a yellow highlighter. Since they were flying VFR (visual flight rules), they had to navigate using the map, just as Robert had done as a cavalry platoon leader, only they would be moving much faster than his platoon ever did. As Mr. Taylor pushed forward on the throttle and the small plane accelerated down the runway, Robert could feel the exhilaration of being pushed back into his seat. When the wheels left the ground, he turned and looked back at the Dallas skyline. He could see the shimmering glass of Fountain Place, the famous I. M. Pei building, fading from view behind them.

"You know, Robert, I learned some important life lessons in the Army. I suspect you did as well."

"Yes, sir," Robert said. "The Army can put you in tough situations, and you just have to figure it out."

"That's why I think you'll get through this most recent setback." Mr. Taylor paused while he adjusted the throttle and levelled the plane. "I mentioned life lessons because the most important thing I learned in the Army is the importance of having a plan. We used to say: if you fail to plan, you plan to fail."

Robert grinned. "I heard the same thing. I guess some things in the Army never change."

"That's true. I've reflected on that over the years, and while I think one's goals will naturally change over time, I've learned that it's important to always have clear goals, so that you can plan accordingly. And, of course, if the goals change, you change the plan."

"Yes, sir. I think that's right."

"Alan had the goal of becoming the first black partner at Underwood & Crockett. He now thinks that's not going to happen, although I think that judgment is premature."

"I don't know much about the process, Mr. Taylor, but I think you're right. This year only one person was promoted to partner early. I think Alan's still on track to be promoted on schedule. He's done very well at the firm."

"I hope you're right. Do you mind if I ask what your goal was in joining the firm?"

"No, not at all. I went through a bad divorce back in Georgia. My child visitation order is horrible. I just wanted to get out of Georgia. Did you ever hear that Davy Crockett quote about 'Y'all can go to hell, but I'm going to Texas'?"

"I doubt there's a Texan alive who hasn't heard that," Mr. Taylor said. "But don't you think leaving a bad situation is just that: getting away from something, not striving for something?"

Robert didn't answer, and they were quiet for a while.

"It's beautiful up here, don't you think?" Mr. Taylor said. "I never get tired of this view. And it's nice to have the sun at our backs, isn't it?"

"Yes, sir."

As he watched Mr. Taylor check the controls and survey the route below, Robert thought about his own "failure to plan," about all the decisions in his life that he had drifted into: marrying Janelle, going to law school, losing his way in Panama, leaving the Army and Georgia and coming to Texas, joining Underwood & Crockett. And, of course, his relationship with Megan Miller—his latest poor decision.

"I think I understand what you're saying, Mr. Taylor."

"About what, Robert?"

"About how running away from something isn't really a goal. It's an escape. I guess I've failed to take the time to plan my life and career the way I used to plan field problems." Robert's voice carried a hint of sadness.

"Well don't beat yourself up, Robert. Most people don't. But we all should. I heard a quotation once that I've never forgotten, although I'm sorry to say I can't remember who said it. It goes something like this: 'Some people spend their entire lives struggling up the ladder of success only to find—at the top—that the ladder is leaning against the wrong wall.' "

"Wow. That sort of nails it, doesn't it?" For a few minutes Robert said nothing as he studied the map and the terrain below, trying to determine where they were.

"We're about forty miles west of Fort Worth now," Mr. Taylor said. "Until you get the hang of it, Robert, it's hard to navigate around here because everything's so flat—no mountains to use as landmarks. I typically look at the highways."

"You know, Mr. Taylor, I think I've moved my ladder a lot, but I haven't found the right wall yet." Mr. Taylor glanced at him knowingly, and Robert continued, "Do you mind if I ask how you do it?"

"Set goals, you mean? Well, I think everyone is different. And I haven't always been good at it. In fact, I've moved my ladder quite a bit, too. What I try to do now is to constantly consider my priorities and to ask the Almighty for His help."

"That sounds pretty simple."

"It may sound simple, but it's not. Wasn't it Aristotle who said 'the unexamined life is not worth living'? It takes examination. And, for me, prayer." Mr. Taylor turned and looked at him. "I'm sorry, Robert. I didn't mean to get so preachy."

"No, sir. I appreciate what you're saying. It's helpful. I haven't been so good about praying lately. It never seems to fix things."

"I don't think it's intended to 'fix things,' Robert. I think it's about building a relationship with our Lord. When Alan was born, it became clear to me that taking care of my wife and child was the most important job I had. And I knew I needed His help with that."

"I haven't done a good job with that either," Robert said.

"I'm sure that's not true, Robert. And I'm also sure you're a good father. Sometimes, marriages just don't work out. There are a million reasons why." Mr. Taylor paused, as if trying to decide what to say next. "You know, Robert, we all have setbacks and disappointments in life. My father used to say that a man shouldn't be a prisoner of his past. His mistakes are just lessons learned—not something that warrants a life sentence." Robert grinned but said nothing, and Mr. Taylor continued. "I've always thought that a mistake that makes you humble is better than an achievement that makes you arrogant."

"Well then, I guess I have a lot to be humble about," Robert mumbled.

"Come on, Robert. Things are never as bleak as they appear." For several minutes they said nothing. Deciding he needed to lighten the mood, Mr. Taylor brought up college football, which led to a variety of other topics: the performance characteristics of the Cessna 172 Skyhawk, how the terrain below changed dramatically as they flew west from Dallas, stories from their respective Army careers. As they spoke, Robert began to ponder what Mr. Taylor had said and why he'd even bothered to do so.

What a wonderful man, Robert thought. He didn't need me to navigate today. He just wanted to get me up here so he could share his thoughts. So he could try to help me. And he's right: I've got to start focusing more on what's important. I've got to stop drifting into decisions and start making them with an end goal in mind. My first goal is to be the kind of father that my dad was and the kind of man Mr. Taylor is. And, of course, I can't let Tom Jackson down in the meantime.

# CHAPTER THIRTY-SIX

SINCE HE HAD been gone most of the day, Robert called Sharon as soon as he returned to his duplex. She had finished her review of the stock purchase agreement and asked him to meet in the morning to discuss her concerns. He was reluctant. After all, barely twenty-four hours had elapsed since he had been unceremoniously fired and escorted out of the building. But Sharon assured him that Davis Burnet and Hugh Williams would be in court and reminded him he was collaborating with her in support of a firm client. So, he agreed to meet at 8:30 a.m.

It was unsettling to return to the offices of Underwood & Crockett. His memory of the snide smiles and suspicious glances was fresh. But the receptionist was cordial—more cordial than he had expected. She explained that Sharon had reserved a conference room on the forty-first floor—three floors below the one on which Davis's office was located. Clearly, Sharon had arranged everything to put him at ease, including—in all likelihood—telling the receptionist to be cordial. But—he was still uneasy.

As the receptionist escorted him to the conference room, she bantered on about how much she loved working at Underwood & Crockett. Does she know I was just fired from this place? he thought. Maybe I'm reading too much into things. Maybe nobody at the firm is even interested in why I was fired.

Entering the room, Robert was surprised to see Diana sitting next to Sharon. Simultaneously, the two women looked up.

"Get a cup of coffee and have a seat, Robert," Sharon said. "We have a long list of things to talk about. There are features of this agreement that are going to be challenging."

Robert placed his cup onto the table and sat down, squirming a bit in his chair. "But the price was more than Tom expected, wasn't it?" he asked.

"That's true. But almost thirty percent of the price is contingent on the performance of the company during the year following the closing. It's called an earnout."

"Is that a problem?"

"Well, yes, it is. Mr. Jackson will have no authority following the closing, no access to information. In short, he'll be at the mercy of Darden Industries with respect to whether the company achieves the goals that are the prerequisite to the payment of the additional amount. And, he'll have to trust Darden Industries to be fair in their accounting practices. If they play games with the numbers, it could reduce the earnout or possibly eliminate it altogether."

Robert must have appeared puzzled, so Diana tried to help. "An earnout is a contingent payment, Robert. If the company fails to achieve the goals listed in the purchase agreement, then Mr. Jackson won't get the additional payment. And remember, the buyer—in this case Darden Industries—is in control of the company and the keeper of the accounting records used to determine whether the conditions for paying the earnout have been met. Bottom line: Mr. Jackson can only hope they manage the company properly, so that it achieves the stated goals, and hope that they are honest in how they account for things."

Robert groaned, dropped his head, and closed his eyes. He noticeably inhaled and exhaled before looking up. "I see. So if they manage the company poorly and/or cook the books, Tom would lose a significant portion of his compensation."

"That's right. But let me be clear, Robert" Sharon said. "We'll insist on provisions in the agreement concerning how the company will determine whether the conditions have been met, as well as provisions concerning the accounting practices, although I must say it's difficult to draft provisions that a nefarious party can't get around."

For a few seconds Robert stared blankly into space.

Tom is counting on me to look out for him, he thought. And, I have no idea what to do about what Sharon just described. This sounds like a big, fat mess.

Turning back to Sharon, Robert asked, "What should we do, then? Besides those provisions, I mean."

Sharon took off her reading glasses and shook her head. "Unfortunately, Robert, we may be stuck. We weren't involved in negotiating or drafting the letter of intent, which Martin & Howard sent over with the purchase agreement. I'm sure it sounded good to Mr. Jackson—especially the $163 million purchase price. And I'm sure he's confident the company can achieve the financial goals necessary for him to receive his earnout. But I'm not sure he realizes that Jackson Life Insurance Company will be just one of many companies owned by Darden Industries. They could be planning to cannibalize it to benefit one of their other portfolio companies. The earnout makes this deal extremely risky for him."

"Can't we change that aspect of the deal now?" Robert asked. "The letter of intent is nonbinding, isn't it?"

"Yes, it's nonbinding. And in theory we could try to revise the transaction, though it would be really bad form. We would need to have a substantial reason for doing so. And there's another problem: Jackson Life Insurance Company is carrying a tremendous amount of debt on its balance sheet. Its debt-to-equity ratio is significantly higher than those of its competitors."

"Isn't that normal for a new company?"

"It is, but Darden Industries wants the company to be debt-free at closing. Consequently, that debt has to be paid off at closing using a large portion of the purchase-price payment. And so, Mr. Jackson will receive only a few million after that, unless he gets the earnout."

I can't believe Sharon just used the phrase "only a few million" when referring to Tom Jackson. If she had seen him only a few years ago, as an Army captain, holding forth in a concrete-floored bar—a cigarette in one hand and a Balboa beer in the other—telling war stories until closing time to a collection of wide-eyed lieutenants, then she'd realize just how funny that sounds. But—that's not who he is now, is it? Now, he's E. Thomas

Jackson, the CEO of a major corporation that he built. And, he's my friend, who stood in a conference room upstairs less than two weeks ago and asked me to handle the biggest transaction of his life. He's counting on me to get this right. He's earned those millions. And I need to make sure he gets them.

Robert exhaled sharply and then asked, "What if... what if Tom says he didn't understand the earnout part of the deal and threatens to walk away unless it's deleted?"

"He could do that," Sharon said. "But it would come with risk. I suspect that one or more of his employees, customers, or vendors already know about this transaction. Some might already be taking their business elsewhere. Some employees might be looking for new jobs out of fear that they will lose theirs under the new ownership. And, if the transaction fails to close, it might make the company look like damaged goods. There are always people out there who like to gossip about such things. I'm sure there would be some who would say that the deal fell through because something was wrong with the company. That could seriously damage the company's reputation. A seller has more negotiating leverage with a buyer *before* the letter of intent is signed, because the buyer is still in courting mode."

Robert felt sick. He twisted his West Point ring, his hands now wet with sweat. "Oh man," he moaned. "I should have never agreed to take this on."

"We're doing the best we can, Robert," Sharon said.

He looked up to see both women staring at him and realized his comment was insensitive.

"Oh. I am so sorry, Sharon. That didn't sound right. I know both of you know what you're doing. It's just that Tom is looking to me to—"

"Well, he should have called you earlier, Robert. I'm sure he's a smart man, but a seller's negotiating leverage erodes quickly after the process starts." Sharon looked at Robert to see if he appeared to understand what she had just said and then continued, "But I've been doing this for a while, and I have an idea."

"Thank God."

"Well, don't get too excited until we see if it works." Sharon sorted the papers on the table until she found what she was looking for. "Here it is. This is a list of the top salesmen at Jackson Life Insurance Company. Know what they all have in common?"

"Uh, no."

"Each of them served in the Army with one E. Thomas Jackson. And, I'm willing to bet, they're extremely loyal."

"How does that help us?"

"There's nothing in the agreement about retaining employees, including Mr. Jackson. If he leaves, I suspect a large percentage of those top salesmen will leave with him. My father was a JAG in the Army Reserve and spoke fondly of the camaraderie in the military. I'm sure those preppy lawyers in Atlanta don't have a clue about that."

"So you think Tom does have some negotiating leverage?"

"Maybe. I'll explain to Darden's counsel that Mr. Jackson will not be continuing with the company and that he can make no guaranties concerning the continued employment of any of its employees. I'm sure that will be a shock to them. Remember, the reason Jackson Life Insurance has been so successful is that it has an incredible sales team. They outperform their competitors year after year."

"I hope you're right, Sharon."

"It's not a question of being 'right,' Robert," Sharon said, sounding a bit testy. "We have to play the cards we're dealt."

"I'm sorry, Sharon. I didn't mean to sound unappreciative."

During the back and forth between Sharon and Robert, Diana said nothing as she continued to examine the documents arranged in neat piles in front of her.

For the next two weeks, the team of Sharon, Diana, and Robert worked almost exclusively on Tom Jackson's transaction. Sharon involved other attorneys at the firm on issues ranging from tax to employment law, and she associated her friends in Atlanta on insurance regulatory matters. Robert worked mostly at home, reviewing boxes and boxes of documents that Sharon sent over. When he met with them in person, it was in the evening, after most of the Underwood & Crockett employees had left for the night. He made a point of parking his Nova where it wouldn't be seen by any of the lawyers in the firm. On several occasions he asked Diana if she wanted to go to dinner when they finished work. Each time she refused, saying she had too much work to do.

There were numerous long telephone calls with Tom Jackson, which always included Robert, although Sharon did most of the talking. She kept Tom updated on what was going on with the transaction and explained her negotiation tactics for dealing with the earnout and other issues. Robert was impressed with how well Sharon handled not only Tom (which was no easy task), but also the lawyers from Martin & Howard. She was a pro. She never raised her voice, but the force of her intelligence and quiet confidence reassured Tom and intimidated opposing counsel. Unfortunately, Darden Industries continued to insist on the earnout. Sharon was able to revise the agreement to include specific provisions concerning how the company would be operated following closing and the accounting practices it would use to determine whether the preconditions to the payment of the earnout had been met. The Martin & Howard lawyers made that concession in exchange for Tom's commitment to stay with the company following the closing, something the Atlanta lawyers realized they had failed to include in the agreement.

The closing was scheduled for Thursday, March 26, at the offices of Martin & Howard in the C&S Bank Building in downtown Atlanta. The building was old, so the offices were not sleek and modern, like those of Underwood & Crockett. Instead, there was an air about them of "old money": oil portraits of former partners, two of whom had gone on to become federal judges and one a U.S. ambassador; antique oriental rugs that covered squeaky hardwood floors; mahogany furniture; and hallways that had more twists and turns than a labyrinth. Robert, Sharon, Diana, and Tom were ushered into a conference room with a massive table, on which had been arranged stacks and stacks of documents.

Initially, the lawyers from Martin & Howard were gracious—the epitome of Southern hospitality. But before anyone had finished the first cup of coffee, they dropped a bombshell: they wanted to revise the agreement to cut the cash paid at closing by almost $15 million and move that amount to the earnout. Consequently, even more of Tom's compensation would be at risk. Worse still, they wanted to add an additional precondition to the payment of the earnout, requiring at least eighty-five percent of the sales staff of Jackson Life Insurance Company to agree to remain with the company for at least a year following its sale to Darden Industries.

Sharon didn't bat an eyelash. She explained that she and her team would have to confer with their client. She had not expected such a venerable firm as Martin & Howard to propose such a significant change from the terms of the letter of intent. Her parting shot was perfect: "You boys remind me of something written by Emerson, which I read in college."

"So, this is an American Literature lecture now?" the senior Martin & Howard attorney asked.

"Not at all," she said. Smiling, she paused for at least five seconds. "If I'm remembering it correctly, Emerson wrote: 'A little integrity is better than any career.'" Then, in a matter-of-fact—almost dismissive—tone, she said, "Now, we'll need to retire to a private conference room to confer with our client."

A Martin & Howard associate led the team and their client through the hallways of the firm to a conference room far removed from the one they had just left. As the door closed, Tom looked at Robert and asked, "What do you think about all this?"

"To tell you the truth, Tom, I think we need to hear what Sharon thinks."

"You know what? You are right, counselor. And let me say right now that I'm glad you asked Sharon to help us, instead of that tight-ass Davis Burnet." Tom put his hand to his mouth. "I'm so sorry, ladies. Being around my old Army buddy brought back my foul mouth."

"No apology necessary, Mr. Jackson. We've heard worse." Sharon was still smiling.

"I've been meaning to tell you, Sharon. Please call me 'Tom.' 'Mr. Jackson' reminds me of my father." Tom had not forgotten how to charm people, especially ladies.

"Well, Tom, they are trying to negotiate a new deal at the closing table, which I despise. It is truly bad form and something I would never do. One sees that kind of behavior in New York sometimes, but I never expected to see it in Atlanta, especially from an old-line firm like Martin & Howard."

Tom leaned back in his chair so far he was staring at the ceiling. Then he sat back up and looked directly at Sharon. "It's kinda like money and ethics are two cars headed straight for each other on a one-lane road. When they meet, ethics winds up in the ditch."

"I couldn't have said it better myself," Sharon said.

"What they don't know, Sharon, is that I really don't want to sell my company. I started talking to Darden Industries, primarily because my wife wants me to cut back. I've been working like crazy the last few years, and she thinks it's going to kill me. But in all honesty, I'm not ready to leave my guys. I'd just as soon keep things as they are."

Tom's comment surprised the three lawyers. But then Robert remembered what Sharon had said about the potential damage to a seller when a deal fails to close. He waited to see what she would say.

"I understand how you feel, Tom. And I, more than most, hate it when someone changes the rules of the game after it's started. But I do need to ask you a few questions."

"Sure." Tom looked at her with an expression of respect.

"Are you concerned that the failure to close this transaction could have an adverse effect on the company?"

"What do you mean?"

"Well, for instance: Have you lost any employees? Are you afraid any of them might leave?

"No. Our most valuable asset is that we have a team culture. That's what I created, and that's what's made us successful. They're my guys—and gals, too. I don't think any of them would consider leaving."

"What about vendors and customers?"

"The vendors are always kissing my as—. Sorry. Almost did it again. Let's just say I'm not worried about the vendors. And our business is retail. We sell to Joe Six Pack and his wife. And I can assure you, they don't read the business section of the *Atlanta Journal Constitution*. So, no. I'm not worried about that."

"Well, then, I think we go back in there and tell them to stuff it."

Sharon's blunt talk made them all smile. Tom laughed outright.

"I like that, Sharon. Let's tell them to stuff it," he said.

As they walked back into the conference room, Robert noticed the smug expressions on the faces of the Martin & Howard lawyers. After they were seated, Sharon said nothing. She just looked at them expectantly. Finally, the lead Martin & Howard lawyer raised his eyebrows and asked, "Well?"

"Well what?" Sharon replied.

"Have you considered our proposal?"

"We have. Our client finds it unacceptable."

"You do understand that Darden Industries insists on those changes because of what we discovered in due diligence?"

"Save your breath. We're finished here. Our client does not intend to sell to Darden Industries on those terms."

"Are you breaching our agreement?"

"No. We don't have an agreement, remember?" Sharon stood up, and everyone else in the room did as well.

"We'll sue your client, Sharon."

"Go ahead. You'll need to be ready to explain to the Georgia Bar why you encouraged my client to sign a letter of intent when you knew he was represented by counsel."

"I don't know anything about that."

Turning to Tom, Sharon asked, "Didn't you tell me you signed the letter of intent in this very conference room?"

"Yes. That gentleman right over there gave it to me. I asked him if I needed to have my attorney review it, and he said 'no.' He said it outlined what Mr. Darden and I had discussed over dinner and that it was nonbinding, so I shouldn't worry about it."

All eyes turned to the lawyer to whom Tom had pointed.

"I was, uh, I was—"

"Be quiet Jeffrey," said the senior Martin & Howard attorney. He turned back to Sharon; his eyes narrowed. "You know that means nothing."

"We'll see," Sharon said. "I think you might find that Mr. Darden—who values his reputation as a *Christian* businessman—won't want the adverse publicity that would come from a lawsuit in which the defendant, an Army veteran, would assert that he was misled by Mr. Darden and his team of lawyers who apparently have forgotten the Rules of Professional Responsibility." Sharon turned and walked out of the room, followed by Diana and Robert and Tom.

When they reached the street level, Tom spoke first. "That was impressive, Sharon. Do you think they'll sue me?"

"Who knows, Tom? They could, but I doubt they will. There's no signed agreement, and I think Mr. Darden does value his public image.

And, the Martin & Howard boys won't want to be embarrassed by the way in which they treated you, so I doubt they'll advise Mr. Darden to file suit."

"Well then, let's go celebrate."

"Tom," Sharon said, "I believe that's the first time I've ever had a client suggest that we celebrate a deal that's cratered."

"Well, I'm probably your most unusual client," Tom said, his trademark grin on full display.

# CHAPTER THIRTY-SEVEN

THAT EVENING TOM insisted on having what he called his "Dodged-a-Bullet Celebration" at the Sun Dial, a revolving restaurant at the top of The Westin Peachtree Plaza Hotel, a modern, cylindrical building in the heart of downtown Atlanta. As the restaurant rotated, revealing a panoramic view of the Atlanta skyline, Tom regaled the group with stories of the murder trial Robert had prosecuted in Panama. With great relish, he told how the judge, annoyed with the contentious behavior of Robert and the defense counsel, had banged his gavel so hard the head broke off and tumbled across the floor of the court room. That caused Sharon and Diana to turn and look at Robert as if they had never seen him before.

"What can I say?" Robert shrugged. "I was young and inexperienced."

Diana suppressed a smile. "When I heard Alan tell those stories about your murder trial, I never imagined anything like that!"

"That's not all," Tom continued, "I watched the whole thing. Clark, I mean uh, Robert was brilliant. He had the accused crying on the stand and got him convicted. But that wasn't even the best part." Sharon and Diana stopped eating and stared at Tom intently. "After the trial was over, Robert's chief witness said he wanted to change his testimony."

"But the trial was over." Diana looked puzzled.

"Well, that's not how courts-martial work," Tom replied without missing a beat, even though a former Army JAG was sitting next to him. "The general has to review the record of trial and can reduce the sentence or even set aside the conviction."

"That's interesting," Sharon said. "But why do you say that was the best part?"

"Because Robert told the defense counsel about it instead of telling his boss, the Staff Judge Advocate."

Robert squirmed in his chair, not noticing that Diana was smiling at him.

"Tom, I don't think these ladies want to hear any more about that old case."

"Oh, yes, I do," Sharon said. "But I still don't understand why that was the best part. Was that procedure improper?"

"Well, it wasn't by the book." Tom grinned. "But Robert knew that his boss would do virtually anything to please the general who desperately wanted a conviction for the little girl's murder. You see, Robert's boss had been caught, shall we say, *in flagrante delicto*, with another colonel's wife. And so, he was trying to get back in the good graces of the Commanding General. Robert knew his boss would have found a way to bury the information about the witness wanting to change his testimony."

"Oh my." Sharon cocked her head. "Even senior officers were doing that sort of thing? Was it that wild in Panama?"

"Absolutely," Tom said. "That and more. There was another guy who—"

"Whoa, Tom," Robert said, holding up his hand in protest but smiling. "I know where this is headed, so let's not go there." Tom smirked and took a sip of water. "And," Robert continued, "I need to set the record straight. My co-counsel is the one who insisted we should go to the defense counsel with that information, and she was right."

"Watkins was the one who told me all about it," Tom said, turning toward Robert. "She knew it was hard for you because you'd gotten all that praise for the conviction and would catch hell for the reversal. Ladies, Robert here was an actual celebrity on the post until he torpedoed his own case by giving that information to the defense counsel."

"Watkins told you all that?" Robert asked.

"Yeah." Tom raised his eyebrows and shook his head. "You know, you and I both underestimated that woman."

As Robert turned to face Sharon and Diana, he bumped his wine glass, almost knocking it over it. "What can I say? Some of us are slow learners."

Diana was smiling at him, but he couldn't tell whether it was a boys-will-be-boys teacher smile or a sincere I-need-to-get-to-know-this-man smile. He continued, "Can we change the subject, Tom? Please."

"I agree," Sharon chimed in. "This has been most entertaining, and I've gotten a glimpse of an entirely different side of you, Robert, but I'd like to talk about what happened today."

"As I told you, Sharon," Tom said, shaking his head, "I wasn't all that keen on selling my company, anyway. And given the way those bastards treated me, I don't even want to think about what they would have done to my people after they owned the company."

"So, you're fine with everything?"

"Yes. I am. Totally. And let me tell you, I bet J.B. Darden calls me next week to say it was all a serious misunderstanding. You pegged him right, Sharon, about that Christian-businessman stuff. In my experience, when a businessman leads with all that religious talk, saying 'let's pray' before a business meeting and asking if you're a Christian, it's time to hold on to your wallet."

Everyone chuckled at that comment, which transitioned the conversation to other subjects. For the remainder of the evening, Robert tried to decide, from Diana's comments and glances, whether she was interested in him. He would catch her looking at him from across the table but then would recall how she'd rebuffed each of his dinner invitations while they were working on Tom's transaction. He was confused.

Around 10:00 p.m. Sharon explained that she and Diana had changed their flight plans and were flying out the next morning, so they needed to get back to the hotel. Tom drove everyone there in his BMW. Robert rode in front with him; Sharon and Diana were in the back. As they drove up to the hotel, Robert thought about asking Diana if she wanted to get a nightcap, but she and Sharon quickly said good night and goodbye and headed for the elevator.

Robert had booked his flight back for Monday morning, so he could spend the weekend with his mother in Pemberton. There was no reason for him to get back to Dallas any sooner. Not feeling ready for bed, he headed to the bar alone. Following three drinks and a long conversation with the bartender, he went to bed late, so he missed seeing Sharon and

Diana before they left for the airport. He skipped breakfast, bought a coffee to go, and headed for Pemberton.

The drive would take almost three hours, giving him time to think. As he steered his rental car onto Interstate 75 South, his thoughts turned melancholy—something about being back in Georgia, where so much of his life had unfolded, made him sad.

Some career I've got going, he thought. All that talk about Panama last night reminded me of how badly I fouled that up, along with my marriage. Too much ambition and not enough thought. Too little character, until Watkins prodded me to do the right thing. I can't believe Tom brought up Watkins. I haven't thought about her in years. Robert smiled as he recalled his frumpy, assertive co-counsel. Yeah, Tom was right: we definitely underestimated her. She never lost sight of what we were supposed to be doing. And, she was the first person who told me Janelle and I weren't right for each other. I wonder what she's doing now.

Robert drove on for a few minutes thinking more about Panama—the rowdy parties, the fishing, the perpetual summer, and that horrible autopsy he attended while preparing for the murder trial. The memory of seeing that child being dissected like a biology lab project jarred him back to the present and his most pressing concern.

How am I going to find another job? And where? Every law firm in Dallas will ask why I left the much vaunted Underwood & Crockett after only seven months. I don't even know anyone in Dallas other than people at the firm and Alan's family. Maybe I should come back to Georgia. I'd be closer to Ellie and Momma. But that would mean I'd have no chance with Diana. Who am I kidding? I sabotaged that by dating Megan. If I do come back to Georgia, I'm still going to have to explain what I was doing in Dallas for seven months. And, I still have five months left on my lease. Shit. There aren't any good options. I've done it again.

What am I going to do? How in the hell am I going to pay child support? I'm sure Judge Harrington would be only too happy to tell me it's my problem. I don't even want to ask Larry to go before him again, after what happened last time. But if I don't find a job soon, I'll wipe out the meager amount I've saved.

# CHAPTER THIRTY-EIGHT

ROBERT MADE IT to Pemberton by noon, but instead of heading straight to his mother's house, he drove around town, reminiscing about growing up there—parades on Main Street, Christmas shopping at Belk's department store on the square, sneaking a peak at *Playboy* magazine in the back of Atkin's Pharmacy. That memory made him smile. Mr. Atkins knew all the boys peeped at the adult magazines, but he didn't seem to mind. He hadn't forgotten what it was like to be young.

Around 12:30 p.m., he finally pulled into his mother's driveway. Ruth popped out of the back door as if on cue. She'd obviously been waiting for him. As soon as he stepped out of the car, she hugged him tightly, seeming to know—as good mothers do—that he needed it. That feeling of I-want-my-mom has no age limit. She knew her son was hurting and that he needed reassurance everything was going to be okay.

As usual, the aromas in Ruth's kitchen brought back a flood of treasured memories. She had set the table with the good dishes and had prepared a lunch that was normally reserved for Sundays, when lunch was called "dinner." Having her boy come home for a visit was obviously special. After feasting on fried chicken, mashed potatoes, green beans, and freshly baked rolls, Robert insisted on doing the dishes while his mother sat at the table with her coffee. When he was finished, he poured a cup and joined her.

"So, tell me about this meeting you were at in Atlanta." His mother's eyes sparkled over the rim of her cup as they had when she used to ask him about his school day.

"Well, it didn't turn out like we expected. Tom backed out of the deal."

"He backed out?"

"Uh-huh, they changed the terms of the deal at the last minute, and Tom said he'd had enough. He seemed to be fine with it, though. He told us he wasn't all that excited about selling his company anyway."

"So, what are you going to do now?"

Robert knew his mother wanted him to say he was moving back to Pemberton, but instead he said, "I don't know, Momma. I've made so many bad decisions, I think I need to take my time with this one."

"You haven't made bad decisions, Bobby. You're a West Point graduate and a lawyer. How many people can say that?"

"And I'm unemployed, Momma. I got fired from the leading firm in Texas."

"Well, I think you did the right thing. Your daddy would be proud."

"That's all well and good, but I don't know how I'm gonna make my child support payments."

"I can pay them for you."

"No, Momma. I'm a grown man. You're not going to pay my child support. I'll figure something out. I just don't know what that is right now."

"Do you think you might want to work for Larry?" She stared at him and gently bit her lower lip. "He was just selected to be the attorney for the City of Pemberton, so he's real busy. I'm sure he could use the help."

"Momma, that's not the kind of law I've done or want to do."

Ruth looked down into her coffee cup.

"I'm sorry, Momma. I know you're trying to be helpful, but I just don't think it would be a good idea for me to approach Larry about a job."

"Okay. I just thought—"

Robert took his mother's hand and kissed it. "I love you, Momma. You've always been there for me."

Ruth's eyes began to glisten. "And your daddy was, too."

"Of course. Daddy, too. The biggest mistakes I've made in life were because I didn't listen carefully enough to the lessons y'all were trying to teach me."

Ruth's eyes began to fill with tears. "Oh, I just remembered something." She sat up straight and composed herself. "Janelle called, asking about when you were coming home."

"You didn't tell her I'd been fired, did you?"

"Of course not, sweetheart. She just wants to meet with you while you're in Pemberton."

"Meet with me? Did she say what about?"

"No. But why don't you meet her for lunch at the Swanson Inn? It's not crowded on Saturdays. If you want me to call her and set it up, I'll be happy to. I'll probably be keeping Ellie when y'all meet anyway."

"No. I'll call her, Momma. I just wish I knew what it was all about."

Janelle sounded even more distant than usual when Robert arranged to meet for lunch on Saturday, so he was anxious about how things might go. The next day he arrived early at the Swanson Inn, and as his mother had predicted, there were only a few other customers present. He sat down at a table in a quiet corner, ordered an ice tea, and waited. When Janelle walked in, Robert was struck by how old she looked. He had seen her at Christmas and briefly at Junior's funeral, but she appeared to have aged years since then. Maybe she was grieving over losing Junior. She spotted Robert in the corner, managed a half-smile, and headed his way. A weary sigh escaped her lips as she wilted into her chair, looking down before making eye contact.

"Thank you for meeting me," she said. "This is fancier than I expected." That half-smile again.

"We probably should have been doing this more often—for Ellie's sake, don't you think?" he said.

"Well, you were at Fort McPherson in Atlanta and then all of a sudden in Dallas. I didn't know what to think."

"Yeah. I guess I just felt like I needed a new start."

Janelle was quiet until the waitress appeared to take their order.

"I guess I'll have the special and ice tea," Janelle said.

"Me, too," Robert said, with a nod and an expression that indicated they wanted to be left alone.

"I'm sorry about Junior's accident, Janelle. I didn't mean to create a ruckus at the funeral home. I just wanted to see that Ellie and you were all right."

"That's okay. Mr. White is a bit of a jerk. Junior had his moments, too, but he was mostly okay. I'm not really sure why we were together. I guess I just wanted to get out of Daddy's house."

Robert wanted to ask her why she had left him in Panama without any explanation whatsoever but decided that wouldn't be a good idea at the moment.

"Well, anyway, Janelle, I'm sorry for your loss."

The waitress arrived with their orders, and having missed the Southern cooking he'd grown up with, Robert dug right in. Janelle picked at her food for a few minutes without saying anything. And then: "I have cancer, Bobby."

"What? What did you say?"

"I have cancer. I tried to think of a way to tell you, but as usual I came up with nothing. So, I just said it."

Robert raised his hand to ward off the waitress headed toward their table to refill their tea glasses. He was silent for a long while, not sure of what to say. "Janelle, I'm so sorry. Have you gone to see doctors in Atlanta?"

"No. It's too late for that. I'm Stage IV, Bobby, which means it's spread to other parts of my body. I'm not gonna do chemo. What's the point? I'd spend my final days in agony and die anyway."

Although they might not have been "right" for each other, Robert still cared about the mother of his daughter, despite the way she left him in Panama and despite the visitation order she had agreed to.

"What can I do, Janelle?"

"We've got to talk about what will happen with Ellie. I don't want my daddy raising her, and as much as I love your momma, she's not right either. Ellie needs her daddy, Bobby."

Robert was silent. The problems with his career suddenly seemed insignificant, almost childish. It would make no sense to take Ellie to Dallas. But where else could he get a job? Savannah? Macon? Maybe he should follow his mother's advice and ask Larry about a position.

"Does Ellie know?" he asked.

"No. I don't see the point of telling her now. I will at some point."

"Do you want me to be with you when you tell her?"

"No. I have no idea when that might be, Bobby. And, of course, you've got to get back to Dallas." Janelle's irritation at his devotion to his career was apparent in her voice.

"Janelle, you can be sure I'll do what's best for Ellie."

"Can you do that, Bobby?" She sniffled and wiped her nose, her eyes now red. "Or will your job always get in the way, and you'll leave it to someone else to raise her?"

Robert said nothing. He just stared at Janelle for almost a minute.

"I need your promise, Bobby." Her eyes were tired and filled with tears.

"You're right, Janelle. I've got to get my priorities straight. And I will. I promise. But I need to tell you something else." He paused, wondering whether he should tell her. "I got fired."

"Fired? You?" She almost laughed at the implausibility of that news.

"Yeah. I'd rather not go into the details. Let's just say I was asked to do something I wasn't going to do. Anyway, there's nothing holding me in Dallas anymore." As soon as he said those words, an image of Diana, sitting across the table from him in Atlanta, flashed through his mind. "Yeah, uh, like I said, nothing is holding me in Dallas. I'll look for a job in Savannah or Macon or Atlanta. Anyway…" His chin began to tremble, and his voice quavered. "I won't let Ellie forget you or your daddy. And I'll never say anything bad about you to her. I promise."

"Thanks, Bobby. I needed to hear all that from you." A haggard breath parted her lips as she slumped back in her chair. "I think I'm going to go now. I'm pretty tired, and I'm not very hungry. Daddy's watching Ellie, and he's not very good at it." She tried to smile, but the effort seemed too much for her. "Do you want me to bring her by your momma's house this afternoon? She can spend the night, if you'd like."

"Of course. That would be wonderful. I was hoping to see her on this trip."

"I'll keep you posted on how things go with me. Don't worry about paying child support until you find a job. And please don't tell your momma or anyone else what I told you. I don't want to get all those looks on the street or those insincere I'll-be-praying-for-you comments. You know how it is around here. I just want to die in peace."

Robert reached over and took both her hands in his. It was the first time they had touched in years. He looked at her for several moments and then said, "I *will* pray for you, Janelle. I mean it."

Her eyes welled up, and she nodded but said nothing.

# CHAPTER THIRTY-NINE

"WHAT'S WRONG, SWEETHEART?" Ruth asked, as soon as Robert walked through the back door.

"Nothing, Momma. It was just weird having lunch with Janelle after all this time." He turned away so she couldn't scrutinize his face further. "She's going to bring Ellie by this afternoon," he said over his shoulder. "She said she can spend the night. I assumed that was okay with you."

"Well of course it is. That's wonderful. I can't get enough of that sweet child. Oh, I need to tell you something. While you were out, Mr. Jackson called. He gave me his number and asked that you call him back right away. What a delightful man he is. I can see why y'all were friends in Panama."

I guess a part of Elmer lives on inside the new Tom, Robert thought. I've never seen a woman he couldn't charm, even over the phone, even one old enough to be his mother. I hope he hasn't changed his mind and is now upset that his deal didn't close.

Robert dialed the number on the paper his mother handed him.

"Jackson residence, Ruby speaking."

"This is Robert Clark. I'm returning a call from Mr. Jackson."

"Just one moment, sir."

Robert could hear Ruby calling Tom to the phone.

"Thanks for calling me back, man."

"You have a maid?"

"Yeah. Now I know what you're thinking. But she doesn't come every day. We have this big house, and it's too much for Tracy to take care of by herself. Anyway, I'm glad you called. Your mom said you were driving back to Atlanta tomorrow, so you could catch an early flight on Monday."

"Yeah. Say, how'd you get my mom's phone number?" Robert asked.

"There are only two 'Clarks' in the Pemberton phone book, Robert. The other one is your dad's cousin."

"Oh yeah, I guess that's right. Dumb question."

"Why don't you drive up and stay with us Sunday night? I'll be happy to drive you to the airport on Monday morning."

"I wouldn't want to impose."

"You won't be imposing. We can catch up on old times. We've been so focused on this transaction, we've barely had time to talk like we did in Panama."

"That's nice of you, Tom. Would it be okay if I get there around five? I wanted to take Momma to church tomorrow and lunch afterwards."

"Sure. That'll be perfect. I'll grill steaks. Do you still smoke cigars?"

"Of course. You know, that does sound like Panama. I look forward to it."

Robert didn't know what to think as he hung up the phone. Tom sounded genuinely excited to have him stay with them. It certainly would make things easier—and less expensive.

Later that afternoon Janelle dropped off Ellie for her visit but didn't get out of the car. Ellie walked to the front door by herself. When Ruth opened the door, Janelle just waved and pulled away.

Robert and Ellie spent most of the afternoon outside, enjoying an unusually warm spring day. Ellie loved swinging in the tire swing that Robert had hung in a pecan tree in the backyard almost twenty years before. At first, he had hung the tire high enough to practice throwing a football through it. But after concluding his arm was never going to be as good as Mike Griffin's, the quarterback of his high school team, he lowered the tire to use it as a swing.

He watched Ellie's blonde ringlets flutter as she swung back and forth and recalled that terrible evening when he had raced to Gorgas Hospital in Panama—her hair dancing in the breeze coming through the car windows. She had become dehydrated as a result of bacterial diarrhea, something that was common among young children in the military community in Panama. Robert remembered falling to his knees next to her hospital bed, after he was told she was going to be all right, begging God to forgive him for not taking care of his little girl and promising he would do better. Now, as he watched her smile and laugh in the swing, he asked himself whether he had honored that prayer. Wasn't she more important than his job? Janelle certainly saw it that way. Why had he gone to Texas instead of staying nearby in Georgia? Had he simply run away without knowing where he was running to?

As the sun slipped low in the sky, Ruth called from the porch, telling them to come inside and get cleaned up for supper. Darlene and Frank joined them for another one of Ruth's feasts. After dinner they all played Crazy Eights around the kitchen table. It almost felt like old times, together with his family in the house where so much of his life had taken place, warm, safe, and loved.

The next day they all went to church and then to the Swanson Inn for lunch. Ruth was tearful but smiling as Robert loaded his suitcase into the rental car around 2:00 p.m. Ellie hugged him around his waist and demanded to know when he was coming back. He promised her it would be soon. His life was in turmoil, and he knew he had to fix it. Ellie deserved the kind of childhood he'd had, and that was going to be tough to give her, in light of Janelle's news.

The drive to Atlanta took him past mile after mile of agricultural fields, causing him to reflect on how different his parents' lives were from his own. He had been striving for so many years, engaged in all manner of activities—West Point, Airborne School, Ranger School, law school, Army JAG and prosecutor—all of them in the pursuit of what he thought would be a better life. He had been so focused on those activities he had forgotten the lessons from his childhood. His parents understood the inner value of just being alive, enjoying each other's company, sharing each other's joys and sorrows. He didn't really know his own daughter, despite his prayer on that fateful night in Panama. What's her favorite color? What did she tell me her doll's name was? What does she want to be when she grows up?

Robert had promised Janelle that this time he would get his priorities straight. As Interstate 16 merged into Interstate 75 in Macon, he resolved to do just that. His job and his career would have to take a backseat to his most important responsibility: that of being a father.

Tom's house was located on West Paces Ferry Road, only a short distance from the Governor's Mansion. The street was lined with mature oaks and dogwoods, the latter of which were already bursting forth with white bracts arrayed around small clusters of yellow flowers, announcing the end of winter. In the front yards, red and pink and white azaleas bloomed beneath the trees and in flower beds. They reminded him of something his father had told him: in Chinese culture, azaleas are known as the "thinking of home bush." His trip to Pemberton, especially learning about Janelle's cancer, had convinced him he needed to do more than think of home, he needed to *be* home, regardless of how that might affect the life he had envisioned for himself.

A maid who Robert assumed must be Ruby answered the front door. "Mr. Jackson is waiting for you on the patio. I've never seen him so excited. You must be somebody special."

"No. I'm not special. Just an old Army friend."

"I see," Ruby snickered, suggesting she might be aware of her boss's exploits in the Army. "Come this way, please." She led him to a bluestone terrace overlooking a pool and gardens worthy of an English estate.

"At last. You're here. You remember Tracy, don't you, Robert?" Tom walked toward him wearing chinos and a sweater, looking like someone in an L.L. Bean catalogue.

"I do indeed," Robert replied, though he wasn't sure he did. "It's so good to see you again."

Wealth had been kind to Tracy Jackson. Gone was the chubby housewife with mousey brown hair who wore nothing but jeans and T-shirts. In her place stood a well-coiffed, trim blonde, tastefully attired in clothes that must have come from the posh shops in Phipps Plaza on Peachtree Street. Most striking of all, though, was the exquisite, two-carat diamond ring that graced her left hand. Robert's cynical side wondered whether that was the price Elmer had paid for a second chance—as Tom.

"It's so good to see you, Robert," she said, "though I find myself still wanting to call you 'Clark.' "

"I'll answer to just about anything, Tracy. Sometimes, Panama seems like it was yesterday, doesn't it?" As soon as he said that, Robert realized she probably wanted to forget most of what happened in Panama.

"Well, I'm going to leave you two fellas to talk."

As Tracy stepped inside, Ruby appeared with a platter of sirloin strip steaks, which Tom immediately threw onto the grill. For the next fifteen minutes, Tom held forth on the proper way to prepare a steak. The aroma made Robert's mouth water, even though he'd eaten a late lunch. Tom had just finished when, as if on cue, Ruby emerged again from the kitchen with a bowl of tossed salad and tray of steaming baked potatoes. Tracy joined them, and the three of them enjoyed dinner on the terrace, complemented by wine that would have made Alan Taylor jealous, though Tom did not partake. When they finished, Tracy excused herself, and Tom brought out bourbon and cigars and poured Robert a hefty drink.

"Aren't you having one, Tom?" Robert asked.

"Nope. Have you forgotten so soon, Robert? I'm an alcoholic. I don't drink anymore, though I don't mind if others do. And if I remember correctly, you have a fondness for Maker's Mark."

"Good memory, buddy. But I feel funny drinking by myself."

"You're not. I'm having a cigar with you and a Coke. And that's fine with me. It's my go-to substitute."

By this time the sun had set and the night air was beginning to get cool. After lighting their cigars, they settled in next to a fire pit in the backyard. Tom threw on another log, which sent sparks floating up into the night sky.

"Now for the good part," Tom said.

"I don't know, Tom, that meal would be hard to beat."

"Thanks. But that's not what I meant. What I meant by 'the good part' is that now we can talk about what I wanted to discuss with you—not that I don't enjoy the simple pleasure of your company, mind you." Tom's grin was reminiscent of the old Elmer—charming and devilish at the same time.

Robert was unsure what was coming next, so he braced himself for the worst.

"Why did you set me up with that lesbian partner?"

Damn, Robert thought.

"Well, I, uh—"

"Don't get me wrong, Robert. I thought she was perfect. I'm just curious about why you picked her."

Relief.

"Honestly? She is the only partner I trusted. And, she'd previously handled the sale of an insurance company, so she knows what's involved. How did you know she's gay?"

"Come on, Robert. You know me. In the old days I chased my fair share of women, remember?"

"How could I forget?"

"Well, over time you can spot the signs. Anyway, I wanted to thank you. She did an excellent job. The best lawyer I've ever worked with—besides, you, of course. I'll admit, like many guys in the Army, I had my prejudices about gays. But I put all that behind me a long time ago." Tom noticed Robert staring at him blankly. "What? You thought I was going to embarrass you?"

"Uh, no. No. Of course not."

"Bullshit, Robert. You can't fool me." Tom smirked and took a long draw on his cigar.

"So, is that what you wanted to talk about?" Robert asked.

"No. I want you to come to work for me."

"What?"

"Yeah. You remember I told y'all that Tracy was worried that this job is going to kill me? Well, I need an executive officer. I like being the commander, but I need someone to ensure that things get done when they're supposed to, to keep things organized and on track. And, I could use a general counsel, too. All that legal bullshit makes my eyes glaze over."

"I'm honored, Tom. But like I told you with your deal, I don't have much civilian experience."

"That's not why I want to hire you. I need someone who thinks like me. You can learn the legal stuff fast enough. Hell, you can hire your two ladies as outside counsel for all I care. I trust you, and I know what you can do. And, I'll give you some stock options that will make you a wealthy man when we finally sell the company, which I hope will be a long way in the future." Tom paused and stared at him for several moments with his piercing blue eyes. "Well, what do you say?"

"I need to think about it, Tom. I've made too many hasty decisions in my life and wound up regretting that I didn't think things through first. This time I need to—"

"I know. I know. You don't want to do something rash. You have your career to consider. *Et cetera, et cetera.* But what's there to think about, Robert? You need a job. I need someone I can trust. I'll pay you at least what you were making at that law firm, plus stock options."

"That's really generous, Tom. And don't get me wrong. I really appreciate the offer, but I need to find something close to Pemberton. I found out yesterday that Janelle has cancer."

"Damn. Is it serious? What's the prognosis?"

"She didn't say, but it can't be good. She's Stage IV and has refused chemo. She said she didn't want to live her final days in agony."

"Well, I can see why you need to be in Pemberton. You'll need your mother to help with Ellie and all. But you still have to earn a living. Look. I don't want to sound insensitive, but I can help you with being in Pemberton, too."

"What do you mean?"

Tom took another long draw on his cigar and exhaled slowly. "Tracy wants to move to Wilmington Island."

"Really?"

"Yeah. So, I'm going to move the company headquarters to Savannah. And that's pretty close to Pemberton, isn't it?"

"Yeah, but... What about all your employees in Atlanta?"

"I'll keep an office in Atlanta, too. The ones who want to can stay there. But I think most of them will welcome the move. Most of my guys hate the Atlanta traffic almost as much as Tracy does. Basically, she's a small-town girl with new-found, big-city tastes. Oh, and I'm going to get a company jet, or at least a part interest in one. That way we can go back and forth without the hassle of driving."

"All that sounds perfect, and I don't want to appear ungrateful, but could you give me a few days to think about it? I need to see if I can get out of my lease in Dallas."

"Come on, Robert. You can't let minor things like a lease get in the way of where you want to go." Robert avoided eye contact. "Look," Tom continued, "if you can't get out of your lease and you can't sublet the place, the company will pay it. Dallas is a good market. We can use the apartment when our folks need to go out there. Can you leave it furnished?"

"Uh, sure, but it's nothing special, Tom."

"Robert, most of my guys are retired Army. They just want a clean place to sleep, take a shit, and watch T.V."

Robert chuckled. That sounded like the old Elmer. He studied Tom's expression, recalling how he had jumped into action to get him on the next flight home from Panama when his father was dying, how he'd encouraged him when he was struggling to learn the ropes of being a prosecutor, how he'd stood by him and encouraged him when the murder conviction unraveled and Robert's celebrity status evaporated, and, of course, how he had entrusted him with the sale of his company. Then as now, Tom always seemed to be trying to help him.

"You know what, Tom? I don't need any time. I'll take the job." Tom's face lit up. "And—thank you, although those words don't seem nearly strong enough to express how I feel." Robert paused and then said, "I do need a few days to get clear of Dallas, though."

"Take all the time you need. What are you going to tell Diana?"

"What do you mean?"

"Come on, Robert. You know what I mean. I saw you two looking all googly eyes at each other during dinner."

"I don't think she's interested in me, Tom. I asked her to dinner a few times while we were working on your deal, and she said 'no.' "

"Well," Tom said, "it's for sure you wouldn't make it as one of my salesmen. We get told 'no' all the time. It doesn't mean a damn thing. The question is: Are *you* interested in *her*?"

"I think so, but I need to get my personal situation squared away first."

"Fair enough. But you'd better tell her you'd like to see her. If she thinks you're not interested, she may not wait around."

"Good advice. You know, I have this rental car, so you don't need to drive me to the airport. But I do need to get up early to turn it in and catch my flight, so I'd better hit the hay."

"Okay." Tom puffed his cigar.

"Like I said, buddy: thanks doesn't seem nearly strong enough."

"It's gonna be great, Robert. Just like old times."

# CHAPTER FORTY

BY THE TIME Robert made it back to his duplex, the afternoon sun was streaming through the branches of the mature oaks in the front yard, creating dappled patterns of light across the front of the building. It was his favorite time of day—a temporary lull in the turmoil that was his life. Although he was glad to be leaving Dallas, he felt strangely wistful about what might have been if Davis had been different, if he'd avoided Megan, if he'd focused more on Diana. But none of that happened. It made no sense to ponder what might have been: he had too much to do. He needed to get on with it. His answering machine informed him he had two messages: one from Alan, asking him to call him at home, and a second from Barry, also asking for a call. He decided to try Barry first.

"Suncoast Automotive. Glenda speaking."

"Could I please speak with Barry Daniel? This is his friend, Robert Clark."

"Oh! Are you the famous lawyer?"

"Huh?"

"Barry claims he knows a famous lawyer in Dallas named Robert Clark."

"Well, I am Robert Clark, but I'm certainly not famous. Barry left a message on my answering machine, asking me to call him. I'm not sure whether it's urgent or not."

"Oh. Okay. I'll get him for you."

Glenda put her hand over the receiver, though Robert could still hear her yelling for Barry over the noise of the office.

"Well, well. The famous lawyer calls me again." Robert could almost see the grin on Barry's face.

"Why'd you tell folks I'm famous?"

"Aw, just having some fun." Barry chuckled, causing him to cough a few times, the wheezy way smokers do. "Excuse me, Bobby. I gotta quit these damn cigarettes." His voice turned serious. "Your momma called me last week." He paused for a reply, but Robert offered none. "She's worried about you getting fired and all. I just wanted to tell you not to sweat it. I know you'll be okay."

"Thanks, Barry. But as it turns out, Tom Jackson—the guy whose deal I was working on—offered me a job in Savannah."

"I thought you was sellin' his company."

"The deal fell through. Anyway, he's going to move the company headquarters to Savannah, and he wants me to come to work for him."

"Well, see. Like I told you. That'll sure make your momma happy. Why don't you come through Panama City on your way back? We could have us some fun for a day or two."

Robert hesitated. His normal response would have been to say that he had work to do. But he didn't. "You know what, Barry? That sounds like a great idea. I have to pack up and clear out of here, so it'll be Friday before I can get there."

"Friday's good. I gotta work during the week. We'll do some partying, and you can drive to your momma's on Monday. I'm at Seaview Apartments in Panama City, apartment 15. The people in the front office know me. I'll tell 'em you're comin' so they can let you in my place if you get there before I get home."

"Sounds good. See you Friday afternoon." Robert flopped into his recliner. An inner sense of peace came over him.

*Everything's falling into place. Thank God for Tom Jackson.* He suddenly remembered his other message. *I wonder what Alan's going to say? And why did he tell me to call him at home? That's strange. I hope he doesn't get mad that I'm leaving Dallas. He's so high on this place.*

"This is Alan Taylor."

"Hey, man. This is Robert."

"Where the hell have you been?"

Robert immediately felt defensive, as if he owed Alan an explanation.

"I, uh, decided to visit my mom while I was in Georgia. It's not like I have a job to come back to. What's up?"

"No, man. It's all good. It's just that I heard your deal cratered."

"Yeah. The buyer tried to renegotiate at the closing table, and Tom told them to shove it. Did you get an update from Sharon?"

"No. Diana. But the big news is they both quit."

"What?"

"Yeah. They came in the office Friday afternoon and resigned."

"Where'd they go?"

"Nobody knows. Sharon's wealthy, so she doesn't really have to work. I don't know what Diana's up to."

"Wow."

"And that's not all. I quit, too."

"Holy shit. You're not going to sue the firm about not making partner early, are you?"

"No, although I'm still pissed that Davis hung all that crap on me. And get this: Davis and Hugh were sanctioned by Judge Carter."

"Sanctioned? For what?"

"Apparently, Davis abused Donna one too many times. She contacted that asshole John Dickerson and told him she had proof that Davis had seen the infamous letter from Scott & Cranston and had instructed her to shred it and all the other records involving Scott & Cranston's valuations of the company. But she didn't. She gave them to Dickerson. Can you imagine the look on Davis's face when she showed up as a surprise witness at the second hearing? Needless to say, she's no longer employed by the firm. But I wouldn't be surprised if she sued the firm. It's going to be a mess."

"Whoa. Damn."

"It gets worse—or better—depending on your perspective," Alan laughed. "When the judge reviewed all the stuff Donna had given Dickerson, the whole going-private transaction blew up. The court found that Davis and Scott & Cranston and Mr. Russell had engaged in a quote 'manipulative scheme' close quote that failed to establish the fair dealing of the board and the special committee. Mr. Russell was so angry he fired the firm. And he was Davis's biggest client by far."

"Serves Davis right. So why did you quit?"

"Something you said that night we had dinner at my apartment got me thinking. And you were right: I haven't appreciated the sacrifices my dad made for our family. So, I told him I wanted to go flying with him the next time he got a chance." Alan let out a breathy chuckle. "He had that lined up in less than twenty-four hours. I wanted to talk with him while no one else was around. You made me realize I'm in no position to criticize him for failing to fight for social justice. So, I wanted to talk to him like we did in the old days. We had a great time flying. It was like I was a kid again, only I understood so much better what he was trying to tell me."

"He's proud of you, Alan."

"Yeah, I know. But anyway, I've decided to go to work for the Organization of African Unity. You might say I decided to follow my own advice: I've been blessed, and I need to give back." Alan waited for a response, but Robert was too stunned to say anything, so Alan continued, "Want to buy my BMW? I'm selling everything."

"Uh, no, Alan. I can't afford your BMW. And anyway, it's too much car for me." Robert struggled to compose what he wanted to say next. "I admire you, Alan. But don't make the same mistake I've made so many times. Think about what your long-term goal is and whether working for this organization will further that goal."

"You know, Robert, I'm not sure whether this will further my long-term goal. Hell, I'm not even sure I know what my long-term goal is. It just seems to be the right thing right now. Dad reminded me of a quote from Dr. Martin Luther King: 'The time is always right to do what is right.' Like I said, this seems to be what is right for me right now. I think I can help and maybe working in Africa will help me figure out what my long-term goal *should* be. I've decided it's got to be more than having designer suits, a cool apartment, and a BMW."

"So, you've already told the firm?"

"Yeah. Friday was my last day. They acted like they cared, but I know they don't. I've seen it before. They want to act like they're supporting the career of a young black man, but they'd just as soon I leave. They get their liberal credentials burnished. And, they're rid of me."

"Now you sound cynical," Robert said.

"Just keeping it real, man. What are you going to do? I have plenty of contacts at other firms in town that I can introduce you to."

"Actually, I got a job. Tom Jackson wants me to work for him."

"No shit. Well, that's great, man. When do you start?"

"As soon as I get cleared out of here and get back to Georgia." Robert hesitated, expecting Alan to give him a hard time for asking the next question, but knowing he had to ask. "You wouldn't happen to have a new office phone number or address for Diana, would you?"

"Are you still sweet on her?" Alan teased, the way guys do when it comes to matters of the heart.

"Maybe. I'd just like to talk to her before I go."

"You still not believing she's gay, are you? You know I'm right. She may not be Sharon's lover, but she's definitely gay."

"I don't care one way or the other, Alan. I just want to say goodbye."

"Well, I don't have anything for you. Nobody knows where she went. Have you checked the phone book? She's probably listed."

"Duh. I don't know why I never think of looking in the phone book. I guess I could try her at home. Listen, take care of yourself, my friend. I'll never forget how you helped me."

"Yeah, but it didn't turn out so well," Alan said.

"That's not your fault. You tried. Hey, please stay in touch. Will you actually be stationed in Africa?"

"Yeah. My mom's not too happy about that, but Dad is all smiles. And yes, I will definitely stay in touch. I'll probably hit you and your rich friend up for a donation."

"Count on it, buddy."

Robert hung up the phone and immediately began looking for the phone book. Surprisingly, there was only one listing for a "Diana Maguire"; he dialed the number.

"This is Diana Maguire. You've reached my answering machine. If this concerns a matter involving Underwood & Crockett, please contact

Lydia Styles at (214) 555-4000. If this concerns anything else, please leave a message at the beep and I'll call you back when I can."

"Uh, Diana, this is, uh, Robert. I'm back in Dallas. Big surprise: Tom offered me a job. So, I'll be moving back to Georgia. I'd love to see you before I leave. Would you like to have dinner tonight or tomorrow or any night this week? I'll be leaving really early on Friday morning. I'm going to see a friend in Panama City on the way back to Pemberton. Anyway, I hope to hear from you. I'm at my duplex. You have that number."

Over the next three days, Robert called Diana two more times and each time reached only her answering machine, although he left only one more message. If he had said what was actually on his mind, he knew he would have sounded desperate.

To avoid thinking about Diana, he busied himself with packing his books, clothes, and other personal items. He wanted to keep his dad's recliner, so he purchased a replacement for the duplex but otherwise was happy to leave everything behind. Alan surprised him and came over on Wednesday afternoon, ostensibly to help him pack, although they spent most of the time drinking beer, reminiscing about their exploits, including those with Michelle and Megan, and contemplating what the future held for each of them.

Alan seemed to be at peace and yet excited about going to Africa to do what he kept referring to as "good work." Around 6:00 p.m. he said he needed to get to his parents' house for dinner. He invited Robert to join him, and though he wanted to tell the Taylors goodbye in person—and certainly would have enjoyed Mrs. Taylor's cooking—Robert knew he needed to finish packing, especially since he and Alan had made virtually no progress. They promised to stay in touch and shook hands. Alan stopped on the sidewalk in front of the duplex and turned back to announce with a smile that he was giving his BMW to his father. The prodigal son had come home just in time to leave again, only this time it was to do "good work."

Robert wished he were as confident about his own future. He had no reason to doubt that Tom would be a good boss, and yet he had been burned more than once because he failed to understand what he was getting himself into. He knew nothing about the insurance business and hoped that Tom's confidence in him was not misplaced.

Early Friday morning he began to load the U-Haul trailer. Although he had only a dozen or so boxes and his dad's recliner, it took multiple trips, since he was loading it by himself. As he trudged back and forth to the trailer, Diana was on his mind, and it made him melancholy.

How did I screw this up so badly? he wondered. I'm never going to hear from her. So much for Elmer's sixth sense about women. That must've disappeared when he became businessman Tom. Googly eyes or not, she's clearly not interested in me. I should have known that when she always had an excuse for not going to dinner.

Robert loaded the last box and sat down heavily on the floor of the trailer. He took a deep breath and exhaled. I wish Tom had been right. She *did* look at me differently during that dinner in Atlanta. But she hasn't called me back in three days. Maybe she was just amused at dinner with all the talk about Panama and is not really interested.

As he was making one last check of the duplex, the phone rang.

"Bobby?" It was Barry Daniel, sounding uncharacteristically anxious. "Ain't you answering the phone? I done called you twice."

"Sorry, man. I've been loading the trailer. Is everything all right?"

"Uh, yeah. I was just checkin' to be sure you was still stopping by."

"Yeah. Why?"

"Well, I, uh, I thought your momma might have convinced you to drive straight to Pemberton."

"No. In fact, she said a vacation would do me good."

"Well that's good. Okay. See you tonight, then."

Robert hung up the phone, perplexed.

Since he was pulling a trailer, the drive from Dallas to Panama City would take over twelve hours, giving him plenty of time to plan what he needed to do when he got to Georgia. It felt strange to be driving east on Interstate 20—the same highway that had brought him to Dallas only several months before. He had hoped then it would be a new beginning for him. But it had all gone awry. Was it just as Panama had been years before? Had he simply failed to understand what he was getting himself into? Had he again idealized a situation and thought all he needed to do was work hard to make everything perfect? Right. Dallas had turned out just like Panama. Was he becoming what soldiers called a "shit magnet"? Nothing seemed to go right for him.

After many miles and a great deal of thought, he realized that wasn't it.

No. I'm not a shit magnet. My judgment may be clouded at times. But that's totally my fault. I lose perspective because I keep trying to prove myself. You can't assess situations properly if you're too focused on work. It's like that old saying: if you're too focused on the "trees," you lose sight of the "forest."

Yet he knew that wasn't the complete answer. More miles. More thought.

Hard work can't be a bad thing. That's what got me into West Point and took me to the top of the class, which is what got me selected to go to law school. So, what am I doing wrong? I work hard, perform well, and get praised for it. Maybe that's it. Maybe I like the praise too much. I keep moving from one challenge to the next, hungering for more. Shit. I'm a fucking addict, no different from a drug addict—only my high comes from getting praise. And like all addicts, I can't get enough.

Suddenly, things became clear—at least concerning his career. And that helped him put other things into perspective.

I've got to detox. My career can no longer come first. I've relied way too much on Janelle to take care of Ellie. Poor Janelle. What am I going to do when she passes? I'm not ready to be a single father. How am I going to raise a little girl? Momma will help, of course, and I'm sure Darlene will, too. But how am I going to deal with the countless questions a little girl will have about so many things?

He pondered these things as he drove east. The sun was beginning to set behind him.

# CHAPTER FORTY-ONE

"YOU MADE GOOD time." It was Barry Daniel, walking down the sidewalk in front of apartment 15, Seaview Apartments, with a longneck Corona in one hand and a cigarette in the other. "I figured it was you on account of the trailer and all."

"Yeah. I had to rent it to bring Daddy's recliner. I couldn't part with that. It's not full, though. If there's anything you need carried to Pemberton, there's plenty of room."

"Hell no. I love it down here. I ain't even thinkin' about Pemberton no more."

That's obvious, Robert thought. Barry was wearing a bright blue T-shirt with palm trees on the front, cut-off jeans, and flip-flops—an outfit he would have never worn in Pemberton. Only his tattered Braves baseball cap looked familiar.

"Anyway," Barry continued, "get your ass in here. I ordered us a pizza. It'll be here any minute. You still like pepperoni, don't you?"

"You know it." Robert grabbed his gym bag and followed Barry into the apartment. "I sure am glad you don't want to go out to eat. I'm beat."

Barry's apartment was a cut above his trailer in Pemberton. But not by much. Dirty dishes were piled in the sink, and the place smelled like an ashtray. Spot barked at Robert a couple of times as he walked in but soon recognized him and began wagging his tail so hard it looked like it might fall off. The only pictures on the walls were framed school photographs of Barry's daughter, Misty. The furniture probably came from the clearance room of the Goodwill Store. The only thing that appeared to be new was a large television set, which dominated the living room. Barry noticed Robert looking around.

"As you can see, Bobby, I ain't much on housekeeping."

"It's fine with me, buddy. You work hard all day. Housekeeping isn't high on my list either."

As he flopped down onto his stained sofa with threadbare arms, Barry continued, "Let me tell you about tomorrow night. We're going to Club La Vela. The place is awesome. Ain't nothing like it in Savannah or Atlanta. Gregg Allman, the Outlaws, and bunch of other famous bands have played there."

"Sounds awesome. Who's playing tomorrow night?"

"I don't know. But every time I've been there, it's been great. It's a good thing it ain't spring break though. They say you can't hardly get in there then. But let me tell you: it's always full of good-lookin' women." The doorbell rang. "That's probably our dinner. Get you a beer out of the Frigidaire."

After they devoured the pizza, the two old friends consumed almost a half case of Corona and reminisced about growing up in Pemberton, including the time—on a dare—they jumped off the bridge over the Ogeechee River. A lot of water had passed under that bridge since then. Both of them had been through tough times, including divorce and the loss of loved ones. But on this night they didn't want to think about any of that. They only wanted to laugh and recall the good times.

It was 10:00 a.m. when Robert awoke to the sound of Barry snoring and snorting in the next room. It made him snicker. A woman would have to really love that guy to put up with that, he thought.

Barry stumbled out of bed a half hour later and insisted on making breakfast. He did a respectable job, though he kept saying it didn't compare to Ruth's cooking, which was true, of course. Robert just smiled and said nothing. After sitting around watching re-runs of *The Beverly Hillbillies* and *Gilligan's Island*, Barry gave Robert a tour of Panama City Beach, including a roadside view of Club La Vela, a massive white building with arched openings across the front, which gave it a Mediterranean air. It seemed out of place for an area affectionately known as the "Redneck Riviera"—home to water parks, tattoo parlors, bars, crab shacks, and T-shirt shops.

They arrived back at Barry's apartment late that afternoon and immediately began to get ready for the evening. Barry was in the shower so long the steam began to seep out the bottom of the bathroom door. When he finally emerged, he was clean-shaven, which surprised Robert. Robert took his turn to shower and shave, and when he came out the smell of Polo cologne emanating from Barry's bedroom was so strong he could almost taste it.

He's certainly getting ready, Robert chuckled to himself.

When they arrived at Club La Vela, there was already a line out front. Twenty minutes later Barry guided them to one of the bars, where they each ordered a beer and began to survey the scene. Seated at a table across the room was a shapely blonde, wearing a tube top and tight, white jeans, which glowed in the black lights of the bar. Robert thought she looked familiar—a movie star, perhaps. Or maybe it was Diana. But her hair was different and, anyway, he knew that wasn't possible.

"You see anything that looks interesting?" Barry asked.

"I'm not looking. My life is too screwed up right now."

"You got to stop thinkin' like that. You sound like some kinda old man."

"I feel old."

"What about that blonde yonder?"

"I must admit I was checking her out. She reminds me of someone I know in Dallas."

"She looks like she's alone. Why don't you go talk to her?"

"Nah. I don't even know how to do that anymore."

"Oh, bullshit, Bobby. Come on. Let's both go sit down with her."

"I don't know, man. Wouldn't that be kind of creepy?"

"Nah. Come on." Barry grabbed Robert's arm and headed in her direction.

As they approached her table, she smiled—that breathtaking, unmistakable, dazzling smile that was capable of changing his entire day. It was Diana.

"What on earth brings you to Panama City?" Robert's eyes were wide in surprise and recognition. "You... you look fantastic."

"Thanks, Robert. I decided I needed a vacation. Sharon and I quit the firm."

"So I heard. Alan told me."

"And I guess you heard he quit, too. He's going to work for a non-profit in Africa. Surprised the heck out of me."

"Of all the places you could have gone… Were you looking for me?" The words came tumbling out before he realized how they sounded.

"Now what makes you think I was looking for you?" Robert could feel his cheeks flush. "I'm teasing you, Robert." She took a sip from her glass, which had a tiny umbrella poking out of it. "When I couldn't reach you on Friday, I called your mother, and she referred me to Barry. It was sweet that you had told your mom about me, by the way."

"So, you were in on this, you scoundrel," Robert said, turning to Barry. "I should have known something was up. I haven't seen you clean-shaven in years."

Barry shrugged and grinned. "I got a call from this lovely lady on Friday morning. She said she'd been trying to reach you all morning, but you never answered your phone."

"I… Oh shit. I disconnected the answering machine. I guess I was going in and out of the duplex while I was loading the trailer and missed the calls." He turned to Diana. "Why didn't you call me before Friday morning?"

"On the plane back to Dallas, Sharon and I decided to resign, which we did as soon as we got back. On Monday morning we drove to Austin and called on a number of law firms where Sharon has contacts. She's had enough of Dallas and thinks Austin might be a better fit for what you call her 'lifestyle choice.' "

Robert blushed again. "That was a poor choice of words, Diana. You know I have the utmost respect for Sharon."

"Just teasing you again, Robert. But I do think Austin will be better for her. Anyway, I didn't get back to my apartment until late Thursday night. It was a good trip, though. We both received offers from a good firm. She's accepted, but I'm still considering it. I'm not sure what I want to do next." She leaned forward and touched his right hand with her left. Her soft skin felt sensuous against the back of his hand. It was the first time she had ever touched him like that. He looked down at her elegant, long fingers wrapped around his hand. None of them bore a ring.

Barry stood to leave. "I'm gonna leave you two. If, uh, anybody's listening, I'll be at the bar."

For a moment neither of them said anything or looked his way. Then Robert turned and said, "Thanks, man. As always, you've been a true friend. Just come and find me when you're ready to head home."

"I have a rental car," Diana offered. "I can take you back."

"Okay," Robert said. "Yeah. That would be great. Well, then I guess I'll see you later, Barry."

Barry grinned and walked away.

"It's kind of loud in here," Diana said. "There's a deck on the back. Want to go out there?" Robert nodded, and they made their way outside. The night was cool, and the breeze carried a hint of salt air from the Gulf of Mexico. The moon was waxing crescent, though it still made the waves sparkle in the darkness. "Let's walk down to the beach," she said.

The sounds of the club faded, overcome by the rhythmic crashing of the waves. Diana reached out and took Robert's hand, and he again felt a warm rush as her fingers wrapped around his palm. For several minutes they walked along the beach, saying nothing. She broke the silence.

"So, you're going to work for Mr. Jackson."

"Yeah. It's an answer to a prayer."

"I guess so," she whispered, as if she'd lost something, though Robert didn't notice the change in her voice.

"I mean, I have a little bit saved, but I have to pay child support for my daughter. Janelle said I could wait until I get a job, but I know she needs the money."

"So, you saw her while you were in Georgia?"

"Yeah. She's not doing well." Robert started to tell her about Janelle's cancer but remembered his promise. "You know, I think I misjudged her. I think it was her lawyer who came up with the idea of that awful visitation order. Anyway, we agreed we needed to get along for Ellie's benefit. That will be easier now that I'll be living in Pemberton."

"I thought you would be living in Atlanta."

"No. Tom says his wife wants him to move the headquarters to Savannah, which is close to where I grew up. So, I can live in Pemberton and be close to my mom and Ellie."

"That's wonderful news, Robert. Well, I hope your new job works out better than Underwood & Crockett."

"Me, too. Do you think you'll take that job in Austin?"

"I don't know. Do you have any thoughts on that?" She cocked her head, and the ringlets framing her face danced in the breeze.

"What do you mean?"

"Come on, Robert. What do I have to do? Throw myself at you."

He was thankful for the darkness, because he knew his pale face had flushed bright red again.

"I don't understand, Diana. All those times I asked you to go to dinner, and you turned me down."

"We were too busy, Robert. I had to stay focused on the deal. If I'd gone to dinner with you, I would have lost all my focus."

"Now, you sound like me," he chuckled. Diana's eyes widened; she dropped his hand and turned away. "Oh, no, Diana. I didn't mean to sound critical. I get it. When I'm working on a tough assignment, I have to focus, too." She turned around, and he looked deep into her eyes. "No, you don't have to throw yourself at me. I've been interested since the moment I saw you."

"Even when you were dating Megan?"

"I told you before that was one of the dumbest things I've ever done."

"I don't understand that."

"What can I say? I hadn't dated in years, and Alan practically insisted— no, he *did* insist—that Megan and I double date with him and Michelle."

"What about that trip to Galveston?"

"More colossal stupidity on my part." Robert looked out at the ocean for a while and then turned back to Diana. "I'm not sure what you see in me, Diana. It does make me very happy. But I've got to tell you something: I've made a lot of mistakes in my life."

"We all have, Robert."

"Yeah, I know. But mine seem to have long-lasting consequences, like becoming a father. I should have never married Janelle, and now I have a daughter whom I adore, and she has two parents who are divorced."

"No amount of guilt can change the past, Robert. Look at it this way: you're going to be back home with your new job."

"But that's not all of it, Diana. Janelle has cancer. And it doesn't look good." He could feel his eyes starting to well up. "She asked me not to tell anyone, but you don't know anyone from Pemberton other than Barry and my mom. Please don't say anything. Anyway, you don't want to get involved with a guy who's about to become a single dad."

"Maybe I do."

"My life is a mess right now, Diana. I *wish* we could have a relationship. But like you said about focus: I've got to focus on this new job and my responsibilities as a father. It wouldn't be fair to you."

"Why don't you let me worry about that? Did you ever think that I might be interested in you precisely because you are worried about your responsibilities? Most men just want to hop in the sack."

Robert looked down and kicked the sand. "I'm no saint, Diana. I've been guilty of that, too."

"Megan?"

"Yeah. And like I said before: that was stupid, plain and simple."

"That's not really *you*, is it?" Diana asked, her tone indicating she wanted him to answer the question. She wasn't suggesting the answer was "no."

"No," he replied immediately. "That's not me. Sex has just caused me a lot of trouble."

"Seriously?"

"Right. That did sound ridiculous, didn't it? I like sex. Every man does. I've just learned that it's not as important as other things in a relationship." Robert looked down and kicked the sand again. "If I remarry..." He paused, searching for the right way to express himself. "Yeah. I don't know. I guess what I'm trying to say is that if I get married again, I want to do it right."

"Do you want to talk about that? I'd like to know what you think." She stopped and turned to face him. Her eyes sparkled in the moonlight. "Not that I'm suggesting anything, mind you."

"No. I don't mind talking about it. I think I married Janelle out of guilt. I felt like I owed it to her."

"Why on earth did you feel that way?"

"Now *that* is something I don't want to talk about. But I will say that marriage has to be a deeper relationship than anything she and I ever had."

"I've thought about it, too," she said. "I've been asked twice, but it didn't feel right for me."

"I don't know what's wrong with me, Diana. I guess that's how we're different: my feelings have never been a good guide for me."

"Maybe that's because you were focused on the wrong thing. I think couples get into trouble when they think marriage is supposed to be a long-term love affair."

"That's what my parents had," he said.

"Maybe. But I suspect there was something deeper there, too. My dad, for instance, was only interested in my mother because she was beautiful. After she had me and got a little older, he went looking for a younger model. He never saw my mother's true beauty."

"What do you mean?" Robert asked.

"He only saw her outward beauty. He never saw, much less appreciated, her inner beauty. She used to tell me that I inherited her looks, and I should be careful not to marry someone who was only interested in that. She told me to find my soulmate."

Robert had never heard a woman talk like that. He was enthralled and, at the same time, felt inadequate. Obviously, Diana had thought much deeper about relationships than he had. "How will you know when you've found your soulmate?" he asked.

"I'm not sure. I think you've got to focus on the right qualities. You can't get distracted because a guy's handsome or sexy. There's nothing wrong with that, mind you, but there needs to be more. You know how the *Bible* talks about how the two will become one flesh?" Robert nodded like a school boy. "I don't think that's referring to sex. I think it means that each person must constantly defer to the marriage, instead of their own personal whims."

"Did you ever read that book *The Prophet* by Khalil Gibran?" he asked.

"That trendy one back in the seventies? Yeah. I think I did back then."

"He said something about the need to have spaces between husband and wife, so that marriage wasn't a bond."

Diana looked down and then up at him with her gorgeous blue eyes. "I'm not sure that's it, Robert. But mind you, I'm no expert on poetry, and I'm certainly no philosopher. I just think marriage is a relationship and that when you make sacrifices in the marriage, they aren't to each other but to the unity of the relationship." Robert looked puzzled. "In other words, the unity—the two as one—is what each party is committed to."

"You sound pretty philosophical to me." He thought for a moment. "It's kinda like that Chinese symbol of yin and yang, isn't it? The black and the white are individual but together define the circle."

"I never thought of it that way, but I guess you're right."

She took his hand again, but he let go and put both arms around her waist, pulling her close to him. She smelled of bergamot and orange blossoms—a whisper of fragrance, not a shout. Tilting her face upward, she leaned forward. Her eyes were wide and inviting, and then she closed them, waiting for him to respond. He bent down and kissed her. A kiss unlike anything he had ever felt—warm and soft, the kind of kiss that made his entire body tingle. She was so different from Megan. Kissing Megan was like kissing a rubber doll. And he'd totally forgotten what Janelle was like.

Was he screwing this up? He didn't want to let her go, yet they pulled apart. Their breathing was shaky and shallow. He wondered if she had felt what he felt. His question was answered when she put her arms around his neck and pulled his face to hers, again kissing him passionately, her tongue flicking against his. She pressed her body against him, and he worried that she could feel him getting aroused.

God, don't let me screw this up. She's perfect. I can't let her think I'm like those other guys.

"Don't pull away," she whispered. "Hold me close."

They kissed again and again, like teenagers who had just discovered what it was like. They walked to a sand dune that separated the beach from the high-rise condominiums and laid down onto the sand, Diana on top of him. Their bodies were so intertwined and close they could feel the heat of each other, their breath warm across each other's bare skin. He resisted the temptation to explore her body beneath her clothes, though he caressed all that he could reach.

She was first to speak. "Where does this go?"

"I don't know, Diana. I just don't want it to end."

"Do you want to come to my hotel?" She gazed at him, her eyes full of longing. Every cell in his body pleaded for him to say "yes," yet he hesitated, pausing so long she rolled off him and sat up. She stared at the ocean and ran her hand through her hair. "That was a stupid thing to say."

"No. No it wasn't," he said.

"After all I said about finding a soulmate, instead of—"

"Diana, I'm falling in love with you," he said. She turned to him, her eyes glistening in the lights from the condominiums. "I don't want to screw this up. But I've got to get things straight in my own life first. Can you be patient? Do you want to?"

The corners of her mouth began to curl into a smile, though tears began to stream down her face.

"Are you happy or sad?" he asked.

"I'm frustrated."

She paused for what seemed like an eternity, wiping her wet cheeks with the back of her hand. He didn't want to say anything. He was afraid of what she meant.

"I'm falling in love with you, too. I'm frustrated because I've waited so long for this, and now I have to wait some more."

"I promise you I'm going to do everything I can to be worth the wait."

She leaned over and lightly kissed his lips. "I know you will."

# About the Author

*Dawn in Dallas* is the sequel to William H. Venema's first novel, Death in Panama, which is available on Amazon (see: https://www.amazon.com/Death-Panama-William-Venema-ebook/dp/B0725LG8RG/ref).

Bill is a Distinguished Graduate of the U.S. Military Academy at West Point. He also earned an MBA from Georgia State University and a JD from the University of Virginia School of Law. His legal career spans almost forty years and includes time in the U.S. Army Judge Advocate General's Corps, in law firms, and as general counsel of major corporations. Prior to entering private practice, Bill served in the U.S. Army in Germany, Panama, and several stateside assignments. He is a graduate of the Army's Airborne and Ranger schools, as well as the Command and General Staff College. He and his wife reside in Georgetown, Texas.

His website is: www.williamhvenema.com.

Made in the USA
Columbia, SC
21 May 2021